Tell No Lies

Also by Gregg Hurwitz

Tell No Lies

GREGG

HURWITZ

ST. MARTIN'S PRESS ★ NEW YORK

TELL NO LIES. Copyright © 2013 by Gregg Hurwitz. All rights reserved.
Printed in the United States of America. For information, address St. Martin's Press,
175 Fifth Avenue, New York, N.Y. 10010.

www.stmartins.com

LIBRARY OF CONGRESS CATALOGING-IN-PUBLICATION DATA

Hurwitz, Gregg Andrew.
    Tell no lies / by Gregg Hurwitz. — First edition.
        pages cm
    ISBN 978-0-312-62552-8 (hardcover)
    ISBN 978-1-250-02610-1 (e-book)
    1. Executives—Fiction.   2. Serial murder investigation—Fiction.   I. Title.
    PS3558.U695T46 2013
    813'.54—dc23

                                                        2013009881

St. Martin's Press books may be purchased for educational, business, or promotional
use. For information on bulk purchases, please contact Macmillan Corporate and
Premium Sales Department at 1-800-221-7945 extension 5442 or write
specialmarkets@macmillan.com.

First Edition: August 2013

10 9 8 7 6 5 4 3 2 1

For Bret Nelson, M.D., who as a future ER doc had the misfortune of once sharing a dorm room with an aspiring thriller writer.

For twenty years of friendship.

For allowing me to clog his waiting room with fictional injuries, book after book, script after script.

And for guiding my characters through countless ailments, fractures, contusions, knifings, gunshot wounds, pathologies, surgeries, and the odd tension pneumothorax.

We thank him.

Men are disturbed not by things,
but by the view which they take of them.
—Epictetus

Tell No Lies

Chapter 1

The ridiculous thread count made the new sheets feel like warm butter, which is why Daniel had been luxuriating in them since the faux church bells of his alarm had chimed five minutes earlier. Forcing himself fully awake, he rolled to his side and watched his sleeping wife. Cristina lay on her back, dark tresses falling across her face, one arm flung wide, the other curled overhead like *Venus at Her Bath*. Smooth brown skin, bowed eyelashes, that broad mouth, always ready with a smile or a wisecrack. Her pajama top was unbuttoned to her cleavage, revealing three blue pinpoint tattoos on her sternum: the radiation therapist's alignment marks, finally starting to fade.

For whatever reason this morning, the familiar sight of those three dots caught him off guard, a first-thing splash of emotion in the face. Cristina used to talk about getting them lasered off—it *had* been five years since they'd served their purpose—but over time she'd taken a shine to them. Her war paint.

Just like that he was back in the swampy memory of it. How she'd wake up breathless in the middle of the night, her heart racing, unable to draw a full breath. The bouts of nausea that kept her tethered to the couch for hours at a time, her athletic body softening. The doctor's appointment always a week away, rescheduled for this reason or that. And then the incident at the fund-raiser, Cristina in a pale tile bathroom, coughing until her white sundress was speckled with bright blood, her wounded elegance calling to mind a pellet-shot dove. He'd cleaned her up with trembling hands as she leaned over the sink, weak-kneed and faint, and she'd said, "We're at an age now that when people get sick, it doesn't mean they have the flu."

Their relationship up until then had accelerated without brakes. They'd fallen into each other with an instant intimacy, laughing about the right things and serious about the rest. He'd met her in front of a painting at SFMOMA. They'd found themselves side by side, admiring the same piece. She'd gotten him talking, and Daniel had mentioned how his mother loved Lautrec and how he'd been drawn to the bright, bold colors of the dancing ladies even at a young age. He was going on a bit about the Frenchman's debt to Japanese woodcuts when Cris bit her lip thoughtfully, cocking her head to take in the row of paintings on the wall. "You can see how left out he felt," she said, and Daniel was brought up short with admiration.

Was it love at first conversation? Who could say? But after the drinks that followed their dinner, which followed their walk, which followed their spontaneous lunch in the museum's café, Daniel did know one thing: She was the first good reason he'd had to want to live forever.

And now, half a decade later, his feelings were undiminished. At the cusp of forty, and still he got a heady schoolboy rush watching her twist her dripping hair up into a towel or sing under her breath while chopping cilantro or gather her pantyhose around her thumbs as she poised a foot for entry.

He set his hand gently on the slope of her upper chest over the three dots, feeling for her heartbeat. There. And there. And there.

She stirred, those lashes parting to show her rich brown eyes. She smiled, and then her gaze pulled south, taking in his flat hand pressed to her chest. A puzzled furrow of the brow as she frowned down. "What are you feeling?" she asked.

"Gratitude," he said.

———

Daniel ran the steep slopes of Pacific Heights with the same intensity with which he'd tackled them as a high-school wrestler trying to make weight, except now with the complaints of a thirty-nine-year-old body mediating the pace. Someone had once remarked that when you got tired of walking around San Francisco, you could always lean against it. He felt like leaning now. Instead he loped along Vallejo to the edge of the Presidio and jogged the regal Lyon Street Steps, lined with meticulously planted gardens and cast in the shadows of towering trees. He passed a cluster of teenagers up from the night before, smoking their cigarettes and practicing their pouts, and a few early-morning boot-campers he recognized, traders and i-bankers out to break a sweat before the market opened.

Ahead a younger man with rock-hard calves and tapered lats bounded up the steps, and Daniel dared himself to catch up. The stairs blurred underfoot, his muscles straining, taking two at a time, driving into the face of the challenge, and then it was no longer leisure but something more. The age-old urge fired his belly.

Be faster. Be stronger. Be *better*.

Whistling past the guy, he kept on, legs burning, breath scouring his throat, the hill like a wall stretching up and up. But he wouldn't stop, wouldn't slow, not even after the man's footsteps receded into memory. It was never about the man, of course, or this challenge on this day. It was about appeasing the chorus of voices in his head, the ones that had always told him that if he ever wanted a life he could call his own, he'd have to fight his way to it.

Sweat falls from Daniel's locks, dotting the wrestling mat at his feet. The gymnasium is packed, ridiculous for a junior-high meet, but it is that kind of school and these are those kinds of parents. The headgear's strap digs into his chin, and he tastes salt from where he nearly put his tooth through his lip on the last takedown. But he'd completed the move and gotten near-fall points to boot. If he has one thing going for him, it is that he won't allow pain to be a deterrent. His shaggy-haired, pale-skinned opponent is more developed, with real biceps, but even at age twelve Daniel fights as if his life is on the line, as if he is trying to escape from somewhere. He is winning 5–2 with less than a minute on the clock.

They circle each other warily. The kid takes a few open-hand swipes at Daniel's head, but they're halfhearted. His bowed shoulders and weary eyes show that he has already conceded the meet. But Daniel doesn't want to win like this. He wants to clash until the bell. He wants to hear the definitive slap of the referee's hand against the mat, announcing the pin, showing that he didn't back down from a challenge by coasting to the finish line.

A whistle halts the action—the kid's laces are untied. Daniel bounces on his toes to keep loose, his slender frame jiggling. Someone has the bright idea to enhance the time-out by blaring Kenny Loggins's "Danger Zone" through the antiquated speakers.

As the boy crouches to adjust his shoes, Daniel turns to take in the bleachers. There's his mother up in the stands, out of place among all those sweatshirts and done-up soccer-mom faces, her fingers doing an impatient caterpillar crawl along the sleeve of her fur coat, itching for a cigarette. Severe lipstick. Her pulse beating in the paper-thin skin at her temple. She notes his gaze, but her expression does not change, and he knows that her dead-even stare has everything to do with why winning by points is not enough.

The match goes live again, and they circle and slap, the other kid shuffling, exhausted. Their shoes chirp against the mat. The smell of rubber and sweat fills Daniel's nostrils. He watches the kid's legs, the angle of the feet, the bend of his knee. They shuffle-step some more. The clock ticks down, and then—there—he sees his opening. He lunges in for the fireman's carry, but his sole skids on an invisible puddle of sweat and then he is off balance, flipped on his shoulders, and the bigger kid is lying across him. Daniel bucks and flails but cannot wriggle free. Sooner than seems plausible, the referee's palm strikes the mat near his face and it is over.

In the locker-room shower, he replays the moment, except this *time he doesn't slip—he hoists his larger opponent in the fireman's carry and dumps him on his back, and the crowd roars, and there's his mother, on her feet, cheering, her face lit with triumph.*

He exits the building, his hair still damp. The sky is San Francisco slate, overcast and gloomy, and the air bites at him through the slacks and thin sweater of his school uniform. His mother waits, leaning against the car, her arms crossed against the cold, wearing an expression of disgust. No, not disgust—concealed rage.

"You had him on points," she says. "You just had to run the clock."

"I know," Daniel says.

"You could have had the medal."

"I know."

Evelyn's gloved hands light a slender cigarette, lift it to her bloodred lips. "You make things hard on yourself."

Daniel averts his gaze. In the car, behind the wheel, James is little more than a hat and a shadow. He stares straight ahead. This is not his business, and he has a paycheck to earn.

Daniel says, "I know."

Evelyn shoots a disciplined stream of smoke into the darkening evening and opens the rear door to climb in. Daniel takes a step forward, but she halts midway into the car and turns back to him.

"Losers walk," she says.

The door closes neatly behind her, and the car purrs up the street.

Daniel watches until it disappears. Blowing into his cupped hands, he begins the long walk home.

Pausing at the top of the Lyon Street Steps, panting, Daniel turned and looked back. Far below, the younger man he'd blown past struggled up the final leg of his run. Daniel took a few seconds to catch his breath, the raised sweatshirt hood damp around his head, eucalyptus clearing his lungs, stinging his nostrils. The summit afforded a view across the vast forest of the Presidio toward Sea Cliff, where Evelyn presided over her estate, looking down on the city.

He took the stairs hard back down and ran for home, dodging curbside recycling barrels. Victorian mansions alternated with Mission Revivals and the occasional Chateau, the gleaming façades making clearer than ever how Pacific Heights earned its nicknames—either the "Gold Coast" or "Specific Whites," depending on which demographic was weighing in.

Daniel and Cristina's place, though several blocks downsized from Billionaires' Row, was still stunning. Average-sized by the standards of any reasonable town, the midcentury house was a narrow three-story rise of concrete and dark wood with a square patch of front lawn, shoulder-width alleys on either side, and a matchbook courtyard framing a black-pebble fire pit in the back.

Daniel entered, tossing his keys onto the accent table beside the miniature Zen garden with its white sand groomed into hypnotic patterns. Up the stairs to the wide-open second story, the view making its grand entrance through the floor-to-ceiling steel-framed windows in a fashion that—still—made his breath hitch. Backdropping the kitchen, a cascading vista down the hill to the Bay, the Golden Gate forging magnificently into the craggy headlands of Marin, Angel Island floating in an ice-cream haze of fog. And on the other side, beyond the little sitting area they called a living room, a panorama captured the dip of Fillmore and the Haight and the houses beyond popping up like pastel dominoes, forming a textured rise to the one visible Twin Peak. Sutro Tower loomed over it all, sticking out of the earth like a giant tuning fork.

He climbed to their bedroom on the third floor. Red pen clenched between her teeth, Cris was proofreading a printout and wriggling into a pair of jeans at the same time. Her eyeglasses were shoved atop her head, forgotten.

"Your op-ed?" he asked.

She nodded, distracted, not looking up.

"It was great two drafts ago."

"It has to be *better* than great. It has to be a brimstone avalanche of influence that convinces the planning commission that it is not worth their political while to displace sixty low-income families so their cronies can build faux-Italian town houses."

Cristina's job as a community organizer for nonprofit tenants' societies had grown harder each year since the aggressive gentrification of the dot-com era. The hot-dotters had taken over vacant lots and homeless squats, pressing out each fold and wrinkle of the city like an expanding waistline. Now the trendy restaurants and bars of the Divisadero were creeping into Western Addition, and developers were picking off buildings not officially designated as projects and protected with federal subsidies. Including the sixty-unit apartment complex Cris was currently fighting to preserve.

She scribbled at the sheet. "They bought off the asshole landlord, who's helping drive the tenants out. No repairs, nothing. There's a family of six in there that's had a broken toilet for a month, so they have to use the neighbors'. Two black drag queens. You can imagine how *that's* working out. There are elderly couples with nowhere to go. I had a single mom in yesterday, crying, won't be able to afford to live in her own neighborhood. A five-generation Chinese-Filipino family on the third floor—"

"*Five* generations?"

"There's a great-great-aunt in there somewhere."

"Maybe the cupboard."

Her face lightened. For an instant. "This is boring."

"Not even a little."

She slashed out another paragraph. "I have two volunteers and a college intern. We spend six months organizing through churches and schools to get thirty thousand signatures, and then some *associate*"— she spit the word—"bundles two hundred grand in contributions to the right city supervisor and tilts the whole goddamned seesaw the other way."

Her accent edged into her words when she was mad. She sank onto the bed, chewing through the cap of the red pen. Having grown up in a similar apartment building in the Mission, she took her job personally.

"The power brokers," she said. "They matter more than we do."

"Don't say that," he told her.

She looked at him evenly, not a trace of self-pity in her eyes. "But it's true."

Chapter 2

The heat had been shut off again last week, and the walls of the box apartment held the San Francisco cold greedily—the place might as well have been refrigerated. A scorched comet marred the plasterboard above the uneven stove where a grease fire had flared and died. No door to the bathroom. Toilet missing its lid, a prison bowl. The concrete floor like ice even through their shoes, even through the thin mattress they shared each night, fully clothed.

If he hit her just below the left cheek, they'd discovered, it brought up a pleasing raised bruise without causing any real damage. She stood patiently, exposed, her face turned slightly. Waiting. He executed the first blow, taking care not to put too much weight behind it. Her head snapped back, and she smiled, her eyes dazed and distant.

His life, it seemed, had become nothing more than a series of tough runs laid end to end. Lately it had been flipping burgers and onions, the stink of the grill clinging to him, in his pores, coming off his clothes, filling the shower stall when the lukewarm water drizzled over his head. Nine bucks and change an hour, forty-nine cents taken out for Social Security, Medicare at twelve, and SDI—whatever the hell that was—chiseling off another couple pennies. They were almost through the canned meat, but he'd be paid tomorrow and then there'd be fresh cigarettes, a few packs of hot dogs, gas for the tank, a gallon or two of milk. If things got too bad, he could dip into the stash, but that money was reserved for the Purpose, and the Purpose was everything. And so they'd held their vow to abstain even through a few daylong stints with no food at all. That morning he'd found a still-smoldering butt on the sidewalk, and he'd crouched in a bus shelter and smoked it down, watching all the well-heeled folks traipse by.

She was trembling there in the semi-dark, thin arms at her sides. Spread across the floor behind her were their secret plans—maps with red circles, schedules gleaned from months of surveillance, confidential files painstakingly collected.

"Ready?" he asked.

"Mouth now," she said. "Come on, baby."

He palmed the back of her head and struck her, a hard tap of the knuckles, enough to split her lip. Her grin gleamed darkly, red filling the spaces, framing her lower teeth. She tasted her lips, her loose gaze radiating a deep, almost sexual ache. "More," she said. "Give me more."

Again.

This was the really sweet part. The sacrifice. The lengths they were willing to go to.

The grief had caught up to her now, rushing in with the pain. Tears glittering, feather of blood on her chin, her shoulders shuddering.

Sheets of fog stirred at the window, ghost raiments forming and re-forming, diffusing the streetlight's glow. The rumble of a Muni bus down the hill reached them, another hollow stomach, another city beast out to feed.

She breathed wetly. Her eyes glinted like dimes.

Overcome, he lowered his arms, and his fingers flexed at his sides, trying to grasp the ungraspable. He looked at the scattered maps and folders, the underlined addresses, the names on printouts. So much work, so much careful planning, years in the making. He tried to draw strength from it all, tried to let it fuel him.

She hooked his neck with a hand, pressing her forehead to his, the warmth of their sobs mingling.

"I love you, baby," she said. "I love *her*."

He nodded, swiped at his cheeks with the worn cuff of his sweater. "Me, too," he managed.

Her fingertips touched the blood at her lips, checking. "Then make me hurt for her. Make me *feel* it." She pulled away a half step and raised her head regally, bracing.

Still crying, he drew back his fist.

Chapter 3

Quarter to eight and the November sky was already as dark as midnight. For Daniel, navigating the smart car across town felt a bit like driving a shopping cart, but it got great mileage and could ratchet itself into any parking space that might improbably come available. He headed south of Market, weaving through municipal buildings, rusty warehouses, and dilapidated apartments, the worsening neighborhood still a four-star upgrade from the danger zone it used to be. The 22 Fillmore bus, nicknamed the "22-to-Life," rumbled past, heading even farther south to real high-risk territory.

Daniel's workplace loomed ahead. A colossal mausoleum of a building implanted in the mid-seventies, Metro South was as cold and bare-bones functional as an insane asylum or a Soviet ministry office. A subterranean gate rattled open, and then Daniel pulled in to the dungeon of the parking level, complete with sweating concrete walls and flickering fluorescent overheads. He pulled in to his usual spot, then got on the elevator, redolent of industrial cleaner. As the car rose, he drummed his hands against his worn jeans, praying it wouldn't get stuck again.

The five-story building housed Probation, Parole, and various related social services. Last year the city had moved about half the occupants north into newer quarters, so now Metro South gave off a condemned-building vibe—empty halls, groaning pipes, loose floor tiles. The only departments remaining were those purposefully left behind. Like the one Daniel belonged to.

He had a job very few would want. A job that tested his patience, courage, and sometimes his sanity. And yet here he was. No one ever said he didn't love a challenge.

The elevator shuddered on its cables. What a far cry from his past life in a penthouse office managing the family portfolios. He vividly remembered Evelyn's response when he'd told her that he was switching career tracks—to this one in particular.

"Isn't that just like you. The world at your feet, and you trip over it." She turns, buries her nose in her gimlet. "A shrink." She snorts. "Oh, that's rich. Well, I suppose I gave you plenty of material."

He observes the derision in her face; at thirty-five he has learned to regulate his reactions to her. Outwardly at least. Not that it slows her down any.

"What did I do to you that you have to do the opposite of everything that makes sense?" she asked. "Just once can't you take the easy way?"

"Easy's overrated."

She smiles humorlessly, then orients herself toward a more pleasing view. Her sitting-room window looks across the curved cliffs rimming Baker Beach. In the distance a hang glider leaps free of the earth and soars, dangling from rainbow wings, a dot against the choppy expanse of the Pacific. "We've all had hobbies. When I danced for Balanchine as a young woman, I never lost sight of my real responsibilities. And now with your father gone and you the last one." She takes a silent sip, as if her nerves need settling. But Evelyn's nerves never need settling. "This is because of her, isn't it? The illness."

"Yes, but in a good way. It's what I want. I've been lucky. I've made plenty of money—"

"With the job I handed you." The jeer seems not up to Evelyn's

standards, and sure enough her face registers a flicker of regret. Her insults are generally less trifling, better constructed. She turns to the window, her steel-gray hair fastened in a chignon. "You are built for your job. This is what we do. This family has weathered the Great Quake, two world wars, Black Monday, Black Friday—hell, a Black Each Day of the Week—and now you want what? To leave? Forge your own way in the world?" The last, tinged with mockery.

"Yes."

She turns, that silhouette, framed against the double-paned glass, still striking. "You'll never make it."

"Why?" he asks.

She touches her lips to the rim of her cocktail glass as if to nibble it. "Because I couldn't."

He shows himself out. He is at his car when he hears dress shoes crunching the quartz stone of the circular driveway behind him; James is too well mannered to call out. Before James has to say anything, Daniel nods, sighs heavily, and heads back inside.

There has been a set change. Evelyn is sitting on the velvet couch in the sunroom, flipping through a magazine. "You know, Daniel, I've been thinking. Maybe this is a good thing. All this talk about helping others. You and Constanza—"

"Cristina."

"—have been so vocal about good works and charity that it's made me consider my own blessed lot in life. Long look in the mirror, et cetera." A smile creases her face, stopping well short of her eyes. "In fact, you've inspired me to bequeath my estate, my entire estate, to the arts. A museum. Perhaps the opera house. Isn't that something you'd approve of?"

Now, that, he thinks, is an Evelyn-grade assault.

At last her smile is genuine. His mouth has gone to sand, and he feels the familiar fury burning through his veins, but then he blinks and sees her with a moment of pristine clarity, as if a filter had been changed on his camera lens. He sees her as if she were just another seventy-six-year-old lady, sitting next to him at a play or getting off a *bus from the Midwest, a petulant woman-child full of flaws and scars who wants to take her toys and go home. He breathes out and feels the tightness in his chest release, if only slightly.*

"Yes, Mom," he says. "Great idea."

The elevator heaved to a stomach-jolting stop in the lobby, and Daniel passed through the metal-detector checkpoint, dropping his keys into a plastic dish. He rode another elevator to the third floor and stepped out into the corridor. For three years he'd walked these halls, ridden that Clorox elevator. In a few months, he'd be moving on. As he braced himself and headed for the meeting room, it struck him just how much he'd miss all this.

He could already hear the group milling around beyond the corner. Rowdy laughter. A sharp curse. The threat of violence, coursing like the sound of a timpani beneath the murmurs.

His adrenaline flared, a distinct pulse in the blood. Deep breath. Gather yourself.

Here we go.

Chapter 4

"How the hell," A-Dre said, giving Daniel a once-over, "could some-one like *you* help me?"

Anton Andre Powell answered only to "A-Dre" when he answered at all. He'd been sullen in last week's intake session, but his high IQ and quick emotions had convinced Daniel to take a gamble on him for group. Now A-Dre slouched in his chair before the others, wear-ing a stained wife-beater, arms crossed, his dark skin lit with tattoos. Flames up his forearms, *"LaRonda"* written in an Old English font on the side of his neck, prison-ink spiderweb clutching his elbow. A circular burn scar the diameter of a softball marred his left biceps, the skin shiny and bottle-cap-crimped at the edges.

"I'm not sure yet," Daniel said. "Want to stay and find out?"

"What choice I got?" A-Dre sneered.

"There are always choices."

A-Dre sucked his teeth, glaring at the five other group members. The three men, like A-Dre, were large and bulky and loose on their chairs, fingers laced behind necks, spread arms, sprawling legs, taking up as much space as possible. Power postures. Daniel always sat ev-eryone in a circle with no table between them so he could observe each member's body language and take note of these peacock dis-plays. X was stretched out like the men, while Lil hugged her stom-ach, crossed her legs, and hunched forward, an "I'm not here" pose.

The spacious room felt almost industrial; even with the stacks of chairs and shoved-aside desks along the perimeter, there remained plenty of empty tile around their little circle. A set of large windows dominated the north wall, able to be cranked open barely a few inches. Very little fresh air to dilute the smell of damp concrete and floor wax.

A-Dre eyed the old-fashioned chalkboard and its three powdery words: REASON AND REHABILITATION. "What you gonna teach me 'bout choices?"

Daniel said, "Nothing you don't want to learn."

A-Dre weighed this, his face fixed and scornful, older than his twenty-four years. He'd kept apart from the others as they'd shuffled in, ignoring them as they joked about past members who'd completed the group and moved on. The Good Old Days routine always reemerged when someone new cycled in, a way for established members to band together in the face of disruption.

Daniel had sat A-Dre with his back to the door, the position a tough-guy shot caller would least want to take. Keep him off center, break up his usual approach, change his perspective. The guy had certainly earned his stripes in the system. A few years back, he'd been nabbed on possession with intent, and the arresting officer had found in his pockets an unregistered gun and hastily scribbled plans to break his older brother out of prison. He and big bro had been reunited after all.

Daniel turned to the circle. "Why don't you go around, introduce yourselves to A-Dre, tell him why you're here, what you hope to get out of group, maybe offer some advice."

The predictable tape delay. Blinking. Someone coughed. Daniel let the silence govern.

"I'll go," Big Mac finally said, slinging a boot up to rest on the broad shelf of his knee. In one hand he clanked a grip strengthener, bringing swollen knuckles into view. "I got a wife and two kids to take care of, and I've had trouble with the economy, holding down a job—though right now I got a good gig as a waste collector."

X mouthed, *Garbage man,* but Big Mac didn't notice.

"Good gig except when I'm smashing my damn fingers between the barrels." He gestured at the bruised back of his hand. "Anyway, I been in for some short stints, year here, four years there, but still. Four years when you have kids . . ." He shook his head. "That stretch . . . well, I'd been outta work a long time and things were . . . thin. So I tried to hit an armored truck."

For the first time, A-Dre perked up. "Just you?"

"Yeah. I didn't take on the truck. I'm stupid, but not *that* stupid. I caught the transport guard in an elevator, pulled on him. But there were more waiting at the ground floor, and it was gonna go bad, so . . ." A shrug. "No one got hurt." He wiped his mouth. "I'm here 'cuz I'm forty-five years old and I don't want to go back to prison no more." A couple nervous clasps of the hand strengthener—*clank-clank*. "Group don't guarantee that life won't suck or that you'll get everything you want when you want it. It's fucking hard in here. You will have setbacks. Like the counselor says, change don't come overnight. Sometimes it don't come at all. But you show up. That's what you do. You show up."

All eyes shifted to Walter Fang, who realized with evident discomfort that he was next. His gym-strong body was slouched in his chair, the ragged cuffs of his sweater pushed up past muscular forearms. He sat with his coat in his lap, ready to split, eyeing the door when he wasn't eyeing his watch; he generally entered the room slow and left fast. Bright yellow Pumas matched the piping on his tracksuit pants. His hair, gelled and impeccably spiked, gleamed wetly under the sterile, blue-tinged lighting.

"I got busted for assault with . . . ah, ah, intent to kill. The dude shot my cousin. I got him in Portsmouth Square and broke his jaw. And his cheek. And his arm. And his knee. And then I got caught. I was drunk so I didn't run away when the cops came. I do bad when I drink. I try not to go to the strip club because I spend money and I . . . ah, ah, drink there. And if I drink, I miss group, and if I miss group, I go back inside, so . . . ah, ah, no strip clubs. It's been three months, and at the end of every month I don't go to the strip club, I buy myself . . . ah, ah, ah—"

18

He was stuck, so Daniel helped finish the thought. "He buys himself a new pair of sneakers."

Fang nodded and slumped back down in his chair. A-Dre crossed his arms and looked bored.

" 'Kay. My name is Xochitl." She drew it out: *So-Chee.* "But everyone calls me X. This is my seat. Don't take my fucking seat. Let's see. Advice. Use the stairs. They don't break down twice a week." She laughed, showing gleaming white teeth. With long, loose waves of dark hair drawn back by two thin front braids, she would have been beautiful if she weren't so busy looking tough. "I'm workin' on my GED—Counselor here got me into a program." She knocked the binder in her lap, overflowing with her intricate sketches of bejeweled female warriors and elf queens. "I'm only nineteen, so I'm not that far behind if you think about it. I'm gonna be a comic artist and have my own reality TV show and shit, *Droppin' with X,* with hot tubs and—"

"X," Daniel said.

"Okay, okay. I got all the boo-hoo childhood shit, too. Runnin' drugs in my underwear by the time I was five. Had a sick mom I had to support, so I was dealing by the time I was ten. She died, and then I ran away, joined a gang."

"Where you did . . . ?" Daniel prompted.

She flashed that youthful smile again. "Gang shit."

Big Mac gestured at A-Dre. "Tell the man what you got charged for."

X glowered at the room. "Rape. We jumped new girls into the gang, you know. With a stick. Five of us. One to hold down each limb and one to, ya know? It's what was done. Like I said, there were five of us, but I took the fall."

Across the circle, Lil shook her head faintly in disgust.

A-Dre had barely bothered to make eye contact with anyone. He cast an irritated glance over his shoulder, checking the door.

"Okay, Martin?" Daniel said.

Martin shifted in his chair, his broad shoulders rolling like the flanks of a bear. He wore black J. J. Abrams glasses that in another zip code would be hipster cool and was prone to flannel—today was an olive-and-black plaid. Tucked behind his left ear was a single bent cigarette.

"My lady was dying," Martin said. "Skin cancer. It just drilled down and . . . *ate* her. By the end her skin, it was"—his hand hovered around his face and neck, trembling—"patches. The treatments were serious dollar, wiped us out. But the cancer, it didn't care when we ran outta jack. So I knocked off a coupla grocery stores. Bunch of tills, in and out." With a trace of pride, he added, "Took 'em a month to catch me." His faint accent was generic urban, indistinct enough to resist any clear ethnic association. "I only got six years, 'cuz I didn't hurt no one, got knocked to three for good behavior. I was almost forty when I got out with nothing to get out *for.* My lady, she died when I was inside. She was the purest thing I ever knew." He bent his head, brown scalp shining through the throwback buzz cut. His worn shoes showed Magic Marker where he'd touched them up. "Best thing about group is you can't con a con man. We know when we're fulla shit. And we can learn from each other's mistakes."

Lil giggled nervously. "I guess it's just me. My turn." She averted her eyes, biting her lips, adjusting her clothes—always a flurry of movement and discomfort. "I was kind of a lookout or driver sorta for my husband, who robbed banks, and he's . . . um, he's in jail. The robberies, they were always his plan, not mine."

"You'll learn quick," X told A-Dre. "Nothing's ever her fucking fault."

Daniel looked at Lil to see if she'd stick up for herself, but she just offered A-Dre a weak smile, then shoved at her stringy brown hair, inadvertently showing a flash of bruised cheek. If history was a guide, that bruised cheek would not be discussed.

"I, um, was never on my own, really, until now, and so he was all I knew, and so if he said jump, I said how high, and if he said park here and wear a mask, I'd say Zorro or Batman?" Another nervous titter. "And Daniel's been helping me sort of figure out why I might need to look at all that, I guess. I have to remember I'm shooting for progress, not perfection, because sometimes progress is, um . . . slow."

An awkward silence, broken of course by X. "Come on, Counselor," she said. "Give him the speech now."

In group therapy the rules were essential. In *criminal* group therapy, the rules could be life and death.

Daniel turned to A-Dre. "No violence or threats of violence. We meet every Monday, Wednesday, and Friday for two hours. You need to show up on time and sober. You're here for six months, and you cannot miss a single session without a doctor's note. If you're late, it counts as a missed session. If you get asked to or choose to leave two times, it counts as a missed session."

"Can't miss one suck-ass session?" A-Dre said.

"Not one suck-ass session. The routine matters as much as what we talk about in here. Learning to show up, be responsible, accountable. And under no circumstances can you share the IDs of the other members of this group. Nothing leaves this room. We have full confidentiality here."

A-Dre smirked. " 'Cept you. Like you ain't gonna tell my PO every last *word* I say."

"My job's not to trap you or get you in trouble with your parole officer. If you're not a threat to yourself or others, nothing leaves this room. If you mention past crimes that you haven't been convicted for, don't tell us who, when, where, or how." Daniel turned to the group. "Want to tell him the other rules?"

"No standing"—*clank-clank*—"when you're pissed off."

"We don't like, um, jabbing your finger at people."

"No meeting outside group. Or . . . ah, ah, sex with anyone from group."

"No taking my fucking chair."

A-Dre sat like a snake, cold and still, expressionless eyes boring through the far wall, his torso perfectly rigid. Daniel removed one of his business cards, crossed out the listed cell phone, and jotted his new number on the back. He'd already handed out a round of marked-up cards to the others—no sense getting new ones printed, given his impending departure.

He offered the card to A-Dre. "This is my cell. For emergencies only. I'd suggest you keep my card on you at all times."

A-Dre stared at the proffered card for an aggressively long time before taking it.

"What we ask for is honesty and accountability," Daniel said. "If you're honest in here, you'll make progress. If you're not, you won't. It's that simple."

"Honesty, huh?" A-Dre's mouth twisted to the left. Contempt: the only facial expression that occurs on just one side of the face. "Well, lemme drop a little truth on *you*. I don't want to be here. If there weren't no court *man*date, I *wouldn't* be here. Fuck this place."

Right on schedule.

"Okay," Daniel said. "I get it. You feel forced to be here. You hate it. But you're here anyway. So maybe think about what you want to do while you're here."

The notion, dismissed with a flick of the head. "And if I leave?"

"You know the answer to that. Back to court with noncompliance, you'll be revoked to prison. Or. You show up every session, your sheet gets initialed, and everyone's happy. Or at least not incarcerated."

"So like I said, I got no choice."

Martin said, "First week I was scared, too."

"I ain't scared, spic. I don't got no fears."

"That's another rule," Daniel said. "No slurs. Swear all you want, but racial slurs won't be tolerated. Understand?"

A-Dre gave the faintest of nods. "I'm not like you fools. I don't need to be here."

X twisted a strand of hair around her finger. *"Fail."*

"Got it all figured out, huh?" Big Mac said.

"Yeah," A-Dre said. "I do."

"Nothing to learn?" Daniel asked.

"No."

X chimed in again, flicking her chin to indicate A-Dre's neck tattoo. "Your girl LaRonda gonna say you perfect?"

A-Dre lifted his left shoulder in a partial shrug. Not a firm no. Progress. But still not much.

Daniel waited, let him breathe, waited for the words to work their way to the surface.

"I had a friend did this counseling shit," A-Dre said. "Didn't make it. He's back inside."

"Okay," Daniel said. "So therefore . . ."

Nothing.

Daniel finished the other half of the equation for him. "So therefore *no one* can make it?"

A flare of anger. "Maybe so. Sittin' here talking 'bout *choice*. How do you know what it's like to have your back to the wall? To *do what you need to do*?" The last, a staccato beat of anger. "Look, I get it. I'm the one who planned to bust my bro-bro outta the pen. But no matter what bullshit we spew in here . . . at the end of the day, I'm still just a criminal to people like you."

"That's not how I see you," Daniel said.

"Is that so?" A sneer. "How you see me?"

"Like I see everyone. As someone who made choices, some good, some shitty."

"Well, lemme tell you. Bein' in here? With you? It ain't gonna change *shit*. I am who I am because they *made* me this way. *Change*. I don't got the *option* to change. I went to jail because that's what the system does to people like me." He crossed his arms and cocked his head. "My only *choice* was Folsom or San Quentin." He sucked his teeth again and looked away.

Impenetrable. Unreachable. Tuned out.

Daniel scanned the others. They were giving A-Dre and him the floor.

He bit his lip and considered the metal folding chairs, framing a circle much like a wrestling ring. Combatants and rules and timed periods. You hold back, stay light on your feet, gauge your opponent. Do the dance until you see an opening. And then it goes like lightning.

You miss your shot, you wind up knocked on your ass, staring at the ceiling, teeth grinding in your skull. Or your opponent lunges first and you use him against himself, finding a point of leverage and leaning hard, locking out a joint, letting him ride his own momentum down.

And sometimes you go for the full-frontal out-and-out attack.

Which of course was higher risk.

And higher reward.

Daniel could feel his heartbeat in the side of his neck, tapping in the fragile artery, a reminder of the stakes should this go awry. *Just once can't you take the easy way?*

He cleared his throat. Leaned forward, elbows on knees, angling his shoulders, a knifepoint posture. His voice low, aggressive. "You pathetic idiot."

A-Dre stiffened on his chair. Whatever he was expecting, it was not this.

"Letting the world grind you down, huh?" Daniel said. "Nothing your fault. You got your tough-guy marks. Your cheap-ass tattoos."

The others drew slowly upright on their chairs. They'd never seen Daniel take this tack, but they'd seen plenty of times where it led in other situations.

A-Dre wet his lips. "The fuck you say to me, you white-ass piece of shit?"

The sudden electricity amped up Daniel's senses, his skin tightening. One of Fang's shiny sneakers squeaked faintly against the tile. The stale air tasted of rusting pipes, cigarette smoke, the sweet rot of the disintegrating subfloor.

Daniel said, "That spiderweb on your elbow, supposed to show that you got caught in the system, right? You're too dumb to know it used to be a white-supremacy tat."

A-Dre jerked to his feet as if pulled by a hook, the chair knocked over by the backs of his legs, rattling the tiles. His shoulders bulged, arms tensed, veins rising. His neck, a wall of cords.

Daniel implored him silently, *Don't charge me. Have just enough control to let me get to the other side.*

He forced a laugh. "A black man wearing an Aryan Brotherhood tattoo. That's rich."

A-Dre lunged forward, and for an instant Daniel was sure he'd gambled wrong, that he'd misgauged the man and the session was going to end with blood spatter on the floor. But A-Dre stopped over him, arm jacked to the side, forefinger and thumb hammering the air above Daniel's head, punctuating each word. He was screaming, lost in rage.

"Motherfucker, you say one more thing! You say one more thing!"

Daniel kept his seat, fighting every instinct in his body that was telling him to rise, to protect himself. He kept the pitch of his voice the same, not escalating but not backing down, maintaining direct, hostile eye contact. "You just broke three rules," he said, "in ten seconds. Look at you. Your heart's racing. Clenched fists, raised voice. Your jaw's tight. You like feeling this way?"

"Course I don't fucking like it. You're making me—"

Daniel pounced. "That's right. I'm *making* you. *I* did this to you. All this. You know why? Because I'm *smarter* than you. *Better* than you. You're a puppet. I'm controlling your voice, your heartbeat, your muscles—"

"No one controls me!" A-Dre yelled. "It's my body. I act how *I* want to act."

"No," Daniel said. "I made you pop up off your chair and stomp over here, swearing and yelling. Admit it. *I* did this to you, didn't I? *Didn't I!*"

A-Dre drew back a fist. It loomed there, behind his ear, quivering. Lil gave a little cry. Daniel looked up at the cocked fist, the bulging arm, the whole room hanging by a thread.

"Bullshit!" A-Dre screamed. "*I* did. *I did it myself.*"

The words rang off the hard walls. A-Dre's face shifted as the words bounced back off the echo. Registering them for the first time.

No sound in the room. A frozen tableau—six bodies on chairs and one figure standing. A-Dre's chest heaved and fell, heaved and fell.

"You're right," Daniel said. "Which means you can change it."

All the air seemed to go out of A-Dre, the puffed-up chest deflating, the straining muscles suddenly lax and shuddering as if of their own volition. He lowered his arm, shuffled two steps back, and sat.

"Welcome to group," Daniel said. "I'm glad you're here."

Chapter 5

"Daniel Brasher, don't you run away from me!"

Session had ended, and the members finished filing out, mixing with a group of sullen teens from the juvie group up the hall. Daniel turned with a smile as Kendra Richardson, a mountain of a woman, ambled up the corridor after him, bracelets jangling about her wrists. The corridor emptied out, doors banging, elevator dinging, leaving them alone with the faint hiss of the heating vents.

Setting his satchel briefcase at his feet, he gave his program director a hug, disappearing into that delightful blend of Ed Hardy perfume and cinnamon gum.

"Did you sign your termination agreement?" she asked. Then, off his blank expression, "Look, baby, I'm happy if you *don't*."

"What termination agreement?"

"The one that went out to you last month."

"Went out to me where?"

She drew back her head. "Where you think? Your work box, here."

"You mean they *haven't* been forwarding my mail to my house?"

She fluttered a hand at him. "That whole mess again? Remind me the problem?"

They'd been over it half a dozen times. The mail room in the bowels of the building had never been upgraded, the employee boxes no more than a bank of creaky wooden cubbyholes, each with a sedimentary layering of brittle, flaking labels—the remnants of workers past. Daniel had landed a box near the top, just beneath the outgoing-mail cubby, which was labeled OUTG IN MAIL. Which meant that folks accidentally shoved their mail into his box all the time. Which in turn had led him to make multiple requests that all his mail be forwarded to his house so he'd no longer have to sort through his colleagues' mail or the painstakingly addressed letters of various parolees just to get the occasional departmental notice. Kendra's administrative assistant was supposed to check his box to make sure everything was being appropriately routed, though she rarely showed interest in tasks aside from applying makeup and conducting cell-phone conversations at high volume.

"The problem is," he said, "that the only mail I get here is other people's."

"We'll get it straightened out. Just in time for you to head off to your fancy-pants private practice and forget all about us." She flipped her chin sharply away in mock offense. Kendra ran the perennially understaffed department like a benevolent matriarchy; affection and guilt were rarely in short supply.

He said, "First of all, I could *never* forget the woman who gave me my first break in the field"—a slight softening of her rigid neck—"and second, I'm still here another couple of months. Don't go writing my obituary yet."

He'd been steadily downsizing his workload so it would be a smooth transition for the program when he left. At one time he'd been juggling four groups, but he'd concluded three as the members graduated out. Kendra had begged him to stay on with this last group, though they'd need to phase in another therapist to see the members to the finish line. He'd have to tell them soon that he was leaving, give them time to adjust.

After promising Kendra that he'd dig out his termination agreement, he found the back stairs and descended to the mail room. He checked his watch; the hallway chat had put him behind for his already late-night dinner with Cristina, so he quickened his pace. The lights were on motion sensors to save money for the city, the corridors illuminating in swaths as he hurried forward. Sure enough, his mail cubby was stuffed with mail, so he stretched his satchel briefcase open and raked the envelopes in. He'd sort them out at home, bring back what wasn't his on Wednesday.

Sliding out a last stack of mail, he caught a splinter in his knuckle, and then the lights went out on him. He leaned back, balancing the briefcase on one knee and waving a hand to catch the sensor. He had to laugh a bit at himself. What a contrast with the new office suite he was checking out in the morning. Sleek marble and plush carpet and electricity that stayed on when you flipped the switch. After three years of blood and sweat, heartache and small triumphs, maybe he was finally ready to make it easy on himself.

He reset the burglar alarm behind him and headed up the stairs, which gleamed with Lemon Pledge—Cris's doing. Now and then they'd hire a cleaning lady, but every time they brought in someone regular, Cris would wind up tidying the place beforehand, making the woman lunch, and advising her son about college loans. Quickly, the convenience turned into a second job. She laughed about it— what a joke, you hear the one about the overzealous Pacific Heights housewife?—but at the end of the day, she preferred that the Brashers clean their own damn house.

She waited upstairs at the kitchen island, sitting over a glass of wine and a sliced loaf of Boudin sourdough, her hair up so a fan of caramel skin showed at her back collar. She turned at his footsteps, chin to shoulder. "Chicken reheating in the oven, *mi vida*. Five minutes."

He drew near, kissed her between the shoulder blades. "How was your day?"

Her head shook ever so slightly, and then she gave a faint sniffle. The heel of her hand rose to her cheek, and a spot of wet tapped the glossy photo on the counter in front of her. A birth announcement from a childhood friend. It showed a newborn swaddled in a blue hospital blanket, eyes no more than seams in a wrinkled face.

Daniel slid beside Cris, put his arms around both shoulders, and kissed her head as she wiped at her tears.

"Wow," she said. "Talk about self-centered. I should just be happy for them. I *am* happy for them, but I should *just* be."

He adopted his best commercial voice-over tone. "*Guilt: When feeling bad's not enough.*"

She laughed a little, hit his arm gently. "Okay, okay. You know what'll make me feel better? Sending a gift." She reached for her silver laptop, across by the prep sink. "Babyregister-dot-com. I'm sure they have my credit card on file by now."

He waited, watching her.

"I'm okay." She kissed him, a peck pushing his face away. "I'm fine. Two minutes. Chicken."

He walked over to the living-room couch and dumped out his briefcase on the glass coffee table. Flyers and envelopes and junk mail. Sifting through the mess, he searched for the form—no, the "termination agreement." Who named these things? Last week he'd been stuck on hold with a "listening-care associate," which was enough to make him want to—

Finally. A clasp envelope in the distinctive gray of the department.

The timer dinged, and Cris clapped her Mac shut and padded to the oven.

He pinched up the metal clasps, ran a finger beneath the flap, and slid free a single sheet. At first he couldn't register what he was reading—the uneven scratch of the handwriting, the pencil-scraped letters cramped, then spaced, on the unlined white page—but the words came clear, one by one, and his heart did something funny against his ribs. The air had gone suddenly frigid, prickling the hairs at the base of his neck. He blinked hard and looked again, this time the sentences rushing at him.

admit what your done. or you will bleed for it.

Chapter 6

"Uh, hon?" Daniel's eyes, still fixed on the cramped handwriting.

Hoisting the roasting pan, Cris replied with a faint noise in the back of her throat. Then he heard metal thunk against Caesarstone, and she seemed to have levitated to his side, oven mitt on his back; his face must have mirrored the shock vibrating his insides.

She read over his shoulder. "Is that a joke?"

"Doesn't feel like one."

"'Admit what you've done,'" she read. "What are you supposed to have done?"

"I have no idea."

"Disgruntled group member, maybe?" She tugged off the oven mitt, let it slap to the floorboards. "Whatever it is, it's creepy as hell."

Daniel turned the sheet over, his fingers leaving impressions. On the back, the same sloppy handwriting, pencil pushed hard enough to leave grooves in the paper.

you hav til november 15 at midnite

"Last Friday," Daniel said. "November fifteenth was last Friday. The deadline's already passed. That makes no sense."

Cris snatched the torn gray envelope from his lap and flipped it over. Through her teeth she shot a breath strong enough to flutter the envelope in her hand. "It's not for you."

31

"Not for . . . ?" He stopped, his brain still jarred out of gear. "Right." A rush of relief. "So it was outgoing mail that the person accidentally stuck in my box. Intended for . . . ?"

She lowered the envelope for him to read.

jack holley

And an address in the Tenderloin. The city, misspelled, with no state or zip code.

The stamp, unmarred by a postal mark. Not surprisingly, there was no return address.

"So Jack Holley, whoever he is, never got this ultimatum," Daniel said.

He looked up from the couch, and she looked down at him. Her hand, clammy against his neck.

At the same time, they directed their stares to the silver laptop on the kitchen counter.

Side by side, they walked over. Cris flipped the laptop open and keyed JACK HOLLEY TENDERLOIN into Google. Took a deep breath. Her finger hovered above the return key. A faint sheen of perspiration glistened on her cheek.

Reaching across, he clasped his hand over hers and lowered her finger to the key.

The little wheel spun atop the page as it loaded, and then the top search result slapped them in their faces.

LONGTIME TENDERLOIN RESIDENT
VICTIM OF BRUTAL KNIFE MURDER

November 16—Everyone in the **Tenderloin** seemed to know **Jack Holley**. Always a bright smile and a wave on his way to the second-floor walk-up where he'd lived for nearly thirty years. Which is why his vicious murder last night has left this community in shock. . . .

Heat rolled across Daniel's skin. He felt his face flush, his breath snag in his throat. "Not a joke," he said.

Cristina glanced down at the envelope still in her hand, then released it quickly onto the counter, as if it had burned her. Her throat lurched a bit when she swallowed. "Okay," she said. "Now what?"

Chapter 7

When Daniel opened the door, the woman behind it was not at all what he expected. Attractive bordering on stunning—pronounced cheekbones, smooth ebony skin, slender body fitted into a plain white oxford and pressed slacks—and younger than seemed plausible. She couldn't have been thirty. A small hip-holstered pistol bulged her jacket on the right side.

"Thanks for coming so quickly, Detective."

"It's 'Inspector.' San Francisco likes to be special. Which means we get to be inspectors instead of mere detectives." She flashed a quick smile, showing honest-to-God dimples, and it was no longer a question of *bordering* on stunning.

Daniel stepped aside. "My wife, Cristina."

The inspector offered her hand. "Nice to meet you. Theresa Dooley, Homicide Detail. Your husband and I spoke on the phone."

"Glad you're here," Cris said. "Can I get you something to drink?"

"Nah, I'm good." Dooley moved inside with a single swift step, glancing up the two-story height of the foyer. "Now you're *Brasher*, right? As in the Brasher—"

"Yep," Daniel said. "The letter's on the kitchen counter. Right up this way."

As Dooley followed them up, Cris said, "We didn't handle it anymore after . . . you know, we saw what it was. We figured fingerprints."

"Smart," Dooley said.

"I'm a Mission High grad. That's what we learned instead of baking pies in home ec."

"Mission High?" Dooley paused on the stairs. "No shit. I went to Balboa."

Cris's face lightened. "The Buccaneers."

"First time I've heard a Bear call us anything but the Fuckaneers."

"You're armed, so I thought I'd restrain myself."

"Less armed than I was back then." Dooley's grin seemed more for their surprising rapport than at the crack. "Did you know the Hernandez brothers?" she asked. "Linebackers?"

"I'm out of your age range, lady," Cris said. "I knew the *older* Hernandez brothers. Carjackers."

Dooley laughed. "Jesus, those games. Ex-con parents rolling in on Harleys, bumping Tupac. You guys had those rump-shaking cheerleaders."

"Yeah, we did," Cris said. "It was good to get out."

"Yup. I don't see many grads in houses like this," Dooley said. "Actually, I don't see many grads I'm not *handcuffing*."

They hit the landing, and Cris and Daniel slowed, the good mood instantly dissipating. On the kitchen island next to the pan of cooling chicken and Cris's now-drained wineglass, the envelope and sheet of paper were spotlit like objets d'art.

The inspector's face shifted. All business.

Dooley read the letter, then removed a pair of tweezers from her jacket pocket and used them to flip the sheet. "Weird handwriting, huh?"

"The pencil really scraped into the paper," Daniel said. "Like the words were *carved*. A lot of anger behind them. And the spatial organization on the page is off, too. See how it slants there? Plus, some of the letters are too close, others far apart. Might indicate dyslexia."

Dooley chewed her cheek, leaning over the paper. "A counselor, you said, right? Any other insights?"

"Well, it's probably from someone in Metro South. I mean, who would walk a letter to a rear mail room in a random building?"

"Someone trying not to get caught."

"But the person obviously wasn't planning to screw up and stick the letter in the wrong mailbox. He had to figure it would just get picked up with the rest of the outgoing mail and go straight out. Wouldn't be marked until the post office. So there wouldn't have *been* any trail back to the building to worry about."

"Point taken." Dooley fluffed out a large evidence bag. "So who's in your building on a given day?"

"Aside from social-services workers?" Daniel said. "Felons, parolees, juvenile delinquents."

Dooley grimaced.

"We've got Probation and Parole on floors two and three, Anger Management on the fourth, Domestic Violence on the fifth, and—" He caught himself. "Basically, there's no one in the building who *wouldn't* be a suspect."

"Splendid." Using the tweezers, Dooley guided the letter into the Ziploc. "I'll put on my Miss Marple costume and we'll lock everyone in the conservatory until we straighten it out."

Daniel barely registered the joke, his thoughts moving to the people he passed in those corridors every day, rode next to in the elevators, made small talk with at the vending machines. One of them had issued a threat and carried it out with the edge of a blade. For a nausea-inducing moment, Daniel found himself considering the merry band of parolees who composed his own group. A-Dre's scowl leapt up from memory, the heat behind his words: *I am who I am because they* made *me this way.*

Dooley had said something.

"What?" Daniel asked.

She tapped the envelope with her tweezers. "I said, what do you make of the envelope? You said it was the kind used by the department?"

"Yeah, but that doesn't mean it was an employee," Daniel said. "We have supplies stolen all the time. Anything that's not locked down."

"Sounds like you're running some effective rehabilitation over there."

"The news said it was brutal," Cris cut in abruptly. Her arms were crossed as if against a sudden cold, and Daniel realized she'd been missing from the conversation for a while. "The murder," she said. "Was it brutal?"

Dooley paused with the tweezers but did not look up. "Yes," she said.

Cris refilled her wineglass, her hand shaking. Dooley's eyes lifted, taking note of the uneven pour.

Rather than drink, Cris pushed the rim of the glass against both lips, steadying herself. "You've been investigating Jack Holley's murder. Already, I mean?"

"I caught the case, yeah," Dooley said. "That's why you got me."

"Any leads?" Cris pressed. "I mean, are you close to catching whoever did this?"

"I can't really discuss that," Dooley said. "But no."

Daniel watched the inspector navigate the envelope into the second plastic bag. Then glanced over at Cristina, her face as close to blanched as her skin could manage. He said, "I'm sorry I didn't . . ." He trailed off.

"Look," Dooley said, "it's a break. Would've been better a *week* ago, but . . ." She glanced up, caught his crestfallen expression, put it together. "Come *on*. You're supposed to know to check your box every day in case an inept murderer accidentally sticks a threat with a deadline in there?"

Daniel's mouth was bitter, the taste of regret. "So a man died because the mail wasn't sorted properly."

"I consider myself an expert in guilt," Dooley said, "so let me clear this up right now. You couldn't have done anything. This is one of those little cosmic jokes the world plays on us now and again. A tiny tear in the fabric just to show how things *really* are. Which is? Out of our control. Thousands of people die every day because they caught the wrong green light or chose the wrong surgeon. You didn't do this. A knife-wielding motherfucker did this. And you've got no more guilt in the matter than Jack Holley's daughter for not inviting him to dinner that night or his neighbor for not knocking on his door at eleven fifty-nine to borrow a cup of sugar."

She sealed the second Ziploc and shook them both for emphasis. "Now CSI's gonna take a look at these. In the meantime I'll see what I can do about handwriting samples from the reprobates who cycle through your workplace. As you know, mental-health files are confidential, so we'll have to get creative. And we'll regulate the outgoing mail down there in case our suspect's chicken scratch shows up on a letter to his Aunt Shandrika. My job is to answer the key question."

"Which is?" Daniel asked.

"What did Jack Holley *do*?" Dooley pointed at them. "Your job is to take care of each other and not think about this too much. Think you can manage that?"

"One out of two, probably," Daniel said.

They showed her out and got ready for bed, but twenty minutes later Daniel was still lying there, staring at the ceiling, the sheets clinging to him like vines, the dark room choked with toxic images. The mail room with its flickering light and creaky cubbyholes. That cramped handwriting sliding into view as he'd tugged the sheet free. Poor Jack Holley.

Sweating, exasperated, Daniel threw back the sheets and sat up, rubbing his face. The walls held the faintest fragrance of a pumpkin candle they'd burned the night before, the comforting scent now cloying. He felt Cristina's sleep-hot hand on his back.

"You okay, *mi vida*?"

"You're awake?"

"Not really."

"Go to sleep."

He guided her back to the pillow, kissed her temple. After draining the cup of water on his nightstand, he padded down the stairs, clicking on the under-cabinet lights in the kitchen. The heated tiles were warm underfoot, and the Sub-Zero gave off a comforting hum. The knives, magnetized to a metal strip and lined by descending size, were all accounted for. Across the room, the alarm pad glowed a reassuring green.

Safe. It was safe here.

He filled his cup from the filtered tap and started back for the stairs, passing the couch and the glass coffee table with the mound of dumped mail. His hand had just flipped the light switch when he froze. Dread mounted, constricting his throat. Something replayed in his mind, an afterimpression ghost-floating on his retinas. Real or imagined?

Nailed to the floor. Fingertips still touching the switch. Stomach gone to ice. He felt an overwhelming urge just to head upstairs to the warmth of his bed.

But.

He pressed the switch, bringing the lights back on. Slowly, he turned his head to take in that mess of dumped-out mail on the coffee table, limned again in the dim glow.

Peeking from the mound, partially buried, was a second department-gray clasp envelope. And, protruding from the far edge, a third.

On both he could make out a familiar uneven scrawl.

Chapter 8

Swimming in Daniel's San Francisco Giants shirt, her hair taken up loosely in a butterfly hair clamp, Cristina paced furrows in the floor while Daniel sat on the couch over the two neatly positioned, still-sealed envelopes. The rest of the mail he'd swept off onto the Turkish rug. Ridiculously, he was wearing yellow dishwashing gloves, which he'd used to sift through the mound so as to give Homicide Detail's elaborately named "police secretarial assistant" at the other end of the phone a precise number of how many department-gray clasp envelopes he had in his possession.

Two.

Three, actually, but the third with its neatly typed label was in fact intended for him—the termination agreement Kendra had discussed with him in the hall.

The PSA told Daniel to sit tight and signed off, first assuring him that Inspector Dooley would get back to them.

Which left him and Cristina alone at 11:51 at night with two death threats staring at them from the coffee table like cocked guns.

lyle kane
376 bay st
san fransico

And beside it:

marisol vargas
1737 chestnut st #2
san fransico

They'd Googled both names already, finding nothing on Lyle Kane and scattered mentions of various Marisol Vargases, none of which mentioned any crime.

Cris chewed at a cuticle. "I wonder what they're doing right now. Lyle and Marisol."

Daniel was having trouble removing his eyes from the scrawled words. Two names, two lives.

"Sleeping," he said.

"And they don't know. They have no idea . . ."

He laced his fingers, the stupid yellow gloves squeaking together. For some reason he hadn't taken them off. He'd thrown on jeans and a sweatshirt as well, wanting to face the matter dressed. "We don't *know* that these letters are death threats, too."

"They don't look like Christmas cards."

"No, they don't."

Those gouged pencil marks. The envelopes, thin and nearly weightless. Each one, like the first, seemed to hold a single sheet. What the hell did they say?

Cris checked the phone in her hand, as if a call had somehow been missed in the last thirty seconds. "Where the hell could Dooley be?"

A fresh consideration soared in and skewered him. The words stuck in his throat, so he swallowed and tried again. "What if they're dead already? What if their deadlines already passed, like Jack Holley's?" He didn't say the rest: *Then a mix-up over the goddamned mail would have cost two more lives.*

At this, Cristina finally halted. Despite the cool nighttime air, her cheeks were flushed. Through the south-facing window, the city lights gleamed and wavered like something living.

She said, "Should we . . . open them?"

The question had been working at him like an ulcer since he'd laid eyes on those envelopes. He forced a measured answer. "Wouldn't that screw them up as evidence?"

"Not if you use gloves."

"How do you know?"

"*CSI: Miami.*" Cris crouched and set the ledge of her folded arms on the far side of the coffee table. Stared across those envelopes at him. Tapped the antenna of the cordless phone against her lips. "Between your mailbox and here, you've already touched them plenty. The cop told you to use the gloves to count them. It's not like *opening* them's gonna compromise them all of a sudden."

Daniel reasoned along with her. "Whenever the hell Dooley gets her hands on them, she's just gonna do it anyway."

His mouth had gone sour. The mounted clock behind him *tick-tick-ticked*. Cris ran a hand through her bangs and squeezed, hair spiking up between her fingers.

He nodded at her.

She nodded at him.

The first flap, insufficiently moistened, popped up easily.

admit what your done. or you will bleed for it.

The paper trembled in his grip as he turned it over.

you har til november 20 at midnite

A breath shuddered out of him. "That's Wednesday. Day after tomorrow—"

Cris was gripping the cordless tightly enough that her fingers had gone pale. "So Lyle Kane's still alive."

"And Dooley can get to him." He grabbed the next envelope and slid a yellow rubber forefinger under the flap, desperate to see if Marisol Vargas was already dead or if she still had a shot.

The sheet slid out. Same refrain on the front. And the back—

you hav til november 18 at midnite

His heart seized.

Tonight.

"What?" Cris said. "*What,* honey? You're freaking me out."

He turned and looked over his shoulder at the wall clock: *11:54.*

His voice, little more than a dry rasp. "Tonight."

"Where . . . ?" Cris bounded around the table to read the envelope without having to touch it. "Where's she—"

1737 chestnut st #2

"Jesus, that's across from Moscone Park."

Four blocks away.

Six minutes.

Four blocks.

The phone shrilled, and Cris yelped and jumped back, dropping it. The battery lid popped off, but the phone kept ringing as it spun over to tap Daniel's shoes. He snatched it up.

"Dooley?"

"I just got back. My guy filled me in. I was in the garage with no—"

"Midnight tonight he's killing the next person." A rush of words, his voice unrecognizable.

"You *opened* them? Wait. Midnight. That's—" Her breath blew sharply across the receiver. "What's the address?"

He rattled it off, and she shouted it to someone else.

Daniel was standing. "How long to get someone there?"

"We're too far away—we work out of Hall of Justice, twenty

minutes to get there. Nearest station is Northern. I'll have 'em pull a patrol unit off Western Addition. If they roll now, they could get there in fifteen, maybe ten if they code-three it."

"I can get there in five."

"Brasher?" Dooley's voice now cool and hard. "Stay put."

He was moving, taking giant strides across the room.

Cris was behind him, twisting her hands in the hem of the Giants shirt, shifting from bare foot to bare foot, her voice thin with fear: "You sure about this?"

He whipped past the island, tossed the phone on the counter, turned for the stairs. "No."

"You're not a cop, Daniel."

"I know. But a woman's gonna be attacked in *minutes*. How do I not at least go down there, knock on her door?"

"You could run right into the guy."

"I'll stay outside. I'm only gonna warn her, wait in the street with her for the cops. Look—there's no time to go around and around on this. I'll be careful."

Cris reached across the counter. The butcher knife came free from the magnetic strip with a soft ping. She extended it to him, handle first. Her thin arms trembled.

"Just in case," she said.

Chapter 9

Daniel took the Audi for more muscle, rocketing down the cascade of Webster, the undercarriage scraping and throwing off sparks like flicked cigarettes. The park flew by on the left, a shadowy expanse behind chain-link. The buildings' letters zoomed at him through the passenger window, and he slid to the curb, fumbling for the knife. From the dashboard the time glowed menacing red—12:03.

He leapt out, stumbling. Discordant laughter reached him from a late-night congregation on the dark softball fields across the street, but it seemed only to highlight the desolation of the midnight hour. The block, infused with his own dread, seemed postapocalyptic.

The lawned sidewalk strip housed a row of sycamores with pollarded branches, upthrust stumps like the severed arms of scarecrows. His footsteps jarred his vision as he sprinted across, his shoulder scuffing a trunk, sending off a puff of bark dust.

He searched for the street numbers, his wild gaze finally landing on 1737. Dueling columns, cracked steps leading to a wide, unlit porch inlaid with Art Deco tile. Three red doors stood out like something from a game show, the building carved into different apartments, number two oddly on the right.

He jumped up onto the porch and skidded to a stop before door number two, his heart thumping. A brass lion knocker stared out at him, and he stared right back.

Now what?

In his slalom down the hill, he hadn't contemplated much besides Marisol Vargas and the dashboard clock.

Sorry, ma'am, but someone with bad handwriting's coming to kill you, oh, right about now.

It would have to do.

As he reached for the brass knocker, his gaze snared on the narrow strip of black at the seam of the jamb. The door was a half inch ajar.

The killer was already inside.

The night breeze seemed to blow right through Daniel, bones and all.

He lifted his hand to the wood, applied a hint of pressure. The door swung silently inward.

The foyer, revealed by degrees. Side table with bowl. A Jim Dine print, tilted nearly off the wire. Tangled fringe of an expensive rug, one corner flipped back to show the pad beneath.

She'd fought.

His fist ached around the knife handle. His arm, knotting from the tension.

He told his fingertips to apply more pressure to the door, and they did, the view widening inch after maddening inch. Past the foyer, beyond the dark dining room, and through a doorway, a recessed light glowed in the kitchen ceiling.

He blinked, the tableau assembling itself in chunks.

Under the fall of light, a woman on her stomach, cheek mashed to the floor, her temple swollen, strands of hair matted to one bloody cheek. The kitchen doorjamb seeming to cut her off at the thighs. Her arms wrenched painfully back, wrists bound at the base of her spine. Eyes straining, pupils swimming in white.

She was staring directly at him.

With horror he realized that she must have been watching the entire time. Pinned to her own floor, her only view a sideways tilt through two unlit rooms, every last hope glued to the front door creeping open.

Dark tracks ran across the bridge of her nose and down her temple, and it took him a moment to realize through his shock what they were. Tears of blood. She'd been cut?

The woman's lips moved, and somehow he heard her fear-desiccated voice: ". . . help me."

Her imploring stare froze him there in the doorway.

The last thing he wanted to do was go into that house. But how could he leave her there?

From somewhere behind her, footsteps creaked the floor.

Daniel made no conscious decision to enter; his legs just moved him. Sliding inside, he eased the door mostly closed behind him to eliminate the light profile, however faint, from the porch.

There he was, armed with a cooking utensil and two weeks' training in hostage-crisis intervention, in a closed space with a murderer.

He took swift, weightless steps through the foyer, then sliced through the dining room to get out of the sight line, veering for the wall just beside the doorway. As he neared, a large shadow edged into view in the kitchen beyond, but he jerked right and flipped, planting his shoulder blades silently against drywall, just out of sight. Hanging plants all around stained the air with a fecund, earthy smell.

A blurred, masculine voice: "What?"

From the cramped vantage, Daniel could see only a sliver of kitchen, the outer edge of the light's glow, a tumble of Marisol's hair.

He was sucking air. His heartbeat seemed so loud he thought it might give him away.

Breathe. Breathe.

He wanted to get the drop, but there was no time. He'd have to go in blind. Straight jabs so the killer couldn't block his arm.

Just like a wrestling takedown.

But with a butcher knife.

". . . elp me."

Daniel braced himself. A panic beat pounded in his skull. His legs tensed to pivot and leap. *One . . . two . . .*

An instant before he reached *three,* he heard that same hushed voice say, "Here you go," followed immediately by a sickening sound: *Slit.*

Daniel had barely registered the noise when a mist of blood pattered on the visible wedge of kitchen tile.

There came a burbling of breath, then another faint spray of blood—timed with the heartbeat or the lungs.

A hideous rattling against the floor. The unmistakable sound of someone dying, just around the corner. Daniel's hesitation—the final second he'd taken to steel himself—had been the difference between her life and her death.

His heart jerked, a throat-crowding heave.

Even from the far side of the jamb, Daniel saw a sharp flash of light illuminate the kitchen—a camera? He jerked his head back, squinting against the flare.

Before he'd recovered, a dark form strode through the doorway, speeding right past him without taking note. The killer moved quickly but without panic, heading to the front door. The breeze from his movement chilled the panic sweat on Daniel's face. In the gloom Daniel could make out only parts of the man as he passed through falls of weak light from the windows. He seemed to be big, broad, indistinct in loose-fitting black sweats. At his side dangled a wicked-looking blade, a military knife that he swiped across his thigh and back again.

Unaware of Daniel, the man walked on through the dining room and into the foyer.

At once, for no apparent reason, he halted. His back to Daniel, he was nothing more than shadow against shadow, a charcoal silhouette.

Electricity coursed through Daniel. His chest seized. He didn't want to take a breath, didn't want to exhale. If he so much as shifted his weight, it could announce his frozen presence in the darkness.

The man's head cocked. What the hell was he looking at?

The front door. When Daniel had arrived, it was barely cracked. But in his rush to get to Marisol, he'd left it open several inches.

The man's arm shifted inside the sleeve of his sweatshirt, muscle flexing as he tightened his grip on the blade.

He turned.

And stared across the unlit dining room at Daniel in the shadows.

It was a horrifying blank face, nothing more than a polished oval. Wait, no—it was a black neoprene mask that was wrapped tight, removing the features. A missing figure-eight band for the eyes, like a reverse superhero mask. Triangular peak in place of the nose. A circle of breathing perforations where a mouth should be.

The knife spun around the man's black-gloved hand as if of its own accord, flipping across the knuckles, blade catching light. Then the fingers seized it in a new grip, angling it down along the forearm, cutting edge out. A well-practiced hold.

All sound vanished, leaving nothing but a white-noise rush in Daniel's ears. His back—literally to the wall. Nowhere to run. But that also meant the attacker had only one way at him. Daniel slid his heel to the baseboard, gauging the distance. Let him come, then counter hard.

Daniel lifted the butcher knife.

The man took a step toward him, then another, his boots pounding the floor as he wound into a run.

And then, in the distance, a police siren warbled, freezing the man just as he was getting up speed.

He and Daniel stared at each other across the length of the dining room. Daniel's chest burned, and he realized he was still holding his breath.

The masked face dipped a bit, perhaps in amusement, and then the other gloved hand rose from the man's pocket, a small digital camera lifting into view.

Before Daniel could process what was happening, a blinding flash bleached the unlit dining room, turning everything hospital white.

Bright spots, glued to Daniel's eyes, blotted the ensuing darkness. Yelling, he swiped at the air, blinking his way back to visibility. When it came, he saw that he was alone, stabbing at the darkness.

Chapter 10

"How are you doing?" Theresa Dooley asked.

Hunched forward in his chair, Daniel studied his hands. "Better than Marisol Vargas."

Seconds after the killer's retreat, the cops had blown into Marisol's apartment to find Daniel standing with the butcher knife at his feet, arms raised, his back still to the wall. He'd been brusquely cuffed and shoved into a chair, where he'd waited, ineffectively explaining himself and enduring glares from an endless torrent of uniformed officers until Dooley finally arrived to clarify matters. She let him call Cristina who was, by now, frantic.

As Daniel was led out, he glimpsed the body through the huddle of crime-scene investigators. Thin black notch in the throat—the death cut—matched by dueling slits beneath each eye that drained tears of blood down Marisol's cheeks, a gut-twisting depiction of coerced crying. He halted, transfixed by the stiff, painted doll face until Dooley gently prodded him along.

She brought him down to the Hall of Justice at 850 Bryant Street, a city-block slab that housed SFPD headquarters, Southern Station, and the courts and jail. The edifice, thrust up from a scattering of bail-bond shops, overpriced parking lots, and pretzel stands, was less than a mile from Daniel's workplace.

A noise kept reverberating off the walls of his skull. *Slit*. It was the sound of a person being killed a few feet from where he'd stood. And the heart-stopping pop of that flash. It had done more than merely blind him in the moment. It meant that Daniel's face was now preserved in the killer's camera. For what future use?

His adrenaline had ebbed, finally, leaving him spent. The muscle of his left forearm twitched irregularly, a stress reaction he'd not encountered before. He'd been gripping his elbow to make it stop. It finally dawned on him that his nails were digging through his skin, and he looked down at his clawed hand, told it to relax.

In the cramped space of the Homicide Division on the fourth floor, Dooley's office was small and virtually unadorned. Schoolroom-size desk, two chairs, bookshelves housing brittle binders, and a single poster on the wall featuring the SFPD badge, backlit like a superhero logo. No personal photos in evidence, no stained coffee mug, not even a fake fern. Dooley sat on the edge of her desk facing him, her shoulders tugged forward as if bearing weight. Through the bleary, rain-spotted window, early morning leaked over the horizon.

"That's the problem with living in a nice 'hood," Dooley was saying. "No police station nearby. We just couldn't get there in time."

Daniel gave a little nod.

"Marisol's bedroom phone was left off the hook—probably by the killer. That's why none of our calls to warn her got through. He covered his bases. We were late by a sliver."

"So was I." Daniel realized that his hand had again fastened onto his forearm. "I shouldn't have hesitated in the dining room. I should've just charged straight into the kitchen—"

"This is an organized, highly aggressive killer," Dooley said. "If you'd barged in, we'd be dealing with *two* murders tonight."

A tightness clutched Daniel's neck, threatened to force a shudder. "Same request on all those letters. 'Admit what you've done.' So why Marisol Vargas? Why Jack Holley?"

"We haven't linked them yet. Quite a range on demographics between those two. Our girl Vargas is a professor at San Francisco State who lives in . . . well, *your* neighborhood. Jack Holley was a former rent-a-cop who lived in the Tenderloin. As you know, ain't nuthin' tender 'bout that 'hood. They both got the same knifework, though. The bleeding tears. Our boy, he likes making them cry."

"I have a question."

Dooley rubbed her eyes. "Just one?"

"It looked like there was a struggle in the foyer. But the door wasn't kicked in. Marisol had deadbolts, everything. How'd he get her to open the door?"

For the first time, Theresa's face showed her exhaustion. "Same question we had at Jack Holley's. No signs of forced entry at his place either. Doors, windows, nothing. A street-smart ex–security guard who lived at Turk and Taylor, and he just opens his door to a large male stranger?"

"Maybe he isn't a stranger," Daniel said, and one of Dooley's thin eyebrows lifted slightly to indicate that the consideration wasn't a fresh one.

The words lingered until another inspector ducked into the office. Fifties, bloodshot eyes, with white hair and a red fringe of mustache. "Christ, Dooley, have you *slept* since the Holley murder? I can get this. You need some rest."

"Black don't crack, O'Malley."

"So they tell me." He nodded at Daniel. "Brave thing you did tonight. *Stupid,* but brave." Back to Theresa. "All right, then, Pam Grier. What do you need?"

"Besides a newer reference? Pam *Grier*? Do I call you Burt Reynolds?"

"I wish you did. Now, come on, lady, what do you need me to jump on?"

Dooley asked, "What have we heard back from Lyle Kane's house?"

It took Daniel a beat to place the name: Kane was the intended recipient of the third letter.

"Nothing yet," O'Malley said.

"I dispatched a unit there *hours* ago," Dooley said. "Why can't we get a simple confirmation of his safety?"

"I'm on it."

"Also, pull a warrant and have surveillance get a hidden camera up in the mail room at Metro South in case our boy Daniel here gets any more accidental fan mail."

O'Malley gave a curt nod before withdrawing. "Anything you need."

As far as Daniel could tell, the statement was in earnest. It struck him that Dooley was not only the youngest homicide inspector he'd seen tonight but also the sole female and the only non-Caucasian. Photos of the academy classes lined the corridor from the elevator, progressing from the early 1920s; in his stunned, trancelike state walking in, Daniel had focused on all those tiny frozen faces, changing through the years. More color. More women. Except, it seemed, here in Homicide.

"The camera Marisol's killer had," Dooley was saying. "Digital, right?"

"Looked it."

"It used to be the department could put the word out to the Fotomats. Now any sicko with a laptop can print out whatever souvenir he wants in the privacy of his own lair."

"That's why you think he took the picture?" Daniel asked. "For a souvenir?"

"Whether the victims' transgressions are real or imagined, those letters make one thing clear: These are revenge-based killings. So yeah, I think our guy wants to revel in them afterward."

Daniel's mouth was dry. "He got my picture, too."

Dooley nodded solemnly. "I know."

She didn't dismiss the grim fact with any false reassurances.

She didn't linger on it either. Bouncing off the desk's edge, she circled to her computer. "So that mask," she said. "It look something like this?"

She swiveled the monitor, and a Google image of a faceless mask stared out at him, eerily disembodied. He pictured that cocked head, the expert twirl of the knife and felt his forearm muscle give another twitch.

It took a bit of effort to swallow. "Yeah," he said. "Very close to that."

"And the gloves. You said shiny leather with backing straps, maybe Velcro?" Her fingers purred across the keyboard. "Like so?"

He came forward in his chair, pointing at the screen, as if the image were new to her as well. "How did you . . . ?"

"Sounded like a motorcycle mask," she said. "So I figured motorcycle gloves, too. This helps, Brasher."

They stared at each other across the desk.

"Now you can . . . ?"

"Start slogging," she said. "Check motorcycle-supply stores. Ask around the crime scenes if anyone noticed a bike. It's not a lock that the guy's a biker, but it's a pretty good bet he's familiar with them. There are more obvious masks to get, you know?"

"And you can check who in Metro South owns a motorcycle."

"Felons with choppers. That should be a short list."

"Still."

"Yes. A start. *If* any of your convicts bothered to register their bikes. That's the problem with criminals. They're fucking *criminals*. Disorganized messes. They drive unregistered cars, shoot unregistered guns, change jobs like other people change clothes, skip out on rent to crash on their cousin Hector's couch. Outdated, incomplete files. Which makes them harder to track down." She grimaced, cut short her tangent. "What the hell makes you choose a job dealing with these people?"

"These people?"

"Hell yes, *these people*. I grew up with these motherfuckers. Made me want to protect the rest of the world *from* them." She chewed the side of her cheek, her eye contact unremitting. "So that's all you got? Liberal guilt. Save the world. Help the underclass?"

"Nah. Nothing so lofty. It's just what makes me happy. I like a challenge. And I like underdogs. That's who I want to help. The guy who's gotten kicked around. The woman who doesn't think she can have the life she wants."

"How do you relate to that?" Something shifted in her face, recognition dawning. "Right," she said. "Growing up under the heel of the infamous Evelyn Brasher."

Daniel gave a one-shoulder shrug, a tell he immediately regretted. "I had it easy by most standards," he said.

But Theresa was already blazing forward. "So that's what they do in your rehabilitation class? Talk about their abusive childhoods?"

"Sometimes."

"Sometimes. Okay. Let's talk about 'usually.' *Usually* piece-of-shit criminals are just flat-out *broken*. You can't get through to them. You can't fix them. And yet you try."

"With varying success."

"So tonight? When you see Marisol Vargas laid out, sliced and diced, you want to . . . what? *Cure* the guy who did it?"

He wasn't sure when the conversation had turned, but they were on the far side of the bend, staring at a different view. He felt a pulse beating in his temple, a sure sign to keep his mouth closed.

"What's the difference between this motherfucker and the *patients* in those little groups you run?" Theresa said. "That tonight you had to actually *see* what they do before you decide to treat them for it?" She pointed at the poster of the police badge, the department motto written in Spanish. "'*Oro en paz, fierro en guerra*,'" she read in a crisp accent. "Gold in peace, iron in war." Her nostrils flared. "What happened to Jack Holley? What happened tonight? It calls for *iron*."

His forearm was no longer twitching. "*I* was the one with the butcher knife in my hand tonight. So stow the dated 'I'm from the streets' class bullshit and either focus and do your job or let me go home to my wife."

Theresa rose sharply and pounded her hands on her desk, elbows locked. Her face as hard as carved stone, but he could see the emotion moving beneath it now. His words had jarred loose whatever logjam she'd been hammering at.

He pulled back and out of the confrontation, saw them as if from across the room—a cop and an eyewitness, both on no sleep, trying to stay afloat in the aftermath of a gruesome, soul-crushing night. The skin at the side of her neck fluttered. The thin line between rage and grief.

And then he understood.

He took a moment to choose his words. "It's not your fault you didn't check the rest of the mail earlier," he said. "I didn't think of it either."

Dooley's mouth wobbled a bit, and then she pinched her lower lip in her teeth and bit down. Her eyes had gone glassy, and she blinked a few times quickly, discouraging any rising tears. She sat down again. Breathed hard for a minute or two.

"I'm sorry," she said. "I was being an asshole. It's the only thing I've been any good at this week."

"I get it. Don't worry."

She swiveled over and rested her feet on that windowsill that housed no plants or family photos or anything aside from a film of dust. Chewing her cheek, she stared through the bleary glass.

O'Malley swung back through the door, interrupting the heavy silence. He said, "The reason we've got no confirmation from Lyle Kane of 316 Bay Street is there *is* no 316 Bay Street. And? There's no Lyle Kane either. Not in San Francisco."

Dooley gave no indication she'd heard him. Silence pervaded the room. Down the hall someone shouted about replacing the fucking paper in the fax machine.

Dooley put her feet down again. Rotated back to her desk. Rubbed her face with both palms.

O'Malley said, "Sorry. The guy doesn't exist. We got a letter *from* a ghost *to* a ghost."

Visible over his shoulder at the end of the hall, there was a stir of movement. Cris appeared through the windowed security door, her hands gesticulating as she spoke to the PSA behind the Plexiglas. She was still wearing the ridiculously oversize Giants shirt.

Daniel found his feet. O'Malley stepped aside, clearing the view, and Cris stopped midsentence and looked up. Her shoulders shuddered in relief at the sight of him. Instinct made him start for her, but then he remembered where he was and shot an inquisitive look across at the desk.

"Go back to your life." Dooley waved a hand at him. "Alarm on, eyes open, we'll send a patrol car by every few hours."

"And you?"

"Me?" She mustered a laugh. "Me and O'Malley, we'll be here chasing ghosts."

Chapter 11

"Wonderful views of the Transamerica Pyramid." The Realtor's pencil skirt constrained her steps into short, deliberate thrusts. She eased up beside Daniel, and they stood side by side, admiring the city panorama like two villainous politicians in an action movie. A sweep of her manicured hand. "As you can see."

He could see. In fact, the Transamerica building was hard to miss.

It was a gloomy morning, the sun no more than a yellow smudge through churning clouds. Here on the twenty-third floor, they were eye level with Muriel Castanis's "corporate goddesses" who crowned Philip Johnson's postmodern high-rise across the street like ancient Greek gargoyles, three to a side. Ruffled white gowns shrouded the twelve-foot statues, pronounced against obsidian black windows. City residents had long debated the eerie caryatids with their hood-covered heads. Were they angels of capitalism? Prophets warning against greed and privilege?

"You're a therapist, right?"

"Counselor." He didn't realize that he was more comfortable with his current job title until the response was out of his mouth. Another adjustment he'd have to make.

The fawn walls smelled of fresh paint, the clouded glass wall sconces looked brand-new, and the bathroom door had been left strategically ajar to show off the curved slate counter and recessed double sinks. A world away from the rust-stained urinals and powder soap of Metro South.

"How long have you been in private practice?"

"Oh, I'd be starting. Here." He shifted, the carpet sinking pleasingly beneath his loafers. "Transitioning from another job."

"Why the change?"

"My current job's pretty exhausting. I was hoping for something a little . . ."

"Easier?"

The answer, he realized, unsettled him.

"Well," she continued, "I certainly have some friends I could refer to you." A behind-the-hand stage whisper. "Not to mention my mother." Up close, her perfume was overpowering. "This is the first time in seven years that this space has been available. So what a great opportunity to enter a two-year lease . . ."

He tuned her out. He'd made it home from the police station last night—no, early this morning—and managed a few fitful hours of sleep with Cris cuddled into him. After she'd rolled out of bed groggily and headed for work, he'd sat leadenly at the kitchen counter in his boxers, drinking cup after cup of coffee, trying to get his head to change lanes. But no, it was the same film reel of images. A red front door, already cracked. Crimson stalactites hanging from the lower lids of Marisol's eyes. A bulky figure turning around in the foyer, that featureless mask finding Daniel where he hid. And the gloved hand lifting the digital camera, snapping a parting shot.

An image of Daniel preserved in that camera. Right now. Somewhere in the city stretched out before him.

Again he found his gaze arrested by the wraithlike statues across the street. Faceless. Nothing more than shadowed recesses beneath the cowls. A drift in the clouds cast the carved figures in a different light, and again he was yanked back to Marisol Vargas's dining room, frozen in the darkness, trying to vanish into the wall as the killer's broad shoulders pivoted, bringing that ghastly smooth face into view.

Phantom sounds replayed in Daniel's head. The blade across Marisol's throat. Blood pattering on the kitchen tile.

He should've gone through that front door quicker. He shouldn't have paused outside the kitchen before rushing the killer. One second. One second earlier might've saved her life.

A bead of sweat tickled his cheek. He averted his eyes to the Embarcadero and beyond, where the Bay Bridge forged across to Oakland, but still he could see the white smudges in his peripheral vision, the goddesses beckoning like sirens.

The chirpy voice phased back in. "... and you're just a hop, skip, and a jump to Chinatown."

"Right," he said. "I used to work right there." He pointed past the reddish gleam of the Bank of America building to the penthouse office where he and the team used to shuffle Evelyn's assets around on various monitors. "Different building, same view."

He remembered the grind of that old life, the days blurring together as he made money make money, something at which he was genetically proficient. His lunch breaks he used to take in the very courtyard they were looking down on. Sipping coffee on a bench, dwarfed by the centerpiece, a two-hundred-ton sleek black granite sculpture titled *Transcendence* but cynically known the Financial District over as "Banker's Heart." And hemming in the whole affair, trim boxes of topiary, as constrained as he felt in his overpriced suit. A landscape of the mind if ever there was one.

And then meeting Cris, which he would like to say changed his life.

But it didn't. Not really.

What had changed his life was thinking he was going to lose her.

That moment of reckoning, seared into his brain.

They sit, practically levitating above their chairs with anticipation. The words come in jagged and hard, separate pieces of some indigestible whole. When it's over, they blink dumbly at the doctor.

"I didn't even know you could get heart cancer," Cris finally says.

The doctor looks unusually nervous for someone who does this for a living. Perhaps because Brasher money paid for half of the on-cology wing when some great-great-uncle had prostate cancer and the UCSF Medical Center was still fledgling. Or more likely because this is serious fucking business. "A left-atrium myxoma," he says across the desk. "We generally see it on the right side—"

"Well," Cris says, "at least I'm special."

Her heart, assailed. The thought leaves Daniel breathless.

He pushes words through the fog that has enveloped him. "So what next? Surgery? I mean . . . ?"

"For surgery we remove the tumor along with five or so surround-ing millimeters of the atrial septum. But the margins of Cristina's tu-mor are poorly circumscribed, merged with the surrounding tissue. We don't want to cut that much healthy tissue."

Side by side in their chairs, Daniel and Cristina by some unspoken agreement do not make eye contact, but their hands have found each other and they clutch, hard, sweating.

"So?"

"We'll get her on the heart-transplant list immediately and hope for a match."

The rest is gone. Noise and wind in his ears, an arctic whiteout.

Later, at home, in a frenzy of anxiety, he makes the mistake of con-sulting the Internet. Fever. Air hunger. Bloodstained sputum. People gurgling to asphyxiation, drowning in their own fluids.

Waiting is an impossibility. Cris retreats into herself, but he does what he does best, which is tackle an insurmountable problem head-on. Sublimating all his rage and terror into seventy-two hours of phone calls and referrals, he manages to get her into a closed trial at UCSF, phase one of an experimental brachytherapy where radiation seeds are implanted inside the tumor to shrink it. Combined with high-dose rate and external-beam radiation therapy, it's still a Hail Mary pass, but it's the fourth quarter, the clock is running, and they have no time-outs left.

At the intake session before the trial begins, they find themselves alone in the CT scan room for a few austere moments. The tech has left to make adjustments to his adjustments, and Cris lies on the floating table, her skin papery, her lips chapped, the scanner looming over her like a giant Life Saver.

Her eyes flash up, showing a lot of white, to take in the imposing machine. "My own proscenium arch." She does jazz hands out to a top-hat-waggling ta-da. The comic effect, horizontal, is compounded.

He rests a hand on her arm. "Ready for the coming attraction?"

"It feels like I'm already in the morgue," she says, and tears spill sideways down her temples.

He smooths her hair back from her forehead, kisses her dry lips. They have been together less than two years, and maybe this is what they will have.

She is crying freely, finally, reality dawning. "I'm only thirty-three," she says. "That's not even supposed to be half a life."

He is regretting every lost moment, every cross word, every stupid argument. And then he hears himself saying, "When we're through this, we'll do it all differently. Not a second taken for granted. We'll only do things that matter, that we love doing."

She squeezes his hand, presses it to her besieged heart. "I hope we get to," she says.

Her words almost buckle the knees right out from under him. When he finds his voice, a request springs out. "Marry me."

A sea change comes over her. She laughs, bites her lip, swimming in delight. "When?"

"Tonight. In the hospital chapel."

"You're crazy." Her grin turns sly. "Evelyn will lose her mind."

When he calls his mother two hours later outside the tiny chapel, she abstains. "I am not going to come to a wedding at a hospital.*"*

The next day, sitting on the same pair of chairs in a different office, they feel the pinch of metal around their ring fingers when they hold hands. They glance at each other, share a private smile.

"*. . . minimally invasive,*" *the cardiac surgeon is saying.* "*The seeds will be implanted through hollow needles. You can expect some soreness, and the radiation will carry its own side effects. Nausea, fatigue, weight loss, and . . .*" *A glance at her file and a flicker passes across his face.*

Cris is still smiling across at Daniel, but he notes the doctor's expression and stiffens in his chair. "*What?*"

"*I'm afraid you'll lose the baby.*"

Cris's eyes go shiny—an instant gloss of tears. She blinks, and they spill.

"*What baby?*" *she says.*

"And we are open to a carpet allowance should you decide to change the color."

Daniel came back to himself there on the twenty-third floor in the empty office. The Realtor, it seemed, had not stopped for breath. He takes a moment to shed the memory, to let her words register.

"A . . . *carpet* allowance?" After contending with paper-clip shortages and expense-clearance forms for photocopies, the notion seemed extraterrestrial. He couldn't deny the pang of uncertainty. He'd lived this cushioned life before and found it wanting. He'd worked in a space like this, looking out on the same majestic view until it had ceased being majestic. Just how much would he miss the grit and pressure of the group, the room, the broken souls in their combatants' ring? All the guts and shame and ugliness of hard living, and yet all the grace and courage, too. Those moments when a ray of hope broke through, illuminating a hidden path.

And yet the air up here was intoxicating.

"This is a *highly* coveted space, as you can imagine. If you decide to jump on this opportunity, we can have the contract drawn up in—"

"I'll take it," he said.

Her brain seemed not to register this for a second or two of blissful silence. "Superb. You'll have an excellent new start here."

Before leaving, he cast a final glance at the ghostly forms of the statues across from them, indistinct in their robes, featureless and yet looking on, like the Grim Reaper, like Marisol Vargas's killer, like his conscience.

Chapter 12

After securing his future office space, Daniel intended to drive home but found himself steering the opposite way. It was Tuesday—no group—and yet some compulsion drew him, the impulse quickening until he descended into the dim parking lot of Metro South. He detoured, slowing as he passed the narrow spaces on the far wall, a vast array of motorcycles lined up—from Harleys to Japanese rockets, from gleaming chrome to rusted heaps. Dooley's sneer came back to him: *Felons with choppers. That should be a short list.*

After circling the level, he parked in his usual space and climbed out, inhaling the moist garage air. Fragments of the prior night pricked at his nerves, burrowed beneath his skin. He shook off the sensation and started for the elevator when the doors opened and a man stepped out, the shadowed figure slowly resolving.

Daniel halted sharply there before his car, struck by A-Dre's form and bearing. Not dissimilar to those of Marisol's killer.

Okay. The killer had been wearing loose-fitting black sweats. All Daniel could tell was that he'd been tall and well built. Like *all* the men in group. And like many of the men who rotated through the building.

And yet Daniel's flesh tingled from an adrenaline charge. A little stab of PTSD, nothing more.

A-Dre spotted him and halted.

"Why are you here today?" Daniel asked. He'd intended the question to come across as conversational, but there was too much pressure behind it. What did he expect the guy to say? *Oh, just dropping off some more death threats in the mail room.*

A-Dre cocked his head, and Daniel flashed again on that motorcycle mask, tilting to take him in across the length of Marisol Vargas's foyer.

A-Dre approached slowly. "I'm not supposed to be here?"

"That's not what I said."

A-Dre turned away with disgust, taking a few steps toward the far wall against which the motorcycles were slotted. When he stopped to look back, Daniel realized that he had remained in place, pinned to the concrete in front of his car. Waiting to see if A-Dre climbed onto one of those motorcycles.

"You gonna *watch* me?"

"Is there some reason you don't want to be watched?"

A-Dre's upper lip twitched in a literal snarl as he reversed course and came up on Daniel. "Make sure I don't break into one of these nice *foreign* cars." He flicked his head at the Audi behind Daniel.

The Audi that he made sure never to drive on workdays. But today wasn't a workday. Daniel wasn't supposed to be here any more than A-Dre was.

"Nice wheels," A-Dre said. "The counselor biz must be paying well these days."

"It pays fine."

"Not *S-series* fine. No, you got some *dollar.* You dress down, don't you, afore you slum your ass in here? The worn jeans. The faded T-shirts." A-Dre came up on Daniel, breathed down on him.

Daniel took a step to the side, and A-Dre shadowed his move, blocking him again. He was in no frame of mind to engage A-Dre properly right now; he just needed to get away cleanly and quickly.

"Step back, A-Dre."

In his three years of running groups, he'd never had a confrontation with a member erupt into violence. A-Dre crossed his arms, glowering.

First time for everything.

Daniel held the glare well past the point of comfort. Finally A-Dre laughed and sidled off him. "Just playin'."

As Daniel headed to the elevator, A-Dre stood in place, staring after him. A power play. Unless there was some reason he didn't want Daniel to see what he drove. When Daniel got into the elevator and turned around, A-Dre was still there, watching him across the quiet parking lot until the closing doors wiped him from view.

Before the car could rise, Daniel flicked the emergency stop toggle switch and waited, listening. Footsteps ticked across concrete. A pause. And then the unmistakable roar of a motorcycle coming to life.

Daniel stood with his hands pressed to the cold metal doors until the sound of A-Dre's motorcycle faded away.

Hardly incontrovertible evidence. But still.

The toggle switch clicked back loudly, and Daniel rode the elevator up to the lobby, passed through security, and took the stairs to the second floor. Moving down the hall, he found himself in a haze of suspicion, studying each face as it floated past. He hadn't considered how it would feel being back here in the building.

Unsettled, he paused by the out-of-service water fountain to call Cris. "Just checking that you're okay."

"I'm fine, babe."

"Don't sound fine."

"Corrupt landlord, illegitimate eviction notices, driving the families out one at a time."

"So . . . a normal day."

She made a noise of amusement. "How are *you* doing?"

"A bit rattled, still. But okay."

Over the line he heard elderly voices arguing in Tagalog. "I gotta jump, *mi vida,* or there's gonna be a matricide in my office."

He watched a rat scuttle along the seam where wall met floor, then vanish through a crack in the baseboard. "Okay. Just . . . be careful today."

"You're telling *me?*"

Pocketing his phone, he continued to the administrative offices.

The receptionist blew on her painted nails and head-tilted him through to the vast metal file cabinets paneling the confidential-records room in the back.

He dug out A-Dre's paperwork and thumbed through until he found an informed-consent form filled out by pen. Sloppy handwriting, but definitely not a match for the death-threat letters.

Big exhale. He figured he would have recognized that scratchy penmanship if he'd seen it before. Okay. Suspicion averted.

He started out. Halted in the doorway.

There were five more group members.

That creep of paranoia, termites beneath the flesh. *This*, he thought, *is how it begins.*

Back to the cabinets, pulling files for the three remaining men, confirming what he already knew. Then he checked the handwriting of the two women just for good measure. In case—what? This was getting ridiculous.

Sheepishly, he retuned the files, shoved the drawers closed. All right, then. *His* people were in the clear. That was that.

Unless the killer had somcone else write the letters for him. Which *would* be a smart move if you were, say, a seasoned criminal planning a murder.

He gazed at the floor-to-ceiling banks of cabinets. Thousands of files. He recalled his own words. *There's no one in the building who wouldn't be a suspect.*

So what had he learned snooping on his clients like a low-rent Big Brother? Not much.

His gaze snagged on one of the drawer labels: KAAL–KEANER.

That scrawled name—*lyle kane*—bobbed up from the dark waters of his mind. The man who was going to be killed tomorrow night at midnight. The man who, according to SFPD, didn't exist.

Daniel tugged out the weighty drawer, his fingers scrabbling across the tabs. *Kanatzar, Kandt*—then a jump straight to *Kaneko.*

So there was no Lyle Kane on Bay Street or anywhere else in San Francisco, nor was there a Lyle Kane who'd ever availed himself of services at Metro South. And yet a quick glance at the clock brought a mounting dread. Wherever the guy was, the killer had promised to make him bleed in thirty-four hours and change.

And Daniel's little Nancy Drew excursion to the records room wasn't going to affect anything. He headed out, locking the door behind him.

As he passed her doorway, Kendra glanced up from her desk. "You got that form for me, Daniel?"

"No. Distracting night last night. Sorry. I'll get it to you."

She gave him a mock-glum look over her teal spectacles. "One of your group members was just in here dropping off his paperwork. Maybe I should let *him* run the group—"

"Was it A-Dre?"

She seemed a bit surprised at his intensity. "Yeah. Looks like he's in for the duration."

And looks like A-Dre *did* have a legitimate reason for being here on a Tuesday. That made one of them.

Kendra was still studying Daniel with puzzlement as he withdrew.

The rubber tread of the rear stairwell squeaked underfoot. Daniel's jitters made the windowless back corridor of the ground floor feel even more desolate than usual. As he neared the mail room, a hoarse murmuring became audible, bouncing off the white walls. He slowed, on edge.

A few cautious steps brought him even with the door to the janitor's office, which remained slightly ajar. The murmurs issued through the gap. They seemed to be in Spanish, but he couldn't distinguish the words, only a current of husky sounds and the cadence of an accent.

Daniel reached over and gave the door a gentle push. It creaked open, revealing the janitor sitting on a little bench before a set of three banged-up clothing lockers. Hispanic, sleek ponytail, his head bent as he pulled on one sock, then another. A familiar figure around the building at all hours, pushing a mop, hauling trash, making small, meticulous repairs as the structure at large deteriorated all around them.

At first Daniel wondered why the man didn't look up, but then he noticed: His eyes were closed. His canvas overalls were unclipped and peeled down to his waist, the wife-beater undershirt showing off bulging shoulders capped with Gothic-cross tattoos. A bare dangling bulb cast light across his profile, shadowing the thin line of hair extending from his sideburn and framing the angle of his jaw before rising into a pencil mustache. His lips twitched, the stream of words coming with almost schizophrenic intensity.

Daniel glanced around the tiny room. Stained basin in the corner. A stack of drilled acoustic ceiling tiles. An open cardboard box held packs of pens and pads and—yes, there—a set of unused department-gray envelopes. Daniel felt his heart rate tick up another notch. Why would a janitor need so many office supplies?

Daniel started to lean back from the door when the murmurs abruptly ceased and the janitor pivoted his head to fix on him there in the doorway.

"Sorry," Daniel said. "The door was open, and I heard you talking . . ."

No response, just a dead stare. The unvented air smelled of sweat and chemicals. Daniel had to concentrate not to let his eyes dart over to the telltale envelopes.

He cleared his throat, tried to retrieve a name. "Alberto, right?"

"No." The man lifted his heel to the bench and began lacing up a black boot.

The sight of the boot froze Daniel. He rewound to that moment of suspended terror in Marisol's house when the assailant turned and charged him. Dark boots pounding the foyer. But what *precisely* did they look like? That same itch came on beneath his skin, like a scab that wouldn't heal.

He realized that a response was due, so he forced himself back to the present. "I'm sorry—your name is . . . ?"

"Angelberto. On. Hell. Bear. Toe." The man stood and tugged the overalls up over his sweat-shiny skin.

"You work long hours."

"Day shift. Night shift. I am here. I am here until my work is done." He stooped to pick up the cardboard box and walked out, forcing Daniel to step back out of the doorway.

Angelberto locked the door behind him. Daniel waited for him to turn, then pointed at the jumble of supplies in the box. The gray envelopes were right there on the top. "What's all that for?" Daniel asked.

"Mr. Carpenter ask me to deliver these to Domestic Violence on floor five. You can check with him. They're not stolen."

Daniel felt his cheeks flush. "I didn't mean . . ."

But of course he did.

And already those black boots were tapping away down the hall.

He stood there maybe a full minute, gathering himself, the hum of the overheads the only sound breaking the quiet. Then he resumed his walk to the end of the hall, where the mail room waited. It wasn't until he paused at the threshold that he realized how much he'd been dreading this moment. Holding his breath, he entered, the cubbyholes drawing into view.

His mailbox. Empty.

On his tiptoes he poked at the outgoing mail, then finally gave in and started rifling through it. The sight of a gray interdepartmental envelope caused a flash of anxiety, but he turned it over to see a neatly printed label.

He was just shoving the mail back when his iPhone rang, startling him.

UNKNOWN CALLER. He slid to answer.

"What the hell are you doing, Brasher?"

He tapped the outgoing mail stack back into line. "Who is this?"

"Inspector Dooley." The voice lowered a few octaves. "Do I need to inform you that tampering with mail is a federal offense?"

The hidden security camera she'd had installed. He spun in a circle, searching, but saw nothing out of the ordinary.

"Oh, this is *great*." She laughed. "The expression on your face. You find any Scooby snacks in the outgoing mail?"

He smirked at himself. "You should've seen me earlier."

"Jumping at shadows?"

"Today it doesn't take a shadow."

"I can imagine. We're on the same side of town. Meet me at Philz in twenty. I have a proposition for you."

"Sounds scandalous."

But she'd already hung up.

Chapter 13

"So normally there's a whole clever approach where I play on your guilt and appeal to your desire to be a good citizen to leverage you into doing this," Dooley said. "But you're smart and I'm smart, so let's just pretend we did that part already. Good?"

Daniel said, "Good."

They waited for their order at Philz, the best coffee joint in the Bay Area. Outside, the Mission honked and revved in all its sunny, grimy glory, Twin Peaks parting the fog to let through all that color. Vibrant murals of saints, earth mamas, and migrant workers brightened alleys and garage doors. Trolleybus cables sliced and diced the sky above each intersection. Every hair sash a cultural celebration, every panhandler sporting a tattered poncho, every lowrider thrumming gangsta rap that even the rising rents couldn't muffle. More Central Americans lived here than anywhere else besides . . . well, Central America, so if you weren't going in for a mint-mojito iced coffee at one-cup-at-a-time Philz, you could grab a pupusa or Mission-style burrito that would make you change religions.

Inside, Philz was a mash-up of the City at large. A hot-dotter with a BlackBerry implanted in his head bellowed sell orders, the bumper sticker on the wall behind him serving as a personal caption: SUPPORT THE MISSION YUPPIE-ERADICATION PROGRAM. A nanny shoved wailing twins in a double stroller. Two Norteños with their 'banger-red 49ers jerseys eyed Dooley and her two colleagues haughtily. And

Daniel, along for the ride, was doing his best to keep up with the cops' conversation.

"Confidentiality in your department's a bitch," Theresa was saying. "And we can't subpoena all those records. So. If and when we get a bead on a suspect, we may need you to check certain files for us."

"You know I can't do that," Daniel said. "And you have plenty of access to those files. Everyone who comes through our department is a convicted criminal with a parole officer. Talk to the POs and they can pull whatever records you need released. There's a process."

"A process that's more time-consuming."

"Than having me break confidentiality?" A wave of remorse came on at his own hypocrisy—less than an hour ago, he'd been digging through the files himself with less-than-professional motives in mind.

"You *were* rooting through the mail."

"I never swore an oath not to root through outgoing mail."

One of Dooley's colleagues—the one she'd referred to as Rawlins—made an annoyed noise in his throat. She hadn't bothered to introduce either of them, but they seemed to fit the Homicide mold—fifties, white, rugged good looks eroded by age and stress.

"Unless," Dooley said, "the personal safety of another person is at stake."

"Absolutely. And if I find out *anything* like that, your phone will be ringing two seconds later. Believe me."

"So that's what you're doing? Running your own investigation? Tiptoeing into the mail room on your day off?"

"Tiptoeing? Was it really that obvious?"

Theresa charged on. "And this whole 'run-in with the janitor' routine—"

"I'm telling you," Daniel said. "Something's off about the guy."

"Is that a professional opinion?"

"*Yes.*"

"We ruled out the janitor," Rawlins said. "He punched in the night of. Worked a late shift."

"Can't a time card be faked?" Daniel asked.

"Yes. Which is why I made sure to track down someone who personally saw him at the building. Around midnight. Last night. Airtight alibi. We're covering more angles than you can think of, Brasher. It's not the janitor. It's one of the other ten thousand people at Metro South who wear work boots."

"What's a janitor *supposed* to wear on the job?" the other inspector said. "Huaraches?"

"Maybe they're special *teleporting* boots," Rawlins said. "Got him from Metro South to Marisol Vargas's place with a click of the heels."

This was running the risk of turning into a routine.

Daniel held up his hands. Uncle.

Dooley was enjoying all this. "Look, Brasher, I know you stumbled into this thing and wish you hadn't. But it's grabbed you now." She flashed that grin. "So why not use your superpowers for good?"

Before he could respond, the barista called out her name and she skated off to claim her coffee. Daniel stared at the gang tattoo on the guy in front of them—a sombrero struck by a machete, dripping blood. The Norteños were nothing if not subtle. Rawlins's phone chimed, and he pulled it out, deleted a text. When the background screen came back up, Daniel noticed it was a digital clock, counting down. To midnight tomorrow.

The killer's deadline.

Rawlins followed his stare, then pocketed the phone quickly. They stood there awkwardly for a moment. "We can't find a goddamned trace of Lyle Kane." Rawlins's voice was strained, confessional. "Nothing."

"Maybe the killer won't be able to find him either," Daniel said. "He did have the wrong address for him."

"I'd rather not bank on that. The Tearmaker's one highly organized—"

"The *Tearmaker*?"

Rawlins winced—he hadn't meant to drop the nickname. "Brainchild of one of the reporting officers. It's become a cop-shop tag. Can't accuse us of being unpredictable."

"Pretend you never heard it," the colleague said to Daniel, a touch threateningly. "That nickname leaks to the press, it'll blow up. And so will the captain."

Daniel nodded. "I never heard it."

"The *suspect*," Rawlins continued, "is planning these entries, bringing gear, executing clean exits. He's got an eye on the victims ahead of time. Which means he's probably found Lyle Kane by now. Remember—he picked these folks for a reason. Which means *he* knows where to look for them." Rawlins watched Dooley across the shop, stirring sugar into her coffee. "Maybe we'll get lucky and take down the piece of shit before the deadline. We're kicking over a lot of rocks."

"Anything interesting on the mail room's security footage?"

"Aside from you?" Rawlins said. "Nope. But Dooley's lead on the case, and she's good."

"Seems that way."

"Yeah. She may have gotten the job 'cuz she's black and a woman, but I got this shit 'cuz I'm white and a man, so the way I figure, it all comes out in the wash."

The other inspector said, "I'll take her over O'Malley or Gubitosi any day."

Dooley returned, sipping her drink, resuming the conversation as if there'd been no break. "So, Brasher, I get it. The confidentiality end run's not gonna work. Fine. I'm just saying, maybe we can help each other out."

She offered her hand, and they shook.

He started for the door, and she said, "Your drink's not up yet. What's the rush?"

"I have to get across town to see my mother. I'd rather be the one to tell her about last night. No imagining what kind of shitstorm she'll kick up when she hears about it."

"We kept your name out of the media," Dooley said. "How's she gonna find out?"

Daniel said, "She hears about everything that happens in this city."

Chapter 14

Two stone pillars guarded the entrance to Sea Cliff, the affluent neighborhood nestled above the beaches of the northwest rim of the city. Coasting past the mansions with their terraces and stone lions, Daniel felt the familiar tightening at the base of his neck that came on every time he neared his childhood home.

His parents had been married here on a bluff overlooking China Beach. At the ceremony's culmination, they'd released a pair of doves, and two red-tailed hawks had descended from the heavens and torn them to shreds in view of the wedding party—an appropriate metaphor for the marriage. Denis Milner came with money and a business degree, but Evelyn Brasher came with the fortune, amassed by her great-grandfather, who took skillful advantage of Congress-bestowed land grants for the transcontinental railway. Denis adopted the stronger family name, a move that flew under the cloud cover of sixties San Francisco, and adopted the various bank accounts as well. Aside from the two weeks each July he decamped to Bohemian Grove to smoke cigars with Kissinger and Nixon, he worked most waking hours, the better to avoid his barbed wife. When he died of a heart attack at the age of thirty-seven, one society columnist opined that he'd done so merely to escape Evelyn. Daniel remembered his father as little more than a hazy outline and an oil portrait.

As he steered into the driveway now and waited on the leisurely parting of the wrought-iron gates, he recalled the first time he'd brought Cristina here to expose her to Evelyn. This was before she'd gotten sick, before Daniel had switched careers and burned the bridge to the family fortune. They'd been seeing each other just a few months, but the relationship had deepened to a level where he felt he owed her more than some vague details about his background. Little did he know that this first meeting between his mother and his future wife would also be their last.

Evelyn greets them in the dining room, fluttering in a gossamer wrap. She touches her cheek to Daniel's, then offers a firm hand to Cristina.

"Consuelo, is it?"

"Cristina."

"Well, welcome, welcome."

Cristina has brought a little wrapped gift, her grip on it tightening by degrees as the mansion reveals itself. She glances around now at the paintings, her gaze arrested by Toulouse-Lautrec's La Blanchis-seuse, *and her knuckles go white. Daniel has warned her that his mother is difficult and privileged, but he realizes now that neither adjective was sufficient.*

Evelyn follows Cris's gaze and says, "Denis bought that at auction a few weeks before he died."

"Denis?" Cristina manages.

"With one n," Evelyn says. "As in 'penis.'"

That is how hate works when it's stoked to a bright light. It gets cold.

Dinner has been timed for after the Giants game—nothing interferes with Evelyn's enjoyment of her boys in orange and black—and the threesome crests one end of the prodigious table. Evelyn notes the gift Cristina is trying to hide in her lap. "Is that for me?"

Reluctantly, Cris passes over the small package, her face tense as Evelyn opens it.

A set of Toulouse-Lautrec coasters is revealed. Cris twists a finger uncomfortably in her shell necklace from the Haight. The gift-store coasters look smaller than they are, diminished before the real item dominating the wall behind them. Evelyn looks up, her gaze holding something like triumph. "Aren't they lovely," she purrs, and dismisses them to a butler's tray with a wave of the hand.

Roast chicken and baby asparagus are served, along with Riesling from the cellar. "So," Evelyn says, "you work at a soup kitchen?"

Daniel can no longer veil his irritation. "I told you she—"

But Cristina is catching up to the rules of the game. "I'm a community organizer. But I can understand the confusion. Both jobs deal with poor people."

Evelyn's smile turns genuine. Now there is fun to be had. "Do expound."

"I'm working to protect the tenants in a few apartment buildings in Dogpatch. They're displacing all these folks to build loft condos—"

"Ah, yes," Evelyn says, spooning more asparagus. "I believe we invested in that. Didn't we, Daniel?"

The air goes out of the room. Or maybe Daniel is just working harder to find it.

"I don't know," he says tightly. "That's Vimal's division."

Evelyn says, "Well, the owners of the private property have decided to put it to more lucrative use—"

Cris jumps in. "By booting out longtime residents who won't be able to afford to live in their own city anymore."

"Put them in Hunters Point."

"Hunters Point? Might as well move them to Mars. That's like saying you could just live in Oakland."

Evelyn sips from her crystal glass. "I could just live in Oakland if I had to."

A loaded pause, and then both women smirked at the notion. Honest adversaries.

Evelyn said, "Do you have any idea the revenue a construction project like this brings to the city? What do you think subsidizes little tax-exempt hobbies like yours?"

"Aah. Trickle-down economics."

"Can you really argue them, Carmela?"

"Vehemently and effectively. And it's Cristina."

"Mom," Daniel cuts in, "do you really need to trot out the Joan Crawford routine?"

"No," Cris says to Daniel, exhilaration coloring her cheeks. "I got this." All signs of discomfort have vanished from her manner.

Daniel takes a healthy slug of wine before Evelyn resumes the ping-pong match.

"So a few black families get moved—"

"Enough of this city hasn't been taken away from African-Americans already?" Cris says.

"Sure," Evelyn says, "all the parts they moved into when the Japanese were carted off to internment camps." She lets the point land before leaning on it. "The blacks coming here to escape Jim Crow didn't flourish in the Fillmore until the Japanese got rounded up. Every gain comes at a cost, dear. The blacks oust the Asians. The Indians oust the yuppies. The gays, those storm troopers of gentrification, oust the Hispanics. And redecorate—thank God." She dabs the corners of her mouth with her napkin. "So loft condominiums are going up in Dogpatch and the poor are getting the short end of the stick. This isn't new. We dwell on Yelamu Indian land, all of us. How are those boys making out these days? The trains built to carry people here rode on tracks laid down by coolie laborers paid pennies a day. That's how it's always been—"

"So that's how it should always be?"

"No, dear. It's how it will always be."

The plates untouched. The chicken basting in its juices appears suddenly unseemly. The waitstaff clear and withdraw. Just another night at Brasher Manor.

"You can't really think it'll ever be any different?" Evelyn asks.

"I think," Cristina says, the points of her elbows wrinkling the linen tablecloth, "that life is fucking hard. And that we have an obligation to try to make it less hard for others when we can. I think that *most folks do the best they can and try to scrape by. Scrape by enough and it can wear you down to nothing. Ever scraped by, Evelyn?"*

"Oh, this is fun," Evelyn says, not insincerely. "A hard-nosed truth teller. Most people just tell me what I want to hear, but you. You have tits."

"It's an ugly world, Mrs. Brasher. Down off these hills. And I refuse to flourish at the expense of others."

"Oh, honey. We all flourish at the expense of others. And wearing ugly shoes and cheap jewelry does not a thing about it."

Cristina freezes for a moment, genuinely surprised at the slap. And then she does something that cements her place in Daniel's heart. She laughs. And not just a titter or a dismissive snicker—a genuine, lovely, full-throated laugh.

Evelyn watches her anthropologically; she's supposed to be the only one who enjoys these exchanges. She waits for the spell to pass, then says, "Dessert?"

"Why not?" Cris says.

Tea service is brought.

Evelyn nibbles a chocolate-dipped vanilla madeleine. "I understand you're South American?"

"Worse, I'm afraid," Cris says. "Mexican."

"Don't be ridiculous."

"She's being ridiculous?" Daniel says. "You've yet to ask a question that's not poison-tipped."

"Regarding her ethnic background? Come on. Do you think I'd give a damn if you pranced around town with Carlos Slim's daughter? I'm not racist. I'm classist. And for good reason. How are you, with your life, supposed to—"

"Can't we have this vile argument in private?"

"I don't see why," Evelyn says. "It pertains to all three of us."

"I don't either," Cris says. "Why not get it all out on the table?"

"Yes. Let's." Her lipsticked mouth firming, Evelyn rotates her focus back to Cristina. "You were married, were you? Before?"

81

Mother's people, always checking up.

"Mom," *Daniel says.* "Even by your own feral standards—"

"For ten months," *Cris replies.*

"So it didn't count?" *Evelyn says.*

"Not really."

"What's the story of this nonmarriage?" *Evelyn presses.*

Cris chews her lip, considers where to start. "I had a crappy childhood, the kind that people write crappy memoirs about. Neglectful parents, leering uncles, the whole nine. I married out at seventeen with parental consent. He drank. I got pregnant. He got laid off, came home late, belligerent and smelling of rum, and the next morning I wasn't pregnant anymore."

Daniel cannot remember feeling so peripheral in his life. He has been stricken dumb for swaths of the conversation, and not just by an eavesdropper's fascination but by sheer and growing-by-the-second regard for the woman across from him. He is lost in the exchange as if engrossed in a movie. No girlfriend has ever locked horns with Evelyn so proficiently, and it strikes him now that this dinner is a trial to which he has unconsciously subjected Cristina.

"I suppose a smart *choice,*" *Evelyn says,* "would have been not to marry someone like that at all."

"You're absolutely right. But you know what I did instead? I left him and vowed never to let anyone, *no matter who they are, no matter where they live, make me feel worthless again.*"

Evelyn does something Daniel has never seen her do, not in two dozen board meetings and a hundred socialite brunches. She actually averts her eyes.

Cristina stands and sets her still-folded napkin on her plate. "Thank you for dinner."

Daniel rises, follows dumbly in her wake. Exiting the house, Cristina says out of the side of her mouth, "How did you *come from* that?"

Awestruck, he struggles to keep pace down the marble steps of the front porch. "I . . ."

"What?"

"I think I'm falling in love with you."

That wide smile springs up, overtaking her face. She reaches for his arm but then pinches it, so hard he jerks back.

"What was that for?"

Already she is two steps ahead again. "So you never forget."

He paused now before those same marble front steps and looked past the drop at the Pacific. The view was the only thing he missed here, the way the house seemed suspended above the earth rather than attached to it. To the east the Golden Gate Bridge guarded the Bay, the celebrated towers wrapped in fog. The orange-vermilion hue—officially designated "International Orange"—was in fact accidental, the color of a primer coat that just happened to catch the architect's fancy. It matched the autumn foliage of the bookending headlands while announcing the bridge sufficiently for ships, standing out and blending in simultaneously, unique and paradoxical—San Francisco embodied.

This was, if nothing, a city of contradictions. Synonymous with freedom, yet home to the world's best-known prison. The heart of the pacifist movement and the brains of the war machine. The blinding edge of innovation, navigated by cable car. The most East Coast city on the West Coast.

As he approached the house, he considered his and Cris's life together, how they'd always been something of a paradox themselves, how they managed to bring contradictions into harmony, completing the circle.

A middle-aged painter wearing a backward A's cap paused from his work on the front door to return Daniel's nod and let him pass. A trace of burning birch laced the air inside. Striding through the well-appointed halls, he wondered if he really had to be here. Maybe Dooley was right and the news of his appearance at the crime scene hadn't leaked. Maybe he'd overestimated Evelyn's reach into the city.

He found her in the library against a backdrop of leather-bound books, inhabiting a wing chair like a Bond villain, aside from the seemingly anachronistic iPad in her lap. To her side the hearth crackled behind a triple-panel screen, and above hung that solemn rendering of his father, who surveyed the scene with an air of strained dignity.

On the south wall, a larger rendering of *her* father.

Her eyes lifted, one hand rising to fluff the steel-gray hair away from her neck. "Daniel," she said sternly. "What's this about your walking into a murder?"

So much for overestimating her reach.

"I got a letter accidentally—"

"I already spoke to the president of the police commission. I know more about it than you do." She returned her focus to the iPad, tapping and sliding. "I'm going to have a private protection detail assigned to your house."

This was why he came. Evelyn didn't just react to news. She *implemented*.

"We're fine. No need to overreact."

"You walked in on Jack the Ripper, he took your picture, and I'm overreacting?"

"The guy's clearly targeting people who he thinks have *done* something—"

"Like burst in on him in the middle of an evisceration?"

"If we feel threatened," Daniel said, "we'll take care of it ourselves."

"So you're being obstinate and self-denying. Shocking." A series of cartoonish sneers and twangs emanated from her iPad.

"Mom, are you playing Angry Birds?"

"I can't help it. It's so . . . *satisfying*." A reluctant smile. "How are you these days? Still rubbing elbows with *criminals* for a living?"

"For now. I'm making a transition into private practice."

"Thank God. At least that has a *modicum* of respectability."

Her semi-endorsement of the change grated more than he would have thought. No matter how prepared he was, she always managed to find the chink in the armor. Which is why they were in touch only occasionally, a phone call one month, a brunch the next. While the time between served to layer more sand over the land mines, he still had to watch where he stepped.

He moved to switch subjects. "Are you still seeing that composer?" A Portuguese man twenty years her junior with a full head of hair and an impressive collection of formal wear.

"No. He wanted to have a baby. With me."

"You sure something wasn't lost in translation?"

"Well, not *with* me. His sperm would be carried by someone else, and then we'd . . . I don't know, raise it. Can you imagine? At my age? I kept picturing a pale, thin-necked boy standing in the corner of the room coughing. No. I sent Leandro packing back to Braga."

A muffled ringing arose, and she fished around the blanket in her lap and came up with a cordless phone. Scowling, she consigned the caller to voice mail. "We're getting heavy into leveraged-currency bets these days," she told Daniel. "Going long on the yuan, since the Chinese are going to own our country in twenty years. Vimal calls every hour like a nervous schoolgirl. He doesn't have the stones for it like you did."

"A compliment?"

"Backhanded. I am capable of *those*. Especially when I haven't seen you in seven and a half weeks. Not that I'm keeping count. Of course, who knows if you'd have what it takes to make the tough financial calls *now*. All that counseling may have softened you up."

She raised her thin eyebrows to make clear it was a challenge.

The painter entered and tugged off his baseball hat, a display of servility the likes of which Evelyn inspired. "I'm finished with the job, Mrs. Brasher."

"A day late. I'll get you your four hundred dollars."

"The job was for five hundred."

"You took longer."

"Shouldn't that mean I get paid *more*?" He covered with a weak smile.

"As is, you overcharged given my zip code, but I let that slide. We agreed upon a completion date. It wasn't met. My dinner guests last night entered through a half-painted door."

"It required multiple coats for proper—"

"James." Evelyn barely raised her voice, and yet there James appeared in the far doorway. "Please bring me five hundred dollars."

The painter smiled gratefully, and James produced a zippered leather pouch from which he counted five crisp bills into Evelyn's hand. Throwing off the blanket, she rose, crumpling the top bill. She threw it over the fireplace screen into the fire, then crossed and handed the dumbfounded painter the remaining four.

The man nodded once slowly in comprehension, then withdrew.

Evelyn moved her gaze pointedly to Daniel to let him know that the challenge still stood.

"You're really gonna short him like that?" Daniel said. "Just to make a point to me?"

"I'm glad," she said, "we agree that the point has been made."

"Lovely visit, Mom." He started for the door. "See you in another seven and a half weeks."

Outside, he caught the painter climbing into a beat-to-shit pickup. Pulling five twenties from his wallet, he offered them through the open driver's-side window. The man looked from them to Daniel and said, "It's not *your* front door."

"She's my mom."

"Which means?"

"No one should have to endure her but me."

The man turned over the engine, set his paint-crusted hands on the wheel. "I got my own mom to endure, pal."

His tires crackled over the quartz rocks, leaving Daniel holding his money.

Chapter 15

By the time Daniel neared home, the sleeplessness of the prior night had caught up to him, turning the dusk beyond the windshield even blurrier. He groaned when he saw the car double-parked in front of the house next door. And there Ted was, popping into view behind the raised hatchback, shuffling reusable shopping bags and three children and gesturing for Daniel to come say hello. Daniel forced a smile as he pulled in to the garage, then walked out to where Ted waited beside the Subaru Outback—the one he'd gone to great pains to tell Daniel was built at a zero-landfill plant.

"Hey, Ted." Hoping to convey hurriedness, Daniel moved to check his and Cris's mailbox at the edge of their small front lawn. It also gave him an excuse to avoid full eye contact and—he hoped—engagement.

"Daniel, listen, Danika and I are having another implosion-sculpture event in the back courtyard this Friday, and we'd love it if you and Cristina would come."

The last one had been excruciating, everyone standing around slurping white sangria while the air was sucked from a giant steel cube, collapsing it in an ostensibly artistic fashion.

Daniel scooped out the mail and paused, collecting himself here in the gorgeous golden Pacific Heights dusk. He was smitten with more aspects of San Francisco than he could keep track of. And then there were Ted and Danika Shea.

Danika had been third-tier on a start-up that in the nineties had blown up sufficiently to turn third-tier stock options into professional-athlete money. Since then she and Ted had dedicated themselves to a life of unremitting self-focus, each trend embraced with the aggressive, authoritative air of the recently converted. Paleo one week, macrobiotic the next. Almonds for sex drive, açai berries for weight loss, fair-trade coffee for the soul. Cross-fit, suspension training, Bikram that will *save your life.* The celebrity chefs spoken of in intimate terms—*You know how Emeril is with his andouille!* And the causes brandished like weapons or NPR tote bags—carbon offset, female genital mutilation, orphans in Rwanda—each charity-of-the-week paid the same loving devotion as the newest windsurf board or Manchego. Five years ago the home births had started, with candles and doulas and tubs of body-temperature water, all recounted with inappropriate detail in bizarrely riveting holiday newsletters. The products of these mystical deliveries were indistinguishable mop-headed blond boys, Jayden and Lucas, who, armed with metal water bottles, were currently dueling over the head of their younger adopted sister, Simone.

Tonight Daniel's irritation with the Sheas was closer to the surface than usual, perhaps because he'd been worn thin by the past twenty-four hours. Or perhaps it was in reaction to the fun-house-mirror effects his neighbors wreaked on his own values, the contradictions blown huge, the hypocrisies stretched wider. The Sheas were colossal phonies, sure, but Daniel had his own flickers of self-doubt, those mornings when he felt like he was faking it, too, dressing down and going out into the real world. Evelyn's voice returned: *How are you these days? Still rubbing elbows with* criminals *for a living?*

Finally turning to face Ted, he mumbled an excuse for why he and Cris could not make the implosion-sculpture event.

"Well, do your best," Ted instructed. "I mean, this is silly. We live right next door, and we never see each other."

Jayden or Lucas bonked the girl on the head, and she gave out a strident wail. Ted crouched, took Jayden or Lucas gently by the shoulders, and said, "I'm hearing Simone say she doesn't like that."

Daniel used the diversion to slip away.

———

Rain hammered the wall of glass, turning the city lights into smears of orange and yellow and making the second-floor perch of their living room feel like a tree fort. Cris lay curled into Daniel on the couch, reading the *Chronicle* and sipping a Pacífico with lime. His feet were propped on the glass coffee table next to their dirty dinner plates, his knees forming a makeshift desk on which he attempted to fill out the termination agreement. Though he was doing his best to concentrate, his mind kept wandering back to that slightly ajar red door at Chestnut Street.

Except this time, instead of pausing, he kicks right through, tearing it from its hinges. The masked man appears in the kitchen doorway, startled, and then he and Daniel charge each other like something out of a samurai-warrior flick. Barely slowing, Daniel embeds the butcher knife in the would-be killer's solar plexus, and he crumples, and Daniel gets to Marisol, and she's terrified, yes, but still breathing, and he's able to untie her hands and dab the blood from her cheeks, telling her help is on the way, it's all okay now, and—

"You all right up there?" Cristina asked.

"Huh?"

"Your knees are jiggling. I'm getting whiplash."

The room strobed with a double flicker of lightning, and an instant later the rumble moved through the floorboards. The effect of the vast window and downslanting rain turned the world outside into something treacherous.

"Sorry," he said. "I . . ."

"What?"

"I wish I'd gone through her door quicker." He hadn't stated it so starkly yet, at least to his wife, and the words hauled up the emotion from where he'd tamped it down.

Cris reached up to touch his face. "I know, *mi vida*. But who knows what kind of mess *that* would've led to? Maybe Marisol would be dead anyway and I wouldn't have you here tonight." She pushed herself up to face him. "That half hour waiting for your call, Daniel, it felt like a *month*. And I went through it all in my head. The death notification. Your funeral. How I could never live here without you because you're everywhere I look in this house. And how goddamned angry I'd be with you for running out and getting yourself killed."

"Okay. Let's not get angry *now*."

She touched his face again. "Take me upstairs."

He tossed down the paperwork and stood, hoisting her over his shoulder.

"Stop it! Your back! I'm too heavy. And those creepy Shea kids— Grayson and Chase—will see through the window."

He dumped her on the couch, laughing. "*Jayden* and *Lucas*."

She was cracking up now, tugging at his shirt, trying to pull him down on top of her. "Hamilton and Greydon. And their sister, Baba Ghanoush."

Still chuckling, he fell, bracing himself against the arm of the couch. Through the rain-streaked window, a figure in the street caught his eye, the sight freezing the grin on his face.

A feminine form in a bright yellow rain slicker, hood pulled up over her head, standing in the precise middle of the street. But it wasn't just her reckless position that stopped him cold. It was that she remained perfectly still, like one of Castanis's corporate goddesses. Her face was cast in shadow, but the tilt and focus of the dark oval beneath the hood made clear: She was staring directly up at him.

Then she did something that turned the blood in Daniel's veins to frost.

She lifted an arm, dripping with rainwater, and pointed at him.

A car skidded past her on the slippery asphalt, horn blaring, throwing a sheet of water against her yellow slicker, but she didn't so much as flinch. A stone statue pointing, it seemed, in accusation. Accusing him of *what*?

Cris had slid up on the couch to peer over the leather arm. He heard a breath catch in her throat.

The drops running down the pane and the ongoing deluge turned the woman into a blurry outline. Daniel couldn't exhale, couldn't move. It seemed she had frozen him there by some curse.

A fierce rattle beside them broke the spell. He jerked violently, and Cris fell back on the cushions, grabbing her chest.

It was just his cell phone, vibrating against the glass table.

Keeping his eyes glued on the woman, he reached behind him and fumbled for the phone. Finally he glanced down.

A text from UNKNOWN CALLER. Dooley? Thank God.

He tapped the screen, and a photo came up.

Recognition dawned in degrees. First that the startled face, bleached fish white by the camera flash, belonged to him. Second, that his alarmed posture—recoiled against a wall beside a narrow doorway, brandishing a butcher knife—conveyed nothing so much as terror. Third, that the feathering of blood that marked the kitchen tile beyond Daniel's frozen image was Marisol Vargas's last breath, sprayed through the slit in her neck.

When he finally came back into his body and tore his gaze from the phone, the woman in the street had vanished.

Chapter 16

He heard Cristina's worried queries as if he were underwater, the edges of her words blunted and warbling. When he handed her the phone, it trembled in his grasp. The double shock had taken the air right out of his lungs, and he lowered himself to the couch and calmly caught his breath while Cris sprang into action, calling Dooley, forwarding the text message, and firing off a reply text to the picture's sender, only to be answered by a red error exclamation point.

"He has," Cristina said breathlessly, "your number now."

"They know where I live."

"So you think that woman is working *with* the killer?"

"It has to be related. Doesn't it? The timing, my phone going off just then—"

"They found you." Her voice, low with dread. "This quickly."

He thought of his goddamned picture tacked up on that glass-encased staff bulletin board on the third floor of Metro South. How easy it must have been for someone who frequented the building to connect the dots.

Cris had asked something. She repeated the question: "Why was she pointing at you?"

"I don't know. Maybe just to show that they know who I am."

"But she seemed to be, I don't know . . ."

"I have *no idea*."

The text alert on his phone chimed again. The picture, re-sent.

Then again. Again. Again. Populating the screen before his and Cristina's horrified eyes with image after image of that snapshot. A relentless barrage.

"Turn it off," Daniel said.

Cris remained motionless, so he grabbed for the phone and powered it down.

They sat side by side on the couch, breathing. Then Cris rose and began to clear the plates. He followed suit. They washed and loaded the dishwasher and ran the trash compactor, and then Cris turned into him suddenly and they hugged each other tightly there before the sink.

"Dooley got the forwarded text," Cris said into his chest. "She'll pull our phone records and try to trace it. I told her I'd sign off on all that."

He nodded. Clutched the fragile stalk of her neck. "How about the woman?"

"She didn't know *what* to say about that but thought the phone route was the strongest play for her to jump on now. Keep the doors locked, alarm on. Duh."

They listened to the rain beating against the walls, thrumming off the roof.

"How do you think he got your phone number?" she asked. "Our address?"

Daniel reached over and dropped the Pacífico bottle into the slide-out recycling bin. "Records at work."

"Those are supposed to be private."

"It's not exactly Fort Knox. And the building's rife with fucking bottom feeders."

The words flew out, hard-edged, followed by a wash of regret.

Cris just looked at him.

"Come on," he said. "*What?* I'm angry right now, Cris. Do I have to watch my phrasing in my own house?"

"No. You shouldn't ever have to *watch* your phrasing."

"So what's that? I say something when I'm being *threatened* and that means it's my secret truth coming out?"

"Of course not." She started walking upstairs to the bedroom.

"What then?"

She turned, gripping the railing. "When I was a baby, my mom smuggled me into this country on the birth certificate of my cousin who died at three months. I wasn't even *legal* until I graduated high school. And no matter what my last name is now, I will always be that."

"What are you saying? You're worried you can't get past your background?"

"No. I'm worried you can't get past *yours*."

Anything he was going to say next, he knew he'd regret, so he kept his mouth shut.

"There is a killer who has your cell-phone number," Cris said, her voice cracking. "*Your* number. That bastard has slaughtered two people already. Believe me—I get the stakes here. But it still throws me to hear you . . . I don't know, channeling Evelyn."

He took a few breaths, tried to untense his shoulders. "All right," he said. "But we also can't start dragging our histories into this."

"If you're allowed to say stupid shit when you're mad, then I'm allowed to say stupid shit when I'm terrified." She blinked, and tears fell. "Okay? We both need to reserve our right to say stupid shit sometimes."

She stepped down into his embrace, squeeze-hugging him around the neck hard enough to choke off his air. "I want to get someone to guard you," she said. "All the time."

He tugged at her arm a little, and she loosened her grip. She was one stair higher than him, the perfect relative height, her cheek warm against his. At the end of the day, only the faintest traces of her shampoo and lotion lingered, orange blossom and vanilla blending with the delightful, intangible smell of her.

"Let's talk about it," he said.

"What's to talk about? Think what this guy did to that woman's face. And to Jack Holley. He promised he was gonna kill them, and then he just . . . *did*."

"No one's promised to kill me yet."

"He saw you. And then he took your picture. And then he sent it to you on your own cell phone. And probably sent someone to our house. Whatever he's doing, it's escalating."

The doorbell rang.

Chapter 17

The alarm was on, knob locked, deadbolt thrown, security chain hooked. Daniel and Cristina stood on the bottom stair, confronting the front door across the foyer.

Daniel stepped down, crossed the tile, and pressed his eye to the peephole, making out a distorted bulge of a masculine face. He barely recognized the menacing rumble of his own voice. "Who are you?"

"My name's Leo." A clipped, hard-to-place accent. "I—"

"Step back from the door," Daniel said. "To the edge of the porch."

The man complied, coming into better focus through the peephole. Bald, short, and stocky—a bowling pin of a man. His nose seemed smashed against his face, pounded flat from multiple breaks. Rain caught him there at the porch's lip, but he barely seemed to notice.

"What do you want?"

"Mrs. Evelyn Brasher sent me."

Cristina made wary eye contact, her hands up, confused.

"Are you a bodyguard?" Daniel called through the door.

"Not specifically, no."

"Then why are you here?"

"I've dealt with situations like this. On a lot of continents."

"Like what?"

"Like this." The man clasped his hands at his belt line, motionless save for a slight shift of the knee that betrayed his impatience. "How can I put this? I'm overqualified for this particular job."

"You still haven't answered why you're here."

"I told you why I'm here." A pause. Then, "Mrs. Brasher has a lot of money."

"And you want to . . . what? Follow us around everywhere?"

"No. My job is to protect you here. At home. While you sleep. Think of me as a very expensive guard dog."

"You plan on sleeping here?"

"Not *sleeping*, no. But staying through the night."

"No thanks," Daniel said.

He turned from the peephole, but Cristina put her hand up on the door, her arm blocking him. She drew close and whispered, "Marisol's killer has your picture. He has your phone number. He knows who you are. And where we live. You're *my* husband, which means I get a vote."

"I am not taking anything from my mom," Daniel said, doing his best to keep his voice low.

"Your *life* is at stake here," Cris said.

"We can get our own bodyguard." His teeth were clenched. "Through our own contacts."

"That'll take time. We have a problem *tonight*."

Cris, stiff as a plank, up on her tiptoes, their faces close enough to kiss. Trying to have a whispered argument behind the proverbial closed door. A bead of sweat slid down Daniel's side, tickling his ribs.

The gravelly voice came from outside. "You really want to risk getting dead because of some stupid pride bullshit with your mother?"

Releasing a breath, Daniel looked into the patterned whorls of the miniature Zen garden on the table. Cris read the answer in his body language, and the tension eased out of her. She kissed him on the cheek, turned off the alarm, undid the locks, and twisted the knob, but then Daniel put his palm on the door and banged it shut again, hard.

"How do we *know* my mother sent you?" he called out.

The man cleared his throat and said, flatly, "'And *do* try to avoid tangling with Catalina, that angsty wife of his.'"

Daniel lifted his hand from the door in surrender, and Cris, biting back a smile, swung it open.

Chapter 18

The following evening, before parking and unpacking himself from the smart car, Daniel circled the entire garage level of Metro South to check the shadows, as he'd been instructed by Leo Rizk, the man sent by Evelyn. After they'd let him in from the rain last night, the man had proved highly focused and capable. Leo claimed they should now consider their house a fortress, and Daniel had to admit that he felt no small measure of comfort with the guy there. This morning when he'd headed down for his run, he'd found Leo sitting on the stairs with ramrod-straight posture and his handgun resting on his thigh. He'd turned his alert stare on Daniel and said, "No iPod, right? We need you alert and aware out there," and Daniel had lowered his hood to show him that he wasn't wearing headphones. Leo had snapped off a nod and scooted over to let him pass.

The jog had been an exercise in paranoia, Daniel spinning around at the sound of any footfall behind him, his heart rate revving up with the engine of each passing car. It hadn't helped that Dooley had traced the text message to a number assigned to a disposable phone. A masked killer and the faceless woman from the rain—unknown somewhere out in the city, biding their time.

Sitting in his car now with the doors locked, he dialed Cristina. "You're home safe?"

"You called the house line. So that would be yes."

"Oh. Right. Anything weird at work?"

"It *is* the projects. But nothing unusually unusual."

"Leo's there?"

"Indeed. I'm making him tamales."

"Jealous."

"He has a gun. He's guarding our home. He gets tamales."

Daniel signed off, climbed out of the car, and hurried across the garage, braced for an ambush. Not until he'd reached the far side of the metal detector in the lobby did he fully exhale. The walk down the dark rear corridor proved to be another trial of sorts. The motion-sensor lights arranged at intervals clicked on only as he entered the edge of shadow, illuminating the next cube of hallway. So he progressed cautiously toward the mail room, tensed for a hideous revelation. An imagined horror waited in every block of darkness ahead. Marisol Vargas with bloody tears streaming down her cheeks. That smooth, featureless mask of the killer. A woman in an oversize yellow slicker, her face lost to blackness, her arm raised to point in silent condemnation.

By the time he reached the mail room, his shirt clung to him. He approached his cubbyhole tentatively but found only a few flyers. The outgoing mail, empty. He released his breath, a hiss through his teeth. A glance at the clock curtailed any relief.

Four hours and change until midnight, when the death threat issued for Lyle Kane of Bay Street would presumably be carried out.

Remembering that he was on *Candid Camera,* he straightened his spine and stepped out of the mail room. The corridor still gleamed under the overheads, every inch as bright as midday, and he smirked a bit at his agonizing progress on the inbound walk. The janitor's door stood slightly open now, and he tapped it with his knuckles.

"Come in, please."

Angelberto sat on the bench, smearing wood putty onto a square of cardboard with a wide Popsicle stick. He glanced up and made a respectful nod. How ridiculous Daniel's suspicions felt in the light of a new day.

Daniel said, "I just want to apologize for barging in here Monday."

"It's okay. This is not my space. I do not own it. I am only glad to be here to have work." He slapped at the wood putty, softening it.

"Still, you're entitled to privacy."

"A lot of people suspect workers of stealing. I understand. You are just trying to protect the department."

"Not really," Daniel said. "More like I was being an asshole."

Angelberto gave a faint grin, and Daniel realized that it was the first time he'd ever seen the man smile.

"I didn't introduce myself before, Angelberto." He offered his hand. "Daniel Brasher."

As they shook, Daniel noticed a creased Polaroid of Angelberto with a woman and child taped on the open locker door. "That's your family?"

"*Sí.*"

"Beautiful," Daniel said.

"They are in Mexico," he said. "I will bring them here when I save enough for them."

"I hope it's soon. Good luck."

"Thank you, my friend. But I don't trust in luck. I have found that luck gets you nowhere. And so I trust in work."

Daniel said good-bye and withdrew. Hustling down the hall and up the stairs, he realized that the detours had put him a few minutes late for group. As he neared the room, he did his best to clear his head to get ready for the session. But a stomach-turning thought persisted.

Lyle Kane, wherever he was, likely had less than four hours to live.

Chapter 19

"Get outta my *fucking* chair." Xochitl stood over A-Dre, her arms crossed, as he lounged in the chair closest to the door.

He pulled himself up slowly, grinning. "Didn't want this seat anyways. Just wanted to see you get your G-string in a twist."

"You're a douche."

"Not even a douche*bag*?"

"No," X said. "The douche itself. You are the Douche of Monte Cristo. Douchio Iglesias. The Crown Prince of the Kingdom of—"

"Okay," Daniel said. "Let's get going."

A-Dre settled into another chair in the circle. "Why's she get to pick her seat anyhow? It ain't fair."

Big Mac said, "I pack on a thousand calories a minute eating and burn nine-point-one a minute on the treadmill. Life ain't fair. Whoever fed you that line of crap, ask for yer money back."

"I'm so cold," Lil said. "That open window makes it so cold in here."

"Is there something you want to ask?" Daniel prompted.

Her gaze fell to her lap. "Maybe we could . . . Does anyone else want the window closed?"

Walter Fang, who cranked open the window every night upon entering the room, said, "This building, it smells like shit. We need . . . ah, ah, fresh air."

Lil shrunk further into herself. "I guess it's okay."

"Don't guess," Daniel said.

Nothing.

He felt a pang of frustration. "Lil, if you don't ask for what you want, no one can help you."

"Really." Lil picked at her stringy brown hair. "It's not important."

"Why can't she bring a jacket?" Fang said. "Every week she says she's cold. But she never brings a . . . ah, ah, jacket."

"Because she'd rather fucking complain," X said. "I mean, about being cold, about being lonely, about her husband dumping her—"

"How would you feel?" Lil said softly. "I did everything for him. I did everything he asked, and he still left me."

"Shit," X said. "That's *why* he left you."

"You don't know," Lil said. "You've never been married."

"Right, 'cuz a divorce makes you an authority."

"At least I try. I may not look like much, but at least I got hurt. At least I don't just . . . hide like some people."

Daniel nodded at Lil, encouraging her.

"Yeah, getting hurt's great," X said. "Real step in the right direction."

A-Dre's laugh hid a nasty edge.

Daniel hoped Lil would keep sticking up for herself, but instead she mumbled, "You're right. I'm being stupid."

Showing her throat as she always did when pushed.

The other men watched the altercation, staying out of it. Daniel let the room flow, observing, waiting for the right opening.

"You are one weak bitch," X said. "Anyone can walk over you. You play this shit and hope someone rescues you." The man's zip-up hoodie she wore drooped to midthigh, her body swimming in it. For how wiry and small-boned she was, it was amazing how much intensity she could convey. Easy to forget she was a teenager who sketched unicorns on her binder. "Tell me I'm wrong," she said to Lil. "Go on, tell me I'm fucking wrong."

Lil's lips parted, but no words came out. She tipped her head, pulled at her bangs, hiding behind a curtain of hair.

"*Epic* fail," X said.

"Back off her," Martin said.

"There it is," X said, clapping. "She got you to take the bait."

Martin folded his hands. "I'm serious. You should apologize for that shit."

"Okay." X's head swiveled to Lil. "I'm sorry you're such a pathetic bitch."

"We can just drop it." Lil's sandals tapped a skittish beat on the tile. "No big whoop."

X threw her hands up. "See what I mean?"

Daniel finally cut in. "Xochitl, how do you feel when Lil reacts that way?"

"I *feel* like she's a complaining bitch."

Walked into that one.

He tried again. "When Lil complains, what do you do?"

"Call her out."

"Okay," Daniel said. "And what's that do for *you*?"

The trickle of wind from the window barely cut the stagnant air of the room.

"What are you talking about?" X said. "Like what?"

"Like maybe you're glad everyone . . . ah, pays attention to *her*," Fang said. "Instead of to you."

"Oh, *ah-ah-ah-ah*," X said. "You think *ah-ah-ah* that's what I'm doing?"

"Yeah," Big Mac said. "So no one calls out *your* angry ass."

"I'm not saying Lil's perfect," Daniel said. "But you keep the focus on her as much as you can."

X snickered. "Bitches, puh-*leez*."

"So we're *all* wrong," Martin said.

"Fuck *yes*. Look at yourselves."

"You always look out for number one, don't you?" Big Mac said. "Always take care of yourself."

"Hell yeah," X said. For the first time, genuine emotion flickered in her face. "Who's gonna take care of me if not me? Nobody cares about m—" She caught herself. Arms crossed, staring at the wall five feet above Daniel's head.

Daniel completed her thought. "Nobody cares about you."

"I didn't say that. That shit sounds like *her* complaining ass."

"If you don't say it, if you don't admit it, do you feel it any less?"

"I don't feel shit." She dropped her glare, doodled on her binder.

Daniel grabbed an empty chair from the room's periphery and slid it across, opening up the circle into a horseshoe. Steady gaze at X until she met his eyes. "Will you take first shift getting feedback?"

"Fine." The word, an arrow aimed at his head.

She got up and flopped into the chair facing the others, glowering out at them.

Daniel sat back down. "Did you work on your letter?"

"What letter?" X said.

"The letter to your victim."

"Oh. That shit. Yeah." She dug a crumpled piece of paper from her pocket and read in monotone, "'Dear Raped Girl. Sorry I raped you with a stick. I won't do it again. Sincerely, X.'"

Big Mac shook his head, gave a little snort. "Epic fail."

"Yeah," Martin said. "That pretty much sucked."

"If that's what you came up with," Daniel said, "I can see why you'd want to keep the room focused on Lil."

"Ever been in a gang, Counselor?" X said. "Didn't think so. I did what I had to do. And I don't regret it. I could write a bunch of flowery, remorseful shit if it makes you feel better, but I'm just being honest."

"Amen," A-Dre said.

"Honest, huh?" Daniel said. "The girl have a name?"

"Who?" X said.

"Raped Girl."

X blinked twice, quickly. Shifted her jaw. "Sophie."

"I want you to write a letter for next session, but write it from Sophie's perspective."

"Fine." X stood up, made a show of flicking dust off either shoulder. "You say I avoid shit. But at least I talk. You know who avoids *everything* up in here is Fang."

Daniel put it to the room. "Do you think that's true?"

As the others made various noises of agreement, Daniel glanced at the clock, gauging the time to midnight. It struck him that it had been a full twenty minutes since he'd thought about Lyle Kane, Marisol Vargas, or the masked man from the foyer, and he felt a surge of appreciation for a job that demanded every ounce of his concentration.

Returning his focus to the room, he gestured at the empty chair, and after a delay, Fang walked over to it and sat. His shiny sneakers looked spit-polished, every strand of his gelled hair in place. He wore a form-fitting lime green Polo with the extra-large horse at the breast. He pursed his lips and said nothing. It was always hard drawing out a quiet group member, and Walter Fang was one of the most restrained that Daniel had encountered.

"Anything you want to talk about?" he asked.

"No."

"You're squirming in your chair. Is something bothering you?"

"No."

"Okay. What's the best question we could ask you today?"

Fang glanced at his watch, the door, his watch again. "I didn't get the . . . ah, ah, ah, job at Home Depot."

This was bad news. For weeks they'd been working at helping him find employment, running practice interviews in group with everyone providing feedback, and the Tools and Hardware opening at Home Depot was his holy grail.

The others mumbled various condolences, but Fang stared blankly at them.

"Any idea what happened?" Daniel asked.

"Maybe they hate Chinese people," X offered brightly.

Fang ignored her. "They just didn't like me."

"But we worked on the interview so hard," Lil said. "You were doing great—"

"The *interview* went fine."

"What went wrong, then?" Daniel asked.

"You have to fill out a form."

"Okay . . ."

"I didn't hand it in."

"Why?"

Fang tapped his feet, agitated. Wiped his mouth. "I got . . . ah, ah, trouble writing."

"Learning disability?" Martin said.

"My father, he says there are no learning disabilities." He affected a flawless Cantonese accent. "'You know what we call that when *I* growing up, Wal*tah*? We call that *stupid*.'" The minor animation was, for him, an outburst, and he looked momentarily embarrassed that he'd captured the full attention of the group. "When I was young . . ." He trailed off, moistened his lips.

Martin's hands had paused from polishing his eyeglasses on his flannel shirt. "What?"

"They made me sleep on the couch in the living room. I was the second of five and the oldest son, but I was the . . . ah, ah, dumb one. So. I couldn't go to bed until everyone was done watching TV. And I had to wake up with whoever got up earliest. Last one to sleep. First one up. I was like the furniture."

"Your parents never got you," Lil said.

"No, they got me. They just . . . ah, ah, ah, ah . . ." He cleared his throat, hard. "They just wanted someone else. Who did good in school. Who could write the right way. And I can't. Which means I'll never get a real job."

"No," Daniel said. "Your talking about this is great. We know what the problem is now—you have trouble writing. Which means we can work at fixing it. There are occupational therapists who specialize in this."

Fang stared at him for a long time, his head drawn back, chin tilted slightly up. Haughty? Defensive? Daniel waited him out, though the silence was excruciating. Big Mac clanked his grip strengthener, then clanked it some more.

Finally Fang said, "The application form's in my car. If I get it after session, will you . . . ah, ah . . . Will you . . . will you . . . ah, ah, ah . . . Help me?"

He seemed to overcrowd the chair, humming with vulnerability, stripped to the bare nerves. What must it have taken for him to muster the courage to pose the question?

Daniel felt heat rising to his own cheeks, the glow of empathy. "Yes," he said. "I'd be happy to."

When Fang returned to his place, Martin reached over and gave him a supportive smack on the knee.

A-Dre took the center chair next, slouching, arms crossed. "Let's get one thing straight first, Counselor. I ain't gonna be talkin' no shit 'bout my momz. That woman is a *queen*. And I got a question. You told me all them rules I got to follow. What's *your* side of the deal?"

"My side of the deal is I'll be here," Daniel said, "three nights a week, rain or shine. And I'll help you navigate this. We can start wherever you want to start."

A-Dre scratched at the LaRonda tattoo on his neck. "You guys choose."

"Who's LaRonda?" Martin asked.

A-Dre stiffened. "My sister."

"We allowed to make fun of sisters, Counselor?" X asked.

A-Dre's cold stare skewered her. "I wouldn't do that."

"Can you uncross your arms, A-Dre?" Daniel asked.

"Why?"

"It looks aggressive. Angry. Closed off. Intimidating."

"Thanks."

Scattered laughs.

"I mean with the scar and the ink, especially the neck tattoos, people see you and they know to be careful," Daniel said.

"Thass right."

"If I didn't know you, I'd probably think you're a dangerous guy."

"You're some white guy with a degree who can't dress for shit. Why should I care what you think?"

"You want to get by in the world easier, right? In the world are a lot of white guys who dress just as shitty as I do."

"I don't know 'bout *that*," X said. Big Mac chuckled, and they bumped fists.

"I'd like you to try being more open," Daniel told A-Dre. "And it starts with how you hold your body."

A-Dre shrugged and finally uncrossed his arms, letting them dangle awkwardly. That circular scar on his biceps came visible.

Big Mac gestured at the shiny patch of skin. "How'd you get that?"

"When I was twelve, my stepdad burned me with his cigar."

"That's bigger than a cigar," Martin said.

"I burned over the hole with a frying pan."

Lil looked shocked. "Why?"

"Ain't nuthin that nigga do I can't do better."

Everyone took a moment with that one.

A-Dre crossed his arms again. "This is stupid."

"You're unhappy about being viewed as a criminal," Daniel said. "You're in trouble with the law. You want to control yourself better. But most of what we say seems to be useless to you. Why is that?"

"I got a *code*. Men don't walk away from a fight. Men don't back down. And they sure as shit don't share in some bullshit group."

"That code's gonna wind your ass back up in the pen," Martin said.

"Or get you killed," Big Mac added.

A-Dre bobbed his head. "I ain't afraid to die. I *never* been afraid to die."

"Are there any parts of your code you'd consider letting go of?" Daniel asked.

"No."

"Are your choices getting you what you want?"

A-Dre bounced forward angrily in his chair. "Maybe not. But at least I fuck up my *own* self. No one tells me first. No one—" He caught himself.

"What?" Daniel said. "*What?*"

A-Dre rolled his lips over his teeth, bit down. "No one can tell me I ain't good enough."

"Because you always prove it first," Daniel said. "From the minute they see you."

"I can't do shit 'bout how people see me."

"I have," Big Mac said. "Am I better than you?"

A-Dre stared at him. Didn't answer. He was sweating, a sheen covering his arms and face, even the LaRonda tattoo.

"Am I better than you?" Big Mac's voice boomed off the walls.

"No. You ain't better than me."

"Then you can 'do shit' about it, too."

A glimmer appeared in A-Dre's eyes as he processed this, and then the scowl returned. "We done?" He got up and started to swagger to his regular seat.

"Not quite yet," Daniel said.

They all waited as A-Dre retraced his steps, radiating contempt.

"Why do you fight?" Daniel asked him once he'd again settled into the hot seat.

"I like it."

"Why?"

"It's fun. And I'm good at it."

The others laughed.

"I won every fight I been in," A-Dre said. Given his breadth and jutting muscles, this was easy to believe. "You ever fight, Counselor?"

"I was a wrestler—"

Daniel was cut off by assorted hoots.

"A *wrestler*!"

"—rules and shit—"

"—them little bathing-suit thingies—"

It took Daniel a few moments to steer the room back on track. "What are the *good* things about fighting?" he asked A-Dre.

A-Dre hesitated, so Lil jumped in. "Nothing."

"No," Daniel said. "Not *nothing*. Don't give me the shit you think I want to hear. What's good about it?"

"At least you're *doing* something," A-Dre said. "Not just taking it."

"Okay. What else?"

"Gets you respect. Gets you girls. Gets you *stuff* you can take from people. Gets 'em to do what you want."

Daniel got up and starting writing the pros on the left side of the chalkboard: *"Respect. Power. Sexual partners. Control. Money."*

He tossed down the chalk, dusted his hands. "Okay, great. Now let's talk about what happened after."

"Like what?"

"Like what happened next. For you, for the people around you."

X piped up. "Your sis LaRonda."

"You shut your mouth 'bout LaRonda."

It was slow going, but Daniel finally got A-Dre to list some consequences of the fights, which Daniel summarized on the other side of the board: *"Fired from job. Arrested. Jail stint. Broke up with girlfriend."*

Big Mac snickered as the list grew. "Yep, you sure won all them fights, didn't you?"

"Yeah, I did. I got some blowback, sure. But look at all the shit I got first." A-Dre flared a hand at the scrawled list on the left side of the board. *"Respect.* Power. Shorties. Bling."

"How many of those things did you have six months later?" Daniel asked.

A-Dre waved off the question. "Six months later I was in prison."

Daniel set the chalk down in the tray. Asked again, "How many of those things did you have six months later?"

A-Dre's eyes darted back and forth across the chalkboard, annoyed, and then came a softening of his face. He laced his fingers, stared down at his hands.

"None," he said.

Chapter 20

When Big Mac took center chair after the break, he sat silently for a few moments, squeezing the grip strengthener. "I had a setback this morning. I can't be there for my fucking kids because I'm out there working to feed them, right? My daughter's got asthma. My boy needs books for school. Christmas is coming up, and . . . I don't make enough as a waste collector."

"Dude," X said, "you a *trashman*."

"X, the title on my fucking paycheck is—"

"Refuse Procurement," X said. "Know what we call that on Earth?"

"Shut the hell up, X," Martin said. "Let the man talk."

Big Mac took a deep breath, his broad shoulders settling again. "We're always tight. Gas bill, groceries, cell phone—"

"Car always breaking down," Martin said.

"'Zactly. And my wife, I don't ask much of her. Just stay off my back, cook, and clean."

"That's *all* you want out of her?" Lil asked. "You want to be married to a cleaning lady?"

"Hey, fuck off," X said. "I *am* a cleaning lady."

Daniel kept his attention on Big Mac. "Go on."

Clank-clank. Clank-clank. Then, "So she's on me this morning, right? First thing, over the Cap'n Crunch. About the holidays coming up. Get a promotion. It's that easy, right? Like I can just *get* a promotion. And I . . . uh, put my fist through the wall. And she's still going on. So I put my hands on her. Openhanded, but still. And the kids, they're scared of me. I can see it. They're too polite, you know. Even though I've never hit 'em—I've *never* touched them. They're too polite to me, and they clear the fucking table and go into their room until their mom can drive them to school. And I go in there, and they're sitting on their beds like"—his voice caught—"like they don't know what to do. And I try to say I'm sorry, and they just say, 'It's okay, Dad, it's okay,' like they just want me to leave them alone. Which they do. Want me to just leave. And they don't know I'm really sorry. They don't know I'm really sorry."

X's breath hitched in her chest, and Daniel glanced across at her. Big Mac's story had captured her complete focus; it was the first time Daniel had seen her let down her guard. No one else noticed her reaction.

"Look," Big Mac said, "I didn't even *have* a dad. My old man left when I was eight, my mom checked out when I was fourteen, so my kids are one better, but still. This ain't how you think it'll go, right? When you're in the hospital holding them in that swaddle, kissing those tiny feet. You don't hope for them sitting there on their beds staring at you scared like they wished you were gone already. I'm worn down and short-tempered from working for my kids, and then they're scared of me because I'm worn down and short-tempered."

"They should understand," X said. "They should *understand* why you did what you did."

Again Daniel noted her quiet sincerity—something about Big Mac's interaction with his kids had struck her deep—but he didn't want to halt the room's momentum by switching to focus on her right now.

"—my wife," Big Mac was saying. "I love her, but fuck. Riding me, trying to piss me off."

"Is there another explanation?" Daniel asked. "Besides her trying to piss you off?"

"Maybe *she's* tired, too," Lil said. "Or as scared about money as you are."

"I tell her all the time what I'm doing for the family."

"What else do you tell her?" Daniel asked.

Big Mac studied his large, rough hands. "I love her, okay? She knows that. I don't have to say it. She can tell by what I do, how I work to support her."

"So you *never* tell her you love her?" Lil asked.

"There's no point."

"Why not?" Daniel asked.

Silence. Then, "She's just gonna leave anyway." His turtle eyes blinked. "Her. The kids. Might as well get it over with."

"How you know she's gonna leave?" A-Dre asked. His first question about another group member, that tiny initial step into the circle.

Big Mac took a breath, his vast chest expanding. "*Everyone* leaves," he said.

Daniel let the sentence linger. Then he said, "But you don't want them to. You want to be with your family."

"Everyone leaves," Big Mac repeated. "I learned that young."

"If you learned it," Daniel said, "that means you can *unlearn* it."

"But it's what happens."

"Okay." Daniel held up his hands, slowing things down, putting together the emotional equation. "If everyone leaves, then how do you treat them?" A blank stare. He tried again. "You've decided that everyone close to you is gonna leave. So what *else* have you decided about how to act toward them?"

Big Mac rasped his palm across an unshaven cheek. "Don't trust anyone," he answered. "Don't let anyone close."

"If you lived with someone who didn't trust you and never let you get close, what would *you* do?"

Big Mac swallowed once, hard. The pink rims of his eyes sagged. "*Leave,*" he said.

They spent the rest of the session untangling Big Mac's beliefs, pulling at loose strings and seeing what came unwound. X remained withdrawn, lost in thought. She didn't speak at all, not even a single wisecrack, an aberration of mammoth proportions.

As the group readied to go, Daniel remembered Lyle Kane's approaching deadline, now two hours away. The return to cold reality was bracing, and he felt another rush of gratitude for the warmth they'd created in the room.

He cleared his throat. "I just want to tell you that you've been a real bright spot for me in the past couple of days. The courage you show in here, it's . . . inspiring, really."

Big Mac smiled broadly. "Look at Counselor getting all Hallmark on us."

"I know," Daniel said. "Lapse in judgment."

X gathered her schoolbooks quickly and was the first to head out. She paused with one hand grasping the jamb, seemingly on the verge of a classic "doorway moment"—dropping a revelation at the end of a session when there's no time left for scrutiny. She turned only slightly, showing them her profile. The others were still talking and collecting their things, but Daniel watched her, rapt.

"I had a baby when I was seventeen," X said.

The room went silent, the group members freeze-framed in their various positions.

"Gave her up when I went to the Hall," X continued. "She's lost in foster care somewhere." Still she refused to face the room fully. "She'd be two today."

Before anyone could reply, X had vanished.

After the others dispersed and Fang headed to the garage to retrieve his employment form, Daniel took a moment alone to tilt his head back and breathe in the silence. He found himself itching to call Inspector Dooley to see if she'd made headway in locating Lyle Kane, but he resisted; she was no doubt stressed enough, watching the clock as anxiously as he was and bracing for bad news. In the quiet room, he felt the weight of every passing second.

Fang returned nervously holding a coffee-stained piece of paper, like a report card. Reluctantly, he relinquished it, and Daniel took a look.

It struck him immediately that Fang was dyslexic, the scribbled lines calling to mind the death-threat letters and putting a charge into Daniel's chest. But as he'd seen before, the handwriting was quite different, a wide, undisciplined scrawl.

He settled his nerves and worked with Fang to gather information for a referral, watching him write, examining his pencil grip, and taking a history. Though he did his best to push thoughts of Lyle Kane aside, the countdown to midnight pervaded everything like the deep thrumming of a plucked string. Finally he saw Fang off and headed to the common office on the second floor to leave a message for Sue Posada, an occupational therapist he'd met at a continuing-education course. It wasn't easy to find people in that field who would work closely with violent offenders, but he and Sue went back a ways, and she trusted his referrals.

Waiting for her office voice mail to pick up, he tapped his pen against the top page of Fang's handwriting sample—*I went to the park tobay.*

His mouth went dry.

He stared at the word. No longer heard the ringing of the line. Though there was no air-conditioning vent overhead, the room felt suddenly arctic.

He squeezed his eyes shut, forced that unsettling handwriting to inhabit the darkness behind his lids.

lyle kane
376 bay st
san fransico

Back to Fang's paper.
Tobay.
Today.

Bay St

Day St

The phone line gave a staticky silence—Sue's recorded message must have beeped already. Numbly, he hung up. The home screen on his iPhone showed 11:37.

Twenty-three minutes.

Jamming his thumb at virtual buttons, he called Dooley.

She picked up her office line on one ring. "Yes, I'm here. Yes, I'm aware that we're down to twenty-three minutes."

"The killer's dyslexic." Daniel tried to slow his words, to little avail. "He flipped a letter. Substitute *Day Street* for *Bay Street*."

He closed his eyes, listened to Dooley type. Time seemed to stretch out with a dreamlike intensity.

"Nope," she said. "There's no Lyle Kane at 316 Day Street."

Disappointment blew through him. He fought it away, refocusing. What *other* mistakes might a dyslexic make? The errors could be inconsistent depending on the writer's concentration, speed, stress. Closing his eyes again, he pictured that cramped little address. "Turn the *six* upside down. Try *319* Day Street. Is there a Lyle Kane there?"

He heard her hammering again at her keyboard. His breaths came fast and shallow, making him light-headed. The delay lasted an eternity, and then Theresa said, "Nope—"

He bowed his head.

"—but there's a Kyle Lane."

Daniel leapt up, the chair banging over behind him, clattering on the floor. He pulled the iPhone from his face to check the time—down to twenty-*one* minutes—but he could still hear Dooley's voice issuing from the slit of the receiver: "Meet me there, Brasher."

He barged out the door and sprinted down the empty corridors, his footsteps pounding almost as loud as his heartbeat.

Chapter 21

The unattached house pinned down a modest square of grass on an unremarkable block of Noe Valley. When Daniel screeched around the corner in the ridiculous smart car, he spotted an ambulance and four cruisers at the curb ahead, lights strobing. An elderly neighbor stood on his porch in boxers and an unsashed bathrobe, gesticulating into a cell phone, and a cluster of others were being herded away from the curb by a patrolman. The dashboard clock showed 12:03—late again—but the cops had clearly been here for at least a few minutes.

A paramedic smoked a cigarette before the laid-open rear doors of the ambulance, and Daniel made out the gurney still inside, undeployed. Which meant *what*? His gaze jerked to the porch. No body bag in sight, but a fall of light announced the front door as open.

He did a drive-by. The front door sagged crookedly, and even from this distance he could make out a splintered panel from where it had been kicked in. Rolling past, he spotted a couple of uniformed cops convening in the foyer, one holding a clipboard, the other speaking animatedly to someone just out of sight.

Lowering his window, Daniel braked before the patrolman. "Did you get here in time?"

"We don't look busy?" the guy said. "We're out here at midnight just standing around, hoping to answer questions from rubberneckers—"

"I'm here to see Inspector Dooley. I'm the one who—"

"Get out of here so Inspector Dooley can do her job. Move it. And buy a real car."

"He's fine!" Dooley appeared in the open doorway, shouting down the front walk. She beckoned Daniel with a flick of two fingers, a woman used to having her commands obeyed.

The patrolman grimaced and stepped aside to let Daniel park. An angry wind caught him in the face as he climbed out, and he hunched into it as he made his way up the walk.

Dooley waited for him on the porch beneath an elaborate set of wind chimes, looking displeased.

"How's Kyle Lane?" Daniel asked.

"Not here, that's how he is." They paused by the shattered front door. "Not that that stopped this probe here from going all Vin Diesel on the front door."

A young officer ducked his head sheepishly and slapped a clipboard into her waiting hand. She shoved it at Daniel. "Sign the crime-scene log. And follow me."

A grizzled patrolwoman reached over and took the clipboard from Daniel. She cast a wary look at Dooley. "Hang on, now. The lieutenant—*your* lieutenant—told me to keep the scene airtight. You know damn well the press is warming up to this one, Dooley. And now you're marching in a *witness*?"

"He's not just a witness," Dooley said. "He is *inside* this case. Which means he has a vantage no one else does. I need his eyes and I need his expertise, and if adding one more name to the log's gonna get me an inch closer to the Tearmaker"—Dooley lifted the clipboard from the woman's thick hands—"then I'm adding one more name to the log."

She shoved it at Daniel, who signed, then returned it apologetically to the peeved patrolwoman. Dooley took his arm and pulled him inside. The house's bland exterior did not prepare him for the elaborate furnishings. Red velvet flocked wallpaper darkened the living room, and a few bordello lamps, capped with fringed shades, cast a guttering glow across an antique coffee table stacked with art books about Tuscany. An ornate china hutch displayed kitschy Lladró figurines and a menagerie of wineglasses suited to any varietal. On the closed lid of a baby grand, a carapace of framed photos captured different groups of men in various settings—sunning on a beach-house deck, posing beneath the high barrel-vaulted and coffered ceiling of the grand opera house's lobby, mugging for the camera outside a Castro bar.

Theresa watched him peruse the photos. "Yep," she said. "Gayer than a Christmas tablecloth."

One face recurred in each picture, a dark-eyed man in his mid-forties with a wispy ponytail and a receding chin. Kyle Lane.

"Recognize him?" she asked. "From anywhere?"

"No. I've never seen him before."

Through the walls, the wind chimes came faintly audible, the kiss of metal on metal.

"Look at the rest of these pictures." She dropped heavily into the chenille couch and plunked her heels on the coffee table, jangling loose change in a black Wedgwood dish parked on an art book. "Do you recognize *anyone* in those photos? Anyone from Metro South?"

He took his time looking. The sweet, dusty smell of potpourri rose from a bowl on the windowsill. Behind him the patrolmen creaked the floors, bursts of static issuing from the radios strapped over their shoulders. He turned back to Dooley, shook his head, and sank into an opposing studded leather armchair. They looked at each other, frustrated.

"Any idea where Kyle Lane *is*?" Daniel asked.

"No. One of the neighbors he's friendly with said he's never out this late on a school night."

"You think he was taken?"

"No signs of forced entry."

"There was no sign of forced entry at Marisol Vargas's," Daniel said.

"Or at Jack Holley's." Dooley clicked her teeth, a tic of frustration. "Kidnapping's a whole other animal, but we can't take anything off the boards."

"Maybe Lane's just out of town?"

"He was at work today," Dooley said. "Left at his usual time."

"Where's he work?" Daniel asked.

"CFO of a health-food company. Bars with psyllium husk and flaxseed oil, that kind of crap."

"He from the city?"

"Appleton, Wisconsin. Came out here to get his M.B.A. at Berkeley. No criminal record. No connection with the other victims that we can establish. We've been busting ass, looking at *everything*. No leads on what Lane 'did' to the killer—what *any* of the suspects 'did.' From out here? It all looks random."

Daniel laced his hands together, a gesture meant to be calming. But he sensed the sweat on his palms. "If you don't think Lane was kidnapped and he's not out of town, where the hell is he?"

"That's what we in the trade refer to as a 'key investigative question.' " She even threw in air quotes.

A plainclothes officer entered, covering the receiver of his cell phone with the heel of his hand. "Lieutenant wants to know how you plan to handle the broken door."

She heaved a sigh, seemed to sink further into the couch. Then she unfurled her hand. As she received the phone, she said to Daniel, "There are more pictures in the bedroom up the hall. Take a look."

Beat cops still crowded the foyer, so Daniel looped through the galley kitchen. With its bare counters, IKEA cupboards, and Kenmore refrigerator, it was designed for function over form, striking a contrast with the living room. When he stepped out into the brief hall, the ambience resumed—wall sconces, Campari posters, even an Aztec rug adding a flare of color to the white shag carpet. The wind picked up outside, moaning through the eaves, the music of the porch chimes growing more insistent—*ting, ting*.

Faux-antique wood furniture dominated the bedroom at the end of the hall. A jolly sleigh bed, neatly made and overlaid with a dozen or so decorative pillows. The full-length cheval mirror in the corner reflected back the big window across from it and its claustrophobic view of the neighbor's gray stucco wall, maybe two feet from the sill. Leaning against the high mattress, Daniel examined the scattering of framed photos on the nightstand.

A lot of faces, none he recognized.

He pinched the bridge of his nose, frustration cramping his temples. Then he pushed off the bed, his movement captured by the freestanding tilt mirror. Evelyn kept an authentic version in her dressing room, and he paused to take in the familiar design—the classic oval adjusted to a faint recline in its appliqué-embellished wooden frame.

The reflection staring back was an unflattering one. Pale skin, drawn face, his eyes hollow from stress and lack of sleep. In the two days since he'd accidentally received the threatening letter, he'd been sucked down the rabbit hole, and he was quickly losing sight of the way back. He needed to get home to his wife, grab a good night's sleep, and reenter his life.

"What are you even doing here?" he asked himself.

As he turned to leave, his reflected feet remained in place, dislocated from his body. An optical illusion? Puzzled, he halted. Stepped back.

His legs continued, he realized, beyond the tilted bottom frame of the mirror. The twinning bands of his ankles and—yes, there, his feet. But they weren't wearing his shoes.

They were wearing black work boots.

Chapter 22

Daniel's mind lurched, snagging on the reality, grabbing sudden traction, a blaze of white-hot alarm lighting his insides.

Before he could react, the man vaulted out from behind the mirror, that blank-masked face blurring into view. A muscular arm raked the top-heavy mirror forward on its pegs, sending it into violent rotation. Daniel barely managed to lift his arms before the impact knocked him to the floor. Shattered glass cascaded down around him, raining over the back of his head and his shoulders. The mirror, flung horizontally over him, wiped the room and his attacker from view. He saw only the floorboards and pebbled bits of the mirror, spinning and bouncing, a confusion of reflections.

There were two hard footsteps and then another crashing sound from across the room. The window?

Daniel rolled free, his torso grinding glass, the smashed window reeling into view upside down, then right side up. Already the man was gone—he must have bounded straight through the pane.

The cops' shouts issued from deep in the house, and a single clear thought impressed itself on Daniel's brain: *Wait for them.*

He stood. Stared at that glass-fanged window. Judging by the pounding footsteps, the cops had only just reached the mouth of the hall. Precious seconds trickling away.

Don't go through that window.

But already he was sprinting, the broken frame tilting with each jarring step. He leapt through, hanging shards snapping off against his shoulder blades, the sound like breaking fingers. A half second of flight until his shoulder's impact with the neighboring wall knocked the breath from his lungs. He slotted down neatly into the skinny alley. The walls squeezed him at the shoulders, forcing him to blade sideways.

Ahead, the intruder flew toward the backyard. The black sweats, gloves, and smooth neoprene curve of the head turned him into nothing more than a dark outline, a shadow unhooked from its human. A barred gate at the alley's end rose to an arch connecting the low-dropping eaves of the side-by-side houses. From the gate's hasp swung a rusting padlock. The man was trapped in this stretch of alley.

And Daniel trapped here with him.

His peripheral vision caught the cops spilling into the bedroom, framed by the fractured window, and he shouted, "Here—he's out here!"

Accelerating toward the rear gate, the intruder pounced and grabbed the bars halfway up with a resonant clang. He scaled quickly, like a clawed creature. Between the gate and the crowning arch, a gap came evident. Just big enough for a man to wiggle through.

Daniel took off in pursuit, yelling, "He's heading to the backyard!"

As the man reached the top and wormed his torso through the gap, Daniel hurtled up the alley, his shoulders scraping both walls, dry paint flaking off in his wake. The space smelled of tar and reprocessed air, exhaled through a heating vent. Just ahead, the man hauled himself through the gap, stomach, waist, hips vanishing.

Daniel got there and leapt for the gate, but his shoulder clipped the wall and he hit the bars unevenly, sweat-slick hands scrabbling for purchase. The ground swirled below, off kilter. Clinging, he heard from above the yielding purr of tearing fabric, the ring of metal striking ground. Firming his grip, Daniel tugged himself up. He lifted his head to the gap at the top of gate just in time to see the heavy, drawn-back boot unload like a piston into his face.

The sense of weightlessness lasted longer than seemed possible. The bolt of lightning across his temple dimmed in slow motion, darkness catching him before he struck bottom.

The pack of frozen corn retrieved from Kyle Lane's freezer numbed the swollen bulge of flesh on Daniel's brow, but what he really needed was something to take the edge off his frustration. The Tearmaker had vanished in the maze of interlacing yards and alleys connecting the surrounding residences. Daniel's left eye was badly bloodshot, a wispy red claw cupping the iris from below; the sight of it in the powder-room mirror had made him clench the lip of the vessel sink. Now he sat on the chenille couch, Dooley and a trio of plainclothes officers staring at him as if waiting for his head to do an *Exorcist* spin.

Snatches of sentences made their way through the murk.

"—what happens when you have probies clear a house—"

"—were in a rush, Dooley, responding to a potential *murder in progress*—"

"—kick in the front door but don't think to look behind a fucking—"

"—besides which, Brasher shouldn't even *be* here. He can sue the city—"

"If I sued the city," Daniel said, "they'd probably take the money out of my own damn department."

Dooley perked up. "It speaks."

"Barely." He shifted, and another fork of lightning speared his brain.

"Okay," Dooley said. "Take me through it. Step by step. You should be good at this by now."

Daniel rose to literally walk her through what happened. The house crawled with crime-scene investigators, dusting and tweezing. Camera flashes made the hall and bedroom strobe like a nightclub. Threading through the ordered commotion, he gave her every detail he could recall, interrupted at intervals by cops sailing in to deliver updates or receive instruction, which Dooley handed out in efficient bursts: "Move the checkpoints out to Dolores and up to Twenty-eighth." "Clear the rec center and roust the bums in Billy Goat Hill Park, see who saw what." "Start running the prints through AFIS now, wheat from the chaff."

Daniel watched the men watching her and nodding compliantly, and he realized that all of them were half in love with her. And that that was extremely useful to her in the midst of a manhunt.

He resumed his account to Dooley as they continued their walk-through, winding up before the shattered bedroom window.

Dooley leaned out, peering up the narrow passage between houses. "You said you heard his clothes rip when he went over the gate, right?"

"Yes," Daniel said. "Right before he kicked in my face." He studied her thoughtful expression. "You're hoping for a piece of fabric?"

"I'm hoping for better than that," she said. "I'm hoping he tore a pocket."

He still hadn't caught up.

"Shit spills outta pockets, Brasher. Especially when you tear them. Let's have a look-see."

Rather than climb through the broken window, they circled out the front door toward the alley. A few news vans had turned up, and a CHP helicopter chopped thunderously a few blocks away, the power-ful searchlight beaming down like something out of science fiction.

"Guess he'll figure out now I'm getting his mail," Daniel said.

"He'll know you're on his case for *something,*" Dooley said. "Which isn't bound to make him happy." She slipped into the alley, her slender shoulders, even squared up, clearing either side.

The lane between the houses caught light only from sparse win-dows, so their shadows sprang up fast and sharp. The gate loomed ahead. On the far side, an investigator stood atop a ladder, ducked precariously beneath the arch to peer at the spikes, one ghost-white gloved hand gripping a flashlight.

Daniel recalled how effortlessly the intruder had scaled the bars.

The bulk of his muscles beneath the loose-fitting black sweats. The sole of that boot, hammering down toward Daniel's face. The memory made him wince into a fresh burst of pain.

He said, "I wish I'd grabbed his legs and impaled him on the spikes."

Dooley paused. "Aren't you supposed to be a therapist?"

"I'm not on the clock."

They approached the gate, Dooley looking up at the man perched atop the ladder. "How you doing up there, Roscoe?"

"Oh, ya know. One thousand thirty-nine more days till I retire with full pension. Got me a iPhone app counting that shit down for me." The flashlight beam picked across the tops of the bars. "Not finding anything up here. No blood, threads, nothing."

"Mmm-hmm." Dooley tugged the Maglite from her belt and crouched by the base of the gate, scanning the concrete with the beam.

Daniel flattened to the wall to give himself a vantage past her. Dooley moved the shaft of light along the bottom of the fence, illuminating a few weeds sprouting from the cracks in the concrete, pebbles, flecks of rust.

And a folded white square to the side, just beneath the bottom hinge.

Dooley leaned forward and used her pen to flick the small piece of paper out into the open. It landed up on its edge, an open V with the mouth pointed at them. She squatted over it, and Daniel saw her shoulders settle as if under a great weight.

"What?" he asked.

She pressed her shoulder blades to the wall so he could see past to the little rectangle at her feet.

A business card.

His.

As he stared at the crisp font announcing his name, his heartbeat found the bruise at his temple, breathing pain back into it. At once he struggled to find air here in this cramped alley, the walls closing in on him. The cell-phone number on the card was crossed out.

He lifted the pen gently from Dooley's grasp and used it to tap the card over to the flip side. Written across the back in his own hand was his new cell-phone number.

There were only six of these business cards he'd written his new number on.

The six he'd handed out to his group members.

Chapter 23

Despite the chill on Kyle Lane's roof, he was sweating beneath the mask, his humid breath rebounding into his pores. He sat patiently, arms folded across his knees, watching the helicopter, now a half mile away, continue its futile outward spiral. From the beginning, the cops had focused elsewhere, on the surrounding blocks through which he'd presumably fled. His black clothes had served him well for the one quick sweep the searchlight had taken over the house itself. He'd simply tucked himself against the base of the chimney, camouflaged in its umbra.

The eyeholes constricted his vision only slightly, his pupils jerking alertly to track Daniel Brasher as he crossed the front lawn, heading back to that stupid car. Brasher paused for a moment with his hand on the roof, head bent as if to catch his breath. He looked shaken.

After Brasher puttered off, he lay on his back and took in the few stars penetrating the night gloom. The sound of the helicopter continued to fade, and below, on the street, engines turned over and cars drifted away in twos and threes. When it was safe, he lunge-stepped silently across onto the neighbor's roof, then lowered himself onto the lid of a built-in barbecue in the backyard. Through slats in the fence, he could see the crime-scene investigators packing up their gear under the watchful eye of the black lady cop.

He removed the mask, drawing in a lungful of cool air, then tucked it into his waistband along with his gloves. The sweatshirt came off next, revealing beneath a fitted red thermal sporting the 49ers logo. He stuffed the sweatshirt into a trash bin in the side yard, burying it beneath mounds of ketchup-stained paper plates. Tugging down the long sleeves of the thermal, he let himself out onto the sidewalk. As he strolled, he whistled, his fingertips trickling along the hedge of juniper and stirring up the delightfully bitter scent. Turning the corner, he came face-to-face with a beat cop hauling several flexible traffic cylinders.

"Excuse me, Officer," he said, approaching. "Have you seen my cat? She's a tabby named Lady, and—"

"Sorry," the cop said. "No luck finding anything tonight."

"I'm sorry?"

"Never mind. No, I haven't seen your cat."

The cop never slowed, the rubber bases of the traffic cylinders dragging across the asphalt.

He watched the cop go, then continued on his way, picking up the whistled song where he'd left off.

Chapter 24

The sun broke across the horizon, fanning a sheet of gold through the iconic skyline. Daniel was weary, half asleep behind the wheel, the early-morning haze of the city a match for the early-morning haze muffling the steady throb in his head.

If that neoprene motorcycle mask were peeled back, whose face would be revealed? A-Dre's? Big Mac's? Fang's? Martin's?

Or had one of the group members given Daniel's card to someone else? Was the killer an associate? A brother or a boyfriend?

The hooded woman in the rain—Lil or Xochitl?

No matter the explanation, one thing seemed clear: Someone in the group was involved in the Tearmaker murders. Someone who'd shared intimate shortfalls and sins. Someone he'd fretted over and pried at and fought for and against, usually at the same time. He'd pledged to help these people reconstruct themselves. He'd cared for them, bent his own shoulder to their burdens so they could stand straighter.

He'd thought he knew these people. He'd thought he entered the worlds they lived in, dipped beneath the surface, swam in the undercurrents. But maybe he'd been wrong. Maybe he'd understood nothing. Maybe no matter his focus and perspective, he was still just a rich asshole from Pacific Heights.

The shock and dread and the mule kick to his temple had left him in an altered state, washed up on the shore of a landscape at once familiar and alien, a dream version of the streets he was driving through. He cut past the Castro, where Latina drag queens in fishnets and feathers paraded the sidewalks, strutting past bars with inventively uninventive names—the Lonely Bull, the Missouri Mule, Dirty Dick's. He kept on, skirting the edge of the Haight, where painted VW buses and druggie runaways littered the curbs, in search of a lost decade. During the Summer of Love, Janis Joplin strummed her Gibson in a one-room flop pad here, a tambourine's throw from where the Grateful Dead commune tuned in and dropped out. Relics of each era endured, layered like geological strata in storefronts, charting the evolution from beatniks to hippies to yuppies to fauxhemians.

Forging his way north, Daniel sliced through Alamo Square, its picket row of pastel Victorians basking in the first pink-tinged rays of the new day. Beyond their fanciful gingerbread gables rose the green copper dome of City Hall, where ousted Catholic and local sandlotter-made-good Joe DiMaggio said *I do* to Marilyn and where, a couple of decades later, five hollow-point bullets cut down Harvey Milk in the corridors of power. So much glory and shame. So much beauty and horror. A city that burned to the ground six times before its first decade flamed out yet rose from the ashes again and again, a boxer who wouldn't stay down.

He let his imagination soar across the rooftops to the Tenderloin, where dealers in saggy pants palmed Baggies into skeletal hands and tranny hookers batted improbable eyelashes and held cigarettes to their smeared lips, smoking off the night's work. Mere blocks to yet another ecosystem—capitalism-clean Union Square on perennial high polish, ornate Christmas displays already gleaming in the vast picture windows, Neiman and Chanel, Saks and the ghost of I. Magnin. Coppola shot the conversation in *The Conversation* here, but even his surveillance camera couldn't capture the dead-end alley where Miles Archer met his fictional demise or the Palace Hotel, where President Harding was felled by an enlarged heart or a poisonous wife.

A Peter Pan drift took Daniel to Russian Hill with its manic slalom descents, its vertiginous tumble over the brink of Filbert, its manicured floral gardens cupping the curves of Lombard, the second-crookedest street in the city. Steve McQueen's Mustang scorched these slopes in the world's greatest car chase, the fleeing Charger losing an unlikely six hubcaps in the process.

Then on to North Beach in all its gaudy Italian glory. There perched City Lights Bookstore, where Ginsberg howled, the wedged façade gazing nobly across the intersection at the world's first topless bar, if the historical plaque is to be believed. Carol Doda bared her double-D Twin Peaks here at the Condor Club, a skip from Green Street where Philo T. Farnsworth lived up to his madcap inventor's name and conjured into existence the world's first TV. And overseeing all this squalid, soaring history, the fluted column of Coit Tower, the candle stuck in the cupcake of Telegraph Hill.

All those tales of the city. All those separate lives. Misfits and dreamers, transplants and immigrants, victims and outlaws, packed full of hidden fears and sordid impulses, inflated fantasies and rageful desires. They'd come heeding the siren's call, seeking haven, to this sanctuary city thrust into a swirl of ever-shifting tides and mist. A peninsula draped over seven hills, twinkling and glorious, with jutting heights and precipitous drops, a labyrinthine fog-veiled confusion of one-ways and narrow alleys, shadow and light. A microcosm of the human psyche in all its splendor and horror, its seething, brilliant, hideous capabilities.

So many places to hide. So many ways to disappear. All those masks, imagined and real.

And, beneath one of them, a killer.

Chapter 25

As Daniel neared home, the morning light was still thin, the streets suffused with a straw-colored glow. Any reasonable human would be in bed. This category, of course, excluded Ted and Danika Shea, who were on yoga mats on their front porch, doing sun salutations. Ted glanced up from Downward Dog and beamed a wholesome smile in Daniel's direction. Daniel summoned a weak grin and turned into his driveway.

The alarm chirped quietly when Daniel entered the house, and he punched in the code, then rearmed it. In a stupor, he kicked off his shoes and moved quietly upstairs. The sight of the man sitting at the kitchen island, facing away, brought him up short. The stocky form and broad, bowed shoulders, the smooth dome of the skull glistening beneath the muted overhead lights. Motionless.

Daniel froze with one foot above the floorboards until recognition clicked.

Leo Rizk. Sitting still enough to be carved from marble. A pistol remained within reach, a few inches from his right hand.

For a moment Daniel wondered if the man was dead, but then Rizk's shoulder shifted and his head tilted slightly as he brought something to his lips. Daniel drew nearer, noticing the bottle of Blanton's and a second poured glass across from Leo.

He looked from the tumbler to the back of Leo's head to the tumbler. "Expecting someone?"

"You," Leo said.

"I thought guys like you always faced the door."

"Don't have to."

Over Leo's shoulder Daniel noted the faint mirror image of the room in the broad windows opposite. The bottle had been positioned near the counter's edge so that one sliver of reflection captured the top of the stairs.

Daniel circled the island and sat. Two fingers of golden liquid were in the bottom of the tumbler. He let the smoke fill his throat, warm his stomach. "Where's Cris?"

"Upstairs. Fell asleep. She tried to stay awake, but once she knew you were okay . . ." Leo brought the glass to his lips.

Daniel considered the faceted globe of the bottle. His favorite bourbon, neat, how he preferred it. They hadn't restocked Blanton's in the bar since killing the last bottle after a dinner party last month. He couldn't even recall Leo's having brought a bag with him, and yet here he was, wearing fresh clothes, sipping Kentucky single-barrel. They'd given him the code to the alarm and a set of keys, but Daniel wasn't sure when he'd left the house.

"One drink," Leo said. "Every four hours."

"I don't mind," Daniel said.

Leo removed his watch and polished the face fastidiously on his shirt. His nails neatly clipped. No sign of stubble on his shaved head. The gun looked well oiled, the barrel pointed at the refrigerator. Not a fingerprint on it.

"Thank you," Daniel said. "For being here."

"It's my job. I'm paid well for it." The skin of his face was mostly smooth, but parenthetical lines around his mouth and crinkles at his temples showed his age and seemed, in the dim light of the kitchen, to be code for wisdom.

"Thank you anyway."

Leo knuckled his nose, which showed surprising give. A thin rosary-bead bracelet dangled from his left wrist. He noted Daniel's gaze. "Maronite Christians trace their ancestry back to the invading Europeans during the Crusades. Warriors from the start."

"Your people."

"My people."

Daniel got up and walked to the window. The sun still barely a notion to the east. The fog thick as soup, muffling the glow, leaching the color from the sky. All his group members were out there, probably sound asleep beneath the sheets. Except for one. Daniel pictured Kyle Lane's ponytail, the soft face and thin frame of a man seemingly not suited to violence. He was somewhere out there, too, alive or dead, sipping a mai tai or clinging to life with knife slits leaking beneath either eye.

"This fucking city," Daniel said. "This fucking fog."

"They say the fog was so intense that explorers missed the Bay the first few go-rounds," Leo said. "Sailed right past the entrance. And these were men, presumably, who noticed shit."

Daniel turned back to him.

"It's not a city that gives up its secrets easily." Leo finished his whiskey, and the empty glass clicked down on the counter. His steady gaze unsettled Daniel. "What's worrying you?"

"The killer's probably in my group. But I don't know who to suspect."

"Then you'll start suspecting everyone."

"Is that how it works?" The question was half rhetorical; Daniel didn't expect an answer and didn't get one. He tried for something more specific. "How do you keep hold of what matters to you if you suspect everyone?"

"Until your life is at stake," Leo said, "you don't *know* what matters to you."

Daniel wanted to protest but held his tongue, letting the thought settle.

Leo flicked his head, a nearly imperceptible gesture. "What happened to your eye?"

"I got kicked in the face."

"I've had those nights."

"You've dealt with situations like this," Daniel said. "On a lot of continents."

Leo's mouth stretched, still a straight line and yet somehow a smile. "That's right."

"Protecting folks?"

"I've played some defense. I've played some offense."

"Offense," Daniel repeated, trying on the word.

"Yes. To people who have done things I wish I could still call unimaginable."

"And when you find who's to blame—"

"Blame?" Leo used the blade of his hand to nudge the empty glass back into its condensation ring. "Blame doesn't matter."

"What do you mean, blame doesn't matter?"

"Everyone's to blame. No one's to blame. So—there is no blame. Only people who have to be killed."

He slid silently off his barstool, lifted the gun from the counter, and drifted down the stairs. Daniel stood for a time looking at the two empty glasses before heading up to bed.

"Someone in your *group*?" Cristina said.

Despite her tousled hair and sleep shirt falling *Flashdance* style off one shoulder, she was eminently alert, having bounced awake at Daniel's entrance and squeezed him hard enough to make his ribs ache. After checking his bloodshot eye meticulously under the strong light of the bathroom, she'd returned to the bed, where she sat bolt upright in a coil of sheets as he paced to and fro.

"Seems to be," he said.

"I guess now we know how the killer ID'd you so quickly, knew your phone number to text you that picture of yourself." Her words came fast, a relentless, uncharacteristic chatter. "But don't other people have your business cards? Like past group members?"

"Not with the cell-phone number crossed out and my new one written on the back. Remember, I just switched a few weeks ago—"

"Right. 'Cuz AT&T sucks."

"—and I only wrote down my new cell for the group. That card came from one of them."

"But still. It's not a *lock* that one of them is the killer. One of your group members could've given your card to someone else. Or someone could've taken it from them." Before he even thought to raise an objection, she waved him off. "I know, I know, Occam's razor and all that. I'm just saying, the card isn't *airtight* evidence that one of your group members is the killer. It's just very damn likely." Her speech was high, pressured, one of her hands twisting in the other.

He paused. "Honey?"

Her head swiveled over. "What?"

"I'm okay now."

She stared at him a moment, and then a breath shuddered out of her. He walked to the edge of the bed and put his arms around her.

"We've both worked with a lot of dangerous people," she said into his chest. "But this is insanity."

As he eased in beside her and leaned against the headboard, his back tightened, a reminder of the fall from the gate.

Cris noticed his grimace and took his hand in both of hers. "Need me to get you Advil?"

"I don't know. Think it'll make me feel better?"

"It'll make *me* feel better."

"Okay, then."

She scrambled off the mattress, and he heard her clanking around in the medicine cabinet. "So assuming it *is* someone from your group, how can you not tell who it is? You see them three times a week."

Daniel pictured Martin, A-Dre, Big Mac, and Fang. Four large men with more or less the same build. "They're all big guys. Roughly the same height. The killer wears these loose-fitting black sweats, so it's hard to tell his exact shape. And it's not like I've gotten a clear look. He's always busy running or kicking me in the face."

"How about that woman in the rain? Could *she* be from your group?"

He closed his eyes. Saw the blurry outline in the downslanting rain. That lifted finger, pointing at him. Frozen with purpose, even as a car screeched within inches of her. The raised hood hiding the face, just as the oversize rain slicker disguised her frame.

"Yes," he said. "She could."

"Six group members, six suspects," Cristina said.

"That sounds about right."

She came back, palming off the little round pills and handing him a cup of water. "What's Dooley doing about all this?"

"Right now? Having each group member's residence searched by a parole officer. With cops standing by."

"Because a parole officer doesn't require a warrant."

"Right. Can search a parolee's place anywhere, anytime."

Morning leaked around the edges of the blinds, pale lines stretching across the floorboards. Soon it would be time to start the day. A late-morning meeting with Dooley to set a game plan before the next group session. Come tomorrow night he was supposed to be back in that circle, looking at those six faces, an arm's length away. He thought about how safe it felt right now, here in their bed, the whole world blocked out beyond the drawn blinds. "Dread" didn't seem a strong enough word for the ball of twisted metal in his stomach.

"What are you gonna do tomorrow night?" she asked. "About your group?"

"I don't know."

"How can you work with them and suspect them at the same time?" she asked.

"I can't," he said.

They watched the sunbeams' relentless creep along the floorboards, ushering in the threats of a new day.

Chapter 26

Daniel's sweat-drenched shirt clung to him as he picked up the pace, running into the slope, the burn in his thighs intensifying. He'd still not slept—not a wink—each restless minute a razor blade nicking at him, fraying his nerves a strand at a time. He rose with finality around 7:00 A.M., some compulsion driving him to pound the stress from his body with a jog. His hip ached—last night's fall had brought up a plum-colored bruise the shape of Australia—and his temple throbbed, but there was something soothing about the pain and his ability to persevere in the face of it.

Passing a cascade of bougainvillea accenting an overblown Tudor, he heard footsteps behind him. A steady *tap-tap-tap* at first. And then quickening.

Without slowing, he pretended to scratch his cheek, risking a glimpse behind him. A half block back, a husky guy with his hood raised, a tapering band of perspiration marking the front of a gray sweatshirt. The hood covered his face, but his build looked familiar enough to redline Daniel's pulse.

Daniel forgot the pain, his legs finding an extra charge as he strained to listen for the footsteps. Twenty yards behind him? The windows of the mansions flashed brightly, forming a sporadic mirror by which he could gauge the guy's distance back. The man powered forward, big legs like pistons. An intersection left Daniel reflectionless, and when the row of windows resumed, the man had drawn within fifteen yards.

Up ahead loomed the promise of the Lyon Street Steps, but they were isolated against the edge of the forest, the stairs empty save for fallen eucalyptus leaves. No potential witnesses. A final façade of windows would provide Daniel a last glimpse, and then he'd be trapped in the cul-de-sac or funneled onto the narrow stairs, neither situation ideal for taking a stand.

The pounding footsteps, louder now, closing the distance. All but sprinting, Daniel gained the vantage of the final bay window, his own reflection surging into sight first, the pavement behind him brought into painstaking view with each shuddering step.

The hooded man just five yards back now.

The man's arms stopped pumping, and he shoved a hand into the pouch pocket of his sweatshirt, grabbing for something.

Daniel's shirt felt cold and clammy against his flesh. His lungs screamed. His legs strained, carrying him past the window, his pursuer's reflection wiped from view just as the hand started to emerge.

Steps pounding up on him.

Daniel waited, listening, timing himself.

He pivoted sharply, lowered a shoulder, and bulled into the man, a collision of bone and muscle. The guy grunted and tumbled back, arms flinging wide as he struck pavement, the hood falling away to reveal a clean-shaven, youthful face. His hand, yanked free of the pocket, gripped an iPod, which had come unplugged from the headset. The tinny speaker issued forth the assured drone of a financial guru dictating an audiobook—*"magnified losses in derivative trading can be attenuated by"*—until the young man grabbed the iPod and thumbed it off. "What the *hell,* dude?"

Immediately Daniel pegged him as a business-school student or first-year analyst with one of the investment banks. A wave of chagrin. "I'm sorry." He was breathing hard enough that his shoulders rose and fell. "I didn't see you. I was just turning around, forgot something at home—"

The guy stood up, brushing himself off, glaring. "Do you even *live* around here?"

"Yes."

"You know who my fucking parents are?"

Daniel couldn't help but laugh.

He started for home, leaving the guy's complaints behind. The tension hadn't left his body yet, all those fight-or-flight hormones washing through him, heightening his focus, tightening his muscles. Five blocks away his heart still felt lodged in the base of his throat, tattooing an SOS alert.

Chapter 27

Outside Golden Boy Pizza in North Beach, Daniel found Theresa angling a folded slice of Sicilian into her mouth.

"Do you have news?" he asked. He could hear the pressure in his own voice, the anxiety right at the brim.

Without slowing, she held up a just-a-minute finger and continued, the operation resembling nothing so much as an I-beam being delivered into a high-rise. A pungent smell wafted across the sidewalk.

He gave her some chewing time. "What *is* that?"

"Clam garlic pizza," she said proudly, through pouched cheeks. "Just don't try 'n' kiss me and nobody gets hurt."

"I thought we were meeting for lunch."

"Appetizer slice." She finished, sucked her fingertips, wiped her hands on her pants. "You know the squirrel from those *Ice Age* movies?"

"Yeah."

"I pretty much have his metabolism. Someday I'll look like Nell Carter, but till then? Clam garlic pizza." She picked up a battered soft-leather briefcase. "Come on. Let's find a booth somewhere. Don't want to talk on the street."

They crossed Columbus, passing Club Fugazi, a florid theater poster announcing *Beach Blanket Babylon* as the longest-running musical revue in history. A performer in cabaret stockings sat on a planter outside, struggling with a hat the size of a garbage can.

They turned in to Capp's Corner, a checkered-tablecloth Italian joint, and found a quiet table.

Daniel's impatience had reached boiling point. "Well? What happened?"

"We went with the parole officers to roust each of the group members, but naturally everyone was safe and sound. Been in bed all night, they claimed. Just like on the nights Jack Holley and Marisol Vargas were murdered. Of course, none of the killings have occurred when your group was in session."

"That's why the murders were all planned for midnight," Daniel said. "No one expects anyone to be anywhere then." He realized he was twisting his napkin obsessively. "Did they search the houses?"

"Houses?" She laughed. "We're talking shithole apartments or garagelos at best."

"Garagelo?"

"Converted garage with a futon and a space heater." A smirk. "It's how the other half lives. Yes. Every residence was searched top to bottom. Nothing unusual was found. But generally felons whose places can be searched at any time don't leave a bloody knife sitting out on the coffee table. Oh—and big surprise, we didn't find any motorcycles. None of them have registration on a bike either, for what that's worth, so A-Dre must've borrowed or stolen the one you saw him on. Or I should say *heard* him on. Or *mistook* hearing him on."

"Did you find Kyle Lane?"

"Still missing. Didn't show up to work today. Which, in his employment history, has happened exactly never." She regarded her hand, lying flat on the table, as if it were something she wanted to smash.

"Jesus," he said quietly. "Do you think he's dead already or being . . . *kept*?"

Theresa grimaced. The waiter drifted up, flicking open a notepad, but she waved him off. Daniel, too, had lost his appetite.

"So what next?" he asked once the waiter had withdrawn.

"We'll keep eyes on all of them as best we can. Sit an unmarked car outside each of their places. But running surveillance on six people isn't cheap or easy. We've got some budget leeway given the profile of this case, but still. Given we can't be a hundred percent certain that the suspect *is* one of those six, my LT's patience ain't gonna be endless."

"And in the meantime you what? Just wait for another death-threat letter to pop up?"

"We watch every move of those six," Dooley said. "Just like you will in session."

The waiter returned, plunked down two glasses of water, took in the mood at the table, and retreated. Theresa's stare had not left Daniel's face.

He cupped his hands around the sweating glass, the cold biting his palms. "I can't do that," he said. "I'm quitting."

Her nostrils flared. "*What?* Why? The danger? We have a plan for—"

"No, not the *danger.*"

"What then, Brasher?"

"I have a duty to the people in my group. How can I do the job if I'm suspicious of all of them?"

"What do you think I deal with every day?"

"I'm not a cop."

"No," Dooley said. "But you know the suspects like no one else. Which means you are uniquely positioned to stop this."

"It's not that simple—"

"Of *course* it isn't. We don't have the luxury of *simple.* Look, I get your professional concerns. But this isn't black and white. Nothing is."

"Don't some things *have* to be? If we start bending a rule here and a rule there, where are we gonna wind up?"

"People are being *killed,*" Dooley said. "You saw what he did to Marisol Vargas. Hell, you *heard* it from a room over. I understand you're worried how you'll feel if you don't do right by a patient. You think you'll feel any better if someone else's throat gets sliced and you know you might have helped prevent it?"

He thought about the damp smell of potted plants in Marisol Vargas's dining room. The horrid burbling from the kitchen. Those pictures of Kyle Lane framed on the piano, frozen images in an empty house. His grip had intensified around the glass, and he let go, an ache cramping his knuckles. "No. But how I'll feel isn't the point."

"You have your bullshit definitions of right and wrong," she said, "but this is real life. And real life is dirty."

"Is this the lecture part? Because we tried this route once."

"Apparently it didn't sink in, so we're gonna do it again." Her slender frame rose and fell with a silent breath. "There is a way to navigate this. To do right by yourself and by them and to do right in general, too. God knows it's not easy walking that line, but with what we're looking at, isn't it worth trying?"

He stared out the window but still felt the heat of her gaze on the side of his face.

A few moments passed, and then she added, "I thought you said you liked challenges."

He took a sip of water. Set down the glass. Crunched an ice cube between his molars. "*If* I do this—"

She exhaled.

"—I'm not gonna report to you everything that goes on in that room."

"You are legally required to disclose information if a patient is a danger to others."

"Right. But we don't know *which* patient is."

"So what do we do?"

"I'll continue running the group. See what I can figure out and tell you anything as it pertains to the case."

"How will you determine what pertains to the case?" she asked.

"You'll have to trust my judgment."

She simulated a smile, then flashed back to deadpan. "Guess we're stuck with each other, then."

"So where do we start?" he asked.

"With your selection criteria. How do you determine who gets into the group?"

"I assess candidates in an intake session. Group therapy doesn't work for a lot of people. They have to be drug-free, higher intelligence, not too introverted."

"Great," Dooley said. "Guy we're looking for is intelligent, coherent, highly organized. So you prescreened a suspect list."

"But I should've *also* screened out psychopaths," Daniel said.

"Maybe the killer's not a psychopath."

"Or maybe I screwed up during the screening process."

"Do you think you did?"

He considered. "No."

Theresa hoisted the briefcase onto the table and tugged out a stack of files, one for each group member. Flipping through the tabs, Daniel acquainted Dooley with each member's nickname.

"I haven't managed handwriting samples for everyone yet," she said. "And samples taken under duress aren't accurate."

"I already looked at samples," Daniel said. "No matches."

"Are you a handwriting expert?"

"I've had some training. But it's clear as day. No one from my group wrote those notes."

She searched his face. Gave a little nod. "Okay."

"Someone else could be doing the writing for them," Daniel said. "Spouse, girlfriend, accomplice, whatever."

"We've been looking at that," she said. "Of the group, only Big Mac is married, is that right?"

"Yes. Martin *was* married, but his wife died of skin cancer four, five years ago."

She flipped a few pages. "We got no record of a dead wife."

He replayed Martin's phrasing—*My lady, she died when I was inside*—then cast his mind back to the early sessions. "Right. Sorry. She was a long-term girlfriend, not a wife."

"He bullshitting it?"

"His grief over her loss is real. No way he could feign that."

"And Lillian"—she caught herself—"*Lil* was married, too."

"Yes. But her ex-husband's in jail. Bank robbery."

"Not anymore," Dooley said. "He's been out six months." Daniel's surprise must have shown, because she asked, "She didn't mention that?"

"She probably doesn't know he's out."

"That's not what I asked."

Daniel's discomfort registered, finally, as an emotion. Beyond the shock and anger and betrayal he'd felt since finding his business card, he realized there was sadness, too. Over the months they'd been in that room, sweating and arguing and grinding away, he'd developed a genuine regard, even affection, for each of the group members. Beneath all the discussion and stressful analysis, a plain fact remained: He didn't *want* any of them to be the killer. But there was a dirty reality at hand and a missing man and an answer owed to the question Dooley had raised.

"No," he said. "Lil didn't mention it."

"You know who else is out of prison? A-Dre's brother. Just got out last month." She slid a photo across the table. "About the right size and shape, wouldn't you say?"

"Yeah. He's built like A-Dre." Daniel shot a breath up past his bangs. "So he could be the person who wrote the death threats *or* the assailant. Every turn leads to more suspects."

"Welcome to Homicide," Dooley said. "And you wonder why I haven't slept in two weeks."

They ran through the others, Dooley raising what she'd gathered about Martin's girlfriends and brothers, the guy who was likely the father of the child Xochitl had given up to foster care, and myriad other acquaintances and relatives. Daniel contributed where he felt it was relevant and pointedly didn't answer other questions, which was giving answer enough.

"Should I just bring the usual, Dooley?" The waiter, hovering at a safe distance, broke the spell of their discussion.

Dooley said, "Yeah, thanks." Back to Daniel. "In your opinion, who in the group best matches the profile of a murderer?"

"I honestly can't answer that. My gut instinct tells me none of them are capable of this, and yet they've all committed violent crimes."

"Big Mac's offense was the most brazen. An attempt on an armored truck."

"Guard in an elevator."

"Yeah, drew a gun on an armed security guard—"

"—but he surrendered without incident."

"Only when he hit the ground floor and was clearly outgunned." She leaned back in the booth, folded her arms. "Martin was also taken down for armed assault. He held up a number of grocery stores, convenience stores, all that."

"How many robberies?" Daniel asked.

"We busted him for three, but there were a number of others that fit the profile. We sniffed around the cases, couldn't make 'em stick. But still. We have the guy shoving a gun in the face of multiple innocents."

"And A-Dre planning a prison break," he said. "And Lil sitting lookout for a bank robbery. And Fang nearly beating a kid to death. Xochitl raping a girl with a stick. None of them are model citizens. How is this getting us anywhere?"

"You're right," she said. "Why don't we try a different tack? The course you offer. Reason and Rehabilitation. They get to choose their instructor?"

A prickle of heat along his collar. He sensed where this was heading. "No." Reluctantly, he added, "But they can put in for which counseling track they'd like to take. And they can specify a male or a female counselor."

Dooley posed the inevitable question. "And how many Reason and Rehabilitation courses are taught by male instructors?"

He bit the inside of his lip. "One."

"So they could have chosen *you*."

"In a manner of speaking, yes."

The waiter appeared and off-loaded a laden tray—garlic bread, spaghetti and meatballs, calzone, salad. Daniel slid the plates away, the heat and rising scent suddenly off-putting. Theresa, of course, twirled a fork in the pasta and lifted a twined bulb to her mouth.

Daniel said, "You're thinking it isn't a coincidence that the killer whose mail I got 'accidentally' happens to be in my group."

The idea had occurred to him over the past few days, though he'd been holding the ramifications at bay.

"I'm not thinking anything," she said through a full mouth. "I'm *exploring*." She swallowed, set down the fork. "It can go either way. One: The killer was in fact shocked to see you at Marisol Vargas's house, decided to keep a closer eye on you after that. Or two . . ." She let this hang as she wolfed down a piece of garlic bread. "The killer sent you the notes in familiar gray department envelopes."

"They weren't addressed to me."

"But they were in your box. Highly organized suspect. Coincidences chafe me."

"We don't want you chafed."

"No, we really don't. Makes my skin all ashy." She swiped her lips with a napkin. "You always seem to be in the thick of it, don't you?"

Heat rose beneath his face. "Am I a *suspect*?"

"No. That would be way too convenient." She pursed her lips to one side, an unconscious lost-in-thought gesture that struck him as uncharacteristically youthful. "Any idea why someone would want to target you?"

"None whatsoever."

"The woman in the rain? She pointed at you." Theresa leaned forward on her elbows. "Was your wife with you when that happened?"

"She was next to me—" His unease hardened into anger. "*Why?*"

"Could the woman have been pointing at Cristina?"

"Why would she do that?"

"Why would she point at you?"

"So it's gonna be this kind of conversation," he said. "Where we answer questions with questions."

"Why don't you answer my question with an answer, then?" she said.

"I told you: I have no fucking idea. I haven't done anything wrong to anyone."

Dooley leaned away from his glare. "Quite a broad claim."

"Fine. I'll rephrase. I haven't done anything to elicit someone's murderous attention."

"Okay." She bobbed her head. "I believe you, and I'm not inclined toward naïveté. So as I said. Maybe this has to do with Cris. She's got a worse background than you—"

"So do you."

"Your wife works in the projects with a lot of shady characters. She has an ex with a history of violence."

Daniel said, "Careful, Theresa."

She held up her hands. "I'm just saying. We can't locate her ex."

"Well, we know he's not in my group."

"But who's to say he didn't write those letters? Or that he isn't screwing Xochitl on the side or running with Martin?"

" 'Cuz they're all Mexicans?" he said.

" 'Cuz they're all convicted criminals."

He tapped a fist on the stack of files. "We have two feet of documents, a hundred ifs, and nothing concrete. Is the point to grow the leads until we can't keep track of them?"

"The point is to look at every possible option until we nail this guy's ass to the electric chair." She pointed with her fork to the calzone. "You gonna eat that?"

He shoved the plate at her and started to scoot out from the booth.

"When you go back to Metro South tomorrow night," she said, "we'll have folks in position. Someone in the garage to make sure you make it to the elevator. You're safer inside the building past the metal detectors. The suspect's less likely to try something public, but I'm not taking any risks. When you're in session, I'll be in the building. Keep me on speed dial—program it so you can hold down a single key on your phone to call me."

"A panic button."

"You'll still need to be careful in there."

"I always am," he said, sliding out to leave. "It's a dangerous job."

"Yeah?" Her fork paused midway to her face. "Well, it just got *more* dangerous."

Chapter 28

After the lunch meeting with Theresa, Daniel braved midday traffic across the city, heading to a carpet warehouse in Diamond Heights. His perky Realtor had left him a message offering to meet there so they could peruse "approved carpet choices" for his new office. This excursion was of course a pretext for her to get the lease paperwork signed. Comparing Berber to cut pile was a trifling activity on any day, but in light of recent events it also seemed mindless and distracting, and he figured he could use a little of both.

Picking over the enormous rolls, he found himself unable to process the salesman's rapid-fire specifications of dye methods and stain treatments. He couldn't pry his mind from Kyle Lane, tomorrow night's group session, and the host of concerns massed around the two. Eager to get out of there, he demurred to his Realtor, who had a strong preference for a beige frost textured Saxony. Still, she caught him ducking into his car with the paperwork in her hand, pen at the ready. He set the contract on the roof, the time of lease jumping out at him—*24 months*. She must have noticed his hesitation, because she said, "Did I get something wrong?"

"No. It's just a big move."

"A lot of people feel that way," she said. Through oversize sunglasses, her gaze again shifted to his bloodshot eye; she'd been too polite to ask but not too polite to refrain from staring. "The commitment can feel a bit daunting. But keep in mind, if something doesn't work out, you can always terminate and give up the deposit and two months' rent." Quickly, she added, "You would, of course, have to reimburse the carpet allowance."

"Of course," he said, and signed on the unbroken line.

Driving home, weaving north through traffic, he realized he was going to pass within a few blocks of Kyle Lane's house. Almost involuntarily, his hands moved the wheel, detouring him.

Crime-scene tape crisscrossed the front door. As Daniel rolled forward along the curb, the narrow side alley crept into view. He felt his temperature rise, the flashback coming at him hard and fast.

The black-clad form, scaling the gate with animal dexterity. The smell of tar. Daniel sprinting, walls squeezing him at either shoulder. The ill-timed leap, the clang as he'd hit the bars. The killer overhead, nearly through the gap, the black boot not yet withdrawn to deal him the blow to the face. A tearing sound. The ring of metal striking ground—

Wait.

Daniel hit the brakes, the car halting with a chirp.

The ring of metal. Striking ground.

He'd forgotten that part.

He heard Dooley's words in his head: *Shit spills outta pockets, Brasher. Especially when you tear them.*

So something *else* had fallen from the killer's pocket? A key?

But they hadn't recovered anything metal from the crime scene; they'd focused immediately on the business card.

Daniel parked and climbed out, feeling his pulse quicken as he crossed the front lawn. He stood before the alley, peering cautiously up its length. Then he slid between the two houses, angling his shoulders slightly as he walked toward the gate.

He arrived and crouched, exhaling with disappointment. Nothing on the ground.

Backing up, he kept searching in case the object had bounced away.

A downspout brushed his elbow. He followed the corrugated pipe up to where it intersected the gutter, then down to where it met the ground. Dropping to all fours, he peered behind the pipe's mouth. Wedged behind it, barely visible, was a sliver of notched metal.

The edge of a quarter.

Daniel removed a credit card from his wallet and used it to poke at the coin until it rattled free out the other side.

It looked brand-new, the silver face so shiny that even here in the alley it winked back the diffuse sunlight. Careful not to touch it, Daniel drew closer to read the date stamped beneath George Washington's neck—*1967*. Nearly fifty years old.

And yet its condition was pristine.

Was it a keepsake? A collector's piece?

Daniel flashed on being inside Kyle Lane's living room with Dooley, how when she'd set her feet on the coffee table, they'd jangled the change resting in a black Wedgwood dish. Were those special coins? Had the killer stolen the quarter from that dish?

Back around to the porch now, excitement and anxiety quickening his step. The front door was still askew from when the rookie officer had kicked it in. Daniel lifted a knuckle through the slants of crime-scene tape and tapped a splintered panel. The door creaked unevenly open. Bending at the waist, he crab-stepped inside.

The quiet of the house felt strange. A foyer table held a bouquet of browning roses and an empty cardboard box on its side, giving out a spill of packing gauze. Staring at the photograph of the wind chimes on the box's side, Daniel thought about the life interrupted here. Just a few days prior, Lane had placed these flowers in the vase and hung the new chimes, nestling himself into another week.

Down the hall, the wind sucked at the broken bedroom window.

As Daniel moved to the living room, he was drawn to those framed photographs on the piano—Kyle Lane with his wispy ponytail and focused, intelligent eyes. Where was he? What had been done to him?

Daniel crossed to the stack of coffee-table books on Tuscany, the black Wedgwood dish resting atop them as an accent note. Half filled with coins, most of them scuffed and worn. He stirred the mound with a forefinger, but the underlying change, too, looked ordinary enough.

He breathed the silence, making out the faintest jangle of the chimes—*ting, ting*. The sickly-sweet potpourri scent was making him vaguely nauseous, and he had a sudden urge to flee.

He forced an even pace back to the front door and ducked through the crime-scene tape out onto the porch. The breeze had died, the air laced with car fumes.

Ting-ting.

He froze on the wooden slats, noting the dead air, too still to coax music from a wind chime.

Slowly, he turned his head to take in the ornate chime. There it hung from the overhead hook.

Except each suspended metal tube was still packaged in shipping foam, locked in place apart from the others. Kyle Lane hadn't yet had time to free the chimes, which meant it wasn't possible for them to jangle against one another.

What, then, had Daniel been hearing all this time?

Ting-ting.

As the sound registered again, he stared at the chimes, perfectly still, perfectly silent.

Though his gaze never faltered, the phone was lifting to his ear, his thumb speed-dialing. He waited through two rings, and then she answered.

"I'm at Kyle Lane's," he told Dooley. "Get here now."

"Lane's? You're not inside, are you?"

He hung up and stepped back into the house.

He'd been late through a door once, and it had cost Marisol Vargas her life. No matter what waited, he wasn't going to let it wait longer.

An electric buzz prickled his skin as he inched back into the living room. His cell phone rang—Dooley calling back—and he silenced it quickly. He set his feet down carefully, straining to make out the noise again. Ahead in the china hutch, the wineglasses gleamed in all their variety—Burgundies with their fat bowls, pinot noirs with their flared rims. He looked from them to the collection of Tuscany photography books, then eased silently into the simple galley kitchen with its bare counters.

No wine fridge. No wine rack. He checked the cupboards.

No wine.

Ting-ting.

The noise was barely audible, yet he tensed in his shoes. He turned to the back hall, the framed Campari posters and wall sconces, the white shag carpet and the Aztec rug.

A rug. On a carpet.

Given Lane's taste, this seemed an odd choice. Unless he'd been trying to cover something up.

Daniel braced himself and walked over as silently as possible, each step an agony. With the toe of his shoe, he flipped back the rug to reveal the outline of a hatch in the carpeting.

Wine cellar.

Ting-ting.

The sound, rising through the floor.

His heart thudding, he leaned forward and lifted the hinged metal ring from its groove. A drop of sweat ran into his left eye, stinging, but he didn't dare move his arm to wipe it away—*ting-ting*—because any superfluous gesture and he'd lose his nerve. Bracing, he threw the hatch open, the sight ten feet below grabbing at him—*ting-ting*—Kyle Lane sprawled on his back on the concrete floor, his skin so gray it looked nearly reptilian, a bib of blood hanging on his shirt. One of his hands was caked with blood and clamped over his own throat, his sleeve sodden to the elbow. The other hand was nestled weakly in a tangle of silverware that had fallen from its velvet-lined box—*ting-ting*—sounding a meek alarm.

His throat had been sliced, and the only thing keeping the breath in his windpipe was the seal of his own hand.

Slits beneath his eyes drained blood. His legs were twisted, one ankle tied with a strip of cloth to the leg of a knocked-over wooden chair at the periphery of the shaft of light. Wine racks rimmed the small cellar, save one set of shelves devoted to storage, from which Lane had no doubt jarred free the silverware with which he was trying to summon help.

With horror, Daniel realized that Lane had been sounding that same alarm even last night as the cops had creaked the floorboards with their heavy boots. Even as Daniel had arrived and talked with Dooley, chased the attacker, returned to walk everyone through the house yet again. How tantalizing the murmur of conversation must have been overhead. And yet Lane couldn't grunt or scream or cry for help, couldn't even move his hand off his throat without leaking his air and sputtering to death. All he'd been able to do was stir the fallen forks and spoons with his fingertips and pray that someone heard the sound and found him entombed in this concrete box.

The scene below was like the sun—staring at it directly made something burn behind the eyes. It nailed Daniel to the floor, iced the breath in his lungs, turned him to stone. No more than a second or two had passed.

The bulging eyes fixed Daniel. The fingertips weakly nudged the spilled silver—*ting-ting*—a last time, and then Daniel was scrambling down the brief ladder, shouting for help though he knew no one could hear, his panicked voice bouncing off the walls. He slid across the floor to Kyle, his knees scattering the silverware—*ting-ting-ting-ting*—and cradled him, firming his hand on top of Kyle's fingers, helping clamp the throat, his palm instantly warm and tacky.

Kyle's hand went loose beneath his, the muscles no doubt spent. Daniel fastened his grip, trying to preserve the airway. With his other hand, he fought his cell phone out, thumbed CALL—"Where the hell are you?"

"Turning onto the block now," Dooley said. "What's—"

"Get an ambulance here, *now.*"

Kyle clutched at Daniel's collar with his free hand. The words, a drawn-out rasp. "... 'on't 'eave ..."

Daniel let the phone fall, tried to steady him. "I won't leave. I won't leave. It's okay. I'm not going anywhere. I'm not—"

Kyle's arm went limp, giving out entirely, and Daniel felt the next breath hissing through their fingers. He flung Kyle's hand aside and clamped the throat directly. "I got you. I got you now."

Kyle arched his back violently, his heels rattling the floor.

"No, *no*. You're okay. They're almost— The ambulance— You're okay."

A few bubbles emerged at the sticky seams between his fingers.

And then no more.

He heard Dooley barrel through the front door overhead, shouting for him, but he couldn't find his voice to yell back. A few moments later, he sensed her shadow darken the cellar floor, and then she was half falling down the ladder, at his side, checking for a pulse, saying, "He's gone. Daniel. He's gone," but he wouldn't let go.

Eight minutes later when the ambulance arrived, he finally let her pry his cramped fingers from Kyle's throat.

Chapter 29

Breathing in the stillness of Kyle Lane's powder room, Daniel leaned over the faucet, scouring his forearms, the cracks of his knuckles, the beds of his nails. As he scrubbed, the water turned rust-colored in the bowl of the sink. He kept at it, waiting for the water to stay clear against the porcelain.

It didn't.

Through the door he could hear Dooley talking with another cop.

"Okay," she was saying, "so he's interrupted last night when the rook patrolman kicks in the door. He leaves Lane for dead, covers the hatch to the wine cellar, and hides behind the mirror until—"

The yellow glow from the fixtures turned Daniel's reflection jaundiced. The dried blood beneath his nails wouldn't let go. He nudged the water hotter, leaving a mark on the white handle. Then he was dumping water on the handle, cleaning that, too, but the red just spread out, sliding down around the trim ring.

"How the hell," Theresa was saying, "is he getting people to open their doors? Again, no signs of the windows being forced."

A deeper voice carried in from the hall. "Maybe he picks the locks."

"Two deadbolts on the front door," she said. "Two on the back. Medecos. I'm thinking no way he gets through those."

"The victims are letting him in?"

"They're letting him in."

The water burned Daniel's hands, but he kept scrubbing, his fingers

159

turning pink. The door creaked open, and then he sensed another reflection in the mirror, though he didn't look up. He used his thumbnail to dig beneath the other nails, trying to scrape away all traces of color. He felt Dooley's hand rest gently on his shoulder.

"Three," she said. "Three makes a serial killer."

He nodded faintly. "Did CSI get back to you on the coin?"

"Yeah." Dooley blew out a breath, shook her head in frustration. "It's worth twenty-five cents."

"Come on. A 1967 quarter that looks like it just rolled off the coining press? It means *something* to the guy to keep it in that shape." Daniel's hands were a blur, drops spattering the counter. "Maybe it's a special year. Maybe—"

"Maybe it's time for you to get home. I called Cristina, let her know what happened. You should get out of here. What went down in that cellar . . ." For once she sounded unsure what to say.

Gripping the edge of the sink, he took a deep breath. Turned off the water. Finally lifted his eyes to the mirror. "I need to unsee that," he said.

"I know. But we don't get to." Dooley plucked a tiny fringed towel from a holder and held it out.

When Daniel turned and wiped his hands, they left a faint red smudge on the embellished fabric.

He awoke with a fall of moonlight on his face. The bedroom blinds were raised, and Cris was sitting in the round swivel chair, legs tucked under her, staring out at the street through the rain-spotted glass. Pushing himself up on his elbows, he looked across at her dark silhouette. She used to sit just that way during those endless months of treatment when she was kept up by reflux—literal heartburn from the radiation seeds. Something about her bearing now conveyed that same fragility.

Cancer, earthquakes, falling Acme safes. So much calamity and tragedy was inherent and avoidable. Why add human evil to the mix?

The word—"evil"—struck him as dogmatic somehow, but picturing the vivid human mess at the bottom of the cellar ladder, Daniel found himself unable to dial it back. Horror had shifted to a cold, burning rage, a flame inside a block of ice.

Cristina finally took note of him before turning back to the darkened street. "I can't sleep. I keep picturing her out there, waiting for us in that yellow rain slicker. Pointing. I could *feel* her through the blind."

He rose and slid behind her in the seat. Together they watched the dark street. Every so often a car would roll by, headlights illuminating the spot that the mystery woman had commanded just two nights prior.

"I keep seeing her," Cris said. "Then I don't."

He rested his hand across those pinpoint tattoos on her chest, felt her heartbeat tapping against his palm. Quicker than usual. She felt warm, so warm.

Cris squeezed his hand, a little too tight. "What if she was marking us as the next target?" she said. "Singling us out for . . . for . . ."

"We don't know that's what she meant. But we'll be careful as hell just in case."

"That's the problem," Cris said. "I feel so *helpless*. And helpless is goddamned scary."

"Yes. It is."

"I keep thinking about Kyle Lane. What kind of person does something like that to another human? And what do they want?"

Daniel thought about his conversation with Dooley over the checkered tablecloth at Capp's Corner, how their exchange had strayed onto personal ground. The inspector's claim about the group members rang in his head: *They could have chosen* you. True. And yet he'd answered honestly; he'd racked his brain and come up with no theory on why he'd have been targeted. Which left Cris.

"Do you think—" He cleared his throat. "Do you think, Luis . . . ?" The name sounded bare and raw when uttered here in the confines of their safe bedroom walls. It occurred to him that they rarely, if ever, used Cristina's ex-husband's name, preferring euphemisms for that period of time. *In my former life,* Cris would say. Or, *When I still lived in the Mission.*

Cris half turned, showing him her profile. The slope of her nose, the prominent lips, so lovely even now. "What?"

"Do you think he's a threat? Dooley suggested he might be behind this somehow. Maybe involved with someone in my group."

"God, I can't imagine he'd be capable of something like this. He's a bitter, useless drunk. This is way too . . . *ambitious* for him."

"You never know what people are capable of."

"No," she said. "I guess you don't."

They sat, eyes trained on the dark patch of street below. Another set of headlights came along, illuminating the stretch of asphalt. Beneath his arms he felt Cris tense up, but there was nothing there but raindrops tapping the ground. She let out a held-in breath. They watched the gloom some more, waiting for the woman to ghost into existence.

"Can you actually go back into that group?" she asked. "Tomorrow night?"

"I don't know."

"You'll probably be sitting in the same room as the killer. Are you as scared by that as I am?"

He kept his gaze on the street below. His silence, they both knew, gave the answer.

Chapter 30

Pulling in to the underground garage at Metro South, Daniel felt his palms slick against the steering wheel, the back of his shirt sticking to the cheap fabric of the smart car. He climbed out, armed sweat off his brow, and took a look around, gathering himself. A few people were strolling to the elevator, and several more sat in their cars, fussing with cell phones. He pegged no one for an undercover cop, but Dooley had promised there would be several in the building, herself included, playing guardian angel.

In the lobby he passed through the doorframe metal detectors, noting the familiar weary faces of the security guards and wondering at the efficacy of the machines, which he'd rarely heard beep. Riding up to the second floor, he kept his hand on the iPhone in his pocket, ready to call Dooley with a single tap of his thumb. He tensed as the doors parted, but there was no one waiting, coiled to spring. With an exhale he stepped out into the hall. Mixed with the parolees were a couple of cops and parole officers—an undercover could blend in here on the admin floor without even *being* undercover. A passing patrolman gave him a faint nod, and he couldn't figure out if it was code or general courtesy.

He hurried down the hall, eager to sneak in some pre-session time in the records room. After mumbling a greeting to the receptionist, he closed himself in, pulled the six files of his group members, and dug in.

The pages seemed endless—psychosocial and medical histories, police records, victim statements, court documents, probation-supervision reports, pre-sentencing interviews, employment histories. Poring over them, he realized why Dooley had appealed to him to report findings back to her. When it came to his group members, he probably had access to more information than she did. He remembered her complaint about criminals: *They drive unregistered cars, shoot unregistered guns, change jobs like other people change clothes, skip out on rent to crash on their cousin Hector's couch. Outdated, incomplete files.* Even in the face of the stacks around him, he had to admit she was right. Many of the reports were vague or half-assed. More holes than connective tissue.

Flipping through, reading more of what he already knew, he felt his frustration mount, so much so that he didn't notice that Kendra had entered the room until she made a point of clearing her throat. Her arms were crossed, wooden bangles clanking around her forearms, and she was inflicting upon him her program director's frown.

"Doing a little extra research?" she asked.

He blinked up at her. "Yes."

"That scowly cop and her cohorts have set up camp in my building," she said. "She was good enough to bring me up to speed. Some might call it professional courtesy."

"I'm sorry," Daniel said. "It's been . . . consuming. But I should've taken the time to loop you in."

She took note of his discomfort. "So you're Inspector Dooley's inside line on this case?"

"I wouldn't phrase it like that."

"The phrasing is not my concern."

"There's strong reason to suspect that someone in my group is involved in these murders."

"And what if you and Detective Hardcharger are wrong?" She eased forward and hip-sat at the edge of the table, peering over the rims of her rectangular eyeglasses, her neck turkeying around a string of oversize beads. "I know earnestness ain't in vogue these days, but those six people in that room, they rely on you and your positive re-gard, body and soul."

"Positive regard."

"That *is* the term, baby. You and I both read the textbooks. If you don't believe in those folks, who the hell will?"

He knew better than to answer right now.

"If they lose trust in you," she said, "that could mean their free-dom. And they're not the only ones who go down if they slip. There are kids, dependents, wives."

"You don't think I've considered that?" Daniel said. "I want to do right by them. I don't want to fail them. But—"

"I understand this is life and death." Kendra rose, smoothed the fabric of her vividly patterned tunic. "Just don't forget it is for them, too."

Chapter 31

Daniel entered the room late, his head lowered, forging into the banter of the group. He took his chair and a deep breath, finally scanning the ring of faces.

In this circle a killer. Or a killer's accomplice.

As he considered each member's capacity for violence, still-life images strobed in his mind: Black-Clad Man Clinging to Gate; Faceless Woman in Yellow Slicker; Man in Cellar Scarved in Blood. The hairs on his arms prickled. He realized he'd never been scared in the room before. Charged to the gills with nervous anticipation, sure. But not *scared*. In a bizarre way, it gave him a view from the other seats, a glimpse of how group members must feel coming in here, baring themselves, unsure and vulnerable.

X had said something.

"Sorry?"

"I said, what happened to your eye, Counselor?"

The broken veins and bruising from the kick. He'd forgotten.

He cleared his throat, examined the others for any revealing signs. But there were just six curious faces, pointed his way. "I walked into a garage door as it was closing."

X snickered knowingly. "I walked into that garage door once or twice myself."

His first lie paved the way for the second. "I realized I may have written my cell-phone number down wrong for you guys, reversed the last digits. So let's check. Will everyone take out my business card?"

A rustling in pockets. As Daniel watched closely for any tells, the smell of the room impressed itself on him. No—more than a smell. A *taste*. Mold and wet concrete, leaving a bitter trace on his tongue.

Fang produced from his billfold a business card still in mint condition. X's, in contrast, was wadded up in the bottom of her backpack. A-Dre found his in a back pocket, Big Mac in his money clip. Martin nosed around in his wallet, the chain pulling at the belt loop.

Lil read the number from her cell-phone screen, and the others uh-huhed. "Is that right?" she asked. Eager as always for approval.

Daniel nodded, picturing that dropped business card at Kyle Lane's side gate. "You don't have the *actual* business card, though?"

"I input your number in my phone," Lil said. "So I threw it out." He must have reacted, because she rushed to add, "Did I do something wrong? I'm really sorry if—"

"Someone took mine, man," Martin said, splaying his wallet open.

"You don't know that," Big Mac said. "Coulda fallen out."

"No. I keep it here. All the time. Like Counselor said to. But it's gone. Someone *took* it." Martin fanned through his bills, counting under his breath.

"The wallet is *chained* to your body." Daniel realized, too late, that he'd failed to regulate his tone.

"Protectin' all those singles," X chimed in.

Martin gave Daniel a dead stare. "You callin' me a liar, Counselor?"

"Just an observation."

"Who *cares*?" A-Dre said to Martin. "You can have mine."

"Don't you need the number, A-Dre?" Lil asked.

Irritated, A-Dre pulled out a marker, wrote on his palm, then flicked the card over to Martin, who took it, his glare still fixed on Daniel.

"Good thing you never wash your hands," X said, and A-Dre blew her a fuck-you kiss.

Daniel kept an uneasy eye on Martin as the session got under way.

The banter among the members was sharper than usual, everyone amped up, probably in reaction to Daniel's mood. Recognizing the need for a distraction, he decided to transition early to a more formal exercise.

Lil agreed to start in center chair. She crossed to it uncomfortably and sat, fussing at her curly bangs. "It's freezing in here." She glanced at the open window. "Anyone else cold?"

Fang said, *"No."*

"Okay," she said. "Um. What do you guys want to ask me?"

The question was out of Daniel's mouth before he considered it. "Have you had any contact with your ex-husband lately?"

Lil recoiled, wounded. "No. Why would I? He's in prison."

So she didn't know that he'd been released. Or she was lying. What was he hoping to accomplish here? The debate raged in his head—Dooley on one side, Kendra on the other. Inside man or client advocate? Either way he'd have to be smarter and subtler. His blundering inquiries seemed only to put the group members on edge, which in turn made them act more suspiciously.

Daniel noticed the others considering him—his opening question to Lil had been uncharacteristic—so he refocused quickly into a more familiar drill. "Lil, I want you to pick who you like *least* in the group and tell us why."

"Can I pass?"

"Why do you want to pass?" Daniel asked.

"I don't want to say anything that might . . . hurt anyone's . . ."

"Bullshit," Big Mac said. "You're too scared to say. Don't put that shit on us. *We* can take it."

Lil played with her uncombed hair some more, pulling it down over her eyes. "I don't really have anyone I don't like. I, um, think people have a lot of complexities and everyone has good qualities and—"

Daniel pulled his keys from his pocket and tossed them at her. Hard.

Startled, she reared back and caught them. Jarred out of her rote reaction. An early supervisor had taught Daniel that stubborn group members at times required more extreme techniques, and he was willing to reach back to that training to shake Lil up now.

"Answer," he said.

"I have two," she said quickly. Shaken up, she handed him back his keys. "The first is . . . is Walter."

Fang stiffened in his chair. "Me? I barely say *anything* to you."

"Exactly. It's like I don't *exist* to you."

"And the other?" Daniel prompted.

"This should be a big fucking surprise," X said.

"Well, yes, Xochitl," Lil said. "Obviously it's you."

"Why 'obviously'?" Martin asked.

"She's just so nasty."

"And here I thought I was all puppies farting rainbows," X said.

"Why do you think she's nasty?" Daniel asked, trying to keep Lil in the lane.

"Well," Lil said, "because she's unhappy, clearly."

"*Is* she unhappy?"

"*Yes.* She just seems so . . . lonely inside all that anger. And I think of her with Thanksgiving coming up and then Christmas . . ." Something flickered across her face, and she stopped abruptly.

Daniel felt a narrowing of the room, the picture beneath Lil's words pulling into focus. It was what he thought of as the magical moment in a session, that split second when the defenses shift and the chinks in the armor align.

He spoke softly. "The holidays can be lonely, huh?"

And with that, Lil began to cry. Fist pressed to her wobbling lips, tears fording the bumps of her knuckles. Even X was too shocked to speak.

Lil recovered to give a fake laugh. "Okay. So maybe it's not about Xochitl. Maybe I even secretly wish . . ." She looked away. "That I was strong like her."

At this, X's mouth moved—a silent intake of air.

"But I'm not," Lil added quickly. Another dismissive titter. "I guess . . . I guess maybe I want to not be so lonely." A flip of her hand dismissed the notion. "But, I mean, with society's attitudes toward women my age—"

"Weak," A-Dre said.

"—and San Francisco, there are so few straight men here. And. I mean, you go out and you feel bad when people ignore you."

"Will you say the same sentence but replace 'you' with 'I'?" Daniel asked.

Lil cleared her throat. "*I* go out and . . ." A pause to compose herself. "*I* feel bad when people"—her voice dropped to a whisper as the sentiment settled further into her—"ignore me." Her shoulders folded forward; she was on the verge of clamping shut and disappearing.

"So you just stopped going out," Big Mac said. "How long ago?"

"Since . . . since my husband left."

"For *five years*?" Martin said.

"Do you think you might want to try to go out socially again?" Daniel asked.

Lil shrugged. "We'll see."

"It's a yes-or-no question."

"Maybe."

Always equivocating.

"What would happen if you answered directly?" Daniel asked. She started to respond, and he held up his hand. "Wait. Think about it. Don't make me throw my keys at you again. What's the *real* answer?"

"I don't *know* the real answer."

"What's it buy you *not* to answer questions directly?"

She chewed her lip. "Everyone gets frustrated with me."

"That's a *good* thing?" Big Mac said.

"At least I get to be the center of attention," she said, her voice suddenly loud. "This is the only place I have. I live alone. I have no friends at work. I have no *friends*. This . . . this is it for me."

A rare silence fell over the circle. She wiped her nose, looked down at her hands, then finally continued. "I was never on my own before. I always had someone looking out for me. My dad. My husband."

Daniel asked, "What are you afraid will happen if you go out alone? Socially?"

"I can't stand it when people reject me." She tilted her chin to her chest. Quick little breaths.

"Fuck you, Lil," Daniel said. "You're stupid and ugly, and I *don't want you here.*"

She jerked away, her chair screeching on the uneven tile and tilting back on the rear legs. She stared at him with wide eyes.

Daniel said, "Tell me you don't care what I say."

After a pause she said, weakly, "I don't care what you say."

The front legs of her chair lowered again to the floor.

"Tell me I don't know who you are."

A little more conviction. "You don't know who I am."

"Tell me I'm rude and I shouldn't speak to you that way."

"You're *rude* and shouldn't speak to me that way."

Daniel spread his hands. "Maybe you can stand more than you think."

As Big Mac took center chair next, Daniel realized that in the last ten minutes his mind had drifted, finally, from the investigation. He'd forgotten that Lil had failed to produce his business card, which made her—like Martin—suspect. He'd dropped completely into her fears and vulnerabilities, tried to pull her out of the morass and into a new awareness. A connection like that was powerful, powerful enough even to distract him in the middle of a spate of murders. Big Mac's voice faded as Daniel contemplated how quickly the room had reclaimed its veneer of relative safety.

That was when the fight broke out.

Chapter 32

At the fringe of Daniel's awareness, he sensed the escalation.

Big Mac was waxing philosophical from the center seat. "—in the rain, skidded out on the Embarcadero and almost wound up in the Bay. I mean, three more feet and my rig woulda gone off the lip. But I guess it wasn't my time. I guess it wasn't in God's plan."

At that, Martin was on his feet. "God's *plan*? What about the family who died yesterday in the wreck over in Mission Terrace? God decided to pick them instead of you? And the kids starving in Africa or wherever they starve nowadays? God chose them, too? *Huh?* But you, you with your big, important world-peace-making job driving a fucking trash truck, for *you* he decided to take his eye off the Middle East and tsunamis to stop your rig three feet shy so you can live to tote another goddamned trash can, you self-important, bullshit-spouting *fuck*?"

When Big Mac came off his chair, he threw a shadow across the room.

Lil yelped and scrambled away, and even X, Fang, and A-Dre shoved back a few feet.

Daniel barely managed to jump into the ring before Big Mac lunged for Martin. He got a hand on both chests as the two large bodies clashed. The muscle mass of the men was overwhelming, rock-solid torsos like shields, crushing in on him. He was shouting over their shouts, and then Martin's elbow clipped his chin and spun him like a top into an abandoned chair, and then both men stopped as abruptly as they'd begun, staring at him, mortified. The chair clattered to a stop across the room.

Daniel took advantage of the shocked pause, popping back to his feet and pushing them apart toward opposite seats. "Back off."

"Shit, Counselor," Martin said. "I didn't mean to—"

"*Now*," Daniel said.

Both men took a step back but refused to sit, glowering over Daniel's head at each other, simmering rage tangible in the air. In the whirl of his thoughts came images of that form clad in black, its featureless mask cocked, the predatory glare cutting through the shadows of Marisol Vargas's house. He fought for focus. In his distraction he'd let the room get out of control. He owed it to at least five people not to let that happen again.

"Now sit down," he said.

Martin obeyed, but Big Mac took a beat, clearly grappling with himself, the skin of his face tough and lined, like hide. Finally he lowered himself to his chair.

"*Okay*," X said. "*That* just happened."

"God doesn't choose anything. Only people do. And bad shit, it just *happens*." Martin's voice was choked with emotion, though his eyes remained dry. "You don't know shit about it unless your lady is dying of cancer and you're running outta money and you rob a fucking store because this person you love, she's disintegrating—"

X cut in. "Everyone's got a sob story."

"Hold on," Daniel said. Then, to Martin, "Before we get into that, you're gonna have to take responsibility for how you spoke to Big Mac."

Martin took off his Buddy Holly glasses, squeezed his eyes. Sweat glistened on his scalp, visible through his buzz cut. "Okay. You're right. I'm sorry, Big Mac. I'm sorry."

Big Mac said, "Not fucking good enough."

"He has the right to make a mistake, Big Mac," Fang said. "No one's . . . ah, ah, ah. No one's perfect. We all need to have the . . . ah, right to screw up."

Even in the midst of the tension, Daniel felt a stab of satisfaction at Fang's speaking up.

"He stood first, but you came at *him,* man," A-Dre said to Big Mac. "You threw down first."

"This is bullshit." Big Mac stood again. "After he attacked me, I'm not gonna sit here and listen to—"

"This is your last chance," Daniel said. "To sit down."

Big Mac crossed his arms. Kept his feet.

"You're gonna have to leave now," Daniel said.

"No way. I am *not* taking the ding on my record after Martin—"

"Then we'll wait until you do."

They all sat quietly, eyes on the floor, waiting. Big Mac shifted a few times on his feet. Finally he stormed out, slamming the door behind him so hard that a stack of chairs in the corner slid over.

Martin broke the resultant silence. "I'm sorry," he said again.

Daniel said, "That was a helluva reaction, Martin."

"When people talk about God's will, it makes me angry—"

"It doesn't *make you* anything," Daniel said. "You *get* angry."

"Okay, okay. I *get* angry 'cuz I know there's no one looking out for us. No big judge up there who says my lady shoulda died and someone else's shoulda lived. Or that *I* should have to go through . . ." He palmed sweat off his forehead, wiped it on his jeans. "I got out of prison a few months after she died. Even then I couldn't trust myself to get behind the wheel, 'cuz I'd start crying. Couldn't see the road. Sobbing like a baby in the middle of anything . . ."

Daniel thought of Cristina hacking into her fist in that ethereal white bathroom, blood spots on the breast of her sundress.

"She was perfect," Martin said.

"No one's perfect." Lil's hands worked the hem of her shirt. "Like Fang said."

The anger was back. "You didn't know *her*," Martin said. "She was so innocent."

Inflating her, as always, to saintly proportions. All of Martin's defenses—his very self-definition—had coalesced around the loss. He'd placed her memory on a pedestal of steel, making it nearly impossible to chip away at.

Daniel pursed his lips, worked out a route in. "Is your mourning keeping you from doing other things?"

Martin scowled. "Like what? Dating?"

"Living," A-Dre said, his voice a rumble.

The answer, from unlikely quarters, caught Martin off guard. "*Living?* I don't . . . I don't know how to do that no more."

"Don't know how or don't *want* to?" Daniel asked.

Martin looked away sharply. "If I let go of her, then she's really gone. And she was the best thing in this shitty world."

"You can find a way to connect with others."

"I can't."

"So you just stay *frozen*?" Daniel asked.

In his peripheral vision, he saw Lil stiffen, the question landing hard for her, too. Martin didn't respond.

"You've already made a lot of choices to change," Daniel said. "To be here. To not return to crime. When did you decide to give up *that* life? How did that moment happen?"

Martin was quiet for so long that Daniel was on the verge of asking a follow-up to move him forward. But then he answered, his voice low. "When I was inside about nine months, I finally pulled garden duty. Sounds nice, right? Garden duty. But mostly we hauled sacks of dirt and shoveled rock in the field behind the prison. And through a chain-link fence, there was this little prison cemetery. Overgrown. Weeds. All the folks that died in there who no one cared about. No one even missed them. And I looked at all them little wooden crosses and faded stones and thought, it's too late for them." He took a deep breath. "But maybe not for me."

The impact on the others was evident, and Daniel let them take their time with their respective thoughts. After a pause he said, "How about the rest of you? What was your moment for change?"

Lil lifted her pale face and said, "Right now."

In the wake of the fight and Martin's torn-open confession, Daniel called for a break. As the members headed noisily up the hall to the vending machines, he stayed in the room, satchel briefcase at his feet, the exhaustion of the past five days landing on him like a heavy blanket.

He closed his eyes and took a few deep breaths. The chirp of a sneaker on tile jarred him upright. Fang, standing over him. He started, and Fang stepped back.

"Sorry, Counselor." Fang shoved his hands into his pockets. "I was just . . . ah, ah, checking if you were really asleep."

A sudden image grabbed Daniel—Fang flying at him, leading with a military knife. Fang shifted on his feet, and Daniel flinched a little. Fang looked at him, puzzled.

Daniel covered with a cough. "That's okay," he said, though his heart was working double time. "Guess I'm a bit jumpy."

His satchel briefcase on the floor was unsnapped. He hadn't left it that way, had he?

"What?" Fang asked.

"Did you want something?"

"Huh?"

"My bag, you just opened it." Daniel left it somewhere between a question and a statement.

Fang studied him. "Nah," he said. "I just walked in."

The others returned, shoving and joking, then halted, taking note of the mini-standoff. X broke the tension. "It time for Fang to do a spelling bee?"

Even Fang laughed a bit as they found their seats.

Daniel tore his glare from Fang and exhaled slowly, trying to let go of his suspicion. "Now, X," he said. "It's time for you to read the letter you wrote from the perspective of the girl you assaulted."

"Oh. Right." X collapsed into the center chair and gave a pert smile. With her little-girl dimples and thin front braids pinned in the back, she looked angelic. In another world and zip code, she could've been a Catholic school girl. She snapped her gum. Tapped her chest. Then she lifted her doodle-covered notepad from her lap and cleared her throat theatrically.

"My name is Raped Girl. I'm sad I was raped. Too bad I wanted to join the gang, 'cuz them's the rules. Love, Raped Girl."

She set down her notepad and smiled again.

"You're wasting our time," Lil said.

"You're a fine one to talk, Whiny McBitch'n'Moan."

Martin leaned forward, forearms on his knees. "You got all the words for everyone else, don't you?"

"Yep," X said. "Sure do."

"Last session you mentioned your daughter, who you gave up to foster care," Daniel said. "You want to talk about that?"

"What's to talk about? I had to make a choice, so I made a choice. No biggie."

"We ask for honesty in here," Daniel said. "That's the deal."

X shrugged him off.

Daniel said. "Okay, let's move on to A-Dre."

X looked taken aback. "You ain't gonna argue with me? Ask me 'bout poor Raped Girl some more?"

"No," Daniel said. "I'm not gonna ask you about Sophie again today."

Hurt flickered across X's face so quickly he would have missed it if he'd blinked, replaced by her standard mask of wry annoyance. She relinquished the center chair angrily and flopped down in her usual spot.

A-Dre sauntered over, turned the chair around, and sat backward in it, elbows on the metal rail. "What we gonna talk about?"

"Have you thought about what we went over last time?" Daniel asked. "The pros and cons we listed on the board? The ramifications of committing violence?" His last words were a bit heavy-handed, but intentionally so; he was trying to pry something free about the murders.

A-Dre gave an ostensibly straight answer. "Little bit."

"And?"

"That's just who I am."

"A fighter."

"A *gangsta*. No choice when people piss me off. Look at Big Mac tonight. See, that's just how we are."

"How about Lil? If someone pissed her off, would she hit him?"

"No, she'd shrivel up or some shit."

X giggled, and Lil said, faintly, "Thanks."

Daniel pressed. "So it's a choice you're making, right? You make one choice, Lil might make another." Nothing. "Pretend I'm someone who insults you on the street. What could you do instead of punch me?"

A-Dre made a gun with his hand and fired it at Daniel's head. "Pow."

Titters.

In light of the week's violence, the gesture chilled Daniel. "You like that?" he asked. "Playing killer?"

A-Dre looked taken aback by Daniel's tone. "Shit, I'm just fuckin' around. But what the hell am I *supposed* to do when someone pisses me off?"

Daniel took a moment to refocus. "First thing I try to do is nothing. Breathe. Calm my body down."

"Yeah, right. You mean change everything 'bout who I am? That shit is hard."

"Not as hard as *not* changing who you are," Daniel said. "Jail time. Money for lawyers. Screwing over the people who count on you. Not exactly an easy path you've taken."

A-Dre chewed his lip. "You all think I'm a dumb-ass gangsta."

"Do you want to ask us?"

"I know what you'll say."

"Do you want to ask us?" Daniel repeated.

"Well," A-Dre said, "don't you?"

Various nos and uh-uhs from Fang, X, Lil, and Martin. A-Dre looked legitimately surprised by this.

Daniel got in a question quickly, taking advantage of his lowered guard. "What would have to happen for you to say that violence has been a problem for you?"

A-Dre sat for an uncomfortably long time. Then he said, "I don't want all that. Anymore." He waved a hand at the board, and Daniel realized he was referring to the list of cons he'd written up there last session, still there in faded chalk. "But I walk from a fight, fools gonna laugh up in my face. My *friends'll* laugh up in my face."

"Then you need new friends," Martin said.

"Shit." A-Dre sucked his teeth. "Where'm I gonna make new friends?"

"You have some," Lil said. "Right in here."

"Friends? *Us?*" A-Dre guffawed. "You fools *have* to be here. We're all fake in here."

"Bull*shit*," X hissed, her sudden vehemence catching everyone by surprise. She jabbed a finger at the door. "It's all fake out *there*."

She seemed to realize that she'd parted the curtains on her private thoughts, and just as abruptly she withdrew back into herself. Head lowered, sketching on her pad. She'd been different the past two sessions, something blooming in her, striking chords, tugging at memories. Daniel looked over, but she refused to raise her eyes, so he turned back to A-Dre.

"You might be surprised and find that people in your life *wouldn't* laugh at you if you walked away from a fight," he said. "You might even find people who'd be relieved."

"Like who?" A-Dre said.

"Your mom, maybe," Fang said.

Martin gestured at A-Dre's neck tattoo. "Or LaRonda."

"LaRonda's *dead*," A-Dre said.

At this, even X snapped to attention. Everyone took a beat to catch up to this news.

Daniel knew to proceed carefully. "How would she feel about all the stuff we're discussing?"

"Dunno. I don't remember her."

"You don't . . ." Daniel caught his breath. "Do you remember anything about her?"

"She was just a baby," A-Dre said. "She was my stepdaddy's baby girl. And I was five. We was in the tub, and Momz went to answer the phone and left us. *She* went to answer the phone. *She* did. I was five. I didn't know to pay attention."

X's mouth had come slightly ajar. The others—spellbound.

A-Dre's eyes were glassy. "She told my stepdaddy I did it."

"How'd that go?" Martin asked.

A-Dre shoved his sleeve up and showed the burn scar, giving the room a fierce glare. "Like this." He swallowed. Licked his lips. "Now that I'm old, it gets harder to think about."

"Old?" Fang said. "You're twenty-*four.*"

"Yeah," A-Dre said, "but I always figured I'd be dead by now. So I wouldn't have to live with what I done."

A wail echoed back off the tile and bare walls. Unrecognizable.

It took a moment for Daniel to orient himself, to source the sound. It was X, leaning over, hugging her stomach. Silent now.

"X?" he said. "Do you want to talk about it?"

"No."

"Do you—"

"*No!*"

From the hall Daniel heard the tapping of heels and too late realized that they'd run over the session's end. The door swung open, the admin receptionist entering, blowing on her fingernails. "Kendra say she needs your termination agreement."

One step from the threshold, she lifted her head, her forehead wrinkling.

The room had turned into a still life.

Daniel unclenched his jaw. "We are in session."

She lowered her hand. Smacked her gum. Still confused. "Kendra said session ended fifteen minutes ago."

"Does it *look* like session ended fifteen minutes ago?"

She scanned the room, read the faces of the members, and withdrew gingerly.

"*Termination* agreement?" Lil said bitterly.

A glow of heat started beneath Daniel's skin.

"Where are you . . . ah, ah, where you going?" Fang asked.

"Private practice," Daniel said quietly.

The wind made itself known against the thick panes. Outside, blackness.

"So we're not even your real patients," Martin said. "Are we? We're a *hobby*."

"You were *never* a hobby."

"You said your side of the deal is you'd be here," A-Dre said. "Three nights a week, rain or shine. 'Member that? Or was that just some bullshit? Before you go back to your real life?"

Martin stood to leave, and the others followed suit. "Like Big Mac said. *Everyone leaves.*"

It was not lost upon Daniel that Martin was pissed off enough to quote the man he'd come to blows with earlier in the evening.

"I'm going to transition out," he said, "but not before a new counselor is in place who . . ."

Too late. He'd lost them.

X was last to rise. "Everyone's gotta be honest up in here," she said. "But *you*."

As they shuffled out, Daniel pictured the new office, floating above California Street. Plush carpets and gleaming fixtures, that twenty-third-floor view of the Bay Bridge, shrouded in wisps of fog. He tilted his head back, took in the sagging ceiling tiles.

Everyone leaves.

Losers walk.

Chapter 33

Daniel gathered his briefcase and paused in the still of the room, regarding the ring of empty chairs and breathing in the smells of Metro South. For safety's sake he knew he should get out of the building while there were still footsteps tapping through the halls. And yet it took him a moment to get moving.

He headed out into the desolate hall, cell phone in hand, ready to speed-dial Dooley if he were jumped by a masked, knife-wielding maniac. But the way was clear. The elevator arrived—empty—and he leaned against the rear wall, closed his eyes, and exhaled.

The doors banged back apart violently, and his eyes flew open to see Big Mac shouldering into the car, flushed with anger.

As Big Mac advanced, Daniel put his own shoulders to the wall, spread his stance, ready to charge or deflect. He tapped the screen of his iPhone but couldn't risk a glance down to see if the call had gone through.

The elevator doors slid shut, and Big Mac leaned in, his sheer size evident as he all but blotted out the flickering overhead lights. Wrestling background or not, Daniel didn't stand a chance against him if the situation ignited. He angled the phone, let his eyes dart to the screen: CALL FAILED. Of course—no reception here in the elevator. But had it rung through once, alerting Dooley before the line dropped?

He looked up into Big Mac's face. "What do you want?" he asked.

"You shut me down in there." Big Mac's hand twitched in his

jacket pocket, and Daniel pictured that wicked-looking military blade there, just beneath the fabric.

The elevator whirred its descent.

Big Mac's hand pulled free, clenching a mint green paper of thick stock, which Daniel identified on a slight delay—an attendance card. "I need you to sign this."

Daniel released a slow exhale through his teeth. Not quite relief, not yet.

"I don't get this signed," Big Mac said, "it puts me one step away from fucked."

"You know the rules."

"You saw Martin in there. He instigated it."

"Martin took accountability for his part. He apologized and sat down."

"So I'll take accountability now. I apologize. And I need you to sign this."

They hit the ground floor, the doors opened, but Big Mac stayed there, blocking his exit.

"Mac," Daniel said. "Get out of my way."

Big Mac punched the wall, the boom echoing up the shaft.

"Mr. Brasher?" A voice carried in from the lobby. "Are you all right?"

Angelberto.

The janitor paused from his work and lifted the mop from the bucket, resting the wooden handle horizontally across his thighs. The move was not overtly threatening, but the positioning made clear he was ready to use the shaft as a weapon. His considerable muscles shifted as he adjusted his grip and widened his stance.

Big Mac turned, and Daniel used the opportunity to slide past him. Aside from the three of them, the lobby was empty, the surrounding halls unlit.

Big Mac stepped free of the elevator, read the situation, and his shoulders sagged a bit. "Oh, come *on*," he said. "Am I pissed off? Sure. But, hell, it's not like that."

Wounded, he backpedaled toward the front doors, and it was only then that Daniel noticed Dooley lurking in the darkness at the edge of the far hall, watching. He gave her the faintest signal, his fingers fanning to the side—*Let me handle it*—and she withdrew, fading from sight. Big Mac caught the gesture and shot a quizzical glance in that direction, but there was nothing there anymore except the shadows.

He swung his bulldog head back to Daniel. "I thought you knew me better'n that, Counselor." Turning, he banged through the doors, which swung slowly back and autolocked.

Angelberto let the mop head slap to the tile and resumed his work.

Daniel said, "Thank you."

"I did nothing. Just cleaning the floor."

Daniel passed through the now-unmanned metal detectors—nobody was admitted after 9:00 P.M.—and punched the DOWN button of the garage elevator. As he prepared himself for the walk across the dark parking spaces, a new idea struck. He retraced his steps.

"Hey, Angelberto? You're here a lot, right? And down in the garage?"

The big man nodded.

"That man who just left. Have you ever noticed him drive up on a motorcycle?"

"No. I haven't seen what he drives."

Daniel's thoughts landed next on the only male in the group who had failed to produce a business card. "Do you know a man named Martin? Same build as you, big broad guy, glasses and flannel shirts?"

"Yes, him. I do not like him."

"Why not?"

"He is rude. Looks down on me because I am a janitor. While he is a felon."

Martin had never struck Daniel as arrogant in that way. "Have you ever seen if *he* has a motorcycle?"

"Him I *know* drives a car."

"How do you know?"

"His car battery died Monday night. I had to find jumper cables."

"Okay, thanks—" A surge of adrenaline cut short Daniel's words. "What *time* Monday night?"

"After your class let out. I was last one here."

"How long were you with him?"

"Very late. Midnight at least. Someone had moved jumper cables to maintenance closet on fourth floor, so—"

"You sure about that time?"

"Yes, mostly. It may have been even later."

Which meant there was no way that Martin could've been across town at Marisol Vargas's house.

One group member ruled out. Five to go.

Invigorated, Daniel thanked Angelberto and headed down to the garage. He climbed into the smart car, locked the door after him, and let himself exhale fully for the first time since he'd entered the building.

"Hi, honey . . ." The voice from the backseat sent a charge through his blood. In the rearview he saw Dooley lean forward into a fall of light, flipping open her detective's notepad. "How was your day?"

"You're not funny."

"Yeah, but *you* looked pretty funny." She grinned. "Sorry. Trying to keep a low profile until all your Elvises leave the building." The radio on her duty belt chirped, and a voice spit code through the static. She listened, then said to Daniel, "Which is *now*. We are clear for the night."

He shot a breath at the roof.

"How'd it go in there?" she asked.

He filled her in, choosing carefully what was relevant. How Lil and Martin were the only ones who couldn't produce his business card. Martin's swearing that it had been stolen from him. Lil's claim that she thought her husband was still in prison. He left out the near fight in session but told her about Big Mac in the elevator. And finally Martin's broken-down-car alibi the night of Marisol's murder.

"That's great," Dooley said after he gave her Angelberto's account. "We'll keep locking down alibis—or lack of alibis—for the nights of the murders. We'll downgrade Martin as a suspect, but until we get a better handle on what's going on, we'll keep tails on all six group members, just to be safe."

"You guys are watching them? Right now?"

"For the time being. But there are six of them spread across the city, which is a challenge. And remember—they're our lead suspects. Not the only ones. We are covering a broader swath than you can imagine."

"Have you located Lil's ex?"

"No. But A-Dre's brother, we know where *he* is. Here in the city. He fits the physical profile, like I said, so we had to free up another unit to keep an eye on him, too." She jotted a note to herself, then looked up. "Okay. What about the mail room?"

"What *about* the mail room?"

"Any new love letters?"

"I didn't check."

"You didn't check."

"I had a lot on my mind tonight, Dooley, in case you couldn't tell. Besides, I thought you said that the guy would've figured out by now that he was accidentally sending me the death threats."

"I'm not talking about *accidentally,*" she said.

He felt a sudden drop in the temperature, the chill biting at his arms through his thin sleeves. She opened her door, and he got out, too, and followed her across the parking lot. They rode up to the desolate lobby in silence, then worked their way through the dark back halls, motion sensors tripping the overhead lights, each bank turning on with an industrial clang as they passed beneath.

Dooley's breathing quickened, and she kept her hand near the bulge at her hip. She noticed him looking and cracked a smile. "Interiors by Vincent Price."

They continued with caution, but the worst they saw were a few rats, caught off guard by the sudden flood of light. Eyes glinting like dots of mercury, they dropped their crumbs and went boneless to squeak beneath closed doors.

Dooley gave a cough of relief. "Nice place you got here."

"Recession budget."

Finally the mail room came into view. As he stepped through the doorway, his breath caught. There it was, centered neatly in his otherwise empty cubbyhole.

A gray interdepartmental envelope.

Crossing the little room, he heard Dooley's voice vaguely, as if she were underwater: *Don't touch it.*

He went up on tiptoes to get a better vantage and noticed immediately the cramped, dyslexic handwriting. But one thing was different about this letter.

It was addressed to him.

Chapter 34

i no you saw me daniel brasher but how much did you see me? thats okay. you want to be involved? your part of my crusade now too. go tell molly clarke of sarl ctreet to admit what shes done by november 24 at midnite. or she will bleed. YOU tell her personaly or i will slit her throat first chance I get.

It took everything Daniel had to maintain his composure, to stay calm because calm was useful right now. He read the letter but did not touch it. The sheet of paper, held by a pair of latex gloves beneath an LED crime-scene lantern, put him in mind of a valuable item at auction. Plainclothes cops crowded the tiny mail room; they seemed to have materialized through the walls at Dooley's radio alert. A multitude of discussions filled the air, making it hard to think.

"—postmark shows it routed through the Bryant Street Annex post office, less than a mile—"

"—could've dropped it in any mailbox in the area—"

"—smart move, dodge the cameras—"

"—review the footage anyway in case—"

Theresa put a hand on Daniel's shoulder and steered him into the corner. "You okay?"

His face felt bloodless, but he nodded.

"Handwriting's a match with the others. And *not* a match for anyone in your group. But we knew that already."

"Yeah. We did."

"Her deadline's Sunday," Theresa said. "Two days. But we should go right away."

A cop strode into the room, raising a hand as if signaling for traffic to stop. "We got a Molly Clarke at 1601 Carl Street, number 312."

One sentence in particular clawed its way back into Daniel's thoughts: *You're part of my crusade now too.*

Theresa said, "If you can't handle this—"

"I can handle it," Daniel said.

Theresa drew back her head, gave a little nod. "All right, then. Let's go serve Ms. Clarke her death threat."

The police convoy rolled presidentially through the crooked streets of Parnassus Heights. Molly Clarke lived somewhere within a stretch of identical, connected town houses, each pale yellow with white trim, the picture of restraint. Daniel climbed out of Theresa's sedan, found the right porch, and pressed the buzzer for number 312.

Dooley sidled up beside him as he waited impatiently, the other cops forming an arc behind them, adjusting Kevlar vests, checking the slides of their pistols. Daniel could feel the heat coming off all those bodies.

He jabbed again at the buzzer, and Dooley reached out, stilled his arm. "Give her a minute. She's probably sleeping."

Across the street a SWAT van eased up to the curb, and Daniel and Dooley glanced over as the squad unpacked from it. The lead man jogged toward them with a battering ram, and Dooley muttered, "Oh, for God's sake. Boys with their toys. If Clarke doesn't answer, we can rouse a neighbor before Godzilla-ing another door."

As the SWAT members joined the crowd on the porch, Daniel turned back and thumbed the buzzer yet again, staring at the circular mesh speaker. His breath clouded in the night chill.

"Excuse me?" Behind them all, at the top of the steps leading from the street to the porch, stood a woman dressed in eggplant-colored nursing scrubs, her fingers twined through a plastic grocery bag. She was barely visible through the phalanx of broad, geared-up torsos. A laminated ID dangled from a lanyard around her neck, red block letters announcing UCSF MEDICAL CENTER; she must have just finished a night shift.

The police parted, placing her in sudden isolation, making her seem slight and frail. Her pale, watery eyes glanced tentatively at the line of police cars, then again at the gathering on the porch.

She wiped at her upturned nose with the back of her hand, a scared, childlike gesture. "What are all you guys doing?"

Now Daniel could make out the name on her laminated ID.

He said, "We're looking for you."

The grocery bag hit the porch with a slap.

Once SWAT safed Clarke's condo, Daniel and Theresa broke the news to her as gently as possible. It sent her into a tense perch on the arm of her cat-frayed IKEA couch. Baffled and agitated, she claimed no recognition of the other victims and could think of no overlap with Metro South. With sprays of hair twisting free from her ponytail, one untied sneaker, and overzealous hand gestures, she gave the illusion of a woman barely held together, but once they'd talked through the issue a few times, she settled down onto the couch proper and regained a wry, no-nonsense demeanor more befitting a registered nurse.

An alarm sounded on her watch, and she excused herself to the kitchen, where she stirred some chalky white medicine into a glass of water. She noticed them looking and said, "Twice a day."

"Cholesterol?" Dooley asked.

"Even better. Hemophiliac." Clarke chugged down the liquid, grimacing, then placed the glass in the sink. "It's a new clotting-factor protein they're testing over in Hematology. No more needle sticks or mixing vials, thank God. It's still in clinical trials—the job ain't gonna let me retire young, but I do have access. One of the perks, right?"

Wiping her lips, she came back to them and sat, massaging her knuckles, working each one with a gentle squeeze.

"So you have *no idea* what the letter could be referring to?" Daniel asked for what might have been the fifth time. "No idea what you're supposed to admit?"

"No idea. This is insane. *Insane.*"

"What departments have you worked in?" Dooley asked.

"I've moved around, except for surgery," Clarke said. "Most of my career I've been on the medical floor." She shook her head. "I'm a *nurse.* I help people. I've never intentionally hurt anyone."

"What about unintentionally?" Dooley asked. "Gave a patient the wrong dose. Screwed up a protocol that—"

"*No.* No, nothing like that. Pull hospital records if you don't believe me."

"This isn't about us not believing you," Dooley said. "It's about us trying to help you."

"I am honestly at a loss." Clarke took stock of the humble living room, as if searching out solutions in the sparse furnishings. "What am I supposed to do?"

"Honestly?" Dooley said. "If I was you, I'd leave town. The country, even. Sit on a beach somewhere until we nail the guy."

"You have a suspect?" Clarke asked.

"We have six," Dooley said. "And counting."

"Sit on a beach," Clarke said, amused. "Just *leave.*"

"Yes."

"And come back when?"

"As I said, when we nail the guy."

"I'd love to. But I don't have the luxury."

"Why not?"

"I miss a lot of work due to . . . you know, the illness. Some mornings the hemarthrosis—sorry, the joint swelling—is too much. Then there's a random bleeding episode about once a month. Oh, yeah, nonstop shenanigans around here. So. I'm barely hanging on with my sick days. Some days the pain's too much, but I have to go in anyways, because . . . well, because there's no choice, really. If I get fired, I lose my benefits, which happen to include the best, most cutting-edge health care around. Condition like this, nah, I'd be done." The dark smudges beneath her eyes looked more pronounced, or maybe it was just the lighting. "So sitting on a beach sipping piña coladas? Not really an option."

"That's rough," Daniel said.

Clarke shrugged. "You do what you have to do."

"Yeah. But you're doing it well. And there's something in that."

He felt Theresa looking across at him from the adjacent chair, taking his measure.

"Thank you," Clarke said. "Doesn't always feel that way."

"This killer isn't bluffing," Dooley said, seemingly to both of them. "This is life or death."

"So's keeping my health insurance," Clarke said.

Daniel rose and walked to the window, which gave a clear view up Hillway into the heart of the medical campus. To the right rose the curved tiers of the parking structure, like the Guggenheim without the flow and elegance. He knew the grounds better than he would have wished. Many a night he'd driven Cristina home from treatment here as she lay curled in the passenger seat, nauseous and clammy, a wisp of herself. His quick rapport with Clarke, he realized, wasn't just sympathy. He knew something, too, about being up against a wall that felt too steep to scale.

The conversation continued behind him, Theresa running through some specifics. "We'll assign a unit to you. Two officers at your side at all times until the deadline."

"And then?"

"And then we'll figure out what to do."

"Will you be here with me? At midnight Sunday?"

The silence stretched out. Daniel turned away from the window. Molly was looking at *him,* not Dooley.

"Yes," he said.

Chapter 35

Daniel was awakened by yelling. Through the high boil of his thoughts, he realized that Cris was shouting his name. Twisting in the sheets, he came off the bed, tripping over a blanket that still ensnared his legs. Cris stood at the window, the swivel chair knocked askew behind her, her palm smacking the rain-flecked pane again and again.

"There! *There!*"

He kicked free and stood. Darkness cloaked the street below.

"I saw her," Cris said. "The mist, but still. I *saw* her. She's there."

His lungs, still jerking air from the shock. He watched, but the strip where the street should be was nothing more than a black river, a chasm.

Then headlights swept through the intersection and that bright yellow slicker jumped into vivid relief. The face, replaced by shadow beneath the raised hood. The lifted arm, dripping a sheet of rainwater, pointed up at them.

The car skidded on the wet asphalt to dodge the form, the horn blaring. The woman never moved.

The headlights passed, and the form vanished again, leaving them with jangled nerves and the hammering of rain against the window.

Daniel ran for the stairs, nearly colliding with Leo, just now lunging his way up.

"The woman—out on the street again."

Leo reversed course in a single graceful rotation, gliding down over the steps, Daniel so close at his back that a tangled crash seemed imminent. Somehow they managed both flights without colliding, Cris sprinting behind them. Leo half pivoted at the front door— "Lock this behind us *now*"—and then they were out into the wet before Daniel could contemplate his state of undress, the cold blasting through his boxers and the thin cotton of his T-shirt. His bare feet splashed puddles as he raced to the middle of the street, pulling up in the spot where the woman had stood moments before.

Nothing there but the dotted line.

Vaguely, he sensed Leo on the far side of the street, checking behind bushes and parked cars.

Daniel spun a full turn and then another, the neighborhood a shadow-play simulation of itself, familiar yet different from down here at this angle, the houses looming up around him. Rain pattered against his cheeks, running into his eyes, cutting his visibility. The cords in his neck strained, and he realized he was shouting at the darkness like a madman—"*Why are you here? What the hell do you want?*"—and at once a set of headlights leapt from the blackness at his side and a truck fishtailed past, dodging him by feet, brakes squealing. An irate face at the driver's window floated by in bizarre slow motion, mouth stretched with a road-rage roar.

The truck kept on, brake lights fading into the haze.

Next door Ted Shea materialized at an upstairs window, his puzzled expression evident until Danika appeared at his side and cinched the blinds closed.

Rain washed over Daniel. His clothes, plastered to his skin, grew heavy. He stood in the still, dark center of the street until he felt Leo's hand at the small of his back, guiding him to the house, to safety.

Chapter 36

She entered, peeled the yellow slicker off her shivering torso like a second skin, and let it slap triumphantly to the concrete floor, the pelt of a fresh kill. The lights, off as usual to save money. Had she not known to look toward the bare mattress in the corner, she'd not have seen him sitting there, powerful body coiled even as he reclined. His shoulders to the wall, one leg kicked straight, the other knee raised to support his arm. His hand floating past the braced elbow, thumb bumping across the fingertips. His eyes glinted darkly at her, shining fiercely with pride. With purpose.

He sat like that sometimes for hours with the hurt. Planning.

"They scared?" he asked.

"They're scared, baby."

His teeth appeared then.

She went to him, took her knees before the mattress. He stroked her face. She reached for his hand. Curled it into a fist. Looked at him imploringly.

When she let go, his hand loosened, so she formed it again into a hard ball. "When can we do it again, baby?"

He put his thumb on her chin and tilted her face, still damp with rainwater, this way then that, appraising it. "Not now."

She made a whimper of disappointment.

He said, "We want to keep it fresh."

He unfolded his limbs, spreading himself, and she slid up onto the mattress and laid her cheek against his chest. The smell of him, cigarettes and musk. He stroked her hair.

He said, "Soon."

Chapter 37

Daniel stirred and stretched languidly, back arching, limbs sprawling, hands and toes straining for the four corners of the bed. The sheets to his right bore an imprint of Cris's body, and he could hear the murmur of her voice from downstairs and smell Illy dark roast rising through the floorboards. Yawning, he ground the heel of his hand into one watery eye, the nightstand clock blurry but readable, showing half past eleven. Shocking.

He couldn't remember the last time he'd slept in this late. Come to think of it, he couldn't remember the last time he'd slept soundly at all. But the previous night, after trudging back upstairs and drying off, he'd fallen into bed as if from a great height. All he'd sensed before everything disappeared was the gentle stroke of his wife's fingertips along his shoulders.

He staggered down the stairs now, squinting and scratching at his head, his hair apparently standing on end.

Phone tucked between cheek and shoulder, Cris sat at the counter scowling down at the files arrayed before her as if they were a feast she didn't want to eat. Her glasses, once again, shoved up into her hair and forgotten. Seeing him, her face lightened, and she said, quickly, "Call you back," and hung up. "But soft," she called to him, "what light through yonder stairwell breaks?"

"Is it really almost noon?"

"I don't think that's what comes next."

"Sorry. Can't muster iambic pentameter just yet." He paused en route to the coffeepot and kissed her on the head. "How's your morning?"

"Bad," she said. "Though I suppose that's relative these days, what with Little Yellow Riding Hood and all."

"What's going on?"

The phone rang, and she looked at caller ID, then back to him apologetically. He gave her a magnanimous sweep of the hand and poured himself a mug.

"Nyaze," she said, "what do you got for me?" Then, "No. *No.* We can't take the counterproposal to committee on Monday. That gives them too much time to swiftboat it before the vote. We drop it on them late Tuesday, leak something to the *Chronicle* so it's online before they finish reading the cover page. 'Anonymous sources close to the Planning Commission confirm.' . . . Uh-huh. Uh-huh."

He leaned against the sink and sipped from his mug, enjoying the sight of her, the intensity of her words playing the feminine cords in her neck, the blade of her hand accentuating one point and then the next.

At once Leo was at the top of the stairs behind her, standing motionless, arms at his sides. The man seemed not to approach but to *appear,* as if transported. The recessed light gave a good waxy shine off his bald head, showing the grooves and contours of his skull. He wore a rain jacket, though the street glowed with sunlight.

His legs moved at last as he circled to Daniel, giving Cris and her phone voice wide berth. "You slept," he said. It was not a question.

"Yes," Daniel said. "And well. Thanks to you. It's easier to sleep knowing you're downstairs." He gestured toward the window and the street beyond. "No more appearances by the Lady in Yellow last night?"

Leo didn't smile, but his lips pressed together slightly with amusement. "Nothing to report." The accent clipped his words coming and going, another show of efficiency.

"All clear on the horizon?"

"I wouldn't say that."

A few fat drops tapped the window, and Daniel watched with

amazement as the rain began and quickened into a downpour. Leo zipped his jacket, snapped the top button. His black sneakers were tightly laced, double-knotted.

"You leaving?" Daniel asked.

"No. But I won't be in the house. I want to watch the block." Leo faded down the stairs.

"We *cannot* lose Donahue," Cristina was saying. "He's our swing vote. If we lose Donahue, it's over. Have Wu put it in his ear that if he goes against us in the eleventh hour, he's gonna have major voter-bloc disappearance in November. We're talking some *X-Files* shit."

Daniel refilled his coffee and sat on the counter. Cris reached a crescendo, hung up, and made fists in her bangs. She looked at him through the prison bars of her wrists. "You still here?"

He waved.

"I bet you wish you married someone less strident," she said.

"No."

"Really?"

"Yes," he said. "I hate to sound sexist—"

"Is that phrase *ever* followed by anything helpful?"

"—but you're very attractive when you're angry."

"Oh?" She had that light going behind her brown eyes now, limning them with yellow. "So that's gonna be your new sexy-time move from here on out? Make me angry?"

"Correction: You're attractive when you're angry at *other people*."

"I see. How 'bout when I'm angry at you? Not attractive?"

"Daunting."

"Well," she said, cracking the faintest grin as she returned to her papers, "then don't piss me off."

After procrastinating most of the afternoon, he finally got to his run. He started on a downhill, practically tumbling along the slope of Scott Street to Union, where he paused at the crosswalk. The business of Pacific Heights living took place here—banks and bars, restaurant crowds spilling onto sidewalks, mothers with toned arms shoving twin-size sport strollers into boutiques. On a normal week, he and Cris ran errands on Union or slurped oysters at Café des Amis. Watching the current of people out enjoying a lazy Saturday brought to mind just how off course the last week had set him. The orderly procession of commerce, leisure, and luxury now seemed surreal.

The light changed, and he kept on. Up ahead, a forest of sailboat masts crowded Yacht Harbor, the sun polishing the hulls with a postcard gleam. He veered east at the Marina Green, where hippie drummers banged away, lending an inadvertent sound track to a corps of elders enacting tai chi forms with factory-floor precision. Two beautiful Chinese women practiced the fan dance, their movements chopped to a stop-action film by a team of bicyclists zipping past in Italian racing suits, school-bus-yellow Speedos stretched torso-high. The sun winked off the impenetrable windows of the overlooking Mediterranean houses. Easy to forget that most of the marina rested atop a bed of landfill, composed in part of debris from the great quake of 1906. The Loma Prieta rumble, which cracked the earth and paused a World Series in '89, had served as a brusque reminder to the neighborhood denizens. Yet even seven collapsed buildings, sixty-three condemned structures, and four fires had only put the party on hold. That was San Francisco, keeping about her fun, setting up those deck chairs as icebergs loomed ahead. It was a kind of denial, sure, but wasn't everyone guilty of a bit of the same? A week ago Daniel, too, had considered the foundation solid. And now there seemed to be fissures everywhere he looked.

His thoughts stewed, turning toxic, and he ran harder to escape. But his footsteps pounded out names against the pavement: *Marisol Vargas. Kyle Lane. Molly Clarke.*

He ran the curves of the water's edge, hitting the rim of Aquatic Park. A sand-castle competition was in full florid swing, a six-foot palace with more towers than Red Square rising above the field, seeming to transcend its materials. A pod of Dolphin Club swimmers emerged from the ice-gray waters, teeth chattering, skin pale.

Martin. Big Mac. Xochitl.

As he neared the dividing line of Hyde Street, the salt-tinged air wafted over the barks of sea lions who'd taken up residence suddenly and inexplicably at Pier 39 after the last big earthquake. Up ahead a fire-hose torrent of tourists washed through Fisherman's Wharf, the Place Where Locals Dared Not Tread. A shift of the wind brought the stench of the fish brokers' wares, and Daniel put his back to the pier and ran hard for home.

Lil. Fang. A-Dre.

He let the burn overtake his muscles, sweat coating his body as he legged his way back along the waterfront, then upslope toward the house. It wasn't until he double-locked the front door behind him that he realized he'd altered his run today not for the scenery.

He'd done it because there were enough witnesses along the route to deter an attack.

Chapter 38

Daniel dripped sweat up the stairs to the kitchen and knocked back two glasses of water. Cris came partway down the stairs from the bedroom, ducking to bring him into sight. Her hair was taken up in a ponytail, and she clenched a pencil in her teeth; she'd been working all day. For once her glasses were on her face where they were supposed to be.

She released a breath. "Just you?"

"Just me."

"Where's Leo?"

"Watching the block."

"Yeah," she said, turning to head back up. "That sounds like Leo."

His cell phone rattled on the countertop, and he picked up.

A woman's voice said, "Your guy is a *psycho*."

"Wait," he said, pulling the phone away to look at caller ID. The name—SUE POSADA—was out of context here, so it took a beat for him to place it. The occupational therapist to whom he'd referred Walter Fang for his dyslexia.

When he put the phone back to his ear, Sue was in full swing. "—tried to get him going with some diagnostic reading exercises, but he was *totally* shut down."

"Wait. *When?*"

"He left just now. Hang on, lemme check the hall." Some rustling, and then she came back on the line. "I started seeing clients on Saturdays since so many work, but the place is quiet here on weekends. I don't scare easily, as you know."

"I know. What'd he do?"

"Nothing. That was the problem. He did *nothing*. I tried to talk to him, but he just sat there silently and glared at me. He's a big guy, in case you haven't noticed."

"I've noticed."

"Well, something's not right with him. He scared me. I thought he was gonna . . . I don't know. The building is empty today, like I said. And he just *sat* there with this dead gaze locked on me. Wouldn't answer questions, nothing. I asked him to go, and he wouldn't, so I got up calmly and locked myself in my office. I was about to call 911 when I heard him walk out."

"I'm sorry that it—"

"I don't usually work with violent offenders," she said. "I've made exceptions for you in the past. But you know what? *Don't* send me any more referrals."

Before he could answer, she'd hung up.

He crossed to the couch and sat with his feet up on the glass coffee table. Was there anyone in the group he *could* trust this week? Martin and Lil, both missing his business card. A-Dre with his avowed love of fighting. X at turns shut down and volatile. Big Mac's explosion in the elevator. And now Fang, showing an aggressive side in an unexpected context.

This was the problem with finding a suspect in a pool of violent offenders.

Past Daniel's sneaker on the coffee table sat the termination agreement he'd promised Kendra several times over. He stared at it, then leaned forward, finished filling it out, and signed. He'd just set down the pen when he became aware of Cris standing over him, her arms crossed.

"Okay, *mi vida*," she said, "I've been cooped up too long. I'm officially stir crazy."

"And you want . . . ?"

"Peking duck."

"Right now?"

"Right now. I *need* it. In my belly."

He glanced at his watch. "The best Chinese is in the Avenues or the Peninsula, and we're gonna hit rush hour."

"It's Saturday."

"It's San Francisco," he reminded her. "At dinnertime."

"We could get to Chinatown in ten minutes."

"There is no passable Chinese food in Chinatown."

"A rich irony," she said. "But sad for my belly."

"I'll make you something here?"

"Nothing else will do," she proclaimed.

He gave her a wry look and returned his gaze to the termination agreement. Her face appeared suddenly up close, horizontal, angling in front of the paperwork. "*Peeking* duck!" she said.

Covering his amusement, he rose. She stalked him up the stairs, taking Elmer Fudd steps and freezing when he turned around. She pretended to hide behind the door as he stripped and got into the shower. The steam had just reached a copious murk when she stuck her head through the glass door and said, "*PEEKING* DUCK!"

"Okay, okay," he said. "I'll drive you to the Richmond."

Her face withdrew. "Wait," he heard her say. "There *is* that new place in Chinatown."

"Right," he said, stepping out and reaching for his towel. "The one. From that article."

"The weekly paper—"

"That had whatsherhead on the cover?"

"That's the one." She rubbed lotion into her hands. "I think they're by that corner."

"Next door to the joint with the guy with the mole."

"Then it's settled." She scrabbled at the doorknob with lotion-slick hands, finally gaining purchase. The door swung open, and she grinned in triumph. "Peking duck shall be mine."

They left the smart car in an overpriced lot beneath Portsmouth Square, so named because in pre-landfill days water used to lap against its border. The park now felt as landlocked as a midwestern state, six blocks of high-rises obscuring the view of the Bay. For good reason the square was referred to as Chinatown's living room; old folks milled on benches, bickering, smoking pipes, and playing Chinese chess, on welcome break from their tiny rented rooms.

Daniel and Cris held hands, taking a circuitous route to the restaurant, their own little walking tradition. First they cut down to Bush so they could enter Chinatown properly through Dragon's Gate, which set the mood. The stone lion dogs on the arch were supposed to give protection against evil spirits, and Daniel figured he could use all the help he could get right now. An elderly lady with a quadripod cane accosted them with fluorescent yellow flyers—"*Dim sum half off! Dim sum half off!*" Cris couldn't stop laughing as he tried to shake the old lady loose, and he was finally cowed into taking a leaflet.

They cut up from the touristy thoroughfare of Grant to Stockton Street, where the residents actually shopped, and found the place from the article with whatsherhead on the cover by the corner next to the joint with the guy with the mole. Behind a padded swinging door, a bustling circus revealed itself, carts flying to and fro, lobsters balancing in wall tanks, a steam-spewing purgatorial kitchen ejecting waiters balancing overburdened trays.

Within moments Daniel and Cris were whisked to a table, where they confronted each other, breathless from the rush and heady with the smells. Cris snapped her chopsticks apart and rubbed them together to shed the splinters, a cartoon simulation of eagerness. He ordered an Anchor Steam and pointed at various appetizers on the menu, written in traditional Chinese. Each arrived as a surprise.

Preemptively, Cris palmed a few Maalox into her mouth. The radiation treatment had burned her esophagus, so she suffered from bouts of heartburn, exacerbated by spicy food. She eyed a hot mustard dish longingly. Licked a dab off her pinkie finger and closed her eyes into the pleasure of it before a cough caught her off guard. Eyes watering, she sipped some water.

"A Mexican who can't eat spicy food," she said. "I am a disgrace to my people."

Despite the jest, her look of chagrin made him take her hand across the table.

The waiter came back, bearing a noodle dish that Daniel had not yet encountered. When he mime-ordered the Peking duck, Cris all but levitated off her chair with excitement.

"Do you know," she asked once the waiter had departed, "how old macaws live to?"

"Why, are we gonna eat one of them, too?"

"I'm serious."

"Uh, *no*. I don't know how old macaws live to."

"Sixty years," she said. "Some make it to eighty if you take care of them well. People have to make provisions for them in their *wills*." She poked at a dumpling, and he waited to see what she was getting at. "Remember Mrs. Gao?"

"Five-generation Chinese-Filipino family in your building? The great-great-aunt in the cupboard?"

"The very one. She has a macaw she brought over from Manila when she moved here as a young woman. And with everything going on with the building, she's worried sick over it. I guess they don't like change. Macaws."

"Or maybe," Daniel offered, "it gives Mrs. Gao somewhere to put her fear about getting evicted."

"Yeah, Shrinky Dink? Or *maybe* she just loves that bird."

"Or that."

Cris set down her chopsticks. "I'm really worried that I'm going to fail them all. They really might close this building, Daniel."

"Can we . . . help?"

"We can't *buy* our way out of this."

"Why not?"

"First of all"—a tiny smile—"we don't have enough. At least *this*

branch of the family doesn't. I knew I should've married your mother."
She held up a hand. "I know. Bad visual."

"Hideous," Daniel said. "And second?"

"That's what *they* do. The other guys. They just throw money and throw money until everyone's so worn down that they get what they want."

"It's how the world works."

"I know. I keep waiting to get used to it. But I can't. Which makes me naïve, I suppose. Or stupid. Or crazy."

They ate for a time in silence, and then the Peking duck arrived, coasting in on a savory airstream. Cris dug in, fingers and teeth, her mouth stained with a Joker grin.

"This is a few blocks from your new office," she said when she came up for air. "We can meet here for lunch." She read his face. "What?"

"Nothing."

She decimated a napkin. "Never an acceptable answer."

"Sorry. I just thought I was ready to get out of Metro South, shift into private practice . . ."

"But you're not?"

"Not as ready as I thought."

"So why do it?" She waited, but he had no answer close at hand. "It's not the money. We don't need more things."

"Clearly," he said.

"Is it because . . ."

"What?"

"Well, when I was sick, you said you wanted to do stuff that *matters*."

He set his napkin on his plate. "Private practice *matters*."

"Of course it does," she said. "But does it matter to *you*?"

"It's not like I'm becoming a baby-seal clubber."

"True," she said. "And I've heard that positions in the seal-clubbing industry are highly competitive. But you're not answering the question, *mi vida*."

Two busboys swept in like piranhas, picking the table clean.

When the busboys left, Cristina took his hand. "Let me make something clear. I don't care if you're a private shrink or a portfolio manager or a doula, as long as you wake up every morning feeling alive."

"Doula?"

"Okay, maybe that'd be a little unsettling. But you have a—and I know the term is overused—a *gift* for doing what you do. And part of that has to do with the people you work with. Do you think it'll be the same if you're dealing with the kind of folks who can afford private practice?"

"Maybe I'll make more headway with *them*." Wielding a chopstick, he poked at a few stray pieces of rice on his plate. "I've been doing this for . . . what? Three years? And sometimes I don't know how effective I am. The recidivism rate sucks. Maybe Dooley's right. Maybe some people you can't get through to."

"Some people you can't," Cris said. "How 'bout the others?"

"They make gains in session, and then one thing sets them off six months, a year later, and they're right back where they started." He rubbed at a stain in the tablecloth. "I'd be lying to say there aren't days where I wonder what the hell I'm doing."

She watched him for a while, then said, "You didn't used to."

"Maybe the shine's worn off. When I first started running groups, it was so exciting. The adrenaline. But then it turned into . . . real life."

"Yeah," she said. "Real life's hard and unglamorous and a lotta work. It's about hanging in and fighting the right fights and taking two steps forward and sometimes three steps back. But maybe some fights are worth fighting even if you're not gonna win them. Because that *one* time you make a difference, however small . . ."

When he looked up, something at the periphery of his vision, beyond her face, caught his attention. His focus sharpened. Past the length of the restaurant, through the pinned-back kitchen door, in a stairwell leading down into blackness, an oval seemed to float a few feet above the floor.

A shadowed face?

Disembodied.

As if someone were standing several stairs down, head almost level with the floor. Any trace of neck or torso blended into the gloom.

In the kitchen, steam hissed from a fryer, obscuring Daniel's view. He'd gone rigid in his chair. Vaguely, he sensed Cris's hand on his arm, her concerned bearing, the movements of her mouth.

As the mist cleared, a burst of flame erupted from a pan, throwing a flicker of light into the dark of the stairwell.

Enough for Daniel to discern part of the black sweatshirt that had turned the body invisible. And suspended above, the familiar neoprene mask wrapping the head, smoothing it to menacing perfection.

Chapter 39

The featureless head peered, it seemed, directly back at Daniel from across the restaurant. Like a fencing mask—all focus and yet utterly empty.

A chef crossed between stoves, his legs momentarily blocking Daniel's view, and when he'd passed, the stairwell was empty.

Daniel's thighs banged the table as he leapt up, making the dishes jump. He shouted back at Cris—*"He's here! Call Dooley!"*—and then he was hurtling toward the kitchen. A waiter wheeled out of the way, miraculously keeping a tray of beer bottles aloft. Daniel barreled through the kitchen, dodging elbows and complaints, and into the dark stairs.

There had to be another exit down there. If he could just follow, see where the killer was headed.

Ten or so crumbling concrete steps dropped into a disused room split by support beams. Reaching the bottom, Daniel slapped at a light switch to no avail, the crunch of glass beneath his shoes indicating that the bulb had been strategically broken.

With a quick sweep, he took in the space. Storage boxes, cobwebs, an industrial freezer laboring audibly in the near corner. Stagnant air, earthy and damp. Way on the other side, a sheet of light fell through a barely open door and stretched across the dusty floor, carrying with it the changing colors of the street above—bobbing red lanterns, oscillating neon.

He kept one foot on the bottom step, ensuring a clear retreat route in case of attack. Jerking in a few breaths, he tried to adjust to the shifting glow, the patterns mapping across the ceiling, the stairs, his own face. Not only was it disorienting, but it acted as camouflage, blurring the surfaces, melding box with beam, beam with wall. Everything seemingly inanimate and yet alive with movement. He figured that the man had fled through the door opposite.

Angry Cantonese echoed down at him from the kitchen. The seconds were ticking away; he had to keep on or fall back and explain. Pursuing was foolish for more reasons than he could recount. And yet would he have another chance to get this close?

The image of Molly Clarke came to him. Her scared perch on the couch in her little place where she tended her illness and her cats, making do as best she could. A bit more than twenty-four hours to her deadline.

He broke the stillness, running for that far door.

He'd taken no more than two steps when a chunk of the nearest beam detached itself, resolving into human form. The shadowed figure accelerated at him, one arm drawn back for a blow. Daniel turned reflexively away, but the collision of fist to cheek, even glancing, left his ears ringing and deposited him in a sprawl on the moist floor. The black form was on him, a drawn-back glove flashing through the sheet of light and giving off a metallic glint.

Daniel brought up both hands and caught the man's wrists, stopping the tip of the military knife inches from his nose. They struggled, belly to belly, the man's mass pinning Daniel, grinding his shoulder blades painfully into the concrete. The mask drew closer, the man gathering all his weight behind the knife, and through the circle of breathing perforations sighed sickly-sharp breath—tobacco and mint?

Daniel grunted and fought, heels scrabbling for purchase, but the man's strength was overpowering. Though the mask loomed less than a foot from Daniel's face, the figure-eight slit of the eyehole was too narrow and the storage room too dim for him to catch a glimpse of skin, whether brown or white. He could make out only the gleam of

211

pupils and the point of the knife, inches from his cheek, blurring in and out of focus. His attacker bore down. Daniel's strength was waning. Even through the panic, he registered a single thought as he watched the steel tip lower inch by inch toward his straining eye: *The Tearmaker.*

A recollection washed over him—that feeling of being laid out beneath an opponent on the high-school mat, the bleachers whirling into upside-down view, the referee there on his stomach peering in, counting, hand poised to announce the pin. Reaching back twenty-five years, he found the instincts there and waiting, all that muscle memory, all those wrestlers' dirty tricks.

Bracing the man's wrist with the bar of his forearm, Daniel wormed his other hand free and made a fist, resting his thumb above his curled index finger so the tip protruded—a striking weapon. He fought his hand along the front of the face, his knuckles dragging across the mask, and jabbed the thumb into the pressure point at the jawbone, an inch down from where the earlobe bulged the neoprene.

A pained grunt, a waft of stale, minty breath across Daniel's face, and the man's grip faltered. Daniel drove his knee up between the guy's legs, making brutal contact, and the man twisted, the knife skittering away. Gloved hands grabbed Daniel's biceps, slamming him flat on the floor again, and Daniel hit a bridge, arching his back, rolling onto the top of his head to create space. He bucked and flipped, landing on his stomach, waiting for the bounce of the man against his back. Impact. The man reared slightly to adjust, and Daniel pivoted hard from his midsection, leading with his elbow, connecting at the man's temple.

The blow knocked the guy clear off him. The black form rolled once, steamrollering a cardboard storage box, the momentum carrying him seamlessly up onto his boots about ten feet away near that barely ajar rear door. They locked eyes across the span of concrete for an instant as the man seemed to decide whether to fight or flee. Then he swiped the knife from the floor and barged through the door, letting in a flood of light and street noise.

Daniel pulled himself up and stumbled in pursuit, bounding up a short set of metal stairs to come level with the street. The man was not in view, but through strobing traffic Daniel saw an overturned sale table and a woman sagging against a store window, clutching her chest—the aftermath of a commotion.

He took a jogging step off the curb, but a blaring horn sent him leaping back. A bus hissed by on an effluvium of exhaust, the bumper whispering against his sleeve. Another inch and it would have taken off his arm. Startled faces filled the windows—the "Dirty 30" Stockton, crammed to the gills, as always.

Daniel took a Frogger route through traffic, tracking the man's wake. Here a knocked-over trash bin, there a tourist picking himself up off the pavement. Daniel hurdled a fallen sidewalk sign, shouldered through a huddle of shoppers, staring up the sidewalk. Nothing. Frustrated, he spun, scanning the busy street for any sign of the masked man. Through a storefront window, a deadpan butcher hacked robotically at raw chicken parts. Turtles rasped in glass cases. Fish stench rode a current of air from a market.

A crash announced a collision around the corner, and he bolted back into motion. Too late, he spotted the heap of spilled silk dresses and skidded out on them, all traction lost. He pulled himself up, yanking free from a cluster of concerned and angry onlookers, coming face-to-face with a familiar vendor wielding familiar fluorescent yellow flyers—"*Dim sum half off! Dim sum half off!*" Shaking her off, he saw a black form vanish through a beaded curtain up ahead. It took him a few steps to get back to full speed, and then he blasted through the storefront filled with cardboard bins bearing picket sale signs—3 SHIRT $9.99!—and out the back, spilling into an alley just in time to see the dark figure careen onto the street up ahead and dash out of view.

Daniel sprinted after him, his chest burning. With the police en route and multiple witnesses, the advantage was Daniel's; he just had to stay close enough to jar loose a clue, to spot a getaway car or motorcycle. Veering hard out of the alley, he nearly knocked over a trio of would-be diners. No sign of his attacker. Daniel ran the length of a block, then another, strings of red and yellow plastic pennants passing overhead, endless finish lines. Through a gap in the rooftops, he could see the jagged skyline of the financial district a few blocks over. Beyond his future office building, Castanis's corporate goddesses materialized from the black sky, crowning the high-rise. Fog-misted and backlit, dominating the city, they seemed to peer down onto Daniel with faceless focus. Their attention made him and his ragged pursuit seem small and unimportant, an ant before gods.

He did not slow.

His legs carried him back into Portsmouth Square. The moon hung bone white and alert in a net of clouds. Ahead, an elevated bridge led to the tower of the Hilton and the Chinese Cultural Center, providing a vantage onto the whole park. He ran across to the midway point and leapt up onto the wide concrete-block railing, startling a young couple making out on one of the benches. He teetered a moment on the treacherous edge, the twenty-foot drop making itself suddenly known, but regained his balance and looked around. No sign of the man.

Hopping down, he ran across the narrow breadth of the bridge, jumping onto the opposite railing. He saw the black form, too late, on one of the zigzag walkways in the plaza far below. The man paused, the mask staring back. A frozen moment as they regarded each other across the park's expanse. Then the figure turned, bounding over a metal rail and vanishing into the night.

Chapter 40

Giving a police statement took longer than reading a Russian novel. Daniel and Cristina had been separated the first go-round to ensure they didn't purposely or inadvertently affect the other's version of the evening's events. Now they occupied side-by-side chairs in Dooley's box of an office in the heart of 850 Bryant. Cris looked uncharacteristically pale. With his fight-rumpled clothes and adrenaline hangover, Daniel imagined he looked exponentially worse. Key shock points of the night refused to clear from his mind: the first glimpse of that mask through the kitchen steam, the form melting from the storage room's beam, a knife tip inches from piercing his pupil. They reemerged at random, like jolts of electricity.

Cris gripped his hand, tight. He realized his knee was jacking up and down and made an effort to still it.

Dooley asked, "You sure you don't want us to have someone check you for injuries?"

"I'm okay, thanks. *Mostly* okay." Stifling a groan, he rubbed his nape. "It used to be I could hit a bridge without pulling every goddamn muscle in my neck."

"You were less than half your age," Cris said, "and no one was trying to *kill* you."

"Was he spying on you or trying to kill you?" O'Malley asked from his lean in the doorway.

Daniel said, "Judging by the knife he tried to jam through my eye, I think it's safe to say he was trying to kill me."

"But maybe that was in self-defense." Dooley caught herself. "I mean—"

"I know what you mean. If I hadn't gone after him, maybe he wouldn't have attacked me."

"You never got a death threat," O'Malley said. "It's a break in the pattern. Molly Clarke is supposed to be next."

"Anything else you can remember?" Dooley pressed. "Any detail, no matter how small?"

Daniel leaned forward, his skin tacky with dried sweat. Closing his eyes, he walked through the entire fight again. The initial blow. His shoulder blades grinding into the floor. The perforated airholes of the mask—

"His *breath*," Daniel said.

At this, Dooley and O'Malley went on point. "What about it?"

"It was bitter and stale and minty."

"Like some kind of gum?"

"No," Daniel said, the recognition slotting into place. "It was dip. Tobacco. Like Copenhagen."

"The suspect dips tobacco," O'Malley said. "Are you sure?"

"I'm *positive*. You know how smell hits memory."

Cris was first to the logical next question: "Who in your group dips tobacco?"

"I don't know." Daniel cracked his knuckles, one finger at a time. Realized he was doing it. Stopped. "They wouldn't do it in group. We keep the rooms substance-free."

Theresa looked at O'Malley, said, "Have the parole officers pay visits tomorrow, check each suspect's residence for chewing tobacco of any sort."

As the inspector withdrew, Daniel asked Dooley, "What have you heard from your guys in the field tonight? Aren't they supposed to be watching the group members?"

"Best they can," Dooley said. "They can't go into their apartments and stand over them in the bathtub."

"And?"

"There was some lag between the restaurant, when we got word from you, and when we had our guys knock on doors. But Martin, Fang, and A-Dre were home when checked. Lil was out at the time—"

"Lil was *out*?"

"That's unusual?"

"Yes. Where was she?"

"Some sort of church social."

He felt a blip of pride for her, even now.

"And Xochitl was at a movie," Dooley continued. "Our guy lost visual on her for a twenty-minute period, but obviously she's not the one who threw you around the storage room. Of the men, Big Mac wasn't where our guy thought. He'd left his apartment through a side door."

"You don't have people on side entrances?" Cris asked.

"We don't have unlimited manpower." Dooley kept her eyes on Daniel. "It seems implausible, but the others *could* have snuck out and back before their places were checked. Anton—sorry, *A-Dre*—is the only one we can rule out on geography alone. He lives down in the Bayview—no way he could've gotten back there, snuck into his apartment, and answered his door in that time frame."

Two alibis had been established then. Martin with his broken-down car during Vargas's murder and A-Dre at his Bayview place during the Chinatown fight. Which, among the group members, left Big Mac and Fang as options for the man behind the mask. Big Mac, who'd been conveniently untraceable earlier this evening, and Fang, who according to Sue Posada had been acting erratically.

"So A-Dre lives farthest," Cristina said. "Who lives *closest*?"

Daniel blew out a sigh. "Walter Fang. Right in Chinatown."

"Five blocks from the restaurant," Dooley added.

Daniel remembered stirring in his chair to find Fang standing there, right on top of him. The satchel briefcase at his feet, unsnapped. "But if your guys were watching him . . ."

"You ever heard of tunnels connecting the basements of Chinatown?" Dooley asked. "They hid opium dens and torture chambers during the tong wars in the mid–nineteenth century? Escape routes during Prohibition?"

"Of course," Cristina said. "But I thought that was all stuff-of-legend nonsense."

"Maybe. Maybe not. But we found a length of tunnel connecting an alley to the cellar of that restaurant," Dooley said. "Big hole behind the freezer."

A moment of speechlessness, during which Daniel recalled the earthy scent of the cellar. Having various routes in and out of that space would have proved useful to the attacker. He strained to connect the dots. "So you're saying Fang . . . ?"

"I'm saying maybe he got out of his place and back into it before our patrolman could check and see that he'd gone missing. And maybe he knows some of these tunnels or whatever they are and can move around Chinatown unseen."

"But you don't have any witnesses."

"We might." Theresa drew out the pause, as if debating whether to share more. "One of the dishwashers at the restaurant is a convicted felon, a frequent flier in these hallowed halls, and an Aryan Nation piece of shit. When we questioned the kitchen staff, he was edgy as hell. He knows something or is lying about something."

"How can you tell?" Cris asked.

"Despite my youthful looks, I been doing this a long-ass time." Dooley stood and shot Cristina a pointed look. "I know when people are lying."

Cris's expression changed to one of puzzlement.

"So what's your next move?" Daniel said.

"I'm gonna question him," Dooley said. "I want you to watch."

"Through a one-way mirror?"

"You watch too much *Law & Order.*" She headed out, then paused in the doorway. "I want you in the room."

Daniel gave his wife's hand a reassuring squeeze, let go, and stood.

Theresa flashed Cris a flat smile. "Don't worry. I'll have him home by midnight."

Daniel followed the inspector down the hall. She secured her gun in a wall safe, then paused before a double-locked door. "It could get ugly in there, so I'm gonna warn you now," she said. "This ain't Metro South."

Still dressed in a loose-fitting twill cotton dishwasher uniform, Brant Vogel slumped back in his chair, letting his long blond hair fall forward so his eyes peered through the screen of his bangs. One wisp pulled tight across his cheek to the corner of his mouth, his lips pursing as he sucked it. A wiry frame, all sinew and cords beneath his short-sleeved smock. A day's stubble hid the pockmarks on his cheeks, but not well enough. Tattoos sheathed his left arm, the see-no, hear-no, speak-no-evil monkeys totem-poled down the forearm.

Dooley kept her feet, setting her knuckles on the battle-scarred table across from Vogel, and Daniel moved to a corner, leaning against the wall.

Vogel spit out his hair and flicked his chin at Daniel. "Why the fuck's he in here?"

"He's a witness," Dooley said. "You're a witness. Why can't we all just get along?"

"I told you, Officer. I didn't *witness* shit. Any high-order mammal knows that if I didn't *witness* anything, then I ain't a *witness*. See?"

"High-order mammal. That's clever." She gestured at his right arm. "That's a nice clean shave. Getting ready to do some fisting in the big house?"

Daniel noticed that Vogel's arm was in fact shaved smooth.

Vogel lifted up his shirtsleeve, revealing a freshly scabbed tattoo capping the ball of his shoulder. "Had to get ready. I'm doing the rest of it tomorrow."

"Lemme guess," Dooley said. "It'll have skulls."

His lips tightened. Then he gave a little jerk of his head, his bangs parting just enough to provide a glimpse of the small prison tattoo at his hairline—a pinwheel swastika.

Dooley smiled. "I like the new ink. Almost as much as I like your dishwasher getup. Getting paid by a Chinaman these days? That must make all that pure blood boil in your veins."

"We have to make do where we can. They run everything. The chinks and the kikes."

"How 'bout the blacks?"

"Hell, I heard they're letting them in the PD these days."

They enjoyed a laugh together. Then, keeping on with that friendly smile, Dooley reached across the table and gripped his right arm at the shirtsleeve. His lips went thin, but he didn't flinch.

"I know there's something you're not telling me."

He managed a smile, though it looked more like a grimace. "That kinky hair pickin' up my brain-wave frequencies?"

Dooley's face stayed impassive. They stared across the table at each other. Spots of blood appeared through Vogel's sleeve around Dooley's clenched hand.

"You know how many fools have sat in that chair before you?" she asked.

Finally he pulled away, his pride scalded. He peeled back his sleeve, studied the cracked scabs, lowered it again. Then he glared at her through his bangs. "You know how many power-hungry niggers I've faced down?"

She sat. Calmly. Smoothed her hands on the table's surface. "Coon, sambo, darky, bluegum, jig, mosshead, porch monkey, spade. You wanna shock me? You *can't* shock me. You know why? I live in San Francisco in the twenty-first century, and I'm an African-American female cop. I am one empowered fucking bitch. Now, look at me. Look deep into my chocolate brown eyes. Do I look rattled? No. But you, sweet thing . . ." She reached across the table, and he jerked away, but she merely laid two fingers over his pulse at his wrist. "Your heartbeat's racing. Now, why is that? I'm not a gambling woman, but if I were, I would bet it's because you're interfering with a police investigation, whereas I have the force of the United States government behind me. Hard to believe, I know. World turned on its head. But that's where we are. In this day and age. So. You want to get down to business?"

"I don't do business with your type."

"Okay." She pushed back her chair and stood up. "Let's get Inspector O'Malley. Nice white boy. Even has a red mustache. You'll like him. O'Malley?"

She barely raised her voice, but a moment later the door opened and O'Malley entered. "Yes, Inspector?"

"Mr. Vogel here wants to be questioned by someone more to his liking."

"I'm on a case. He'll have to wait in general pop."

"Who's in there again?"

"Just the usual Knock Out Posse members," O'Malley said. "Dark-skinned fellahs, the lot of them."

"Cute," Vogel said. "This is cute."

"Won't be," Dooley said. "In about ten minutes."

"And some Black Guerrilla Family, too, I think," O'Malley added.

Dooley made an oh-no face at Vogel. "That's a lotta black folk."

"They won't touch me," Vogel said. "They don't know who I am. Just another guy caught in the same system as them."

"Is that . . . ?" Dooley circled the table, peered down at Vogel's head. "Lice?"

Vogel sagged back in his chair. "Oh, this is *bullshit*."

"It would be illegal to cohabitate Mr. Vogel with other prisoners if he has lice," O'Malley said.

"I don't got no fuckin' lice, man."

Dooley said, "Two negatives . . ."

"*What?*"

"Never mind. You don't happen to have a razor, Inspector O'Malley?"

"In fact I do. Right here." O'Malley produced an electric razor from his pocket, slapped it into Dooley's palm.

Daniel watched the well-rehearsed act with discomfort. And a bit of admiration.

"Okay," Vogel said. "Hang on here."

He came out of his chair, but Dooley grabbed him and spun him hard, gripping his head from behind. "Missed your chance." She pulled back his bangs to expose the pinwheel-swastika tattoo. "We'll get you cleaned up before we put you in the cage with the lower-order mammals." The vibrating blade hovered inches from his hair.

"Wait! Fucking *wait*, okay? I'll tell you."

Dooley turned off the razor, the sudden silence pronounced.

"Sit," she said.

Vogel sat.

"Talk," she said.

"I found something, okay," Vogel said. "I don't know anything about anything, but I found something the guy left behind."

"Left behind *where*?"

"He used it. To pin that storage-room door open—the one that leads up to the street. Probably so he could sneak in or get out in a hurry. I found it after the fight down there, and I kept it."

"Why'd you keep it?"

" 'Cuz it was money."

"You found *money* propping the back door open?"

"Yeah."

"Where is it?"

"You took it when you processed me. You have *all* my shit."

Dooley gestured at Daniel, and he stayed on her heels out of the room, down a corridor, to a different wall of security glass. She knocked hard, and the desk cop spun around on a pivot chair. "Brant Vogel's personals. I need his personals."

A moment later a plastic shoe box slid into the pass-through. Dooley grabbed it, looked down into it, and her face changed.

She said through the speaker, "Get one of the lab rats down here. *Now.*"

"What is it?" Daniel asked.

She held the plastic shoe box out for him to see. Beside a set of keys and a duct-tape wallet was a roll of quarters. The paper sheath had split, most of the shiny coins spilling out into the box. Daniel leaned closer until several of the stamped dates on the metal came clear—*1985, 1978, 2002.*

And yet every last quarter looked brand-new.

Chapter 41

At half past nine the next morning, James greeted Daniel at the door of Evelyn's estate, wearing honest-to-God white gloves and a new pair of spectacles. James's role had never been precisely defined. More than a chauffeur, less than a personal assistant or house manager, he'd simply been the person who took care of what Evelyn needed for as far back as Daniel's memory stretched.

"She's making you wear *butler* gloves?" Daniel asked.

"These?" James regarded his hands, and Daniel saw now that the gloves were in fact microfiber mitts. "No. I'm polishing the dashboards."

"Oh. I guess even *she* isn't that pretentious."

James's expression changed not at all yet somehow managed to convey irony. He gestured, and Daniel stepped into the lobbylike foyer, following him back. His shoulders ached from the fight on the concrete floor, his neck painfully stiff when he craned to take in the vaulted ceilings. But being here in the embrace of the house was a welcome distraction. An excuse to get his mind off the cellar brawl, the chase through Chinatown, and the roll of inexplicably shiny quarters that had baffled the entire Homicide Division last night.

James removed his new eyeglasses, showing textured pouches beneath his eyes. For the first time, he looked older. He'd aged over the years certainly, but only in shades so gradual they went unnoticed, like afternoon fading into dusk. He'd always seemed fifty-five or thereabouts, frozen in time, a paragon of circumspection and mature restraint. But it struck Daniel now that any reasonable estimate had to put him close to seventy. Noting the slight stoop in James's shoulders and the extra care he took stepping across a raised threshold gave Daniel a pang in the chest.

They drifted through an elaborate set of French doors into the rear garden, where a half dozen rows in they found Evelyn kneeling on her flowered cushion, weeding with well-used hand tools. Each Sunday morning she toiled in her award-winning garden with meager enjoyment. A crew tended it the other six days of the week. She was never relaxed, least of all out here. Daniel often wondered what she got out of her few hours' contribution. A contrived sense of accomplishment? Or was she simply duty-bound? *This is what we do.*

Without lifting her head, she said, "I asked you to be here at eight." Now she cast her gaze up, but only at James. "You want to get him to do something? Tell him to do the opposite." She waved a muddy hand, dismissing whatever James didn't say. "I know, I know." She put on her version of his voice, English accent with a hint of swish, though in reality James displayed neither affect. "'Wonder where he gets that?'"

"May I finish with the cars, or are you going to improvise more of my dialogue?" James asked, with no hint of bitchiness.

"The cars."

James withdrew. Evelyn went back to her weeds.

Daniel rolled his neck, so stiff he could barely look at the sky. "I had a busy night," he said. "And a busy morning."

"I heard."

"Of course you did."

"The story is working its way through the bullpen at the *Chronicle*," Evelyn said. "Should be ready for the morning's front page. They're connecting the dots, putting the murders together, ascribing them to one killer. 'The Tearmaker,' they're calling him. No ring if you ask me, but . . . you know, the business with the eyes. The president of the police commission said it's gonna drop on this city like the Zodiac Killer but without all the cryptogram fun."

"He said that?"

"No, but he would have were he pithier." She plunged a trowel into the moist dirt. "I made a few calls. I've managed to prevent your name from leaking."

"*Our* name."

"No. *Yours.* I don't recall scrambling around crime scenes playing Eliot Ness."

"Eliot Ness?"

"I'm seventy-six. What do you want? Justin Bieber?"

"There are some options between the two."

"Still. What are you doing? There are easier ways to get yourself killed. Xanax and scotch. Exhaust pipe and hose." She threw down the trowel in disgust. "Meet every challenge head-on, is that it? Even other people's?"

He thought about trying to explain to her how impulse and obligation had wound him, pythonlike, into the case. How a sense of duty, however misguided, had dragged him into the thick of it, just as it dragged her out here every crisp Sunday morning to weed a garden that didn't require her ministrations. He'd always hated standing by when others were at risk, but announcing so would sound cloying and self-serving, so he just breathed in the perfume of the prizewinning dwarf snapdragons, which had been pinched and pinched again to save their reblooming for these November weeks. Past the greenhouse and beyond the bluff, the Golden Gate Bridge added a few stalwart strokes to a dour gray sky.

"It's not *safe,*" Evelyn said. "What you're getting into. And running out to dinner in *Chinatown.*" The last word given an extra dose of disdain. "I'd imagine Conchita is still going to the projects every day?"

"Cristina. We're being careful."

"You're going to sit with that woman, are you? Molly Clarke? Tonight at midnight?"

"Yes. With Inspector Dooley and a number of other—"

"Can't you just let the police handle it?"

"The police have asked for my help."

"God forbid you say no to someone else besides me." Her phone rang, and she wiped her hands on her bunched Polo sweatshirt, pulled it out, and glanced at caller ID. Her face soured.

"Vimal?" Daniel asked.

"I swear that man—and I use the noun liberally—needs a wet nurse."

"Why don't you see about bringing someone else in, getting him some support?"

"That's none of your concern anymore, is it?" The phone slipped from her hand and thudded in the dirt. She tried to wipe it off, but the mud from her hands made marks on the casing. "You *left*. Just like your father did." She seemed to be talking to herself more than to Daniel. She tossed the phone aside in frustration and glowered at the surrounding plants. "It's a *mess*. Such a mess."

"What is?"

"I made sure the angel's trumpets were well established before winter. That the soil was drained."

An answer or a new topic?

She rose and reached into the drooping white flowers, putting a yellow leaf on display. "And still the leaves are falling off."

"Spider mites?"

"I pay a *crew* of gardeners—well, you don't want to *know* what I pay them. They have one job in this world. *One* job. I have given them that luxury. And they can't keep spider mites from my flowers?"

"So fire them."

"I did. This is the third company."

"Mom, you can't just sit up here on this hill and *pick* at people."

"*What else do I have to do?*" Her hand flew up as if to block the words, but they'd already escaped. She turned away, chagrinned, and began stripping dead leaves from the angel's trumpets with fierce twists of her wrist. "I *like* being wealthy," she said into the bush. "The summers in Costa Brava and my brunches at the St. Francis. But I know there's more to it. I know my money protects me. I know these servants would just as soon tear me to shreds as bring the tea service." She laughed, a hollow noise. "But they don't. There's an order, and I like my place in it."

He watched her frail shoulders rise with an inhale.

"One morning last year, I locked myself out of the house. I wasn't done up, my face wasn't on. Bathrobe. James had the day off. No staff here, nothing. Neighbors—not home. And I had to leave the community and go to the corner, that filthy liquor store, to call for a locksmith. And the guy behind the counter jerked his thumb at me and said, 'Get in line.' Just like that. He treated me like . . . like some old lady."

"Mom—"

"I'm not *special*. I know that." When she turned to face him, her eyes were steely as ever, though rimmed red with emotion. "But I don't *ever* want to feel that way again."

His mouth had gone dry. With effort, he swallowed. "So you want to stay up here in your castle? Only interact with people you control?"

"*Yes*," she said. "And *yes*. I'm not like you, Daniel. You're not like me. You never were. When you were in second grade, we brought you back a sterling letter opener from Paris. Very expensive. You took it to school for show-and-tell, and when we picked you up, we discovered that you'd given it away to one of your little friends. Were we angry! We said, 'That was a *very* special present. Didn't it mean anything to you?' And you said, 'Of course. That's why I gave it to someone.' " She laughed. "Do you remember that?"

He felt a grin touch his face. "I remember getting grounded."

"We tried to teach you the value of things." She shook her head, set her dirty hands on her hips, her eyes everywhere but on him. "Looking back, I suppose . . . I suppose I'm proud of you."

"At one point," he said, not unkindly, "that would have mattered a lot to me."

"Was I really that awful?" she asked.

"You gave me a great gift, Mom."

"What's that?"

He said, "You taught me how to fight."

She took this not as an insult but as he'd intended. She regarded him a moment, then patted him affectionately on the chest and started back for the house.

Chapter 42

By 11:00 P.M. they dispensed with any pretense of not watching the time and Molly Clarke retrieved her digital alarm clock and set it on the rug, where they could view it like a television set. Theresa and Daniel occupied the same cushioned chairs they'd sat in before, leaving Molly more room on the couch to shift nervously.

"God," she said. "It's been surreal. Being at the center of this . . . this *thing*. This morning I made the mistake of turning on the TV. The reporters seem gleeful, almost, to have this to talk about. The Tearmaker. A city in panic. Like it's some *video game*. But I'm the target. I'm the one who . . ." Her voice trailed off.

"We have two cars outside," Dooley said. "Men at all the entrances, in the stairwell, at the elevator. No one's getting in here." Her Motorola squawked, and she turned down the volume, held it to her ear. A quick scowl. "Copy that."

Molly had come off the couch, standing on bare feet. "What? What was that?"

"Our guys in the field. All the suspects seem to be accounted for. Asleep in their beds."

"Unless they snuck out," Clarke said. "It's hard to watch every window, every door, isn't it? I mean, you said there are six of them. And that's just the ones you *know* about."

Dooley put on a smooth smile. "We've dedicated a lot of resources to this, Molly."

"Why can't you just hold all the suspects in custody for the night?"

"Uh, because this isn't the Soviet Union." Dooley caught her tone. Generated a placating expression. "Look—we're gonna keep you safe."

"Then why's there an ambulance on standby outside?" A sudden beeping issued from Clarke's watch, and she literally left the ground. Settling, she grabbed her chest, twisting her sweatshirt above her heart. "Jesus, Mary, and Joseph."

She headed into the kitchen and stirred her medicine into water, the spoon dinging around the glass.

Daniel said quietly to Dooley, *"What?"*

"Everything's fine."

"I can read your face, Theresa."

"I don't like this. I don't know *what* I don't like, but something's off. He *knows* you're getting the death threats on time now. And he knows we're looped. There's no way he's getting in here. But he doesn't strike me as someone who bluffs."

Clarke turned to face them from the kitchen, wiping her lips. "What are you guys talking about?"

"The Giants," Dooley said. "Lincecum's been losing velocity on the two-seamer."

Clarke finished what was left in the glass and returned to her vigil on the couch. At the half-hour mark, they gave up on small talk. At 11:46, Clarke sobbed quietly for a few moments, then fell quiet again. At 11:57, she broke the silence again. "Countdowns are horrible. It's like I'm waiting for the place to blow up."

Dooley said, "We had the entire building safed by—"

"I know. But still." She bit her lip. "Someone wants to *kill* me. And I have no idea why."

11:58.

"Do you have any idea how helpless that makes me feel?" She pressed a hand to her mouth, breathed awhile.

11:59

"I guess we never can know what we do to affect other people,"

Clarke said. "Maybe I was rude to someone on the bus. Maybe I didn't tip a waiter enough. Or maybe something worse. I could've demeaned a patient or—"

"You can't blame yourself for being targeted by a psychopath," Dooley said.

"I'm not blaming myself. I'm just . . . I don't know. I don't know *what* I'm doing."

They watched the clock in silence.

The red digital lines reconfigured.

Midnight.

Clarke made a noise in her throat. No one spoke for the entire minute. Daniel could hear Clarke's quick exhalations. The smell of Dooley's perfume—something light and citrusy—lingered.

The clock changed again.

"Okay," Dooley said, standing. "Okay."

Clarke's hands stayed clasped in her lap, but her fingers were trembling.

Daniel took note, then said to Dooley, "Maybe we can sit awhile longer?"

Dooley let out a breath and eased back down into her chair.

They waited, avoiding one another's eyes, watching the clock until 12:30 and then 1:00. Finally, by some mutual unspoken agreement, they all shifted and rose.

Clarke looked pale with fatigue. A bit unsteady on her feet, she walked them to the door.

Dooley paused. "We're gonna keep a full team on through the night," she said. "And you'll have someone with you tomorrow."

Sweat glittered on Clarke's forehead, and she raised a palm and wiped at it.

"You'll be okay," Daniel said.

Clarke's eyes fluttered. She fell hard against the wall, banging it with her shoulder. Then she toppled to the floor.

"Shit," Dooley said. "*Shit.*" She leapt up, grabbing for her radio.

Daniel was on his feet, too, instantly, rushing for Clarke, who lay sprawled flat on her back. Her body stiffened, arching onto her heels and the back of her head. Vomit streamed down her cheek. Daniel hit the floor hard on his knees, leaning over her, using his finger to clear her mouth so she wouldn't choke. She convulsed violently and arched again, this time to her side like a speared fish. Eyeballs prominent, pupils dilated, purple creeping beneath the surface of her face.

Frantic, he cupped the back of her head to protect it. "Get them in here now."

"I called!" Dooley shouted. "They're here–they're here!"

He felt her breeze past him. She flung the front door open, yelled. Footsteps thundered up the hall, and two paramedics burst in.

The lead man said, "Hemophiliac, right? Do *not* hit or jostle her."

They moved Daniel brusquely aside and knelt over Clarke, sliding a large-bore IV into either arm. Black-and-blue marks dappled her thin neck. Wine-red splotches moved across the whites of her eyes, spreading like storm clouds. Her rigid body convulsed in bursts, as if the bones were trying to pull through the skin. Her bulging stare held a terrible awareness—she was experiencing every second of this.

"Subconjunctival hemorrhage, ecchymoses—"

"Run the saline wide open."

"Call the ED, tell 'em to get factor eight on standby."

"Pressure here. And here."

"Gentle . . . gentle . . ."

"What tripped her?" Dooley said. "*What tripped her?*"

The skin of Daniel's face tingled, a thousand needle pricks. He lifted his gaze to the stretch of kitchen counter visible through the doorway. The medicine canister rested beside the empty glass marked with milky residue.

"The meds," he said. "He put anticoagulant into her meds."

One of the paramedics paused, mouth still to the phone. "Pull vitamin K, and FFP from the blood bank. It's bad." He hung up, helping lift Clarke onto the stretcher. "Step back. *Move.*"

Daniel and Dooley skipped out of the way.

As Clarke passed, she arched again, her head twisting to the side. A tear of blood rolled over her eyelid and streaked down the pale skin of her temple.

Chapter 43

The following morning the Brashers' kitchen felt like a tomb. The dawn chill wouldn't depart the walls and floor. And the *silence*. Leo sat at the top of the stairs facing the front door below. Perfect posture, rigid spine, hands on his knees. Swimming in one of Daniel's button-ups with the sleeves cuffed, Cris stood at the counter, sipping the mint tea reserved for when she and her stomach were upset and staring blankly out at the early-morning haze muffling the Bay. And Daniel slumped in the tree-house alcove of the living room, gazing through plate glass at the ticky-tacky houses on the swelling chest of Twin Peaks. All those little boxes looked just the same, sure, but pop them open and you'd get a good dose of Left Coast variety. All the colors of the city, a rainbow array of ethnicities. A story beneath each roof, the inevitable tribulations and heartaches, charmed interludes and quiet tragedies. And yes, barbarity, too. Like, say, poisoning a hemophiliac with superwarfarin in an effort to make her bleed out beneath her own skin.

Molly Clarke had been rushed to the hospital, mercifully located a half block away. She'd been quickly stabilized in the emergency room and moved to the ICU, even managing to sit up and take fluids after a few hours. As a UCSF nurse, she'd received extra attentiveness, her colleagues cycling through to check on her, and she'd been left in good company with around-the-clock guards. Dooley had made arrangements for her to be moved to another hospital out of the area, where she'd check in as a Jane Doe. When Daniel had finally headed out of the ICU last night, Dooley had jogged to catch him at the elevators.

"I know it feels like we're being outplayed, but you saved her life today."

Daniel gestured at the crowd of cops and medical staff up the hall. "We all did."

"You made the call to wait with her longer. You saw she was still scared, that she needed us there. If we'd left when I wanted to, she'd have bled out alone in the apartment while I patrolled the lobby."

He could tell by the set of Dooley's mouth that this was hard for her to say.

"We have different jobs," he'd told her, "which means we have to have different concerns. Mine aren't any more noble than yours."

The words echoed now as he sat at the window. He, Leo, and Cris remained spread throughout the second floor as if fearful of proximity, facing different directions, trapped in their own bubbles of dread.

A soft thump sounded at their front door.

Before Daniel could turn his head, Leo was on his feet—impossibly quick for such a sturdy man. The noise carried Daniel up off the couch, and Cris whirled, her mug clanking down on the marble.

Leo said, "Stay here."

His footsteps light down the stairs. The creak of the front door. Cris and Daniel watched each other. A beat. The door thumped closed. Footsteps back up.

Leo appeared, holding the newspaper. "You're gonna want to see this."

Daniel reached him in a few quick strides. The florid headline: SERIAL KILLER LOOSE IN THE CITY. And the subhead: *"Tearmaker Claims Fourth Victim."* A picture of Molly Clarke, who was listed as being in critical condition.

He felt the heat of Cris at his shoulder, then heard a quick intake of air.

"That's her?" Cris said. *"That's* Molly Clarke?"

"Yes," he said. "Why?"

"I know her," Cris said. "She *treated* me. During some of the radiation sessions."

His grip tightened on the newspaper. A horrible notion tugged at him.

Leo had faded back a few steps, giving them space.

Cris shifted her weight, and the pinpoint tattoos on her sternum came visible, a mini-constellation. "What does that mean?" It was clear she was doing her best to stay calm, but still, the realization had brought up a flush of fear on her neck, her cheeks. "That *can't* be a coincidence. Can it?"

He looked down at the screaming front page. The newspaper print left a smudge on the meat of his thumb. He felt the air go out of him.

"I'm not sure." He swallowed dryly and moved toward the stairs. "But I'll find out."

Chapter 44

A conference room in Homicide had been cleared out, a makeshift war room dedicated to the Tearmaker. When Daniel arrived, Dooley got one look at him and told the others to take a coffee break. As he surveyed the inner sanctum with awe, she paced like a great cat before a dry-erase board sporting a spiderweb of connections between map locations, photos of the victims, and rap sheets of Daniel's group members. Stacked on a rear table were sheaves of motorcycle registrations and profiles for the employees of Metro South—even some for workers in the neighboring buildings. Clearly, SFPD had pulled out all stops; assembling this much data must have required a staggering number of man-hours. An array of mounted TVs, tuned to local stations and CNN, popped up visuals about the Tearmaker, the nickname also looping through the news crawls. One reporter had resorted to scared-man-on-the-street interviews about the newly branded killer. Dooley's expression—fury iced with disgust—made clear how she felt about the nickname's leaking. Daniel found himself watching the screens with horrified interest until she muted them so he would focus.

He trudged over and sat in a chair near the latest case files, taking a moment to shape the cyclone of thoughts that had consumed him on the drive over. Trying for patience, Dooley waited. In the background the slick logo of the Tearmaker—a hockey mask with tear tracks—finally vanished from ABC7, replaced by footage of the Gilroy Garlic Fry at AT&T Park.

Daniel spread his hand on the nearest stack of papers. "Marisol Vargas was a professor." His throat was raw, his voice soft and scratchy. "But her field—it was something medical, wasn't it?"

Dooley finally stopped pacing. She lowered herself into a chair carefully, as if she'd grown suddenly fragile. "Public health."

"Did she ever work at UCSF?"

"No. Not full-time at least."

"Look into it," Daniel said. "There'll be a connection. And Kyle Lane. An M.B.A., right? Where'd he work before he moved to the health-food company?"

Dooley grabbed a file, scrabbled through the pages. Then stilled.

Daniel said, "UCSF, right?"

She gave a little nod. "Grants and funding."

"For the oncology department."

"Doesn't say." Dooley tapped the file, her forehead lined with thought. "So there's a medical connection between Clarke, Lane, and Vargas. How does Jack Holley fit in? He was a security guard."

"Did he ever guard—"

"Nope. Not UCSF, not any hospital. From the beginning I oversaw his case *myself,* remember? I know his entire employment history."

"Call and check."

"Daniel—"

"Trust me."

Keeping her gaze on Daniel, Theresa picked up a phone, poked at the numbers with the end of a pen. As she routed through various menus and departments, Daniel zoned out. His blinks grew longer and longer, and then Dooley was repeating his name.

His head snapped up, the sore muscles of his neck making him grimace. "Huh?"

Her eyes were intense, alive. "I had the security firm search every single one of Holley's time sheets. Seems they swung him off his usual job for a one-week period. He usually worked jewelry stores—that's why we missed it—but they got a request to beef up security at UCSF Medical during some big animal-rights protest. The dates were . . ." She flipped through her notepad.

Daniel said, "Fall 2009."

Dooley's mouth fell open a little. "October fifth through eleventh." She wet her lips. "Daniel? You want to tell me what the fuck is going on here?"

He took a deep breath. Readied for the plunge. "The paper this morning. Cristina recognized Molly Clarke. She was treated by her."

"Treated?" Dooley said.

"There were closed trials at UCSF," he said. "Experimental therapy—the radiation seeds?—for heart-cancer patients."

"Cristina had *heart cancer*?"

"Yes. It's rare, but she got it."

"And?" Dooley was clearly fighting for patience.

"The study is the connection. Between the victims."

"But *why*?"

His frustration flared. "I don't know."

"If the victims are connected," Dooley said, "then Cris is connected, too. You'd better—"

"We have a guard at the house," Daniel said. "Before I left, I asked him to stay at her side at all times."

Dooley was still putting it together. "If your wife was involved in the study, that means the killer *meant* for you to get those first death threats. Those envelopes weren't *accidentally* put in your box—he just wanted it to look that way. And if the suspect's in your group like we think . . ."

"Then he—or she—*chose* me. Just like you guessed before."

"Why would they have wanted to involve you like *this*? I mean, you're not just another victim. You're the goddamned focal point."

"You said you can tell when people are lying, Theresa, so look at me closely." He leaned forward. "*I have no idea.*"

"Maybe Cris does."

"I'll talk to her."

"I'll do the same." She rose, tugged open the door, and shouted into the hall, "I want every warm body in here! We just got our first no-shit lead."

Dooley's questioning of Cris gave them nothing more, and after she was finished, Daniel got on the phone with her. She was rattled and bewildered, and he promised to keep her abreast of any developments. Cris wanted to run down the hill for a few things—the last week had left the refrigerator and cupboards sparsely stocked—and he made her promise to keep Leo with her at all times.

At Dooley's request he stayed on in the war room. DAs were called, judges pinned down, and leads flew across monitors and phone lines. The inspectors braced for a dogfight from the pit bulls on the hospital's legal team, but they proved cooperative, supplying information readily as the subpoenas came in. Predictably, human-resource files were turned over first, patient records to follow. Over the course of the morning and afternoon, the picture slowly resolved.

On her sabbatical in 2009, Marisol Vargas had consulted with the oncology department, acting as a project manager for a smattering of studies. During his tenure at UCSF, Kyle Lane had secured and over seen the funding for numerous trials, and Molly Clarke had served as a dedicated nurse during that period for oncology, hematology, and infectious diseases. The only project all three had overlapped on was the experimental brachy study in which Cris had participated.

And yet the inspectors' initial pass through the records of the trial, aided by hospital administrators, had yielded no red flags.

"So," O'Malley said, "who's gonna get the next death threat?"

Daniel grimaced at the thought of another gray interdepartmental envelope arriving in his mailbox.

"Let's consider anyone who played any role in that trial to be at serious risk," Dooley said to the room. "Study coordinators, doctors, the principal investigator, secretaries, chief of staff, the hospital CEO.

Put them on alert and get them out of the area. I don't care if they bitch and moan—after Molly Clarke we are taking no chances."

"Where are we supposed to tell them to go?" Rawlins asked.

"If they're doctors, to their summer homes in Tahoe. If they're broke, to the Motel 6 in Daly City under an assumed name. I don't give a shit, as long as they're not findable until we can get our arms around this thing."

"If the Tearmaker has an issue with some study that took place, why hasn't he attacked the hospital itself?" O'Malley asked.

Dooley said, "Lotta witnesses, lotta security, what with all the animal-rights crap and stem-cell research and abortions."

"No," Daniel said. "That's not why." All eyes moved to him. "It's because this is personal. It's about *individuals*. 'Admit what you've done,' remember?"

"So we're back to the patients who croaked," O'Malley called out, and Dooley cringed a bit.

Most of the study participants had been fortunate like Cris—a testament to the treatment—but two had died. Rawlins was running down information on the deceased in case a relative was nursing a vendetta.

Dooley crossed to a bulletin board and pointed to a row of mug shots—Big Mac, A-Dre, Fang, Martin, Lil, X. Every one of them captured in an unflattering light, pasty and dangerous, up to no good. In two dimensions, thumbtacked to cork, they looked so different—like suspects. Lines fanned from each picture like sun rays, connecting to lists of names broken into subcategories: *relatives, known associates, cell mates.*

Dooley said, "I want *every last connection* checked until we find one that leads back to that trial. Understand?"

Several mumbled assents and the room wound back into motion. After finishing his third cup of surprisingly decent office coffee, Daniel excused himself to go to the bathroom. He washed his face, stared at a reflection he barely recognized. He'd not fully considered the toll the past week had taken on him, and the physical evidence was appalling. Stress etched in each line of his face. His crow's-feet pronounced. Bloodshot eyes. Two-day growth.

When he returned to the beehive of the war room, he was shocked to see that all activity had ceased. The cops were transfixed in their chairs from some newly hatched revelation.

Dread filled his chest. He said, *"What?"*

Dooley was staring at her laptop. "Come here."

He did.

"Look familiar?" She pointed at a PDF file—a scanned form, filled out by hand.

MOTHER: *viviana olvera*

FATHER: _____

PATIENT NAME: *francisca olvera*

PATIENT AGE: *fore*

There it was. The handwriting from the death threats. The words that had set the machinery into motion.

"Viviana Olvera," Daniel said. "She filled out this form."

Dooley's voice cut through the buzz in his head. "We got the *writer* of those death threats. But maybe not the author."

"Why's the father not listed?" he asked.

"Maybe she doesn't know who he is," Rawlins said. "Or he's illegal, married to someone else, in prison, whatever."

"*Mamá*'s hitting up the free clinics, applying for financial assistance, so it was probably better not to document a man and a second income," Dooley said.

"But this is . . . this is *good*, right?" Daniel said. "There's an address here." He pointed farther down the screen.

"Building was torn down in 2010. We ran her through the system. Which wasn't helpful, given she's not *in* the system. According to the doctor's notes on the kid's intake session, the mom's illegal. That's the problem with this. No marriage records, birth records all fucked up, family tree missing all the leaves and branches. Someone pops out a kid three feet across the border . . ." She rubbed her face with her palms. "And no father."

The blank line seemed to stare out at them: FATHER: _____

Dooley shook her head. "So. The million-dollar question is, who's the babydaddy? Because that masked motherfucker's *pissed*." She handed Daniel a sheet of paper, still hot from the printer, that contained a grainy photograph.

A little girl with a spontaneous smile, brown skin, and beautiful almond-shaped eyes. Crooked teeth, some missing, some still growing in. Frizzy dark hair fought into a style of sorts, a rubber band securing a side braid. The thin neck of a fawn. She wore a stained plaid dress with a hole beneath the collar. She was in the throes of an awkward stage, but her energy was so pure, so earnest, that the sight of her was arresting. The kind of kid with music in her laughter.

"Indistinct ethnically," Dooley said. "Could be half black, half Chinese, half anything."

"Which means the father could be Fang," Daniel said. "Or Big Mac."

"Or Martin or A-Dre," Dooley said. "I know they're alibied for certain nights, but I'm not ruling out anyone a hundred percent. A-Dre's brother could be hooked into this, and you could've been rolling around with *him* in the restaurant storage room while A-Dre cooled his heels at his pad. Francisca Olvera could be a cousin, a niece, a friend's kid." She tapped a pencil on the table to accent each possibility. "All we know for sure is that the killer has *some* connection to the group. That's all."

"You're focused on the men," O'Malley said. "But how 'bout Xochitl's kid she gave up for adoption?"

"They tested Viviana Olvera to establish blood type for transfusions," Dooley said. "No question she's the biological mother."

"The age doesn't work out for X's kid anyway," Daniel added.

O'Malley again. "Where are we with Lil's convict ex-husband?"

"Joined a biker gang in Montreal," Rawlins said. "Gubitosi tracked him down. So Lil's ruled out."

"Not *ruled out*," Dooley said, her irritation making clear this line of reasoning had been cause for previous discussion. "Until we get something airtight—and I mean *NASA-shuttle* airtight—we don't *eliminate* suspects. We"—and here the other inspectors joined in weary chorus—*"reduce the likelihood of their involvement."* Dooley blinked, half annoyed, half amused. "That's right. And we divert resources accordingly."

Daniel asked the question that had been scratching at him since he'd seen Francisca's face. "How'd the girl do? With the medical treatment?"

Dooley and O'Malley exchanged a look, as if just now remembering that Daniel had come in late. "She wasn't in the study," Dooley said.

"What do you mean?" Daniel said. "The form you showed me. That was for the trial."

"She was enrolled," Dooley said. "But at the last minute, she got bumped."

All the heat in Daniel's body seemed to rush to his face. His hand dimpled the printout.

"There was a scene," Dooley said. "And guess which security guard escorted mother and child off hospital premises? Jack Holley."

"What . . . ?" Daniel had to clear his throat and try again. "What happened to her? Francisca?"

"There's a morgue record in the database," Dooley said. "January seventh, 2010."

Something curdled in his stomach, a sickness spreading up through his chest, out into his limbs. "Where was she treated?"

"We're still digging," O'Malley said. "But as you know, medical records are tough. We'll pull subpoenas, start serving every clinic and hospital in the city, but it could be a slog. You saw the crappy job Viviana Olvera did filling out that one form. These people are happy to take advantage of the system, but they don't like being *in* it."

Dooley pushed back in her seat. "He's right. Mom's illegal and broke. Dad's MIA. Records of the kid are gonna be sketchy at best."

Daniel's voice, so hoarse he was having trouble getting words out: "That's why she was the easiest one to drop."

He pictured the woman in the yellow slicker, braving rain and traffic, pointing up at him and Cris in their bedroom. Viviana Olvera. A grieving mother.

Dooley stood, concerned. "What's going on, Daniel? Do you know something about this?"

Already he was running back to the bathroom, his gorge rising.

Chapter 45

Occupying the nineteenth floor of the Mark Hopkins Hotel, the storied Top of the Mark held a unique place in San Francisco lore. With its Art Deco flair and wraparound views of the city, the venerable sky lounge attracted rich tourists, pedigreed locals, and the occasional young couple willing to pay a cover charge for dim lights and fussy waitstaff. Many a merger had been lubricated here by offerings from the famed hundred-martini menu and more than a few engagement rings passed across the starched periwinkle tablecloths. John Barrymore had once brought his pet monkey here, the story went, to show him the view. The lounge was a sentimental favorite of not just simians but the Ladies Who Cocktail as well.

True to James's tip, Daniel found his mother there on an upholstered settee, facing the span of jetliner windows as if she were piloting the whole building in for landing on the choppy night waters of the Bay. A coiffed friend of hers whom Daniel half recognized sat in a club chair, two gimlets pinning down the roundtop to the side. Daniel said, "I need to speak to you alone."

"Darling, I—"

"*Now.*"

Stiffly, the other woman rose, fingertips adjusting her necklace and conveying offense at the same time, and then Daniel and Evelyn were alone. Evelyn sipped her gimlet, returned to the view. "That was forceful. Perhaps you should sit down."

"I'm fine."

"Yes, you seem perfectly in control."

"The closed medical trial Cristina was in at UCSF, the one that saved her life. A child was bumped out at the last minute." He paused, almost afraid to continue. "Did you do it?"

"Maybe you should sit down."

"I don't *need* to sit down."

A waiter came over, hands clasped, all impeccable decorum and curated blond hair. Most anywhere else in the city, you could glance around and feel like you were at the UN, but up here on the nineteenth floor, the clientele and staff were, save for the Hispanic barbacks, tennis-club white. "Is everything all right, Mrs. Brasher?"

"He's my son."

"I'm sorry. I didn't recognize you, sir."

Daniel sensed the waiter's retreat. He kept his stare on the side of his mother's face; Evelyn craned her neck for no man.

"I called Bill Emerald," she said. "You remember Bill. Head of development for the hospital?"

Daniel tamped down a surge of impatience that threatened to explode out of him. "And . . . ?"

"He told me that the trial was full. That he could get someone bumped."

His voice was shaking. "What did you say?"

"Do it."

"Just . . . *do it*?"

"Of course," Evelyn said. "It's what you wanted." She granted him a brief glance. "I really think you should sit down, Daniel."

He sat.

They looked out at the tycoon view, the night-lit towers of Grace Cathedral, the shiny Bentleys at the Pacific-Union Club across the street. To the north, the rotating beam from Alcatraz pierced the fog, an alien probe taking the measure of the land.

"That's *not* what I asked for," he said.

"You came to me for my help. You said, 'I've never asked you for anything in my life. I'm asking you to help me save her.'"

"But I *never* knew that someone would have to be . . ." He couldn't finish the sentence.

"You asked me to get it done. So I got it done. What did you *think* would happen?"

"I thought they'd make room for her."

"There's only so much room, Daniel. You knew that."

"I *didn't* know that. I did not."

"Then why did you come to *me*?"

"Because you . . ."

Evelyn nursed her drink. "That's right. Because I know people. Who are beholden to me. For favors. Do you have *any* idea how much money we have given—*generationally*—to that medical center? You must. There is an auditorium at that hospital with our family name stamped on it. Our money poured the foundations for half the institutions in this city. You grew up between our box at the opera house and Director's Circle dinners for SFMOMA. And you claim not to know how this works?"

He sat, leaden and speechless, part of the chair.

"Everyone has a price," Evelyn said. "Yours was the life of your fiancée."

"I didn't know," he said. "I *never* knew."

Evelyn touched the rim to her lips. A delicate sip. "Did you tell her?"

"What?"

"That you were going to come to me for help. Did. You. Tell. Her?" She waited patiently.

"No," he said.

"Why not?"

It wasn't quite a rhetorical question, but it was clear that no answer would be required. When he'd gone to his mother for help, he hadn't known the contours of the course of action she would take, but he'd known that Cristina would not like the shape of it. So he'd kept it from her.

And, in some manner, he'd kept it from himself.

Evelyn finished her drink. The waiter appeared to ask if she wanted another and she said, "Please." It arrived sometime later, and she rested her hand on the elegant glass stem but did not lift it from the table.

Daniel said, "So you did it just to lord it over me? To show me what a hypocrite I am?"

She shifted in the chair, rearing slowly, shoulders squaring to him. "Is that *really* what you think?"

"I don't know what I think," he said. "Why did you do it?"

"I did it because no matter how shitty a mother I am and have been, you're still my son. And when you came to me, broken and devastated and lost, I would have done *anything* to take away your pain."

He rose, his legs numb beneath him all the way to the elevator. The car sank down and down, and then he was out onto the street. The city looked just the same, of course.

It was as it had always been.

Chapter 46

The ring of Daniel's phone interrupted his stupor at the wheel. He'd called Dooley and given her the bones of the revelation, and from what she'd heard in his voice, she must have known he was in no shape to flesh it out at the moment. Then it had been ten silent minutes bumping over the hills of the city toward home, his dread mounting as he neared the conversation to come.

And now the ring, shrill as a scream in the confines of his car.

A voice, lined with annoyance and concern: "Where *are* you?"

Kendra Richardson. His boss.

A panicked glance at the clock showed 8:24 P.M. It was, he realized, Monday night. Session—long-forgotten session—was supposed to have started almost a half hour ago.

"Got a group here waiting," she continued. "Or did you forget?"

"I'm not . . . I can't . . . I can't come in."

"Look, I know there was a gaffe last session. After how things ended, your timing to not show up isn't exactly ideal."

"Move it to tomorrow night. I'll be there then. Tell them for me."

"You know how essential consistency is."

"Kendra. You have to take my word for it. I *cannot* do this right now."

"You've never pushed a session."

"I need to tonight."

He hung up and turned onto his street. The block was throbbing—a valet in front of Ted and Danika Shea's and several attendants waiting with champagne glasses on silver trays. Nearing his house, he slowed. A parked car blocked his driveway, and he felt his agitation and self-rage bubble over. He screeched to a stop and climbed out.

"Take your car, sir?"

"No—I need you to move that SUV."

"I'm so sorry. Is that your residence? I think that's a VIP guest of the Sheas. She parked there before we showed up, so we don't have the keys."

Daniel charged toward the side gate, past the officious staff—"Kir royale? Crémant d'Alsace?"—and into the crowded backyard. Aside from a spotlit cube of metal the size of an industrial dryer, the yard was mood dim, and Daniel had a hard time locating either host. From all sides he was assailed with gourmet-hipster fare wielded and announced with great aplomb—short-rib sliders, sustainable sea bass on risotto crackers, endive spoons smeared with lemon-herb goat cheese. Nostrils quivered over chilled Napa Valley whites. The conversations pressed in on him, about what people *weren't* eating and wearing, what *wasn't* cage-free or grass-fed or sweatshop-stitched. He pushed past a stocky gentleman announcing through a full mouth that he'd been working on opening his navel chakra, and he spotted Danika across the way, waving her arms like a well-heeled carnival barker, the event about to commence. A hush fell over the yard as a sculptor wearing strategically torn jeans threw a switch, and the large metal cube crumpled in on itself with, Daniel had to admit, some majesty. But the pointlessness arrested him. He knew that it was his own self-loathing turned inside out and vomited on everything around him, but he couldn't help himself.

Ted was shaking hands and clutching elbows as if he'd actually accomplished something himself, and Daniel neared, calling across the bobbing heads, "Ted. *Ted!* I need a car moved so I can—"

"You made it!" Ted shouted, parting a circle to fold Daniel into its embrace. "Daniel's a smart guy, used to work in finance—let's ask *him*." He shoulder-squeezed a lanky-haired man at his side. "Wes here runs a Web site on social and environmental awareness, and he's started a boycott on gas stations that import from the Middle East. Until *all* our troops are home—"

"Look, Ted, there's a car blocking my driveway—"

"Come *on*, Daniel. Take a second. This is important. You *must* see the value in a boycott like that." Ted's face was alcohol-flushed, and Danika had appeared at his side. The discussion was public now, and there were stakes. "I mean, isn't it a wonderful—"

"—valets don't have the keys—"

"—hit Shell and Exxon and Chevron where it hurts? In the pocketbook?"

"—emergency, really need to get home and talk to Cris—"

"If we can get *enough* people to—"

"It won't matter!" Daniel said.

The others reeled back a little. Ted came at him, patting the air, all strong chin and hopeful diplomacy. "Let's just calm down here."

"You're already calm," Daniel said. "I'm the one who's worked up."

"What *possible* objection could you have to a Web site that—"

"Because it's *naïve*, Ted. It doesn't *matter* if you boycott the Middle East for gasoline. Where are you gonna import from? *Nigeria?* With their great environmental and human-rights record? So you'll boycott Chevron until they . . . *what?* Bring in crude from Russia that's really Iraqi oil sold through Baltic middlemen? It's a *global commodity*. Where you gas up your fucking flex-fuel Honda isn't gonna change anything."

At some point the string quartet had silenced, ceding the stage of the backyard to Daniel's rant. The people nearest wilted; those farther away stood on tiptoe.

The lanky-haired man shook his head in disgust. "You object to social awareness?"

"No. I object to social awareness as *wardrobe*."

"Then *what*?" Danika said. "We do nothing about anything? Is that your plan?"

"We admit," Daniel said wearily, "that we're all full of *shit*."

"No," some brave soul in the back called out. "Just you."

"Really?" Daniel spun, gesturing at the party. "You're here to watch the air get *sucked out of a metal cube*. How many LED lightbulbs to offset that energy expenditure? That's what we do, though. Buy conflict-free diamonds and eat net-free tuna and feed our guilt with *righteousness*. Who are we kidding anyway? Ourselves? Each other? Half our focus goes into consuming and the other half into making that consumption look principled."

It was true, sure, or at least a version of true, but the truth could be used like a baseball bat. There was a sweetness in yielding to his anger this way. A *relief*. He was swinging that bat, smashing up the scenery, and he didn't want to stop.

Color rouged Danika's cheeks. "Not *us*," she said. "We have been extremely—"

"Danika. You recycle your tinfoil and fly to Europe three times a year. You and Ted and your three au courant children have a carbon footprint the size of *Godzilla's*. It's *inherent*. We want to be good people and do good things, but we also like our *lives*. And we want what's best for ourselves and people we love, and no matter how hard we try, there's no unhooking that from the rest of the planet."

His anger had deflated, and he detected a note of pleading in his own voice. A hush had fallen across the yard. He caught sight of the rise of his and Cristina's house, the drawn blinds of the bedroom window, returning his mind to the task before him. The party had chilled into a spine-arching silence, every face directed at him.

"Now," he said, "will whoever parked in front of my driveway please move their fucking SUV?"

Chapter 47

Daniel keyed in the alarm code and trudged up the stairs, patting Leo the Sentinel on the shoulder as he passed. The lights were off on the second floor, the table elegantly set, candles flickering off the glass and marble. Cris sat at the end, seemingly unable to repress a smile. A margarita waited at his place, and at the center of the table were fresh-cut roses and a silver-plated dome cover resting atop a platter.

"I figure," she said, "with everything going on, we could use one night to catch our breath. And to remember what it's like to be together alone. Or *almost* alone. Right, Leo?"

Leo's voice lofted up the stairwell: *"Right."*

"Cris . . ." Daniel said.

"I want to just relax and talk about what our lives are gonna look like when all this is over. Sit and have a drink, *mi vida.*"

"Cris. You have to put all this away."

She gestured at the silver dome. "I have something special for you."

"Not tonight."

He drew nearer, and she saw him, and her face changed.

He started talking before he lost his nerve, the hard facts spilling out of him. He barely heard the words as he was saying them; they were lost beneath the white rush in his ears. But he registered a set of impressions. A glitter on his wife's cheek. An abrupt, clogged inhalation. Her chair sliding out from the table at a sharp angle. And then she was standing, taking a half step away from him, bent at the waist, the vertebrae showing at the back of her neck. Her face, war-zone numb, the eyes gone.

"What did you *do*?" she broke in. "That girl is dead. Because of *me*." She doubled over, clutching her stomach. "And I had no choice in it."

"I never knew that someone else would be kicked out of—"

"That's the worst part," she said. "You didn't even *know* what you did."

"When you were sick, you were terrified, too—or don't you remember? You knew I was going to *everyone* I knew for help. What do you think that meant?"

"I don't know."

"That's how the world works, Cristina. Whether you want to see it or not. We are *privileged*. Our luxuries—our *lives*—rest on the sacrifices of others. We get opportunities other people don't. And no matter how much we try to dress that up or dress it down, it's still true." Each breath thundered through his rib cage. "What my mom did for me, I did for you."

"What if you *couldn't*? That girl—her parents—they didn't *have* that power."

"So what are we supposed to do? Pretend we *don't* have it? Not take care of each other because other people can't take care of their own? You can't separate it. How many patients didn't get into the closed trial at *all* because of education or geography or timing? What if I'd called two days earlier and we'd gotten your paperwork in before that girl? Is that different?"

"It is," she said fiercely. "It *is* different. I don't know how. I don't know why. It just *is*." She lifted her glimmering eyes to him. "And you know it, too. That's why you kept it from me."

"The only thing I didn't tell you is I went to my *mother*. Who you uniquely hate."

"I don't *hate* her. I pity her. She's a privileged—"

"You know what, Cristina? You're privileged, too."

She was weeping now, openly, her words a blur. "You said you had a picture. I want to see her."

Reluctantly, he pulled the crumpled paper from his back pocket. He started to smooth it out, but she snatched it from him. She looked at the printed photo, and a noise escaped her. "What was her name?"

The word came out dry and cracked: "Francisca."

Tears spilled down Cris's cheek, one after another, silently. "That was my nana's name." A drop tapped the picture of the girl, that gaptoothed smile, the frizzy braid, those oversize brown eyes. "She could just as well have been my cousin, or my niece. If I didn't marry you, *I* could be that mom filling out the—"

"But you *did* marry me! You did. And I was born to Evelyn and Denis Brasher. We can't rewind our circumstances."

"Look at her face." Cristina held up the paper. "Even in the middle of what we were dealing with . . . How could you do it?"

"She didn't have a face then!"

All life, all warmth, seemed to vanish from Cristina's body. Her features a mask he didn't recognize. She turned her stare from him and moved to the steps, minding each one as if walking through darkness.

The bedroom door closed upstairs, and he stood for a time, staring at the floor, reminding himself to breathe. Some impulse seized him, and he went to the table, lifted the silver dome.

Beneath, centered on the platter, the wand of a home pregnancy test.

The sight vibrated him, everything humming with sudden resonance. The cravings. The nausea. The nervous excitement lighting her face as she'd waited at the head of the table.

With a trembling hand, he lifted the wand. Even by candlelight, the plus symbol was clear.

Chapter 48

The buzz of the cell phone against Daniel's thigh jarred him awake on the couch, and as he lurched up, digging at his pocket, the memory of his fight with Cris flooded in at him. And that pregnancy test, which on any other night would have been cause for celebration.

"Counselor? Counselor? You there?"

He moved the iPhone from his face, read the time on the glowing screen: *1:14 A.M.*

The voice came again. "It's Fang, man. He's in deep trouble."

"Martin?"

"He called me. Guess he couldn't reach his sponsor. He was on the edge. Heading to a club. I couldn't talk him down. I'd go after him, but I got work early—"

"Shit. Where's he going?"

As Martin gave the address, Daniel shoved his feet into his shoes. Pulling on a jacket, he dialed Dooley, who sounded wide awake.

He asked, "Is someone on Fang?"

"Not at this second. With no new deadline, we can't go twenty-four/seven on six suspects. Why?"

He told her.

"And you're gonna go meet him?" Dooley said in disbelief. "At night. Alone. On his home turf, blocks from where you were attacked, maybe by him?"

"If Walter Fang goes into that club, his life falls apart. It's that simple."

"This could be a ploy to draw you out."

"Yeah."

"Is it worth the risk?"

He pictured Fang on the chair, foot nervously tapping the tile: *I do bad when I drink*. Three months of hard-fought sobriety.

"It's the job. Stay by the phone in case I get stabbed."

Dooley's sigh sounded like a growl. "I'll send a car to meet you by the club."

"Ask them to park, wait, and watch. I need to talk to him in private."

He hung up and ran for the stairs. A dark form midway down made him jump back. With everything that had gone on tonight, he'd forgotten about Leo.

All-knowing, all-hearing Leo. Where had he learned that skill—when to assert a comforting presence, when to give space? From navigating countless crises, no doubt. This life-shifting upheaval for Daniel was for him just another day of work.

"Want backup?" the shadow asked.

"No, thanks. Stay with Cris. Just . . . make sure she's safe."

"You tell her you're going?" Leo asked.

"You've heard enough tonight to know the answer to that."

"Maybe she'd want to know before you wind up dead in some Chinatown alley."

Daniel tried to slide past, but Leo encircled his biceps with a giant hand. His grip was gentle, but the force behind it was evident. Their faces were close there in the narrow stairwell. It was dark, but Leo's pate caught a streetlight glint through the window.

"You're gonna be a father," Leo said.

Daniel shook free and kept on down the stairs.

Daniel gunned it to Grant Avenue, pulling over on a seedy stretch several blocks from the touristy thoroughfare. It was the oldest street in the city, and tonight it looked it. He braved the club, which was more like a glorified bar, for a quick walk-through. Seeing no sign of Fang, he returned to his car and waited.

He looked up and down the curb, pegging a sedan a half block away for an unmarked police car. Shadow in the front seat. Knowing that a cop was there was a comfort, though he felt a familiar pulse in his stomach as he waited. What if Dooley was right and this *was* a planned ambush?

Before he could dwell on the point, he spotted Fang among a crew of young Chinese men who emerged from a side street and started for the club. Daniel got out, jogged after them. "Walter? *Walter?*"

They turned. They were dressed similarly—athletic wear, vibrant sneakers, low-slung designer jeans. It occurred to Daniel just how outnumbered he was.

A guy wearing rose-tinted sunglasses slapped Fang on the shoulder. "The fuck is this *gweilo*?"

Fang froze, an elk in the crosshairs.

Daniel licked his lips, which had gone dry. "I'm a friend of his father's," he said.

Fang eased out an exhale.

The guy tilted his head to Daniel respectfully. Then, to Fang, "Meet you inside."

The others kept on toward the club, leaving Daniel and Fang alone on the street. Fang's head was lowered, and he was breathing hard—an almost-raging bull.

"I'm mad at you," he finally said.

Daniel flashed on the masked face in the restaurant stairwell. Then on the picture of Francisca Olvera. That little-girl face, as ethnically blended as the city itself. *Could* Fang be her father?

"For, ah, ah, ah . . . for abandoning us."

"So take it out on me," Daniel said. "In group. Not on yourself."

Fang looked across at the neon sign above the awning. Then down at his banana-yellow sneakers. "You're already gone. You . . . ah, you blew us off tonight."

The hurt in his eyes was undeniable.

Daniel stepped closer, within stabbing range. Past Fang's shoulder he could see the undercover cop, now out of the car, leaning against the door, having a smoke and pretending not to look over. A half block suddenly seemed like a long ways.

"I'm sorry for that," Daniel said. "I had a personal matter come up that I had to handle. But don't use that as an excuse to fall off the wagon."

"You're leaving anyway," Fang said. "What do you care?"

"If I don't care about you, what the hell am I doing out here at one forty-five in the morning?"

"It's your *job.*"

"Yeah, I'm killing it with overtime right now."

Fang gave the slightest smirk.

"Five more days sober," Daniel said, "and you can buy yourself a new pair of Jordans."

Fang's mouth twisted. "*Jordans?* Man, you are the most unhip person I ever met." He turned for the club.

"Where's your chip?" Daniel asked. "Your sober medallion?"

Fang glowered at him, then dug the coin from his pocket. An imprinted circle inside a triangle read 3 MONTHS.

"A lotta work to get that coin," Daniel said. "Night after night."

"Gimme a break."

"No," Daniel said. "This is it. A dividing line. Think about where you'll be tomorrow. Think about what it's gonna feel like when you wake up."

Fang rubbed his thumb over the coin. Then he turned and hurled it. It pinged off something in the darkness. "I want to . . . ah, ah. I want to go in. I'm going in." He rolled his muscular shoulders, let his hands slap to his sides.

"What do you expect me to do right now?" Daniel said.

"Try 'n' argue me into not going in."

"What if you don't need me to?" Daniel asked. "What if you can make this choice on your own?"

Fuming, Fang pouched his lips, looked away. Maybe his anger over Daniel's departure had been what had made him act so bizarrely shut down in Sue Posada's office; after all, it had been the day after the receptionist had accidentally spilled the news to the group. And now that anger was driving him back to the bottle.

"Whatever choice you make, you'd better be ready to live with it," Daniel said. "Because right now. This moment. Your whole life can change."

Up the street the club door opened and the guy with tinted sunglasses leaned out. "What the hell, Walter?" he shouted.

Fang gave Daniel a final glare and stepped at him, bumping his shoulder as he brushed past and kept on, walking away from the club. Daniel closed his eyes and let out a pent-up breath. He heard the friend swear in Cantonese and the club door bang closed. Then he turned and watched Fang storming away, head ducked, hands shoved in his pockets.

The sight, he realized, warmed what was left of his heart.

Chapter 49

"Cris, look. Open the door. Come on."

"It's a new day. Let's talk about this. Or fight about it. Or whatever you need to do."

"I'm sorry, okay? I *didn't know*. How the hell was I supposed to know what exactly my mom was gonna do? How am I responsible for that?"

"Don't you think this is getting a little stupid?"

"Are you there? Are you okay in there? You're *pregnant*. Shouldn't you eat something? I just want to make sure you're all right before I leave. I have to meet Dooley soon."

"Look, I know I fucked up, and I'm really sorry. I should've at least told you I was going to my mom to ask her for help."

"Okay. I gotta go in ten. I don't *want* to, but . . . Leo's here if you need anything. I guess I'll see you—or I guess I'll talk to you later. Through the door again. 'Cuz this is really fucking productive. Sorry. I . . . Sorry."

"I'm not leaving unless I hear you're okay. So you're gonna need to say something now. Or I'm coming in there."

At last a faint voice floated through the door. "Go away," it said.

Chapter 50

Designated "The Original Cold Day Restaurant" on its plates and mugs, Tadich Grill is the oldest eating establishment in the state. It predates Coit Tower and the Golden Gate Bridge and does its best to conjure the past, from the dangling Art Deco light fixtures and brass accents to the brash, white-jacketed staff. Daniel found Dooley toward the end of a sailboat-length handmade mahogany bar that had survived the move from Clay Street a half century ago. She stuck out among the lawyers and financial consultants sitting shoulder to shoulder. Even more professionals lined the walls, flicking lint off their dark pinstripes as they waited for stools to free up.

She'd held a chair for him, a midday miracle effected no doubt by her flinty cop demeanor. On the starched napery before her sat the trademark bowl of lemon wedges and half loaf of sourdough, as well as sand dabs, oysters, and bowls of clam chowder *and* cioppino. She slurped at a half shell and said, "Couldn't make up my mind. Plus, I eat when I'm stressed." She made a have-at-it gesture toward the array of plates.

He shook his head, his appetite having gone missing since he'd seen the printed face of Francisca Olvera. "You're more stressed than before?" he asked.

"Uh, have you watched the news? The Tearmaker: bigger than Bundy. Anderson Cooper and Brian Williams, top billing on Drudge. Jon Stewart even riffed on it."

"Where are you with the case?"

"To start with the physical evidence," Dooley said, "the shiny new old coins are still baffling. Did he work for the mint? Is he OCD? We're looking into acids, coin collector's gear, but we don't even have a strong working hypothesis." She spooned some clam chowder into her mouth. "Molly Clarke is stable, moved, and hidden. We've tracked down and relocated other workers involved with the medical trial, key hospital staff have raised their security—"

"The *girl*," he prompted.

"We are looking into everything we can find on that kid. Which ain't much. O'Malley and Rawlins zeroed in on a couple of clinics that treated her, found the place she died. They're running down staff from four years ago, but there's a lot of turnover, and those they've found don't remember particulars. A lot of sick kids between then and now, unfortunately. The father is still unknown, and the mother— Viviana Olvera—fell off the fucking radar, probably to help plan *this*. But it's a huge break. Thanks to you. And your wife. How's she doing in the face of . . . ?"

The smell of mesquite wafted over from the grill. Daniel said, "She's been happier."

"Because of your mother's involvement?"

"And mine. In going to my mother."

Dooley stopped chewing. Or at least slowed. "You never told her."

"No."

After a respectful pause, Dooley tore a hunk of sourdough from the loaf and swiped it through the remnants of clam chowder. "There's a long list of people we need to protect here. Anyone who had anything to do with Francisca Olvera getting bumped from that study. And your mom? She's the one who pulled the strings."

"I'll talk to her."

"Get her out of town. We haven't received the next death threat yet." Her gaze was focused, intense. "Could be anyone."

"I've got group tonight. I'll check my mailbox."

"We already took the liberty. Nothing in there from yesterday or today."

He said, "So we wait?"

"Wait," she said. "And look over our shoulders."

The wing chair enfolded Evelyn like a cloak, the library air redolent of leather-bound books and smoldering birch from the fireplace. She glared out at Daniel. "You have *got* to be kidding me."

"You made the call, Mom. You got Cris into the study. Which means you're a potential target, too."

A dismissive flare of the hand. "Oh, honey. Getting victimized— that's for *other* people."

"Mom. I've seen this guy. Up close. Believe me: You don't want to be up here on a cliff in a house with three hundred windows."

She studied him for a few moments, then said, "James?"

An instant later he was in the doorway.

"Pack us," she said. "We're going to the Fairmont."

James eased back out of view.

"Mom, this is serious. You need to leave the city."

"What's the killer gonna do?" she said. "Storm the penthouse at the Fairmont?"

They argued for a few minutes, but she was resolute as ever, and soon enough Daniel found himself in the quartz driveway leaning against his car, watching James supervise a raft of attendants wielding hatboxes and matching luggage. The town car departed, and James ran back to the garage, and moments later there Evelyn was in the backseat of her ridiculous 1938 Bugatti coupe with its Batmobile aerodynamics and magisterial snail-shell wheel wells. It pulled even with Daniel, reducing the smart car to a tricycle.

"I'd imagine Chiquita was upset at last night's nonrevelation," Evelyn said over a slab of tinted window.

"Cristina. And yes."

"Well. Thank you for seeing me to the room. I'm sure you'd rather not, but your sense of duty is admirable."

He followed her across the city to the peak of Nob Hill, where he left his car with the fifty-dollar valet and rushed into the mob of waiting hotel staff. He was recognized by the manager and ushered into the elevator with Evelyn and the penthouse staff, which included a butler, a trio of housekeepers, a massage therapist, and a chef, and then they were riding up to the most expensive hotel suite in the United States.

Occupying the entire span of the eighth floor, the penthouse featured respective bedrooms in purple, cream, and peach, and a living room so large it dwarfed the grand piano. JFK had stayed here, as had Tony Bennett. Daniel recalled his mother once complaining that she'd been unable to secure a weekend due to a booking by King Hussein of Jordan. Or had it been Gorbachev?

The staff acquainted Evelyn with recent upgrades, taking notes on clipboards, making wine selections, adjusting thermostats in various rooms. Daniel grew impatient, exhausted by the pomp and spectacle. They passed through the vast dining room with its silver-and-black chinoiserie wall covering, the chandelier and sconces glimmering with thousands of bits of Czech crystal. The lofty rotunda of the library featured gold-leafed constellations against an azure sky, and they'd added a secret passageway behind the books of the second story. No, Mrs. Brasher would not be needing use of the Ferrari California. Yes, roast suckling lamb would be ideal, as long as it was boned, at 8:00 P.M.

As the butler set out the Tiffany china and the housekeepers arranged fresh-cut flowers in Chinese porcelain vases, Evelyn retired to the nearest bedroom.

Daniel found her sitting on the bed, framed by an immense David Hockney. Spread on the duvet beside her was a hotel spa robe, Evelyn's initials freshly stitched at the breast.

"Well," he said tightly, "I'm gonna get back to my day, then."

"So soon?"

He paused at the door. Struggled to keep the hostility from his voice. "I've got work."

"You won't stay for dinner?"

"I'm assuming you'll be well looked after in my absence."

"But, honey." She gave a wry smirk and flung an arm across her forehead in mock Lichtensteinian despair. "It's all just so *inconvenient*."

Chapter 51

Cris trudged downstairs, her face drawn and gray. She still wore Daniel's button-up shirt, but the cuffed sleeves had fallen to cover her hands.

Leo sat at the counter, gun resting near his hand about three inches from his pinkie, a placement he had calculated punctiliously, no doubt, as the ideal distance for a grab-and-aim.

She crossed to the sink and vomited neatly two, three times. Leo rose, handed her a dish towel, and returned to his stool. Wiping her mouth, she ran the water and the disposal, then filled a glass and sipped it. She turned to face Leo.

He said nothing.

Frustrated, she clicked on the small countertop TV and flipped until a news reporter appeared outside a nondescript house, her dark hair whipped by the wind.

"*—proving baffled by the so-called Tearmaker killer, who has struck seemingly without regard for demographic or geography, including here at the Noe Valley residence of Kyle Lane. An SFPD spokesperson announced that they are working hard to uncover some method to the madness—*"

She pointed the remote again, and the screen blinked to blank. Another sip of water. She looked at Leo.

Leo looked straight ahead.

Cris said, "Well?"

He spread his hands flat on the marble, as if examining a mani-cure. "When I was a child in the seventies, Syrian army special forces entered my country. They supported Sunni militias. Unleashed them. My entire family was tortured and killed. My mother and sister, raped and murdered. My father, dishonored and shot. Two brothers. Seven cousins. Three aunts, an uncle."

Cris's throat bobbed. She set down the glass. Her hand had moved instinctively to her belly. After a moment she nodded for him to con-tinue.

"I've done a lot of things for a long time now," Leo said in his same clipped, even voice. "But I will never for the life of me under-stand what you rich, safe people fight about."

Chapter 52

The group members were there waiting, arrayed in the chairs as Daniel entered the room. A thin current of air from the cracked window met him in the threshold, cooling the nervous sweat at his hairline and throat. Despite the usual protections in place around Metro South, he was on edge.

One of these six was likely a relative of a little girl in whose death he'd had a hand.

He sensed the weight of the stares on him and rehearsed again the opening words he'd planned. Turning, he closed the door behind him.

That's when he saw the tin of Skoal dipping tobacco in the trash can in the corner.

The green circular label—LONG CUT WINTERGREEN—was pronounced against the liner bag. The sight locked him up. Brought him back to the death match in the restaurant storage room, the knife tip inches from his eye, the sickly-sweet tobacco breath pushed through the perforations in the black mask, washing across his face.

He set a hand against the closed door. His mouth moved before he could consider the words. "Whose Skoal is this?"

Puzzled silence emanated from behind him.

He turned. "There's a tin of dipping tobacco in the trash. Whose is it? Anyone here dip?"

"No, Dad," X said, leaning back in her chair nearest the door.

"We got POs busting into our houses at all hours, searching us in front of our *families*." Big Mac shot a glare at Daniel. Was it accusatory? "Now we gotta get cavity-checked for fucking tobacco?"

"Cavity-checked," Daniel said, meeting Big Mac's glare, "might be overstating it."

"Why you care anyways?" A-Dre asked.

"I want to know who's using stimulants during session." A feeble explanation, which he regretted the instant it left his lips.

They all shook their heads or stared at the ceiling, annoyed.

"Looks like no one," Martin said.

"So someone else came in here to . . . what? Use the trash can?"

"What's your problem, Counselor?" Big Mac asked.

"My problem is that I ask for *honesty*." All his pent-up rage steaming out. "And *someone* in here isn't being honest with me."

The members looked a bit shocked by his quick anger.

"Honesty," X repeated, with a pointed glare.

Excellent. Thirty seconds into session and he'd alienated the room further.

He made a mental note to ask Dooley to check the tin for fingerprints, collected himself, and took his place on a hard metal chair.

Before he could say anything, Lil rubbed her bare arms and asked, "Is anyone else cold?" and Fang muttered, "Here we . . . ah, ah, go again."

Daniel blinked a few times, trying to get his head in the game. The face of Francisca Olvera was branded into his brain, and he looked for a match in the features of the members around him. He saw her in every one of their eyes—the pressure of the situation distorting his perspective.

The expressions ranged from aloof to hostile. Last session had after all featured a fight and the revelation of Daniel's impending departure. Fighting through distraction, he said, "I owe you an apology."

So far, so good.

He drew out the pause, studying the faces to see if anyone was reading something else into the apology. Something more intense, involving a girl who'd died nearly four years ago. But the reactions were tentative, unreadable.

Big Mac hunched in the chair opposite, bringing into view a nasty bruise swelling the back of his hand. Another trash-can mash-up? Or an injury sustained in the restaurant brawl? He was wearing a mustard Carhartt jacket and—of course—generic black work boots. Daniel thought about the undercover cops posted around the building, Dooley teed up on CALL on the iPhone in his pocket. How long would it take them to crash the room if the situation combusted?

He had zoned out, he realized, looking at those boots, and he reeled himself back to the room. "I should have brought up earlier that I'll be leaving," he said. "I'm sorry that you found out the way you did. It was unnecessarily jarring, and I should have handled it better. But I will see you through this transition and make myself available to you for no cost at my private practice after I leave."

"For how long?" A-Dre said.

"As long as it takes."

Lil nodded first, and then a few of the faces softened.

But not Big Mac's. "You got something to answer about," he said.

Daniel felt his mouth go dry. "What?"

The hand strengthener had made a reappearance, Big Mac clutching it in his bruised fist like a security blanket or a badge of honor—*clank-clank*. "What happened last night?"

Big Mac's gaze moved from Daniel to Fang, and Daniel realized he was referring to the episode at the club. Martin must have filled him in. A relieved exhale hissed through Daniel's teeth.

Fang crossed his legs, sneaker to knee. A self-conscious twitch of his neck, not quite a shrug. "It was . . . ah, ah, no big deal. Nothing happened."

At Fang's words Daniel's thoughts pulled into abrupt focus. The edges of his perception blurred, and all at once there was nothing outside these four walls, no closed trials, no little girl dying of heart cancer, no featureless killer.

He zeroed in on Fang. "Nothing *happened*? What are you talking about?"

Fang stiffened, his forehead wrinkling.

Daniel ticked the points on his fingers. "You trusted Martin enough to call him. You trusted me. You made a great choice. You *didn't* go into the club. You *didn't* get drunk. You *didn't* get into a fight or blow your sobriety or wind up in trouble with the cops. You *didn't* miss your session tonight." He paused. "*Everything* happened last night."

Fang settled back into himself, blank-faced, but Daniel had learned to read him well enough to see his mind at work. He also knew to move on and give Fang some time with this new interpretation, so he asked Lil to take center chair.

She settled into the seat and cleared her throat softly. "I went out to a church social," she said, her hand fluttering around her bangs. "And I put my hair up so I'd look, um, less ugly."

"I think you have a pretty face," Martin said.

She laughed it off. "Martin, that's why you have glasses." She leaned forward, cramping her shoulders inward. "But I wanted to try at least. To see. After, you know, the stuff we talked about last time."

Noises of encouragement from Big Mac.

A-Dre even chimed in. "All right, girl."

"No," she said. "It was *awful*." Her eyes started leaking. "Every-one ignored me. And I had a panic attack. I went out to the parking lot and almost passed out. It was . . . *humiliating*."

X played a tiny violin with her thumb and forefinger, but Lil ig-nored her.

"I can't go back," she said. "*Never*. It just proved that I'll never be happy again."

Daniel's thoughts had once more gravitated back to Francisca Olvera, and there was a tape-delay pause before he forced himself back to the room and prompted Lil. "You'll never be happy again because . . . ?"

Lil kicked her feet glumly. "I'll never find anyone."

"And you'll never find anyone because . . . ?"

She hugged her stomach, shivering. "No one will want me."

"No one will want you because . . . ?"

"No one will want me because I have nothing to *offer*, okay? I have nothing to offer someone."

A few of the chairs creaked. The wind whistled through the gap in the window.

"All right," Daniel said. "I'm going to speak your thoughts back to you. And you just see how they feel and respond as if you're Xochitl."

"Oh, great. That's great. Compare me to *her*." Lil cast her gaze upward. "Can't you just leave me alone? Just *once*? After what I went through, do you really have to pry at every inch of everything?"

"Who are you looking at?" Daniel asked.

She lowered her gaze quickly. "No one."

"You're looking up. Like you're a little kid."

"Oh. You mean . . ." She hiccupped in a breath. "I don't want to talk about my father."

"Okay. Then can we try this exercise instead? You're a grown woman now. You can make grown-woman choices for yourself."

She hesitated, then nodded rapidly like a kid.

Daniel cleared his throat. "No one wants you. You are never gonna be happy."

She blinked, and tears fell. Martin started to come to her defense, but Daniel shot him a look and he shrank back in his chair, his round, broad face contorted with empathy. X leaned forward on her chair, rapt.

"You're not allowed to be at peace," Daniel continued. "You're not allowed to be *liked*. You're a failure. No one talked to you at this social, which means no one will talk to you at *any* social."

Lil was sobbing freely now, and Daniel felt a stab of concern that if she didn't turn the corner, this would all go horribly awry. He was on the verge of pulling back when she said, quietly, "That's not true."

He seized on her words. "*Why* is it not true?"

"It's just one social," she said in the same tiny voice.

"*What?* I can't hear you when you talk like a little girl. Answer as if you're Xochitl. You ever hear her talk that way?"

Lil flashed fierce eye contact. "It's just one *fucking* social."

The men stirred. Daniel sensed X smile, but he kept his attention on Lil. "But *everyone* at that social did better than you."

"No. They did *not*. There were thirty woman there, and not *all* of them got talked to either." The fear wasn't gone from Lil's voice, and she retained a note of pleading, but her back had straightened out and there was more power behind her voice.

"So what? It'll go just as shitty next time around."

"I can *learn*! I can learn to do better. I can do *whatever I want*!" Her eyes aflame, she squeezed her hands together between her knees, drawing ragged breaths, her clavicles pronounced beneath her collar.

He lifted his hands, palms out. "You're right. You can."

Lil covered her mouth with a fist, surprised at herself and maybe a little scared.

"Okay," he said. "Good job."

"That's it?"

"That's it. Now, next time you go to a social, your aim *isn't* to meet a man."

"Then why . . . ?"

"Your *only* aim next time is to smile. Look people in the eye. Say hello. And pay a compliment to three people, men or women."

"What good'll that do?" Lil asked.

"Change don't come overnight," Big Mac said.

Still lost in thought, Fang gave the faintest nod. His face stayed impassive. Was he thinking about the choice he made last night outside the club? Relating it to what Lil was facing now?

"But if it goes bad?" Lil rubbed her arms against the draft. "The panic attack. When I got nervous at the church, when I couldn't breathe . . . And then out in the parking lot, I thought I was gonna die. I'm not sure I can risk feeling that way again."

"What you felt was caused by heightened stress and arousal," Daniel said. "Increased adrenaline made you hyperventilate. You got short of breath, which made you breathe even more and threw off your CO_2 balance. You got dizzy and light-headed, verged on collapsing. That's all."

"That *wasn't* all. It was *real*."

"Stand up," Daniel said.

Her lips pressed wide and flat, an attempt to beat back her fear. After a pause she rose.

"Breathe," he told her. "As hard as you can. More. Faster. *Faster*."

She panted heavily, her face growing pale, keeping on until her chest bucked and she wobbled on her feet.

"Stop!" he said. "Now breathe into your hands. Get carbon dioxide."

She leaned over, breathed into the bowl of her fingers. A few seconds later, she straightened back up. "I feel better. So quickly."

"You make it happen," he said, "which means you can fix it, too."

She stepped back and collapsed into her chair, her face washed of color but exuberant, too, in the small triumph. She was crying again, but her tears were different; they signaled a release. She managed a nervous laugh, then shivered, wiping at her face. "It's cold in here."

Fang got up, crossed the room, and closed the window for her.

Chapter 53

As the group members milled around during break, Daniel pulled his iPhone from his pocket to text Dooley, and a few coins fell to the ground. SND CSI AFTR SESSION, he tapped in. TIN OF SKOAL IN TRSH - MYBE PRINTS. After double-checking that her number was teed up to call in case of emergency, he reached for the fallen change.

A quarter lay there on the cracked tile. Staring down, he was called back to the perfect, shiny coins found at the crime scenes.

He stood abruptly. "Anyone have change? I want to grab a Coke."

The members dug in purses, pockets, and chain wallets, change spilling into palms to be appraised. Everyone else offered up normal, grubby coins, except Big Mac, who held his Velcro wallet at a tilt so he could peer inside the change pouch.

Daniel collected a few quarters, stalling as long as seemed plausible, then headed for the door. Paused. "Big Mac, you have a quarter?"

The blocks of Big Mac's hands resealed the wallet. Clenched it. "You got enough."

"I think they raised the price," Daniel said.

Big Mac's gaze didn't falter. "They didn't raise the price."

Daniel stopped partway to the door, frozen in the standoff.

A-Dre said, "Man, you one cheap-ass motherfucker, you can't give the man a quarter."

Big Mac stared a moment longer, then rooted in his wallet and flipped Daniel a coin. His heart still thudding, Daniel caught it in the air. He didn't open his fist until he was alone in the hall.

The coin was grimy and worn, just like all the others.

Sipping a Dr Pepper, Daniel reclaimed his chair. "Big Mac, you want to take the hot seat? Talk about the fight last session?"

"No. X has been dodging her turn, and it's bullshit."

"Fuck *you* I'm dodging."

"We all come in here and talk about our shit. Lay it all out. And she plays games every time she's in that chair."

"I don't play no games. Just because I don't go all Weepy Oprah and shit."

Daniel put it to the room. "What do you think?"

"Hellz yeah," A-Dre said. "Get her skinny ass in the chair."

"She's been . . . ah, ah, getting away with doing nothing."

"Fine." X stood up and sat so hard the chair clanked. "*What?*"

"Let's talk about Sophie," Daniel said.

"This shit again?"

"Yes. Talk as if you're her. Think how she's feeling right now."

"She's *feeling*—"

"As if you're *her*," Daniel said.

X shot a breath, crossed her arms, slid down a few inches in the chair. "*I'm* feeling happy 'cuz it's been *two years* since that shit happened, and I don't dwell on it every day like *some* people."

"Think of Sophie as a person," Daniel said. "Think about how it affected her life."

"I'm Sophie." X produced a shit-eating smile. "I get my feelings hurt when people call me Raped Girl. But most girls get raped, so I guess that makes me, I don't know, a fucking *baby.*"

As the others let her have it for being a pain in the ass, Daniel leaned back in his chair, the band of metal cool against his shoulder blades. It was the same shut-out feeling he'd experienced standing outside the closed door of his and Cris's bedroom today.

"What is the most important thing we ask for in here?" he said sharply. "Honesty and accountability." The words boomeranged back and struck him hard. Physician, heal thyself.

"I'm *being* honest," X said. "Y'all just don't like hard truths."

"BS," Lil said. "After *I* sat up there and said what I went through—"

"Boo-fucking-hoo, Lil. 'Oh, no one talked to me at a church social—' "

"—you're scared to even take a look at—"

"I'm *not scared*!" X had come to a crouch above her chair, her face flushed. She eased back down, bit her lower lip. "Fine. *Fine*. You wanna know how it affected her life?" Her nostrils flared, her chest rose and fell. "She wants to not think about it every fucking minute of the day. Reliving the pain. The concrete against her cheek. The expression on the girls' faces—on *my* face—when I held her down. She tells herself it's no big deal, girls get raped all the time. She toughens up. She never, *ever* wants to be helpless again. But she's scared all the time. She can't go into a room with other people without her heart rate going up. She has to . . . has to sit by the door. So she can get away if she needs to. It hurts when she has sex, like a knife going into her. *That's* how she fucking feels. Okay? *Okay?*"

Stunned silence. The room without air. A ceiling vent blew unevenly, and the pipes groaned in the walls.

When X spoke again, her voice was as quiet and small as Lil's. "She was so pretty. I wanted her to be wrecked like me." Then her face broke, and she started keening. Arms crossed at her belly, rocking herself up and down, wailing.

It took Daniel a moment to find his voice again. He was about to speak, but Lil rose first and crossed the circle. She crouched before X, set her hands on her shoulders, and X tilted forward into her arms.

Chapter 54

Daniel's footsteps sounded off the walls of the garage. After session he'd waited in the room until a CSI inspector, disguised as a janitor, retrieved the tin of dipping tobacco from the trash can. The inspector had found only smudged partials; run through a mobile scanner, they'd brought up nothing in the system. Another tantalizing clue leading to another dead end.

Daniel cut through the rows of vehicles, climbed into his car, and sat for a time with his hands and forehead on the steering wheel. Utterly spent.

Removing his iPhone, he texted Dooley: SAFE.

A moment later, the phone buzzed in his lap. I KNOW. LOOK UP.

It took his eyes a moment to adjust to the gloom, but then he spotted her in a sedan parked against the far wall. Through the windshield she gave a little wave. He waved back.

She smiled. He smiled back. It was good to see her face.

The phone vibrated with another message, but he could see her hands, could see it wasn't her.

DANIEL BRASHER.

An unknown caller.

The chill of the garage settled in around his neck. He stared at the screen, waiting for the next message.

ADMIT WHAT YOUV DONE. OR YOU WILL BLEED FOR IT.

YOU HAV TIL THANKGIVING AT MIDITE.

He looked across at Dooley. Her expression had changed, a reflection no doubt of his own. As she got out and hustled toward his car, he looked down at the phone, clenched in his hand.

Through a shell-shocked haze, he realized that he was the first target who actually *knew* what he was supposed to admit. Which of course raised a question that the others hadn't had to consider.

His thumbs were shaking, so it took several tries and two autocorrects to input his reply. ADMIT TO WHO? WHEN? WHERE?

As expected, the error message popped up in its cheery little thought bubble. Invalid number.

Dooley tapped the window. He unlocked, and she slid into the passenger seat. He handed her the phone. Heard her lips make a slight popping sound. She was on the radio right away, but her words were a blur beneath the hum in his head.

Thanksgiving.

Two days.

Chapter 55

"Cris? You there? Look, I'm sorry to tell you through the door, but the next death threat? It's directed at me. The deadline's Thanksgiving at midnight. Leo is safing the entire house now with SFPD—they want to check *everything* because of how it went down with Molly Clarke. They're starting on the ground floor. But you'll have to open up soon."

"Still here. Look . . . I realized something today. In session. I yammer on about honesty and accountability all the time, but I wasn't being fully honest with myself. Or with you. And if we can't do that with each other, then what's the point, right? If we can't share *everything*. Including the ugliest, most shameful truths. So."

"Okay. Here goes."

"When I thought I was gonna lose you, I felt utterly helpless. And terrified. I couldn't imagine what the next fifty years would look like without you in them. Or maybe I could and I didn't think they would be fifty years worth getting through. But more than that, with everything you were going to go through and you being scared and in pain and I couldn't *do* anything—I couldn't do a fucking thing to lessen your . . . your . . . Sorry. Hang on. Give me a . . ."

284

"No matter what I *think* I think about rules and choices—all the sanctimonious bullshit—I would've done *anything*. To spare you that. To make you well. And you're right. I didn't care how it got done. I just wanted you to be alive. I always thought—*hoped*—that I was different from my mom and, yeah, the people I see in group. But I'm not. Because for your life? I wasn't thinking about morals and fairness and laws. I would have done whatever I could. And I would again."

At last the knob turned and Cris filled the slice at the jamb, her face flushed. Then the door pushed open with a creak, and her arms were out and she was pressed tight to him, squeezing his neck, her body warm. He dipped his face into the scent of her.

She squeezed him tighter. "The next death threat? It really came in against you?"

He nodded, their cheeks slick against each other.

"Our situation, it's reversed now," she said. "*Your* life at stake. And while you were talking, it hit me . . ." She swallowed hard. "*I* took a favor from your mom, too, with Leo. I didn't ask any questions. I just said yes. Because *you* were at risk." Her breath came hot against his ear, a low whisper. "I realized that I would, too. I'd do anything to keep you safe."

Chapter 56

They made love in the morning, streamers of hay-colored light escaping the lowered blinds and texturing the rumpled sheets. Cris rose and fell through blocks of semi-shadow, her swollen mouth, her breasts, her arched shoulders sunlit and then lost to vagueness. She leaned on him, palms pressing his shoulders, the fringe of her hair sweeping his throat, every sensation new and heightened as they discovered each other all over again. Her hands left red marks at his chest, his on the slope of her waist. And then they slowed, him looking down at her now, and then slowed more and more, eyes locked, mouths parted, until they were barely moving at all.

They showered together, Cris leaning against his back, arms wrapping him. After they dressed, she said, "I need to see the water."

Leo agreed to tail them at a safe distance, and they strolled downslope for the marina, holding hands, just another couple out for another stroll on the first blindingly spectacular day in months. Tomorrow was Thanksgiving.

Admit what you've done. Or you will bleed for it.

But admit it *where*? Was he supposed to announce it to the city? A press conference seemed ridiculous. Dooley kept the idea on the table, reminding him that they had until midnight tomorrow to weigh options. "Don't worry," she'd said with a smirk. "He hasn't killed anyone early yet." Cris had halfheartedly raised the idea of leaving town, hopping on a plane for somewhere, though they both knew that wouldn't happen. Dooley needed his help, they had Leo at the house, and besides, fleeing the investigation and his group seemed so craven. Plus at *some* point, he'd have to come home and face what needed to be faced.

He tried to force himself into the present. After all, this stroll could be his last. He and Cris didn't speak; they just walked beneath the cloudless sky and felt the sun doing its best against the biting breeze. All was right with the rest of the world. Labradoodles pranced by on designer leashes. Boy-men zipped past on scooters and mountain bikes, messenger bags slung over their shoulders. The Palace of Fine Arts made Cris beam every time it appeared, so unexpected and anachronistic across from the overpriced homes of Baker Street. It was young for a Roman ruin, the last man standing from the 1915 Panama-Pacific International Exhibit, San Francisco's post-earthquake, "We're still standing" bash. The mirror surface of the fronting lagoon doubled the frieze-intensive octagonal dome, the effect breathtaking beneath the canopy of flawless blue.

They picked their way up a narrow spit of land past the Golden Gate Yacht Club right to the water's edge, where in a stroke of quirky genius, a master stonemason had installed a wave-activated acoustic organ sculpture. Dr. Seuss tubes, wound through Lego blocks of granite from a demolished gold-rush cemetery, gave off an intestinal gurgling that was nothing short of hypnotic. Daniel and Cris sat on an icy slab, looked out at the choppy gray, and listened as the world's largest seashell sounded off.

Kite surfers were out in force, skipping across the water like evolved life-forms. Beyond rose the craggy outline of the Rock, where the Bird-man kept no birds, Machine Gun Kelly did perfect time, and Al Capone languished, his brain a syphilitic stew. To the west, at the base of that lionized suspension bridge, jutted Fort Point, where dripping-wet Kim Novak had lolled weakly in Jimmy Stewart's rescuing arms, faking it.

Everyone's got a con, a pinch of deceit, a green light at the end of the dock. And a dream, however grand or modest. A way they want it to be and an angle to get there.

Daniel thought of Francisca Olvera's heart giving out, of a positive pregnancy test resting on a silver platter, of a death threat rendered on the screen of his cell phone. All the terror and loss and vulnerability of the past week rose up, threatening to overwhelm him. He closed his eyes and listened to the pipes and water, a horn section in the round. The whale song vibrated through him, and for a moment he felt without limits, without boundaries, held in the vast belly of the sea itself.

Cris's hand loosened in his, letting go for the first time since they'd stepped out into the city together. She gently grasped his wrist, repositioned his fingers. Tugging up her shirt, she placed his spread palm over her navel.

Feeling the heat rising through his wife's body, he realized just how modest his own dreams had become.

Chapter 57

Later in the day, Daniel was eating a sandwich over the sink when Cris flew down the stairs from the bedroom, flipping her cell phone closed against her chin. "We have to go. Can you— Leo? Can you come with us?" She was grabbing keys, a sweater, swinging the shot put of her purse over an arm. "I need you both to—"

Daniel caught her at the shoulders as she rounded the kitchen island. "What happened?"

She stopped, lips trembling. "The planning commission vote came in. They're taking the building."

With clapboard siding and fresh yellow-and-brown paint, the projects in Western Addition look surprisingly upscale, like dormitories or military housing. Three stories, town-house-connected. Residents out on the stoops and curbs, talking and pointing across the street where moving vans and beater trucks had assembled before the much larger apartment complex Cris had spent the past eighteen months fighting to protect. For once, rival gangs were present within eyeshot of each other, though they kept to opposite sides of the street. The Knock Out Posse, who owned these blocks, moved freely, but the few Sureños who'd made their way up from South Van Ness with their blue kerchiefs, do-rags, and Dallas Cowboys jerseys, minded their curb. Maybe they had relatives getting kicked out, or maybe they were just here for the street theater—the trail of tears leading out the laid-back double doors of the lobby. Families with hastily packed cardboard boxes, an elderly black man gesticulating angrily with a cane, arguments in various languages, and a few universal sobs. A scattering of bored cops were out, along with a few men in suits bearing important-looking papers on clipboards. Not a single reporter.

Daniel coasted through the crowd, practically nudging folks aside with the front bumper, Cris at the window like a dog frantic to escape. Leo throttled behind them in his tank of a Ford Bronco. Parking was a mess, so Daniel let Cris out and kept on with Leo. By a miracle they found meters close to each other a block over. A quarter bought a whopping seven minutes, and Daniel was broke at fourteen minutes. Leo palmed him some spare change to max out the meter, and they jogged back to find Cris.

She was sitting on the crowded curb across the street, arms resting on her knees, staring despondently at the ongoing eviction. Leo lingered nearby as Daniel lowered himself beside her. They watched, Cris wiping her cheeks at intervals.

Even the gang members looked melancholy. "Way of the mothafuckin' world," one remarked sagely, and Cris said, "Stow it, Rags."

At the base of the telephone pole beside them was a streetside altar—flowers, a mini–teddy bear, and a photo of a young teenage girl with long lashes and soulful brown eyes, wearing a confirmation dress. The wooden pole was still pitted from where the bullets had been dug out. The unacceptable, right here, every day.

Cris interrupted his thoughts. "This used to be the *Fillmore.* Not just 'the Fillmore.'" She lifted her arm, pointed southeast. "The Church of John Coltrane was over there. The devout brought instruments, sat in with the band. For three decades they fed the homeless. Then the landlord doubled the rent. Gone. And right here"—she jerked her head north—"the old Winterland Arena. All those psychedelic light shows. Hendrix played there, 'member? The Doors, Zeppelin, the Dead. The night they closed, Bill Graham rode onstage on a giant joint. Today . . . apartments. And now the apartments are going, and I protest *that*. Maybe I *am* stuck in the past. Maybe your mom's right. Dot-com was just the latest gold rush. And now the *new* new economy, Web 2.0." Her hand circled, tracing a rising spiral before falling limply to her lap. "This is how it's always been, and this is how it'll always be, and I need to just grow the fuck up."

An elderly Filipino woman exited the complex and made halting progress across the street, heedless of honking cars. An antique birdcage swung at her side. Various family members trailed, holding lamps, trash cans, suitcases with broken clasps. The woman was steered toward a rusted car, but she demurred, veering off to sit at the edge of a planter, the birdcage on her thighs. She mumbled through the bars to the white macaw as her family members pleaded and gestured.

Releasing a sigh, Cris rose. She and Daniel walked over and cut through the cadre of frustrated family members. Cris leaned down, tried for eye contact. "Hello, Mrs. Gao."

The woman didn't lift her gaze. She kept mumbling in Tagalog. A disinterested grown-granddaughter type translated. "She say Dinky does not like change."

Cris stared at Mrs. Gao helplessly as she continued to mumble.

"She say Dinky has delicate stomach." The granddaughter chewed her gum, half listening, then chewed it some more. "Dinky is too old to move. Dinky will die of heartsickness."

Mrs. Gao finally raised her sagging eyes to Cris, her lips still moving.

The granddaughter examined a chipped fingernail. "She say, 'Why can't you do anything?' "

Cris finally left for home with Leo, Daniel staying behind to help the Gaos load up a succession of vehicles that appeared, one after another, with roof racks embellished by ingenious bungee-cord configurations. Given Cris's pregnancy, he didn't want her hauling boxes up and down the stairs.

He thought about how lovely it would be to be alive when the baby was born.

Too late he noticed the parking-enforcement officer patrolling in a tiny wheelbarrow of a vehicle, even more ridiculous than his own smart car. He set the final suitcase on the curb and ran, digging in his pockets for the change Leo had given him.

He spotted the ticket on his windshield and cursed. But when his gaze lowered, all petty aggravation evaporated. In his palm were a few quarters, spit-polished and brand-new.

His stomach roiling, he poked them apart, exposing the dates.

They were all over twenty years old.

Chapter 58

Speeding across the city, Daniel reached Dooley.

"Where are you?"

"Coming up on your house, actually," she said. "I was gonna stay with you, drive you over to Metro South later."

"Do *not* go in. Leo Rizk—the guard at our house? Who my mother sent? He's involved. He gave me quarters—brand-new-looking. Like the ones at the crime scenes."

"Okay, just hang on." Her breath whistled across the receiver. "Spell his name."

Daniel did.

She said, "If he's a suspect, we need to call for backup, surround the house."

Daniel flew down Webster, bottoming out the car, throwing sparks. "There is *no way* I'm leaving him with my wife. Meet me at Lafayette Park by the tennis courts on the east side. That's the most secluded area. It's two blocks from the house. I'll get him there."

He could hear Dooley's car screeching into a U-turn. She said, "We need to do this slowly and properly."

"Dooley, I'm getting this guy out of my house and away from my wife. You can be there or not."

He hung up, dialed again, running the math in his head. Leo had access to their house, their schedules, and—given his background—God knew what else. A true inside man who'd somehow earned

Evelyn's trust. He'd appeared on their doorstep immediately after the woman in the rain, as if he'd been waiting. He was a different build from the killer—too short—and he'd been with Cris during Daniel's run-in at Kyle Lane's house, but if he was working in concert with a group member—

Leo picked up after the first ring. "Yes?"

"Leo, I need you to meet me up the street at Lafayette Park by the tennis courts. Dooley uncovered a new clue. We know who the killer is. And we need your help."

"I shouldn't leave the house. Or Cristina."

"I'm the one with the death threat on my head."

"And she's a pregnant woman. Not to mention a great way to get to you. If, say, the killer wants to ensure you'll go to a set location at midnight tomorrow, all he's gotta do is grab her."

"Dooley has a tail on the killer right now," Daniel said. "He's in Bayview. It's safe. Get here now."

He hung up and veered onto Washington, the park zooming into view. The patch of not-quite-level ground surfed a hump between steep rises, the surrounding streets lined with pricey Victorians. He found a spot and jogged toward the tennis courts, where Dooley waited in the thickening dusk, thumbs hooked through her belt like an old-school sheriff.

"He's on his way," Daniel said.

"I have backup coming."

"They'll scare him off. He's a hard-core trained operative."

"No shit. I just ran him. He's got no record. As in—*no record*. Who the fuck is this guy you let into your house?"

"My mother hired him for us. She's generally good on due diligence."

Dooley whistled. "The rich are not like me and . . . me."

Leo's bald dome appeared first, bobbing over a rise of grass. He cut past a dog chasing a Frisbee and threaded through a few folks reading on beach towels, heading for where they waited in the least populated part of the park.

Daniel looked at Theresa. A bead of sweat tracked down her neck. She smiled tightly.

Leo approached, spread his arms wide, a rare broad gesture. "What?"

Daniel sidled to Leo's left so the man would have to turn slightly away from Dooley. Over Leo's head on Gough Street, he saw two cop cars pulling up to the curb.

Daniel said, "We found a clue that linked us to the killer." He held out his fist. Opened it.

In his palm, Leo's shiny coins.

Puzzled wrinkles appeared in Leo's forehead.

Dooley's hand moved to her hip. There was the faintest snap, and then she said, "I want you to put your—"

Leo spun, so fast it was like a cartoon blur. His foot swept Dooley's calves, and she went down. Her gun remained precisely in place, aimed at him, except he was now the one holding it. His hands whirled, the magazine falling to the dirt, the lead bullet popping from the chamber, and then the slide clicked back and forward, the spring assembly bounced in the air, and the barrel came free of the slide.

The gun, field-stripped in about three seconds, lay in pieces on the ground at Leo's feet.

Empty-handed, he blinked twice, seeming only now to realize what he'd done.

Daniel barely had time to register what had happened. But one thing was clear: If Leo was going to do something bad, he'd have done it already.

"Sorry, Officer." Leo extended his hand, hoisted Dooley to her feet. "Didn't want anyone to get hurt."

"Who the hell *are* you?" Dooley asked, crouching to retrieve the parts of her gun. "You don't exist."

"Of course I don't exist," Leo said. "There's a guy you can call in the 202 area code who can explain to you why that is. Until then, you want to tell me what this is about?"

The backup officers crested the hill to their left, and Dooley waved them off in disgust.

"The change," Daniel said. "These perfectly polished coins. They were found at two of the crime scenes."

"Those?" Leo said. "I got those coins from your mother."

Daniel's mouth moved, but no words were coming out.

Theresa said, *"When?"*

"I met her at a restaurant before she hired me. I had no money for the meter. She gave me change from her purse, just like I gave it to you." Leo stepped back, suddenly concerned. "But that's not the key question right now."

"What's the key question?" Dooley asked.

Already Daniel was running for his car, dialing his cell phone. "Who's watching Cristina?" he said.

Chapter 59

The phone and the doorbell rang simultaneously, awakening Cris where she'd dozed off on the couch. She started for the phone, but a commotion on the porch diverted her attention. She hesitated before tentatively starting down the stairs.

Midway to the first floor, she heard a frenzied pounding on the door, then a woman's moaning: "Help me. God, oh, God, he's after me. Please open up! Please help me!"

Cris rushed down the final steps and peered through the peephole. A head loomed in distorted close-up—a Hispanic woman, her face battered, strings of hair caught in a trickle of blood running from the corner of her mouth. She cast fearful glances over her shoulder, then rapped on the door again. "Help me, *please*! Please let me in! He's coming after me!"

At five o'clock the sky still held enough light for Cris to see past the front yard to the empty street. No pursuer was in evidence.

She turned off the alarm, gripped the deadbolt, started to turn.

Then froze.

The woman's wails came through the door, her fear tangible. "What are you *waiting* for? He's gonna kill me! Look what he did to me! Please help!" The words flooded out between bursts of panting. "He's almost here! Please . . ."

The foyer tile, a plain of ice beneath Cris's bare feet. Her thin arms trembled. She stared at her hand on the deadbolt, nausea swelling as the woman's wrenching sobs washed through her.

Just when the cries reached a pitch Cris thought she couldn't withstand, they were abruptly severed, as if someone had hit PAUSE.

With dread, Cris moved her eye again to the peephole. The woman's face remained there, but it held a perfect stillness, the bruised mouth set in a confident sneer. Her tongue flashed into view, tasting the blood on her bottom lip.

Cris eased out an uneven breath. She took a slow step back. And then another.

The door rocked in the frame, a resonant boom that rattled the miniature Zen garden on the accent table. A cry escaped Cris's lips, and she instinctively covered her ears.

The kick, way more forceful than anything the woman could have managed.

Another boom, this one even louder. But the reinforced wood held.

Cris stepped back again.

Silence.

Then the sound of footsteps running away.

Two sets of footsteps.

Cris's wavering hand found the stairs behind her, and she lowered herself to the bottom step and let the fear shudder out of her.

Chapter 60

They found Cris in the foyer seconds after her would-be assailants had fled. Daniel, then Theresa, Leo, and six uniformed cops had spilled into the house. Radios blared. Additional cars were dispatched through the neighborhood, but there was no sign of Viviana Olvera or her partner.

At least now they knew how the Tearmaker had gotten his victims to open their doors. By sending Viviana first to ring the bell and feign terror that her attacker was close behind. Her freshly beaten and swollen face, glimpsed through the peephole, had convinced each victim to unlock the door. The Tearmaker probably waited just out of sight, ready to lunge once the deadbolt was retracted.

Cris's hands were still shaking as Daniel helped her upstairs and explained to her about Leo's getting the shiny coins from Evelyn.

Cris asked, "Do you really think your mother has some . . . *involvement* in all this?"

"I have no idea. Dooley's going to my mom now."

"You need to go, too. She's your mother."

"I need to stay with you."

"Leo's here now. Door locked. Alarm on. I'll be okay. Go see what the hell Evelyn has to say for herself."

Daniel's neck had knotted up, but he still managed to nod.

He followed Dooley across town in his own car because he was due at Metro South in a few hours. At the Fairmont, Dooley made an aggressive entrance, and Daniel had to intervene to settle the head concierge, who finally divulged that Evelyn had made an early dinner reservation at the Tonga Room on the lower level.

They rode the elevator down, Dooley badging the hostess at the podium as Daniel bulled past into the humidity rising off the indoor faux lagoon. The place was a Disney-Polynesian explosion, with tiki totems, bamboo screens, and thatched-grass umbrellas beneath a ceiling strung with colorful lanterns. He spotted Evelyn and James sitting alone at the lagoon's edge and started toward them.

As he neared, four large men rose from surrounding tables to encircle him, and he almost took an adrenaline-charged swing before realizing that they were his mother's security detail. James sorted the mess from one end, Dooley from the other, Evelyn relaxing all the while in her chair and slurping a concoction from a fruit-laden glass the size of a fishbowl.

By the time Daniel and Theresa took up chairs opposite Evelyn, a monsoon rain was showering the lagoon from sprinklers in the ceiling, and then a barge of a stage floated forward and a stout woman in a tropical wrap dress began warbling out "Bali Ha'i." Daniel had to shout over the commotion, his explanation about the coins seeming only to enhance the confusion. Evelyn sipped on and ignored the cell phone lighting up at intervals beside her pupu platter. The singer was belting out the crescendo now, each lyric sending darning needles through Daniel's temples, and then the mechanized skies cleared and the barge retracted like the shrinking head of a tortoise and there were just the three of them—mother, son, and homicide inspector—blinking at one another in the sudden semi-silence.

The screen on Evelyn's phone lit again, and, exasperated, Daniel said, "Why aren't you answering your phone?"

She twirled a diminutive umbrella in her manicured fingers and said, drunkenly, "Because Vimal keeps *calling*."

Dooley held up her hands, signaling time called. "Let me put this bluntly, Mrs. Brasher. Until we can clear this up, you are a person of interest in multiple murder investigations."

At this, Evelyn pulled back her head and laughed. Not her calculated titter, but genuine amusement. Then she reached for her sequined clutch purse. Dooley stiffened a little, but Evelyn merely unsnapped the gold clasp and dumped the contents onto the tablecloth. Lipstick tubes and change rolled everywhere, many of the coins bright and polished. Evidently pleased with herself, she tossed the emptied purse aside.

Staring at the shiny coins where they'd landed between the spareribs and the crab Rangoon, Dooley and Daniel remained speechless.

"In 1938," Evelyn began grandly, "the St. Francis Hotel began washing all their coins after complaints that dirty change was soiling the white gloves of their female patrons. A tradition that persists to this day." She paused for a dramatically timed sip of mai tai. "So as much as it truly pleases me to be 'a person of interest in multiple murder investigations,' I feel obliged to point you in a not-so-wrong direction."

Dooley leaned away until the chair caught her shoulders with a thud. "I can't believe we missed that."

"You were asking the wrong class of people." Evelyn set down the empty bowl of her cocktail, plucked up a lustrous dime, and displayed it like a guitar pick between thumb and forefinger. "In San Francisco, darling, *everything* comes down to money."

Chapter 61

With her marble columns and classic brown brick, the St. Francis Hotel is known as the Grand Dame of Union Square. Hammett used her as the model for the St. Mark in *The Maltese Falcon,* and Daniel observed—as he and Dooley passed beneath the historic master clock in the lobby and wound their way up the grand staircase—that not a whole lot had changed since then.

In short order they found themselves in the so-called cleaning closet at the end of a narrow little hall by the general cashier, where, surrounded by machinery from the twenties and thirties, they listened with strained patience as Arthur Carroll, master coin washer, explained the process. With his duck-headed cane, wire-frame glasses, and cleanly parted white hair, he was a stalwart gentleman, precisely how Daniel would have envisioned a master coin washer.

"See this giant silver-burnishing machine? It was built before ball bearings were invented, so it runs on grease cuffs. The change goes through with lead buckshot and 20 Mule Team Borax, which froths into a kind of gray meringue. Removes all the grime of the outside world."

Daniel had to concede that Arthur's enthusiasm was infectious, if exhausting. Dooley opened her mouth, but the man was off and running again. "After the coins are rinsed, we move 'em to these trays here, where they're dried under two-hundred-fifty-watt bulbs. Then they go out to the front desk, the restaurants, and the gift shops. I'd say almost fifteen million dollars has passed through these machines in my forty-nine years." Arthur adjusted a sleek wrist splint that looked futuristic in this context peeking out from beneath the cuff of his Brooks Brothers shirt. "Here we are, fifty miles from Silicon Valley, and everything is totally mechanical."

"And who else," Dooley said, stepping forward as if needing to physically enhance the interruption, "is allowed in here?"

As they'd sped from the Tonga Room over to the St. Francis, Dooley had called O'Malley in the war room and had him check the employment records of all the major suspects. Not one had worked here in any capacity, and cost and location sharply reduced the chances that any of them patronized the hotel. So she and Daniel hung, now, on Arthur's reply, hoping to bring to light a spider thread of a connection.

"No one," Arthur said. "No other staff, no guests, no tour guides. It may not look like much, but it's my little domain."

"Who else *works* in here with you?"

"For forty-six years, not a soul," he said, with fierce pride. "But then my eyesight started going and then my wrists. Arthritis." He lifted the splint. "So a few years back . . ."

"Yes?"

"I started bringing in a worker now and again to help."

"From where?"

"I was a bit embarrassed," he said. "I'd never needed help before. But washing the coins takes four or so hours. And it must be done two to three times a week, so you can imagine the—"

"Mr. Carroll," Dooley said, "I need to know everything about the worker you used. We've traced a clue in a murder investigation to this room, and I need your help."

Arthur's eyes flared a bit at that. He removed his spectacles and polished them with the inevitable old-fashioned hankie, produced from his back pocket. "When my symptoms were bad, I picked up workers from time to time to help me. I did it early in the morning, before work. I didn't want anyone to know."

"Workers," Dooley said, hitting the plural. "Picked them up *where*?"

"Along Cesar Chavez. On my morning commute in." His head dipped slightly, the first erosion in his stately posture.

Cesar Chavez Street was where day laborers lined up with their torn jeans and worker gloves, waiting for foremen or contractors to swing by on their way from Home Depot and throw them in the back with the lumber. They were paid in cash, off the books. Which meant no employment records. Which meant no trail that SFPD could trace in the databases.

They breathed the grease-tinged air of the windowless room.

Arthur said, "I know it's illegal—"

"Don't worry about *that*," Dooley said.

"—but I can assure you I learned my lesson. Money started going missing, so we stopped. And I had to come clean with management. They were quite understanding, actually, which made it worse. I was worried I'd be replaced, and as you can plainly see, this job means everything to me. But they agreed to hire on temp workers now, legitimately, to—"

Dooley cut him off before he could get up another head of steam. "Do you remember the workers you used?"

"Not very well."

"Did you use some regularly?" She fired the questions over the top of her flipped-open black notepad.

"For a while. Then they'd disappear. You know how that goes. Or perhaps you don't."

"How many in total?"

"Maybe eight or nine."

"All men?"

"Yes. It's physical work. A lot of hefting." He raised his splinted wrist. "So, as a rule, I'd pick the biggest man."

Dooley removed from the back of her notepad a set of small suspect photos and spread them on a workbench—the familiar six-pack identification test. Big Mac, A-Dre, Fang, and Martin were there, as well as two other faces Daniel placed from the war-room bulletin boards—Lil's ex-husband and A-Dre's brother.

Arthur donned his glasses again and examined them. "I don't know."

"You don't *know*?" Dooley said. "How long ago was this?"

"The first worker was probably three years ago. The last maybe nine months ago."

"And the last one stole the money?"

"Yes. Maybe others, too. That's just when I noticed. In hindsight it was foolish in more ways than one."

Dooley pointed again to the photos. "Look again, please, Mr. Carroll."

He did, bringing his nose within inches of them, his lips bunching. "I honestly can't say."

"You remember the ethnicities, though," Daniel cut in. "Right? Black, Chinese, Hispanic, Caucasian?"

"No." Arthur scratched at his hair. "A few were Hispanic. But the others? It was a year, two years ago. And I'm nearsighted past a few feet. Examining coins isn't kind on the eyes."

"You wear glasses," Dooley said.

"Simple close-range magnifiers. These are all I wear in the office."

"But you worked with those men. Here in this tiny room."

"The coins are important. Their faces weren't." He seemed to hear himself and gritted his teeth. "I was worried about myself, about not being found out, forced out." Instinctively, he moved a liver-spotted hand to the splint and gave it a protective squeeze. "I suppose I resented them. I didn't want them to be here. I didn't want to *need* them. They got in the back of the truck and then they hoisted bags and poured and sorted, and I did my best to pretend they didn't exist." He lifted his white eyebrows. "I didn't realize that was the case, but it was. I'm sorry." He moistened his chapped lips. "And I'm sorry I can't help you more."

Dooley asked, "Do you have security cameras back here?"

"No. But in the elevator. We have to use the elevators because of the weight of the bags."

"You used the elevator with *all* the workers."

"Every one, yes."

"I need security footage from the elevator for that entire period."

As Arthur picked up an old-fashioned wall-mounted phone and spoke with security, Daniel checked his watch. His group session at Metro South began in a little more than an hour. He tapped the glass face, and Dooley nodded.

They thanked Arthur Carroll and waited downstairs on a leather couch near lobby registration. Fifteen minutes later the security director approached with a brown grocery bag filled to the brim with DVDs.

"That it?" Dooley joked.

The man smiled tightly. "The first batch." As he turned back for his office, he said, "You *did* ask for three-plus years of footage. Be grateful we burn backups."

She produced that dazzling smile. "Grateful I am."

As his loafers clicked away, Dooley poked a finger into the brown bag and peeked inside. Settling back to wait beside Daniel, she shot a sigh at the ornate ceiling. "I'll tell Media Forensics to cancel Thanksgiving."

Chapter 62

Xochitl sat on the hot seat, picking up where she'd left off, the others looking on attentively from all sides.

Still winded from his sprint to arrive in time, Daniel sat erect in his chair, giving her the focus she deserved. Because it was his first group session since that death threat had dinged into his iPhone, Dooley had added even more security measures around the building. Undercover officers at every entrance and several on each floor. She'd gone so far as to insist on waiting out the session in the empty room next door. Before they'd parted in the garage, he'd reminded her that the deadline was not until tomorrow at midnight, and she'd replied, half jokingly, "That's just when he's gonna *kill* you. A maiming or kidnapping could happen whenever."

Settling into the session, he had to confess that the thought of her right there beyond the wall did ease his discomfort a notch or two. But as he surveyed the faces around the ring, dark thoughts simmered beneath the surface, threatening to bubble out of his mouth. *Any of you ever work cleaning coins at the St. Francis? Who tried to kick in my front door yesterday and kidnap my wife? Whoever knows Viviana Olvera, raise your hand.*

"Last session was crazy-ass," X said, interrupting his reverie. "All this feeling and shit just pouring out of me. And now I can't put it back. It's just splattered out everywhere. On the carpet, the walls 'n' shit. I got all teary at a car commercial yesterday. Pathetic. I'm like

307

Lil's ass now. Next thing I'll be going to church socials." Some snig-
gers. "But seriously. Now that all that shit's spread out where I can
see it, I don't know what to do with it. I'm *angry,* too. Not just weepy.
I'm angry at the ones who did it to *me.*"

"You have to find forgiveness," Lil said.

"That's *bullshit,*" Martin said.

X looked taken aback by Lil's recommendation, too. She directed
a challenging glare at Daniel, as if he'd been the one to suggest it.
"You think I can forgive being fucking *raped*?"

"I don't know," Daniel said. "I've never been raped."

"Helpful," A-Dre chimed in.

Big Mac said, "You got a degree for that, Counselor?"

Daniel ignored the digs, not wanting to be sidetracked. X was still
focused on him. "Why should *those bitches* get forgiveness?" she
said. "I never got none from Raped Gi"—she caught herself—"from
Sophie."

"What do you want?" he asked.

"A G6. No—a Hummer limo with Chris Brown in the back. Then
I could run them bitches over." X flicked her nails against her thumb.
"I don't fucking know what I *want.*"

Daniel said, "What do you want for Sophie then?"

"I want . . ." X thought for a moment, and then her eyes welled
up, seeming to catch her off guard. "I want her not to hafta be so
angry all the time."

Daniel looked across at Big Mac, Lil, and Fang, hoping someone
else would step in, but they just stared back, intent on letting him lead.

"That's a great start," Daniel said. "I know what else *I* want for
you."

X wiped roughly at her cheeks. "*What?*"

"I want you to gain power over what happened to you instead of
letting it have power over you."

"It *doesn't* have power over me."

Daniel got up, crossed the small ring, and sat in X's empty seat—

the chair nearest the door. She tensed, glaring at him, her hands turned to claws against her jeans.

Daniel spread his arms. "I want *this* not to scare you anymore."

He got up and returned to his own chair, and even from the corner of his eye, he could see X go slack with relief. She scurried across the circle and reclaimed her spot.

"What a load of *shit*." Martin's eyes, magnified by those bold-framed glasses, held a quick anger. "Forgiveness. Acceptance. *Closure*." Each word imbued with disgust.

"What's the alternative?" Big Mac asked.

"How 'bout not being in denial?" Martin said. "Respecting our history. Acknowledging the shit that was done to us."

Fang said, "You're talking about—"

"Yeah," Martin said. "I'm talking about my lady."

The choice of noun, this time, in this context, tripped something in Daniel.

My lady. Not my *wife*. Not my *girlfriend*.

The draft from the window cooled the sweat that had broken out across Daniel's back. He lifted a hand from his lap, gestured for him to continue.

Martin folded his arms across his black-and-red flannel shirt. "I don't *ever* want to let go of what happened to her. She was *everything* to me, and she was *eaten up* by the"—and here Daniel detected the faintest pause—"skin cancer."

A cascade of memories flooded through Daniel. Martin, adamant in his chair: *She was so innocent*. And earlier, as he'd explained his story to A-Dre: *The treatments were serious dollar, wiped us out. But the cancer, it didn't care when we ran outta jack. So I knocked off a coupla grocery stores*.

Daniel thought of Dooley next door, right beyond that wall. The iPhone in his pocket, pressed reassuringly against his thigh. But he had one shot at this and one shot only, and so he found the point of weakness and pressed.

"She was so vulnerable," he said.

"Yes," Martin said.

"And you were so helpless."

Martin's Adam's apple bobbed. He gave a small nod.

"What was the worst part?" Daniel asked. "Of *all* of it?"

Martin's breathing had quickened. "She'd wake up at night. Terrified. Her heart racing. And it got so she was afraid to go to sleep. And me, too. I got scared to fall asleep, too." He pulled off his glasses, pinched his eyes.

Daniel said, "You didn't want her to be scared and alone. Not even for a second before you could wake up and comfort her."

Martin nodded into his hand.

"She was so little," Daniel said.

The others came alert, confused, but Daniel held on Martin, who was hunched over, his face still lowered into the brace of his hand.

And then he nodded again.

Daniel felt the walls of the room fall away, and then the other group members vanished until there was only a tunnel of space connecting him and Martin.

"It wasn't skin cancer," Daniel said, reaching slowly for his iPhone. "It was even worse."

Martin's shoulders shook, his head lowered, his fists pressing into his buzz cut. "Her *heart*." He sucked in a wet inhale. "We went to clinics and hospitals for different rounds of treatment. Every fucking doctor had another story. We pulled her out of preschool—"

"Preschool?" X threw up her hands. "The *fuck*?"

"I thought it was your *wife* who died," Lil said.

Martin didn't register either of them. The glasses slid back on, and, still curled over, he lifted his gaze, freezing Daniel's hand midway into his pocket. There was a darkness behind his eyes that Daniel did not recognize. Martin's arms bulged, and his foot tapped a slow staccato on the cracked tile, his body tense and snake-coiled. Daniel had seen a lot of people under incredible duress, and he had no doubt that if he moved for the phone, Martin would explode. He kept his hand in place, fingers dug halfway into his pocket.

The other group members were stunned into silence, aware that something beyond their grasp was transpiring. The current of air from the window carried with it the smell of car exhaust, and somewhere far away a driver was laying on the horn. Daniel remained perfectly still; the slightest movement would bring everything crashing down. Martin's black eyes, distorted through the lenses, had gone sharp, boring through Daniel, pinning him to the metal chair.

Daniel pressed his hand another millimeter into his pocket. At once there was a shiv in Martin's fist, low at his side next to his thigh. A carved wooden blade to get past the metal detectors, sanded to a high gleam. The knife was hidden from most of the room, but Lil, beside him, noticed and blanched.

Daniel considered the phone at his fingertips, the undercover cops in the hall, Dooley camped out one room over, but they were all out of reach. Martin was maybe five feet away on the opposite side of the ring. With a single lunge, he'd be on Daniel, blade through his throat.

Martin shifted, his fist tightening around the wooden handle. "It's time," he said.

Chapter 63

Blade still concealed at his side, glare fixed on Daniel, Martin set his weight forward on his boots, preparing to spring from his chair.

"*Wait*," Daniel said.

Martin paused. Lil stifled a cry in her throat.

"I think," Daniel said, "that *I* should take center chair."

Martin sat still for a very long time. Then he bobbed his head.

Daniel's skin felt on fire, a dry heat baking through him. Keeping his eyes on Martin, he moved very cautiously across to the hot seat.

Big Mac said, "The hell?"

A-Dre cast out his arms. "Someone wanna tell us what the fuck is happening up in here?"

"Counselor's got some things he needs to get off his chest," Martin said.

"Like something *illegal*?" X asked.

"Nah," Martin said. "He never committed a crime, because he didn't *have* to." His eyes, pronounced beneath the lenses, swung to Daniel. "Ain't that right?"

Daniel met his gaze as evenly as he could manage.

"All of us did what we did for someone we loved," Martin said. "A-Dre for his brother in jail. Lil for her husband. Me for my daughter."

X held up a hand, tried to cut in. "What *daughter*, Martin? This shit is freaking me out."

But Martin raised his voice, bulldozing over hers. "Fang for his cousin who got popped. X started dealing to support her sick mom. Big Mac needed money for his family."

"Don't put that shit on me," Big Mac said. "I ain't no victim. What I did was *wrong*."

"We can't make excuses because . . . ah, ah, we got it rough."

"That *is* some boo-hoo shit, Martin," X said, and A-Dre nodded.

Martin adjusted his grip around the wooden knife, still hidden by his side. The sleeves of his flannel were torn off at the shoulders, revealing the bulging, shiny arms of a weight lifter. "What then? We did it because we're *evil*?"

Lil's voice quavered with fear. "Because we made dumb choices."

Big Mac said, "We can't just do whatever we want because we care about someone."

"Let's talk about that a minute," Martin said. Beside his thigh, the filed-down tip of the shiv ticked over to aim at Daniel. "Can *you* do whatever you want because you care about someone?"

Daniel took in a jagged breath.

"Can you?" Martin said between clenched teeth.

Daniel said, "I have better options, yeah."

"Better options, huh? Meaning when the shit hits, you can always pull the cord on your golden parachute and sail out of trouble. When your wife got sick, you didn't *have* to rob no bank. You could just call your old lady, couldn't you, *Brasher*?" Martin turned, speaking to the others. "That's right. He got his wife a treatment that saved her life. By bumping my daughter out."

"What's he *talking* about?" A-Dre asked Daniel.

When Daniel hesitated, Martin said, "Honesty and accountability. Ain't that what you say, Counselor?"

"Yes," Daniel said. "I did. I got my wife into a closed medical trial."

X looked devastated. "Did you *know* his daughter would get left out?"

"No, he didn't," Martin said. "And that makes it worse. All those people. The nurse who shuffled the files, crossed out one name and wrote in another. The accountant who rubber-stamped it. The security guard who threw my woman and child out on the street when they went begging. It was so little a part of their lives they didn't even *remember* it. No one thinks they did anything wrong, because that's just how it *works* for them." His muscular shoulders gathered around his neck. "So imagine my surprise after I did my time and paid my debt to society when I got out to see that Daniel Brasher was teaching Reason and Rehabilitation. Educating us crooks on how to make better choices."

Martin's fuse was burning down, rage tightening the skin of his face, veins popping in his neck. Daniel turned slightly, pushing his fingers farther into his pocket. He'd just touched the edge of the phone when Martin said, "Put your *fucking* hands in your lap."

Daniel put his hands up quickly.

"The hell?" A-Dre said.

Martin lifted the knife into view, and an electric current ran through the chairs, jolting the others upright. He cast an eye at Big Mac and A-Dre, who'd gone rigid. "Everyone scoot your chairs back. Everyone but you, Counselor. Back up more. That's right."

Daniel stared helplessly at the mounted chalkboard. Thought of Dooley just beyond it, a few feet through the wall. The noise of the chairs moving would not alert her any more than the raised voices would; she was well aware that a lot went down within these four walls. His only hope was to survive until session ended or to send a text without Martin's noticing.

Martin aimed the knife at the others. "First person who moves gets this in the throat, okay? So we're all gonna just sit here. Sit here and listen. Tell them I'll do it, Counselor."

"He will," Daniel said. "So let's just sit and listen."

"Oh, not *you*. You're gonna have to *answer*, too." Martin tapped the side of the blade against his forearm, studying Daniel. Then he asked, "Could you have shot her in the head?"

"What?"

"My four-year-old daughter. Francisca. Could you have taken a gun and put a bullet through her head?"

Daniel's throat had gone dry, turning his voice hoarse. "No."

"Right. That's not how rich folks do things. Instead you make calls and pull strings and go back to your three-story house in the Heights. But it's the same thing, isn't it?"

"Pulling strings and shooting a little girl?"

"*No.* You didn't kill *a* little girl. You killed *my* little girl. You chose your wife over my baby's life. *Say* it."

"You're right," Daniel said. "I did all that was in my power to get my wife into that trial. And I didn't consider everything that meant. Hell, I didn't consider *anything* that meant. And I'm not saying that was right or fair or virtuous, and I won't try to justify it. But would you have done any different?"

"Of course not," Martin said, grief spilling into his rage. "But you *got to*. You *got to* do it."

Martin's last words cored Daniel out, left him hollow. He reminded himself that this was the man who had drawn a blade across the throats of three people and poisoned a fourth. If there was a time for Daniel to feel guilt and remorse, it was not now, with his own life and five others hanging in the balance. He tried to grope his way back to his role here in this room, as a counselor. And the rules he tried to work by: Don't force a group member. Let him lead. Wait for an opening.

"I need to make it right for her," Martin said.

"And this will do that?" Daniel asked.

Martin pressed a hand to the side of his head, the knife rising, and at the periphery Daniel heard the chairs creak as the others tensed. Martin's face contorted, approaching a sob, but he fought away the grief, a scowl hardening his features again. He took a wary look at the others, his fist reclamping around the handle of the knife. He rocked a bit in the chair, a wrestler bouncing to keep loose on the mat. Sweat coursed down the sides of his neck.

"You have *no idea* what I went through," Martin said, rocking some more.

Daniel pictured tears of blood draining from the eyes of Marisol

Vargas, Kyle Lane, Molly Clarke. Martin had wanted them to feel what he felt. The grief. The loss. The fear.

Martin moved the knife deftly, switching hands. He stood swiftly and took a step toward Daniel. Lil gave a faint shriek, and Fang stood up. Daniel tensed in his chair, coiled to rise, but Martin took another big stride, leading with the knife, and closed the distance in a single lurch.

The blade was at Daniel's throat, indenting the skin just shy of its breaking point. The room, as still as a tableau. Daniel waited for the surface tension to pop, the rush of wet heat to claim the hollow of his neck. Martin stared down at him, biceps flexing. His mouth firmed with determination, and Daniel watched the killing impulse move down the man's bulging arm like a ripple. It had just tensed Martin's fist when Daniel fought words out against the pressure. "Then *tell* me."

Martin paused.

Even over the surge of panic static filling his head, Daniel could make out the heightened breathing of the others. He forced out the words, "Tell me what you went through."

Martin lifted the blade from Daniel's throat, took a few steps back, and sat again in his chair. His eyeglass lenses were fogged at the bottoms. He twirled the knife in his hand.

Everyone sat silent, on the razor's edge.

Though soft, Martin's words carried a weight behind them, as if pushed out from his core. "She'd lost so much weight you could count her ribs. Like something from a war movie. Or Africa. Twenty-two pounds. And the fevers. Her head would get so hot it'd burn my hand. We had to cool her off with ice, but she hated it. The cold. And we couldn't explain to her that it was for her . . . for her . . ."

Daniel said, "For her own good."

Martin breathed for a time.

"They took so long to change her sheets. At the last hospital. She was in too much pain to get up and go to the bathroom, and if we were late with the bedpan . . . Her sheets were dirty, always dirty. I couldn't take care of her. I was her father, and I couldn't take care of her."

The others listened, wan and tense and hanging on every word. A-Dre started to say something, but Daniel held up a hand, palm out, and he closed his mouth.

"That's why you're doing this," Daniel said.

"*Yes,*" Martin said. "I have to make it right for her now."

Daniel caught the phrase coming around a second time—*have to make it right for her.* A desperate little plea, a fissure into Martin's pain. Daniel sensed an underlying truth, that perhaps this whole blood-drenched pageant wasn't merely about justice but *regret.*

Daniel wanted desperately to interject, to take control, but as hard as it was, he firmed his mouth and ran the mantra: *Let him lead. Wait for an opening.*

A few moments later, Martin started up again. "In her last days, she couldn't take it. We were dead broke, but we had the money for another round of chemo. I'd *gotten* her that money, I'd done what I had to do, but she just said, 'Daddy, I'm so tired. Please don't. Please don't make me.' And I was so mad. I'd done *everything* for her. Risked my life even to get the money, all for her, but she was still . . ." He halted.

And Daniel saw it there, the back half of the equation. "She was still going to leave you," he said.

That tiniest of taps seemed to knock Martin into a different lane. For the first time, tears fell, though his face stayed blank. "I was so angry with her for that. She was lying there in dirty sheets, wasting away, and I couldn't forgive her. I couldn't forgive her."

He sat motionless, tears streaming.

Daniel said, "What do you wish you'd told her?"

"Not *told her,*" Martin said. "*Done.*"

Daniel tried to catch his balance after the misstep. "But you did so much for her."

"No." Martin's head rocked side to side. "No."

He was working his way up to something, and Daniel paused again, giving him time and runway. Martin clenched the makeshift knife so tightly that his hand had gone bloodless.

Daniel said, "What do you wish you'd done for her?"

Martin's barrel chest heaved. "She wanted princess toes," he finally said. "There was this pedicure place up the block from the clinic. Forty bucks to bring the lady in. And I told my little girl she didn't need it. I was so angry she wouldn't do the chemo, and she was begging me, but I told her no, that if she wouldn't let us spend the money on treatment to save her life, she couldn't spend it on having her fucking toes painted. My little girl was lying there sick in dirty sheets. And I told her no. That she couldn't." Tears dripped off his chin, pattered on the floor. "She died with unpainted toes because I was mad at her."

His palms went to his face, the knife clattering to the floor, then he collapsed from the chair onto his knees, hunched and weeping on the tile.

After a breathless pause, Daniel slid the phone from his pocket and keyed a few buttons.

A moment later the door flung open and a stream of undercover officers, led by Dooley, poured inside. Martin remained on his knees, rocking himself as if in prayer, the whittled shiv lying just beyond his reach.

They took him without a struggle.

Chapter 64

After the explanations, the witness reports, the phone calls to Cris, after the hushed conversations with group members, Kendra, and an endless array of cops, Daniel found himself at Dooley's side in the basement of Metro South, filling the doorway of Angelberto's little janitorial office. A fan of uniformed cops waited behind them in the hall, edged into sight sufficiently to announce their presence.

"Why'd you lie?" Dooley pressed Angelberto. "About Martin's alibi? You told Daniel you were with Martin and his broken-down car at midnight. No—you said at *least* until midnight. Which is a little tricky, since at that time he was across town cutting Marisol Vargas's throat."

Wearing his loose-fitting overalls, Angelberto sat on the bare wooden bench before his open locker, blinking down at the oil-stained floor. Terrified. "I did not lie. I did not." He pointed at a plain-faced clock nailed to the wall above his locker. "It was midnight. I remember I came back upset that it was so—" His long eyelashes fluttered, and he pressed his hand to his chest, as if on the verge of heaving. "Oh, *por Dios.*"

"What?" Dooley said.

"*Es noviembre.*"

"Yeah. It's November. Speak English, hombre."

"The first Sunday. It was—*¿cómo se dice?*—the clock change?"

It seemed impossible after the last two hours that anything would catch Daniel off guard, but there it was, another jolt. "The end of daylight saving time," he said.

Angelberto's bare arms were coated with sweat. "I change the clock late."

"So it wasn't midnight like you thought," Daniel said. "It was eleven P.M."

Dooley smacked the doorframe with her palm. "Which left Martin plenty of time to get to 1737 Chestnut Street."

Angelberto looked grief-stricken. "I am sorry. So sorry for what I have done."

Dooley's cell phone shrilled, and she answered and uh-huhed a few times, gesturing Daniel a step into the hall. She hung up and said, "Looks like they located Martin's girlfriend, Viviana Olvera. Let's go."

Daniel cast a glance back, wanting to offer some piece of comfort, but Dooley was already blazing away past the uniformed cops toward the garage.

He left Angelberto there on the bench with his shoulders slumped and the wall clock looking on.

On summer mornings when the coastal fog blows in to shroud the land, Sutro Tower is the only piece of the skyline that rises into visibility, beaming TV reception into the folds and divots of the city. When the wind around Mount Sutro has its back up, it can knock a grown man over, and it staggered Daniel now, causing him to take a quick step off the curb behind the police barricade.

They were up past Gardenside Drive on an impossibly steep street, embedded in the fog belt that claimed the hill. As if the incline, smothered visibility, and wind weren't disorienting enough, the Muni line ran right past them, buses heralding their approach with strained rumbling before sailing out of the mist like ghost ships. The medicinal taste of eucalyptus suffused the air, and through breaks in the soup, Daniel could make out patches of green below and the vague outline of the buildings of the UCSF Medical Center, a bulwark to the forest.

SWAT had geared up and filed into the apartment building a few minutes earlier. Dooley paced behind the sawhorses impatiently, radio at the ready. "The hell's taking them so long? I thought the landlord confirmed a sighting."

"Maybe she's not there anymore," O'Malley said. "Remember, that apartment's been checked a handful of times. Nobody saw anyone but Martin."

"That's because no one was looking for anyone *but* Martin." Tapping the radio to her lips, she stared at the building's exterior. The place was Section 8, voucher-subsidized for low-income tenants, and it looked it. A stained concrete rectangle, like a domino set on its side, standing out in the otherwise well-tended neighborhood.

An eerie screech reached them from above, the banshee howl of the wind whipping through the tower, raising goose bumps on Daniel's arms.

Viviana heard the quiet scraping of boots in the corridor outside, and she knew. Tears rose to her eyes instantly. It was over, Martin either dead or captured. Even in this box of an apartment, she felt suddenly dwarfed, as if the walls were rising all around her, the ceiling growing ever distant.

She'd prepared for this aloneness, this end, but *knowing* it, feeling it roost inside her chest was nothing she could have prepared for.

First Francisca. Now Martin.

She could sense them out there, countless men with guns and gear, readying, doing their best to be silent, invisible. All this, for her.

She pictured Martin's face, so clearly she could have reached out and touched it. He'd never given up. Not once.

She rushed to the worn mattress and flung it up, exposing an open hatch in the floor that led down into the crawl space. A few cockroaches scuttled among pipes and rebar. Nestled to one side was their stash of folders. The secret plan.

She dropped in, letting the mattress fall just as she heard the boom of a boot or a battering ram meet the front door. Darkness claimed her. Bodies stormed the room overhead. Men shouted. She was on her knees and elbows, breathing dust, doing her best to flatten her body and squirm forward. The folders slipped beneath her, tearing, their contents scattering—maps and hospital files, schedules and reports. In the darkness she felt a glossy photo bow under the heel of her hand, a prized death snapshot of One of the Responsible crying blood, either Marisol Vargas or Jack Holley.

From above she heard someone shout, *"The mattress—check beneath the mattress!"*

She scrabbled forward even harder, but the papers slipped beneath her hands, her feet, giving her little traction.

All at once the world yawned open again, light blazing down on her from the hatch.

"Here! Here! We got her!"

She lurched for the darkness ahead, but gloved hands seized her around her ankles. As she was torn backward, bellowing, her arms slid across photos of the dead, crumpling them into the grime.

Outside, Daniel's unease had reached a fever pitch when Dooley's radio squawked. She ducked from the gale, shielding herself behind the thick gray trunk of a Monterey cypress rising up out of the sidewalk. Radio at her cheek, she plugged the opposite ear and looked up into the jagged crown of leaves. She made a fist, pumped it, stepped back into range.

"Found her in the crawl space beneath the apartment. They'd widened out a vent so she could slip down there during searches."

The two of them waited tensely, watching the building. From the heavens came another moan as wind moved through the prongs of the tower.

Finally the glass lobby door opened, Viviana stepping forth sandwiched between two SWAT officers, her hands cuffed before her at her waist. They led her down the stairs onto the sidewalk and toward the sawhorse en route to the caged squad car.

Daniel steeled himself.

Something was wrong with her face. As she neared, he saw that it was a patchwork of swells and bruises, the skin stretched shiny tight across one cheek, her lip dotted with a broken scab. He didn't want to confront her but didn't want to step away either, and as she passed right before him, she pulled to a halt.

Her head rotated toward him. She wore torn sweats and a ragged T-shirt, and he could smell the grime of the crawl space on her. Behind him he heard the roar of a Muni bus laboring up the hill. He thought she might spit in his face, but no, she just stared into him, wearing an expression that bordered on smug.

The ground shook with the approaching Muni bus, so her words were lost, but he read her battered lips. They said, *You'll see.*

The Muni bus emerged from the fog.

With a violent shake of her shoulders, she twisted free of the SWAT officers and lunged off the curb. There were shouts and commotion, but already she'd scampered out of reach. For a moment Daniel thought she was making a futile escape attempt, but she halted in the middle of the street. Then she pivoted back to face them.

She kept her eyes on Daniel, the faintest smile haunting her lips as the bus grille wiped her from sight.

Chapter 65

Daniel and Cris stood on their square of front lawn the next day, seeing Leo off. He had nothing with him, no overnight bag, no toothbrush in his pocket, as remarkably self-contained a person as Daniel had ever encountered.

"Sorry I mistook you for a murdering psychopath," Daniel said.

Leo's mouth shifted a little in amusement. He offered his hand, big enough for a man twice his size, and Daniel shook it.

"Thank you for everything you did for us," Daniel said. "I'm not sure how to repay you."

"I was already paid," Leo said.

"I didn't mean like that."

Leo said nothing. This was clearly not a language he was comfortable speaking.

Cris moved to hug him, and he went board straight, his shoulders up around his ears, his arms half raised, held out to the sides but not settling on her. She released him, tapped his vast chest with her palm. "Don't go getting all sentimental on us now."

Leo headed off toward the street. His Bronco was nowhere in sight; he generally parked a few blocks away.

Daniel said, "See you."

Without turning, Leo said, "Hope you won't need to."

As he vanished around the corner hedge, Cris started inside. Daniel had just reached the porch behind her when a Subaru Outback pulled up next door, wearing an upside-down kayak on the roof like a Robin Hood hat. Ted Shea climbed out and began fussing with straps. He caught sight of Daniel, and Daniel lifted an arm in greeting.

Ted slid the kayak off the car and moved up the walk, slamming the front door behind him.

Daniel thought, *Win some, lose some.*

He found Cristina upstairs cooking pumpkin pancakes, though it was midday. After Viviana Olvera's suicide last night, Dooley had asked him back to 850 Bryant to cross every last *t* on the mounting crime-scene reports. By the time he'd driven home, the dew-wet street had already picked up the faintest gleam of the sun, barely tucked behind the eastern horizon. He and Cris had slept an unbroken sleep for the first time in recent memory and woke up late enough that pancakes at 2:00 P.M. made sense.

He came up behind her, embraced her around the waist, and she spun in his arms, mixing spoon in hand. "Three things you're grateful for," she said.

He placed his hand on her shirt, above the small grouping of radiation tattoos. "You're alive," he said. "I'm alive." He slid his hand down to her stomach, noticing for the first time the tiny bulge. "And this."

The house phone rang. Still holding her, he reached across to answer.

The familiar voice, sharpened with anxiety. "Daniel. I need to see you. I need you here."

"Mom, can't we just—"

"*Immediately,* Daniel. I'm still at the Fairmont."

The line clicked. Troubled, he set down the receiver. Cris looked up at him inquisitively.

"It's Evelyn," he said. "Something's wrong with her."

"More wrong than usual?" Cris asked.

"She sounded really upset." He searched for his car keys. "Want to come with me?"

Cris turned back to the pancake mix. "Not particularly," she said.

A slew of reporters waited outside the Fairmont, jockeying for position. After valeting, Daniel slipped through a side door to the lobby and found the concierge. "This about the Tearmaker case?"

The concierge's lips flattened. "No, Mr. Brasher."

"What's going on?"

"Perhaps you'd best talk to your mother."

He rode up to the penthouse, his concern rising steadily with the altitude, and stepped into the vast embrace of the living room. Evelyn sat centered on a banana-curved couch longer than a stretch limo, the scale of the piece and the vaulted ceiling diminishing her. No one else was present—no James, no butler, no housekeeper—which only amped up Daniel's worry all the more. Her ring-intensive fingers were wrapped around a glass, and as he drew nearer, he caught a waft of scotch.

Her hands jiggled the glass, the ice cubes musical against the crystal. "Celestina couldn't be bothered to come?"

"Cristina. Been a long week."

"I suppose I haven't generated much goodwill there."

"No, Mom. Not really."

She took a few unladylike gulps. "I heard the news. That's why my not-so-secret service detail is gone. It's all over the TV, the papers. You were instrumental."

"Inspector Dooley told me they'd keep me out of it as long as they could," Daniel said. "How'd you find out?"

"The president of the police commission phoned this morning."

"Ah, yes. Your inside track."

"Not for long." Her eyes shifted about, returned to the glass.

He watched her watch the scotch for a moment, then said, "Want to tell me what this is about?"

"It's gone, Daniel."

"What is?"

"All of it."

The meaning dawned, slowly. The family fortune, gone. That's what all those panicked phone calls to Evelyn from the office had been about.

"Leveraged currency bets," Daniel said. "Vimal."

"That's right. Though they were my call. He tried to advise me to pull back." She took a sip from the glass, her hands trembling. "Let it never be said I didn't make my own bed. And so now . . ."

He realized he was still standing but felt no urge to sit down. It seemed the kind of news better handled on his feet. "Now what?"

"The Sea Cliff house will be gone. I owe the note on the villa still, so that's . . ." She waved the glass, another residence gone. "We've been feeling it the past few months already. Cash-flow problems, I believe they call it. The interior decorator who redid the master suite is suing. Can you imagine? A Brasher, sued by an *interior decorator?*"

"So everything . . ."

"Gone. The properties, the holdings, the stocks. I'll be down to those dreary retirement accounts your father insisted on funding dozens of years ago. Those can't be touched in . . . bankruptcy." Her mouth puckered at the word.

"How much in the retirement accounts?"

Her hair was mussed slightly in the back, the departure from her usual impeccable appearance making her seem somehow frail. "Not enough."

"How *much,* Mom?"

"They'll throw off a couple hundred thousand a year." She tapped the rim to her lip and sneered. "He must be grinning from the grave."

"People have been known to live on that."

"*People,*" she said.

He walked over and tried to pry the glass from her hand. She held it tighter, turning the moment intentionally comical as he tugged at it. Finally she let go and flopped back on the couch, giving him a mock glare. He considered her glass. Took a sip. She cracked a reluctant smile at that.

"You were smart," she said. "You *chose* to leave the family money behind. On your terms. Having something taken away is so . . . maddeningly *pathetic.*"

Daniel looked out onto the terrace, where a layered Moroccan fountain burbled pleasingly before a jaw-dropping view of the Trans-america Pyramid. He knew that Castanis's corporate goddesses were out there, too, their impenetrable, shadow-cloaked faces observing this fall from fortune as they'd observed thousands before and would observe thousands to come.

A Moroccan fountain. On a roof terrace. For the love of Mary.

He ran his fingers through his hair. "How much is this place costing you?"

She told him.

"A *night*?" He took another swig of her scotch. "Are you kidding me? Okay, first things first. Let's get you out of here. Where's James?"

"I don't need *James*." She rose, wobbled a bit, then steadied herself. "I can pack myself." She disappeared into the master suite. There was a great clanking of hangers and rattling of pill bottles, and then she emerged. "Okay. I have no idea how to pack. I'll send James back for my things." She laughed at herself, and it turned into the faintest sob before she caught herself. "Did I ever tell you the story about the day they pounded the last rivet into the Golden Gate Bridge?"

"No, Mom."

"April twenty-seventh, 1937. My mother was there. She was pregnant, so I suppose I was there, too. It was a big occasion, as you can imagine. They'd made a special gold rivet, said to be worth four hundred dollars—back *then*. During the ceremony the pneumatic hammer pounded the rivet into place, but the soft gold couldn't withstand the pressure. It came apart, sprayed slivers across the spectators, fell into the Bay. So." A tilt of her head. "They used an ordinary steel one." She turned to a wall mirror and began fussing with her hair, smoothing down the back, then making microadjustments. "When Mother told me that story, I used to think she was saying, 'This city has always had an uneasy fit with wealth.' But maybe it means something else." She reapplied lipstick and turned to face him. "At the end of the day, steel is stronger than gold, isn't it?"

He studied her a moment, then nodded.

"I'm scared, Daniel."

He had never heard her say it.

"I don't know who I am without money," she said. "I don't know how I'll live."

"I'll help you."

"How?"

"Put you in one of my classes with felons."

She dabbed her nose, and a laugh escaped. "Maybe you're not so useless after all." She shook her head as if shuddering off water, released a deep breath. "The press caught wind. They're waiting for me downstairs."

"Should we ask the manager to sneak you out the back?" Daniel asked.

"No, darling." Her sparkling laugh was not entirely drained of humor. "Losers walk."

He had to admire that. He countered with another of her favorite sayings. "You make things hard on yourself."

She didn't smile, but he could read her amusement in the way her lips reshaped themselves. "I've been told that easy is overrated. I supposed I'm about to find out." She pulled back her shoulders, faced the door, squaring herself up. "Will you . . . will you walk with me?"

He couldn't help but think of his group members, struggling to gain power over a past they'd let define them. A-Dre and Big Mac, trying to turn a new page. Fang walking away from the beckoning neon sign of the club. X in that chair, owning up to her remorse. Lil braving a church social despite the trembling in her legs, the loss of breath, the fear she might die of panic in a parking lot. How much they had taught him.

Evelyn took an unsteady step, and he turned slightly, offered his arm.

She took it.

Side by side, they rode the elevator down in blissful silence. The mood of the lobby was restrained, the staff elegant and respectful. Each time she wobbled, he righted her.

And then they stepped outside.

The press swarmed. He felt her hand tighten around his biceps, the nails pinch into the skin, but she smiled easily into the wall of cameras and microphones. Steadily, he kept moving her toward her car.

A bald newspaperman worked his way in front of them. "—truth to the rumors that your fortune has dissipated overnight—"

"Nice tie, Bob," Evelyn said. "I see you've graduated from pastels."

An aggressively made up TV reporter lunged to the forefront. "Multiple reports have confirmed that you're now broke."

"No," Evelyn said. "Just less rich."

James eased the Bugatti forward, and Daniel steered her out of the scrum and into the backseat. She slammed the door, and he found himself looking at his reflection in the dark tint of the window.

He was about to turn away when the window rolled down and her hand reached through, caught his forearm, and held it a moment. "Happy Thanksgiving," she said.

Chapter 66

Another hard rain bounced off the street below, making it gleam beneath passing headlights. No moon, no stars—no sky, even. Just a ceiling of mist cutting the tops off the houses. Daniel set his hand on the cool glass of the bedroom window, staring down at the spot where Viviana Olvera had once stood, her face hidden beneath the raised yellow hood. Closing his eyes, he relived the thud of the Muni bus striking her. That faint little smile she wore, as if she were recalling an inside joke. That battered face, the lips shaping those two words:

You'll see.

Cristina sat on the bed behind him, work files spread across the duvet, chewing a pencil and contemplating the next windmill to tilt at. She looked up at him. "You hungry?"

"Does it matter?"

"What does that mean?"

He grinned. "What do you want?"

She tapped the pencil against her lips. "Peking duck?"

"Should we see how many questions we can ask each other in a row?"

That voluptuous wide grin. "Chinatown or the Richmond?"

"Do you think anywhere's open at nine o'clock at night?"

"Would you mind calling around?"

"Is this pregnancy craving thing really for real?"

She set down her pencil, and her face changed. "Are you still scared?"

His smile faded. They listened to the rain tapping the window. Then he said, "I keep waiting for the other shoe to drop."

"You're looking for her," she said. "On the street. Just now."

"I guess I am."

"I do, too. Even though it makes no sense."

"Fear doesn't have to make sense," he said.

A deep breath lifted her chest. "I think it's just hard to believe that this thing is really over."

The phone rang, shrill off the walls.

It rang again. They kept their eyes on each other, even as Daniel crossed to the nightstand and answered. He didn't need to hear the voice to know it would be Dooley.

"We're doing the post-arrest interview," she said. "Don't want to give Martin time to work out his story. And something came up."

A trickle of dread, like a fingernail down his spine. "What?"

"He claims that another person was kidnapped. And is still alive somewhere, alone, like Kyle Lane in that wine cellar."

The trickle down his spine turned to ice water. He couldn't figure out how to make his mouth work to ask the question, but Dooley continued, answering it anyway.

"We don't know who it is. All the people from the study are accounted for. At least the ones we can think of. We've been pressing him hard for a name, a location. But."

"*What*, Dooley?"

A heavy sigh blew across the receiver. "He says he'll only tell you."

When the sally port of the jail swung closed behind Daniel's car, sealing him momentarily from fender to bumper, it produced a perfect claustrophobic dread. Then the front gate slid away, revealing a waterlogged stretch of asphalt, and he remembered to breathe again. A guard escorted him inside and upstairs, where Dooley waited, reminding him that though Martin had demanded that no one else be in the room, she and others would be listening to every last word and that Daniel should do anything to draw him out.

He was ushered into a dank room with a stall terminating in a shield of ballistic glass that looked onto the mirror image of a facing stall. A coaster-size speaking hole in the glass rendered jailhouse phones unnecessary.

He waited, counting the seconds, working to stay calm.

A metallic boom announced the opening of an out-of-sight metal door, and then a rustling of chains came audible, Jacob Marley sounding his approach. Martin appeared in the doorway, his broad form barely contained by an orange jumpsuit. The spartan surroundings only accented the dark frames of his glasses all the more, and he gave a mysterious smile as he fixed his gaze on Daniel and shuffled forward in his shackles to claim the chair opposite. A guard waited until he was situated, then vanished out through the still-open door as prenegotiated.

Martin's voice was husky, close to a growl. "Are you thinking about all you have to be thankful for today?"

"Among other things."

"They told me about Viviana." He wet his lips. "I'm all alone now. Facing the death penalty. You know, pay for my bad choices. Maybe I'll get lucky. Life in prison." Each sentence tinged with that generic urban accent.

"Do you have something to tell me, Martin? Or not?"

"I *am* telling you. About you. And me. See, I'm your photographic negative." He tried to spread his arms, but since his wrists were shackled to his waist chain, all he could manage was a flare of his elbows. Even physically he was in many regards Daniel's opposite. Brown skin, swollen muscular build, close-shaved head with that bristling hair.

"You have everything," Martin said. "I have *nothing*."

"You looking for sympathy?"

"No. Just understanding. That's why I wanted you to find those letters in your mailbox. I wanted you to *learn* what it feels like to be helpless. Because that's how it feels. You don't *understand* why someone's in a study, say, and then she's not."

"But you found out, didn't you?"

"I had nothing to do with my life *but* find out. And plan. I checked your mailbox every day after I put the letters there, but you didn't pick them up. So I kept with the deadlines, figured you'd tune in at some point. I didn't expect you to show up at Marisol Vargas's—you must've gotten the mail late that night. I figured you'd have a shot at Kyle Lane since you had that letter in plenty of time, but the coast was clear. At least on the front end. Then, once you caught up all the way with Molly Clarke . . . well, creativity was called for."

"So it was all about teaching me a lesson?" Daniel asked.

"From the moment you were born, you had no notion of reality. Your whole life. Even when you *die,* you'll die in clean sheets." A breath caught in that wide chest. "When someone you loved got sick, what did you do? You picked up the phone. And then your mom did. You spent money. You pulled in resources. I wanted you to know for once what it feels like to have no resources. No safety net. No idea what would happen next. That is all I ever wanted. Was for you to know what you were doing when you didn't *care* to know you were doing it."

"Did you actually kidnap someone before group yesterday?" Daniel said. "Or was this just an excuse to get me here and spin the same record?"

Martin tilted his chin to his chest. His shoulders shook, and Daniel thought he was sobbing until he heard the low chuckle. "Oh, *I* didn't kidnap anyone."

"You're full of shit." Daniel rose to leave. "You're wasting my time."

"Am I?"

"Yeah. It's over for you, Martin. You're at the end of the road."

He didn't move his head, but his glittering eyes pulled north. "Oh, no," he said. "It's just getting started."

Something in his tone froze Daniel halfway to the door. He turned.

"Look at my record," Martin said. "You have already. No kidnappings. No murders. You *saw* me in the room. You were right there, and I had a knife to your throat. But I couldn't do it. And I couldn't kidnap anyone either."

Daniel focused to keep his voice steady. "So now you're *not* the killer? You're innocent, that it? I've heard that a time or two, Martin."

Martin's lips were drawn back, shaped like a grin but utterly humorless. "Oh, I'm not *innocent.*"

"Was someone kidnapped or not?"

"Yes."

"*Who?* Who'd you kidnap, Martin?"

The dark smile returned. "I gave you a deadline. Thanksgiving at midnight." His head pivoted, slowly, to take in the wall clock to Daniel's left side.

Daniel followed his stare—10:31 P.M.

He felt his heartbeat as a deep ticking, a bomb counting down. He pictured again the pert little smile that Viviana Olvera wore as the bus bore down on her.

"I made you a promise, too," Martin continued. "I said to admit what you've done. Or you would bleed for it. Well . . ." He rolled his bottom lip between his teeth. "I didn't say it would be *your* blood."

Heat rolled through Daniel's body. He stepped toward the glass, knocking the chair aside. *"Who?"*

Those magnified eyes took his measure.

"Who's been kidnapped, Martin?"

He bit his lip again. Released it. Smiled from deep inside his own hell.

The ammonia reek of the room clogged Daniel's throat. He stepped back into the embrace of the stall, gripping the ledge of a desk. "What did you do? What the *fuck* did you do?"

Martin's stubbled cheeks bunched in an alarmingly youthful grin. "Thanks for driving all the way over here, Counselor."

Daniel punched the ballistic glass. *"What did you do?"*

"Just remember to control your breathing," Martin said. "Calm your body down. That's the first step."

Dooley was through the door, pulling Daniel back. "We got two cars en route to your house now."

Martin kept his gaze trained on Daniel. "You made a decision before. One life for another. But *this* time *I* made the decision. Now you'll know what it feels like not to be able to make that choice at all."

"Tell me what you did!"

Dooley wrapped Daniel up from behind with surprising strength, but he knocked her away and sprang at the glass.

Martin wiped his face on his shoulder, then turned his head. "Guard! I'm done. *Guard!*"

"Tell me! You fucking *tell me* what you did!"

Dooley was back at Daniel's side, grabbing his arm. "He's useless, Brasher. Let's go. Let's get to your house."

On the far side, two guards stormed in, took Martin by either shoulder, and hoisted him out of his chair. He kept his eyes on Daniel the whole time. As they dragged him away, he just laughed, a creaking of the chest that followed Daniel as he stumbled out into the corridor.

Chapter 67

The chirp of the phone was muffled inside a fold of the duvet. Rubbing lotion into her hands, Cris emerged from the bathroom, trailed by a curtain of steam from the shower. Adjusting Daniel's Giants shirt at her shoulders, she climbed onto the bed and dug out the phone. It was slippery in her lotioned hands, but she juggled it up to her cheek.

"Cris? Cris, listen. We've been calling and—Just— The cops are en route—"

"Wait, *mi vida*. To where?"

"To *you*."

She bolted off the bed, his words fading beneath the seashell rush in her ears. Leo was gone, the alarm off. The threat was supposed to have passed. They'd *told* her it was over.

Daniel's voice faded back in. "Get in the bathroom, lock yourself in, and wait. Stay on the line with—"

Through the window, down against the dark asphalt of the street, a flash of color caught her eye.

A yellow slicker.

It lay flat in the middle of the road with the hood up, splayed out as if its owner had simply evanesced.

A passing car ran it over, the street falling back into darkness as the brake lights vanished. A strangled noise escaped Cris's throat, and she heard Daniel saying, "What? *What?*"

She spun around to run and collided with a padded wall behind her where there should not have been a wall.

Black sweatshirt.

The phone spun from her slick hands.

She didn't want to lift her eyes, didn't want the fabric to take form as a chest, a person.

But she did.

Staring down at her, a featureless face, little more than a dark oval. In her terror it didn't register at first as a mask. But then it resolved— the narrow slit of an eyehole. The sharp triangle of the nose. The perfect circle of the perforations, like an alien mouth.

Before she could react, she was seized, hands gripping her shoulders, crushing her. Screaming, she brought her knee up hard, connecting with his crotch, and the pressure at her shoulders relented.

A cough of a grunt, carrying with it the stink of evergreen-laced tobacco. The man cringed, doubling over. Twisting away, she slashed at the face, her nails scraping harmlessly across the neoprene but catching resistance at the exposed band of neck.

She raked.

He reeled back, swinging for her head, and she ducked, the dumbbell fist sailing over her head, passing through the lifted sheet of her hair. And then she was flying, her bare feet gaining traction on the floorboards.

She half fell down the steps, barely keeping her legs beneath her. Already she could hear him behind, banging into the bedroom doorway. She blazed across the second floor, shoulder-checking the wall at the top of the stairs to halt her momentum. Knocked into a quarter turn, she caught a Tilt-A-Whirl flash of the man, encased in black, gliding like a ghost, closing in on her.

She was off the wall seconds before he smashed into it. And then she plummeted down to the ground floor, three, four steps at a time, spilling onto the foyer, rolling over her shoulders and bouncing vertical again.

She banged into the front door, grasping for the knob, but her lotioned hands slid uselessly over the metal, failing to turn it. Yelling in frustration and rage, she wiped her hands on the T-shirt, tried again, the knob giving up a quarter turn and then slipping again.

Boots thundered down the stairs behind her.

Frantic, she looked around, seizing on the miniature Zen garden. She shoved her palms into the neatly combed white sand, grit sticking to the lotion. The porcelain planter slid off the accent table and shattered as she pivoted back to the front door.

The black form reached the foyer, blurring.

She reached for the knob, sandpaper hands firming her grip—yes—and turning it. She yanked at the door, a blast of fresh air and the distant sound of sirens flooding through the crack, but then a boot hammered the wood panel at her side and the knob flew from her hand, the door smashing back into the frame.

She wheeled around to see a black glove clubbing through the air toward her temple, and then her head snapped and the foyer went murky. Rag-doll limp, she lolled in a powerful brace of arms, dragged backward toward the rear of the house. The drapes of her bangs swept across her eyes, but still she could dimly make out the sight of that front door shrinking from view, step by jarring step.

Chapter 68

Daniel's knuckles ached around the wheel, and sweat stung his eyes as he followed the lights-and-sirens police convoy heading north from 850 Bryant Street toward his house. From the horrifying, fragmented sound track he'd heard on his end of the line, he knew that Cris was gone. She'd be at another location soon enough, arms and ankles bound, throat bared, awaiting the midnight deadline.

So why the hell were they blazing toward Pacific Heights, playing catch-up instead of trying to skip ahead to the Tearmaker's next move?

The Tearmaker. Martin was ruled out now. If he hadn't taken her, who had? Daniel tried to focus his racing thoughts on the last group session, mentally zooming around the circle to consider each face. Fang, Big Mac, A-Dre, Lil, and X—they'd all looked genuinely bewildered, even scared, during Martin's breakdown.

Who then?

He could see Dooley's sedan up ahead, flasher magnetized to the roof, siren blaring. In the wail he heard Cris's own scream, the crack of the phone striking the floorboards, and his hands clenched the wheel harder. His gorge lifted, and he hunched forward, thinking he might vomit or pass out or both, but the veil of static lifted from his vision and he straightened up, set his mind on the task before him.

Which was *what*?

An image sailed out of the panic spin of his thoughts—that empty tin of Skoal in the trash can.

If none of the group members had dropped it there, who had?

Who else had access to the building and passed through the rooms? He remembered waiting for the CSI investigator after session as the man, disguised in a janitor's jumpsuit, had scanned the tin for fingerprints, finding nothing but useless smudges.

A notion bubbled at the base of Daniel's brain.

As they neared Market, his thoughts had reached a high boil, and he peeled out, away from the others. Screeching off onto a side street, he redlined the car toward Metro South, a few blocks away. The garage gate was locked, so he slammed up half on the curb and ran for the lobby door, tugging his keys from his pocket.

The door yawned open, and he was inside the unlit building, his pounding footsteps echoing off the high ceiling. He wound his way through the back corridors, tripping the lights at intervals, revealing one empty stretch of tile after another. Caught in the flash of illumination, a rat reared up on its hind legs, and Daniel nearly stomped it flat as he sprinted by, closing in on the janitor's office.

With a single kick, he almost took the door off the hinges. Not until he stepped inside and surveyed the row of rusted clothing lockers before the thin wooden bench did he realize that his phone was ringing and ringing.

He answered, breathing hard, the gasoline reek of industrial cleaning products burning his chest.

Dooley said, "Where the hell'd you go?"

"Angelberto—the janitor. Rawlins told me he had an airtight alibi for the night of Marisol Vargas's death. Who alibied him?"

"I don't know."

"Call Rawlins *now*."

He clicked off. Confronted the flimsy lock dangling from the hasp of the center locker. He overturned a toolbox in the corner, found a hammer, and beat at the lock. It gave way, and the tall metal door creaked open a few inches. With a knuckle he swung it further ajar, light from the hall brightening the interior by degrees.

The phone rang again, and he pressed it to his ear as the locker's contents came visible. That yellowed Polaroid of Angelberto with his wife and child. Wads of dirty clothes. A few crumpled balls of fluorescent yellow paper.

And two spare pairs of familiar black work boots, speckled with paint.

Dooley's voice at his ear: "Martin," she said. "*Martin* provided Angelberto with the midnight alibi the night of Marisol Vargas's death. They alibied *each other*."

In the bottom corner of the locker, a paper cup brimmed with shiny, new-looking coins. Beside it, resting atop a short stack of gray interdepartmental envelopes, was a canister of rat poison.

Daniel lifted the canister to the light. Beneath the rat skull and crossbones, a red band of a label proclaimed, WARNING: ANTICOAGULANT. DO NOT CONSUME. He thought of Molly Clarke arched like a dying fish on the floor of her town house. A hemophiliac's worst nightmare.

The canister slipped from his hand. His eyes ticked up. On the locker shelf staring back at him was a tin of Skoal Long Cut Wintergreen tobacco.

"It's him," he said.

Through the phone came a screeching of tires. "We'll run down an address, call SWAT, blast in like a wrecking ball."

"If he's there," he said.

But she'd already hung up.

He stared down at those balls of crumpled paper. Fluorescent yellow. He reached for one, unfurled it against the thigh of his jeans.

Across the top in bold print: *"Dim Sum Lunch Special!"*

He flashed on the elderly lady in Chinatown, accosting him and Cris with fluorescent yellow flyers—*Dim sum half off! Dim sum half off!* She'd been no more than a block from the restaurant where Angelberto had made his appearance, where Daniel had fought for his life in the storage room.

He dropped to his knees, paddling at the dirty clothes, teasing apart the mound filling the locker's bottom. More and more crumpled flyers spilled out with the undershirts and socks. He surveyed them there on the oil-spotted floor. Fifteen, twenty flyers.

As if the pushy woman handed Angelberto one every day. As if he crumpled it, shoved it into his pocket, and kept on. A routine.

Every day. Leaving his place. Which had to be near the restaurant from the article with whatsherhead on the cover by the corner next to the joint with the guy with the mole.

A place where Cris could be held right now, trussed like an animal awaiting midnight slaughter.

Again Daniel heard the echo of his wife's cry coming through the phone. The animal grunt of the Tearmaker, of Angelberto, exerting himself. The patter of light footsteps. And then heavy ones, banging in pursuit.

Wiping sweat from his eyes, Daniel plucked the photo of Angelberto's family from the locker and started for the broken door. Stepping over the scattered tools, he hesitated, looking down.

Then he reached for a box cutter, weighing its heft in his palm. He extended the blade, testing it. Thumbing it back into place, he charged out.

The clock above the lockers showed 11:23.

Chapter 69

Running red lights, screeching through traffic, clipping a few vehicles in the process, Daniel made it to the edge of Chinatown in twelve minutes. Dooley texted that they were still trying to run down a current address for Angelberto, and he texted back that he was searching, too. Traffic slowed, and there was no parking, so he left his car in the middle of Grant, blocking traffic, horns blaring after him as he ran up the block. Paper lanterns floated overhead, wafting on strings. Aside from the few tourists out for a nontraditional Thanksgiving meal, the sidewalks were bare. He found the corner where the elderly tout had waylaid him with her flyers, but there was nothing there except a trash can and a homeless guy with two Jack Russell terriers.

He pulled up short, staring in disbelief. Somehow he hadn't considered the possibility that the old woman wouldn't be there, nailed to the sidewalk at this late hour. Closing in on the homeless guy, he pulled out the picture of Angelberto's family, thrusting it forward. "Have you seen this guy? Anywhere?"

"Nah, man. How 'bout a buck, something to eat?"

Daniel spun, enraged, keeping fear at bay. A glowing yellow sign across the street caught his eye—DIM SUM HALF OFF! The lights were still on, bright overheads showing every last detail, the crumbs on the counter, the cracked vinyl booths. A klatch of elderly women rimmed a table in the back.

He sprinted across the street, a car screeching up to hip-check him off the bumper. More horns. He kept on, leaping up onto the curb. The restaurant door was locked, and he banged on the glass, flat-palmed.

The ladies' faces pivoted to him in unison, and he recognized the one at the head of the table. She shook her head and returned to the game of mah-jongg.

He hammered the glass with a fist, and the woman rose with irritation and came around the counter, leading with her quadripod cane. She unlocked the door and threw it open, startling him with her perfect English. "You're gonna break my glass!"

"This man. Have you seen this man?"

"You're banging on my window like a crazy person!"

The wall clock over her shoulder showed 11:38.

"Look at this photo. Please. It's an emergency. Have you seen this man?"

She scowled down. "Yes. I see him every day."

"Do you know where he lives?"

"Why would I know where he lives?"

He looked past the owner at the three other old women who regarded him, fingers resting on their game tiles. A social meeting of the town elders.

"Can I ask them? Please, can I . . . ?" He gestured, stepped inside. "Have any of you seen this man? Here, in the photograph?"

Blank stares.

He heard the thump of the cane behind him, and the woman trudged up next to him, her head not much higher than his elbow. She spoke to the others in Cantonese, and the photo was passed around the circle. Each woman examined it with excruciating care. They spoke back and forth. The tortoise pace of the proceedings was torture; it was all Daniel could do to keep himself from shouting at them to hurry up.

Finally a matriarch with pearl-drop earrings, liberally rouged cheeks, and a dignified bearing gave a terse nod and spoke to the woman at Daniel's side.

"What? What's she saying?"

"He rents a room from her cousin's aunt's friend. The woman's named Mrs. Lai-Wing."

Relief was so intense it took the air from his lungs. *"Where?"*

Another exchange. Then the woman at Daniel's side lifted her cane and aimed the four rubber points through the back of the restaurant. "Waverly Place at Clay, red house with the shingles falling off. She rents out the basement in-law suite."

"Lai-Wing have no in-laws," the matriarch added. She smoothed a few stray hairs back toward the loose bun at her nape. "Lai-Wing lucky girl."

"Thank you." He grabbed the owner's shoulders, kissed her on the forehead, then charged past her even as she shouted after him. He ran through the brief kitchen and out into an alley, skidding on a mound of rotting vegetables. Waverly Place was a historic two-block stretch of Chinatown, once nicknamed 15 Cent Street for the price of the haircuts given there. Daniel shot out the end of the alley, knocking over crates of cabbage and pinballing off a Dumpster onto the main drag. He rushed past the three- and four-story Edwardians with their intricate balconies, flags, and signs in traditional Chinese, a fluttering banner announcing it as the "Street of Painted Balconies." Between an employment agency and a temple, he spotted the dilapidated red house.

No cop cars. No unmarked sedans. Just the house and him, facing off in the cool Chinatown air.

He paused in front, hands on his knees, panting.

Up the slender alley to the east, almost lost to shadow, was a battered worker's van. Just beside it, concrete steps down to a subterranean door.

Fear scratched at his chest from the inside.

He pulled out his iPhone, checked the time: 11:47.

Moving silently up the alley, he brought up Dooley's number. Pressed CALL.

"Where the hell are you?" he whispered.

"We got the place. We're outside now. SWAT's ready to steamroll."

"I don't see you." He approached the van in a crouch. Coming into view behind, parked haphazardly beside a low wrought-iron fence, was a rusting motorcycle. The final confirmation. He stared at the bike, reminding himself to breathe. "Where *are* you guys?"

"A shithole north of Sunnydale. Are you here?"

He tried to swallow but his throat was too dry. "*Sunnydale?* You— No. I'm in Chinatown at Waverly. Red house by the intersection of Clay."

He crept closer to the van. Dangling from the rearview mirror, a Metro South parking pass.

He rested his palm on the hood.

Still warm.

Dooley said, "All his last-knowns show him at—"

"He's *here*, Dooley."

He hung up. Turned off the phone. Removed the box cutter from his pocket and slid the blade out as far as it would go.

Then he crept around the side of the van and descended the worn steps to the peeling door below.

Chapter 70

The door to the basement apartment was slightly ajar, the latch resting against the jamb, as if someone had made a hurried entrance. With full hands. Inset glass squares in place of a peephole afforded Daniel a partial glimpse of the living suite. Unfolded futon with no frame, electric hot plate in the corner, clothes strewn on a water-stained carpet.

The peeling paint poked into his fingertips. The hinges were mercifully quiet. And then he was standing inside.

Empty.

He retracted the blade, his mind whirling. Ten minutes left, maybe less.

He pictured Marisol Vargas pinned to her kitchen floor, leaking tears of blood, and then her face was replaced by Cris's and his brain mostly shut down, stopping him there two steps onto the rotting carpet.

You'll see.

He waded through the stark terror that had descended over him, telling himself to look for any hint of a clue. The folding closet doors were open, nothing inside but scattered take-out cartons and pizza boxes. A few unwashed bowls were stacked unevenly by the hot plate, and the place stank of fish. Hardened spaghetti lay in a clump near an overturned dish in the corner, red sauce splattered up the wall. Through the bathroom door, he saw the cracked bowl of the toilet, the tank lid missing, a wire hanger jerry-rigged to serve as a

trip lever rising into reach. Here beneath the city, the primitive surroundings seemed not just of another world but another *time*.

A moist, earthy reek emanated from the bathroom. And the faintest stirring of air. He drifted into the cramped space and stood on the
curling linoleum. The mold-speckled shower curtain breathed out at
him. Then sucked away. He stared, bewildered, as it bulged and withdrew like the wall of a lung.

His thumb rode the box cutter's slide forward again, the razor ticking out millimeter by millimeter. The curtain breathed at him some
more. Bracing himself, he raked it aside.

A jagged, man-size hole penetrated the tile wall. Wall studs remained like exposed ribs, a narrow space dropping away.

His breathing came fast, ragged. He tried to calm down but found
his body unwilling to obey. Taking in a gulp of air, he stepped into the
tub and leaned through the mouth, the protruding tiles biting into his
shoulders.

A narrow shaft dropped ten feet into what appeared to be a tunnel.

Only one way left.

Down.

Pocketing the box cutter, he climbed through and lowered himself
as quietly as he could manage, splinters pricking his hands. He
dropped the last few feet and hit dirt, nearly toppling over.

He shot quick looks in either direction. The tunnel was impressive,
tall enough that he could stand without crouching. He remembered the
myths of the passages running beneath Chinatown, the shaft Dooley
had discovered leading into the restaurant cellar. Those apocryphal
tong opium dens and torture chambers, the Prohibition escape routes.
With their ancient beams and rusted bolts, the crumbling walls looked
old enough, but a few joists were held in place by newer metal brack-
ets. The perennial handyman, Angelberto had reinforced them himself.

The intestinal walls radiated a wet chemical stench, like an infested
pond. Daniel spun in a slow circle, his breath clouding about his head
in the chill. Mine-shaft lights dangled from snarls of extension cords,
hung at intervals, barely cutting the gloom. One fork was visible,

several paces ahead. A trickle of air brushed his cheeks, carrying with it the faintest noise. A woman's whimpering.

Cristina.

The sound of her burned his nerve endings straight through to numbness. Leading with the box cutter, he started toward the split in the tunnel. His fear had turned to something physical, needles pricking at his arms, his face, the back of his neck.

He reached the fork, stepping around the first bend to stare down a brief length intersecting another passageway. To his right an adjoining room came visible, sunken several feet off the main tunnel system. The old ceiling had crumbled, beams smashed down at angles, but around the wreckage was new buttressing. In fact, the room had been partially excavated and rebuilt, concrete poured to firm the dirt, a few lengths of rebar stubbed up.

Movement at the tunnel intersection ten or so yards ahead drew Daniel's attention. Paralyzed with disbelief, he watched as Angelberto moved backward through the visible stretch, dragging an empty plastic tarp behind him. He wore the familiar black sweat suit and work boots, and the motorcycle mask was shoved up, crowding his forehead. Whistling, he passed from sight.

Daniel stood breathless, a statue.

The whistling, a skin-tingling merriment, found resonance off the tunnel walls.

Then it stopped.

Firming his grip on the box cutter, Daniel watched the brief stretch of intersecting tunnel.

A puff of air blew into sight.

Breath.

And then Angelberto stepped back into view. He regarded Daniel, head cocked, puzzled. Mist huffed again from his mouth.

It took two tries for Daniel to get the words out. "It's over," he said. "Martin's in jail. You know this."

"The wife." Angelberto spit brown, wiped his chin. "She will pay me. The money from the robberies. She has money still."

"She's dead."

"I don't believe you."

"Suicide. She stepped in front of a bus when they came to get her."

Angelberto considered this, his face tensing, those thin lines of facial hair bristling. "Either way," he said. "You have seen me." He removed the lock-blade military knife from his pocket, unfolded it, and started calmly for Daniel.

Daniel half turned, putting his heels to the sunken room so he'd have space to leap backward and parry. The lip of the packed dirt pressed through the soles of his shoes. The moist subterranean walls muffled all sound from the world above. "The cops are on their way," he said. "Right now."

"That," Angelberto said, "I do not believe. If that was the case, you would not be foolish enough to come down here alone."

A shift of the air brought Cris's muffled cries, sending Daniel up on the balls of his feet as if he'd taken a cattle prod to the ribs. Angelberto observed his reaction with neither pleasure nor sympathy. He drew nearer and paused.

Daniel kept the box cutter ready but low at his side. He dug the Polaroid from his back pocket, flipped it onto the dirt between them. "You want money to bring your family here, right?"

Angelberto looked down at the photo. Back up at Daniel.

"Think of them," Daniel said. "Your wife. Your son. Would they want this?"

Angelberto's shoulders lowered, the blade dipping. Somehow Daniel could hear the rumbling of the Bay, water against the bed of the city.

"Oh," Angelberto said. "You don't understand. You think I care."

The reaction, reflective and almost mournful, caught Daniel off guard. He kept his gaze fixed on the knife. "About what?"

Angelberto said, "About anything like that." The blade stayed low, but he lunged, one of those big black boots striking Daniel in the chest, propelling him backward off the lip.

He felt the impact, not yet pain, but a battering-ram thud. There was a tearing sound, a rending of flesh, and then his concrete-filled head rolled drowsily to the side and he saw the slick, gleaming spike of rebar rising up from his left shoulder, impaling him.

He moved, and his nerves finally awakened, pain screaming through him.

White static clouded his vision, then cleared by degrees.

He sensed Angelberto's shape up past the ledge, the dust filling his lungs, a fallen ceiling joint just out of reach above. His feet squirmed and kicked against the pain, but from the waist up he could hardly move.

Pinned to the floor.

The blood-wet metal bar warm against his cheek.

Another muffled scream traveled down the shaft to match his. His wife, trapped in her own agony.

Angelberto's voice carried down. "I'll be right back." His shadow lifted.

The boots tapped the earth, treading away toward Cristina.

Daniel realized he was bellowing unintelligibly. The white static returned, fuzzing the edges of his thoughts. Somewhere in there was the warning Dooley had issued in another context, another universe: *Usually piece-of-shit criminals are just flat-out* broken. *You can't get through to them. You can't fix them.*

He tried to breathe, found it nearly impossible, his chest cramping around the wound. A memory of his own words to Cristina returned to mock him: *I would do* anything *to keep you safe.*

Well, he thought. *Then fucking do it.*

The slightest movement set off such intense pain that he risked passing out. He cast about for any mental tool but could focus on little aside from the quick jerks of his lungs. He ran the equation: Increased adrenaline led to hyperventilation led to shortness of breath led to overbreathing led to diminished CO_2 led to dizziness led to fainting.

So.

He slowed the rise and fall of his chest.

Deep, even breaths.

Grunting with pain, he reached across his chest and felt for the point of penetration. The rebar rose through the meat of his trapezius just above his collarbone.

Flesh and muscle, then. No bone.

Which meant he had a shot at worming off the hook.

Gritting his teeth and yelling, he strained to lean forward off the rebar but the razor-blade flurry set off inside the wound sliced his will to pieces. Once he'd regained the ability to think, he realized that he couldn't yank himself free; the angle was wrong. He'd have to lift himself vertically up off the metal post.

Impossible.

Through the haze of pain, he heard Cris's cries intensify. Angelberto had reached her.

He breathed in the moist reek.

He thought about Dooley and SWAT, across town in Sunnydale. Theresa had probably dispatched patrolmen to this location, but they'd have to find the basement apartment, the hole in the shower, the tunnels beneath. There wouldn't be time for that.

He concentrated, the fallen ceiling joist above his head coming into focus. If only he could grip it and lift himself free. He tried to raise his left arm, but the pain shut down the muscle, left it dead, a raw slab of meat. His right hand shook as he forced it up. His fingertips barely brushed the wood. No way.

His arm fell away.

He lay defeated.

Cris's whimpers reached him again, and his right hand moved before he ordered it to. Working the buckle of his belt, then yanking the leather strip. He did his best to keep the rest of his torso frozen as he hoisted his hips and tugged the belt free, but the sensation was blinding.

Sweating, grunting, sobbing, he flipped the buckle over the angled joist above him, gripping both ends of the looped belt in the fist of his right hand. Before he could give it any thought, he yanked, hoisting his torso up off the ground. Every muscle, straining, ignited. A roar scoured the inside of his throat. The white static returned, blotting out all sight, all sound, all sensation.

When it cleared, he was sitting up, blood draining down his side and back, matting his T-shirt. He rolled to his knees, then rose.

Picking up the box cutter where it had fallen, he stepped up into the tunnel and headed for his wife.

Chapter 71

There was no time for surprise or strategy. Daniel staggered around the bend in the tunnel and saw Angelberto up ahead in another cleared roomlike hollow, this one more intact. Knife in hand, he was crouched over Cristina. His broad, hunched back blocked her head and torso from view, but her white legs, bound at the ankles, bucked and bucked against the recently poured concrete floor. To the side he'd arranged a cluster of mine-shaft lights and a digital camera, which looked tiny perched atop a heavy-duty tripod, the setup present no doubt to record proof of death for the payment he still believed would come. The knife moved down and out of sight toward Cris's head.

"*No!*" Daniel said.

Angelberto rose and spun. Cristina's face flashed into sight behind his boots. A slit beneath one eye drained blood, mixing with her tears, but her face looked otherwise unmarred. She stared at Daniel, sobbing, unable to speak.

Wielding the box cutter, Daniel lumbered toward Angelberto, who stared back, expressionless. If he was surprised, he didn't show it. As Daniel neared, the janitor squared to face him. His gloved hand snapped once, repositioning his grip on the knife, the blade angled down, parallel with his forearm, razor edge out.

Firming his grip on the box cutter, Daniel stepped into the cleared space, the concrete suddenly firm underfoot. His shoulder throbbed, fire running down the nerve lines, rendering his left arm useless. Burgundy drops pattered onto the floor, the tops of his shoes. A dizzy spell washed over him; he had only a few minutes before the blood loss would leave him powerless.

Last time he'd made the mistake of watching the weapon, so now he watched Angelberto's eyes, his body.

The men circled each other warily.

Shuffle step. Feint. Shuffle step. Feint.

As in a wrestling ring.

Daniel kept his focus on the larger man's legs, reading the pattern of movement. Left knee bent in a partial crouch. Quick push off the foot, weight shifting to the right leg, body rising slightly, then coiling to the point of decision.

Daniel remembered from his countless hours on the mat that the knee broadcast intent. When that right knee started to rise again, it signaled another shuffle. If it stayed bent and started forward, it signaled an attack.

He ignored the knife, watched the knee.

Shuffle step. Feint.

Cris corkscrewed to watch even as wisps of hair fell across her eyes and stuck to her cheek. Her sobs had turned hoarse.

"Don't worry," Daniel told her. "You're gonna be okay."

Shuffle step. Feint.

Angelberto said, "How do you know?"

Shuffle step.

The right knee paused, coiled. Made the faintest swivel toward Daniel, preparing to drive. Then Daniel did something counterintuitive. He stepped into the charge.

The movement caught Angelberto off guard even as he lunged. Keeping his weight low, Daniel sprang back, pivoting on his left foot, a bullfighter fanning his cape. His momentum carrying him forward, Angelberto swung forcefully, the knife arcing past Daniel's cheek, inches from flesh. Driving off his rear foot, Daniel flicked the box cutter at Angelberto's throat, the big man twisting to dodge the blade.

They stood facing each other again, the same distance apart as they'd begun.

"Because," Daniel said, "you're already dead."

Angelberto's head bobbed, and a fine crimson spray misted from his throat. He gasped, his hand rising to clamp over the slit in his windpipe. The lock-blade knife fell, clanging against the concrete. Choking, he dropped to his knees. Then collapsed on his side.

Light-headed, Daniel stepped forward. With the tip of his shoe, he nudged Angelberto's hand away from his throat. A sheet of blood spilled from the exposed box-cutter slash. Growing weaker, Angelberto reached again to cover the cut, and Daniel toed his hand away again, then stepped on his palm. Angelberto stared up at him, beads of perspiration sparkling in his pencil-thin mustache and beard. His other hand flopped over and cupped the top of Daniel's shoe.

And then slid off.

Daniel staggered to Cris and fell onto his hip beside her. He didn't have the strength to cut her wrists and ankles free, but he pulled her head into his lap and she curled into him, fetal and sobbing. Tears of blood dripped from the slit beneath her eye. He tried to cover it with his thumb to stem the bleeding, the crying, but then he realized: He couldn't.

He fought unconsciousness, holding her as best he could.

It seemed a very long time until they heard shouts approaching up the tunnel.

Chapter 72

Daniel waited nervously in the exam-room chair. He turned his head too quickly, and a dagger stabbed up the nerve line toward his ear, finding the back of his jaw. It had been almost two months since the tunnels, and there was less pain every day, but that still left a good amount to go around, especially in the mornings when he woke up stiff. Though the rebar had sheared through nerve and muscle, the long-term prognosis was good. The front and back wounds were impressive, jagged keloid scars, each the size of a silver dollar. Beneath the shiny purple skin, the flesh was still boggy and gave off a deep ache that kept him up some nights, but it had healed over well enough, and now his body just had to do its job.

So much had happened in the time since he and Cris had emerged from the earth beneath Chinatown, though nothing could compare to the weight of those preceding eleven days. The story had exploded pyrotechnically, the afterglow lasting through several news cycles. Each revelation seemed to find its way above the fold or onto a Web site's home page. Two days too late, CSI Media Forensics had released a security still shot from the Fairmont elevator showing Angelberto riding up to Arthur Carroll's coin-cleaning closet, his shoulders bulging under the weight of the bags of change. The Tearmaker, unmasked. The mastermind, meanwhile, awaited trial. According to the *Chronicle,* Martin remained on suicide watch in the jail behind 850 Bryant. The article mentioned that the guards had restricted his right to send letters.

Dooley had protected Daniel as best she could, minimizing mention of his name in news conferences, but a few dogged reporters had sounded out the magnitude of his involvement. He had his fifteen minutes of fame before being gladly demoted to "husband of potential victim."

Theresa had come by the house to check on them, wearing her uniform to show off the new hash marks—the youngest lieutenant in the history of the department, according to the press release. They'd sat at the kitchen counter sipping coffee, but the spaces between words seemed to stretch out. Afterward at the front door, they'd talked about getting together again, but they all knew it was a social pretense to ease the sharpness of the good-bye. Pausing at the threshold, Dooley said, "Forget it. It's Chinatown," and they'd laughed a little. "Anything you need," she added, and he said, "You, too, Theresa." After they shook hands, he stood on the porch and watched her drive away.

To commemorate the New Year, he'd paid a visit to his future office, bringing a few boxes of books, a lamp, and an overpriced desk set, but he hadn't felt ready yet to inhabit the space. As he continued to put days between himself and the events of late November, he figured he'd make the transition in earnest.

This morning Kendra Richardson had called. Hearing his former director's voice caught him off guard. The near-violent end to the last session had accelerated his departure; he'd not once been back to Metro South. After the pleasantries, Kendra had been sure to remind him that several group members were graduating tonight should he want to stop by. She'd reminded him, too, that he still owed her the damn termination paperwork.

Now he sat nervously here in the heart of the UCSF Medical Center, the hospital smells bringing him back to visits past, the torturous hours he'd spent on the stiff waiting chairs of the radiation suite waiting for Cris to emerge.

But it was all different today.

On the exam table, Cris rustled up onto her elbows and shot him a wink. The scar beneath her eye remained, a thin stroke of purple, but she claimed that she'd grown to appreciate it. *An accent mark for the radiation tattoos,* she'd said. *What good is a body if it doesn't look lived in?*

She glanced from him to the monitor. "You *sure* you want to know, *mi vida*? We can always go lavender for the walls."

The ultrasound technician repositioned the wand on Cris's baby bump and paused to await Daniel's response.

"Yeah," he said. "I want to know."

The tech looked at Cris, who nodded.

"You're having a baby girl."

Cris gave an exultant little cry, and then she was wiping her face. "God, I'm so hormonal," she said. "It's not like there was a *bad* option. 'Sorry, ma'am, but you're having a *calf.*' "

"A lot of people get emotional when they hear," the tech said, cleaning the gel off Cris's stomach.

Cris lay back on the table and cried a little more.

Softly, Daniel said, "What?"

"I never thought I'd get to do this," she said.

He reached across, took her hand. The tech put away the cart and departed. The door swung shut, leaving them with the sudden quiet. Cris stared up at the ceiling, blinking back tears. He marveled at her profile. Her hair was rich and shiny, her skin smooth. She'd never looked more alive.

"What do you want to name her?" he asked.

Cris chewed her lip. "Francisca."

"Like the girl," he said. "Like your nana."

Cris smiled.

"Like the city," she said.

Driving away from the hospital into the bitter January gray, Daniel got a call from the high-strung manager of Evelyn's new building, his words a continuous flow, his manner toggling between anxious and indignant. After attempting to shoehorn in a few responses, Daniel said, loudly, "Okay, I'll be right there," and hung up.

He glanced across at Cris, who'd observed, amused.

"Something about requiring a building permit for construction," Daniel said. "He and Evelyn are at loggerheads."

"Shocking."

"Can we go?"

"Do we really need to?" Cris asked.

"She's my mom," he said. "And she's scared."

Cris looked out the window. "I'll wait outside."

They drove across to Nob Hill, Evelyn's second-favorite neighborhood and the highest summit in the city. Here on the "Hill of Palaces," she'd found an old brownstone that some enterprising soul had carved into little condos. Her non-corner apartment on the second floor had a partial view of Grace Cathedral.

As they pulled up, Cris took note of the building. "A significant downgrade," she said. "But hardly the Bowery."

He double-parked, and they climbed out. Through the lobby door, he could see Evelyn inside, animated, her finger pointing at the sour face of the manager.

Cris leaned against the outside wall to the side of the awning. "I'll be right here."

He went in, Evelyn's shoulders sagging with relief at the sight of him. "I don't understand why I need *another* permit to change the crown moldings in my own—"

The manager shook a clipboard emphatically. "The board has been very consistent on the requirements for—"

Daniel held up his hands. "Is this really what this is over? A one-page form?"

Both aggrieved parties said, "*Yes.*" The manager added, "And the board vote, which will happen during Monday's meeting."

Daniel took the clipboard. "I'll fill it out."

"I needed a permit to replace the kitchen counter," Evelyn said. "A permit to add soundproof glass. And now this? A permit for *crown molding*? I just don't see why this little power play is necessary."

"Because, Mom. You don't own the building. So you have to abide by the rules, no matter how annoying they might be."

"Are they *designed* to be annoying?"

"In part," Daniel said. That didn't win him a warm parting glance from the manager, but it drew a faint smile from Evelyn.

She waited until the office door banged shut behind the manager, then said, "I miss James."

"I know you do."

"Thank you for handling the form," she said. "And that bitter queen."

"Last time I was here, I met his wife and sons."

"Oh, like that means *anything*." She checked her watch. "I have to be at the club for lunch."

"I see you're really adjusting to your lifestyle as a pauper."

"Meg is hosting," she said by way of explanation.

"Well, then."

An awkward pause.

"We're fine, thanks," Daniel said. "Cristina's starting her second trimester."

"Oh, come on. There'll be plenty of time for all that doting and blithering once the thing is born." She checked her watch, then turned toward the elevator. "I need to put my face on."

Her face already looked on, but he nodded, and she took her leave.

He walked out and found Cris there, her eyes closed, her face tilted up to the sun. He watched her for a moment until she opened her eyes and said, "Stalker."

"What now?" he asked.

"Peking duck."

He laughed and held up the clipboard. "Let me just fill this out."

A cable car topped the rise, accompanied by that distinctive clanging. Daniel started in on the permit form, but Cris touched his arm so he'd look up and soak in the sight of the car coasting over the brink.

The conductor, his cap and gloves from another era, went nearly horizontal to engage the brake. The injury rates for conductors were off the charts—knees and backs giving out, hands turned arthritic around the giant pliers of the grips. There were so many easier ways to get folks up and down a hill, but the city charter included a provision that cable cars, the only mobile national monuments, could never be outlawed.

And besides: Easy was overrated.

The cable car drifted past, unveiling Grace Cathedral, imposing on the outside but free-spirited within, with its Keith Haring AIDS altarpiece, its stained-glass windows of Einstein and FDR, Frank Lloyd Wright and John Glenn. Secular luminaries inside a house of God topping a hill populated with the mansions of rail barons.

The closer one looked, the less the city made sense. It burned and shook, rose and fell, and at times even defaulted on its obligation to remain underfoot. It made things hard on itself. In that stubborn persistence were a host of annoyances and contradictions, but a kind of beauty and character, too.

Daniel returned his attention to the clipboard.

A few moments later, he heard Cristina say, "Jesus Christ, doesn't the woman know how to hail a cab?"

There Evelyn was at the curb, one hand raised feebly in the air; she must have moved past without noticing them. Taxis zoomed by, taking no notice. She tried again, but the commotion of the street seemed to overwhelm her.

Daniel glanced for the doorman, but then a familiar earsplitting whistle sounded from right beside him. Cris took her fingers from her mouth and pushed off the wall as a taxi yanked to the curb.

Evelyn glanced across, surprised at the sight of Cris suddenly there at her side. Cris opened the door for Evelyn, held it.

The two women regarded each other.

"Thank you," Evelyn said. She paused, the hint of a curve in her spine, then gave the faintest nod. *"Cristina,"* she added, and climbed into the taxi.

Chapter 73

Hesitating in the hall outside the door, Daniel was more nervous than he could ever remember being. He listened to the familiar patter of the room. X's laughter. Big Mac's booming voice. A-Dre getting worked up over something. Finally gathering his courage, he stepped inside.

A chorus of greetings went up.

"Counselor!"

"Mister . . . ah, ah, Crime Fighter."

He smiled and gave a nod to the new counselor, a pleasant if tired-looking woman in a worn skirt suit. "I'll give you the floor," she said, rising.

"Thank you."

The counselor shook X's hand and then Fang's. "Good luck out there. My door's always open."

When she left, Daniel smiled at the two of them. "The big graduates."

"Yeah," A-Dre said. "Us other shitheads gotta keep draggin' our asses in here."

Everyone laughed more than seemed called for, probably to break the tension. Daniel looked around, finding his bearings. He noticed that Lil's hair was up, her skin clean, and she wore a flowered shirt.

"Lil," he said, "you look beautiful."

She waved him off. "You're getting paid to say stuff like—" She caught herself. Dipped her head. "Thank you."

"No new members?" Daniel asked.

"Nah," Big Mac said. "After Martin they're gonna let the original crew ride it out until we all graduate. Enough disruptions, you know?"

"I know."

"Why don't you sit down?" A-Dre said. "Stay awhile."

In his nervousness Daniel had remained on his feet. He said, "Because X is in my fucking chair."

She cracked up, clapping her hands. "Come on. We got some stuff to show you."

He sat. "Like what?"

She pointed.

A-Dre was holding both hands clamped around his own neck.

"You hafta guess," X said.

Daniel said, "A-Dre's gonna strangle himself?"

"Ta-*daaa*!" A-Dre flung his arms wide. His neck, clear of any tattoos. Daniel stared in disbelief at the place where "*LaRonda*" had once been inked.

"I had that shit lasered off," A-Dre said. "My cousin has a place. You think that motherfucker hurt going *on* . . ."

"*And* . . ." Lil said.

Fang had his hand over his heart, as if reciting the Pledge of Allegiance.

"No," Daniel said, grinning. "*No.*"

Fang removed his hand, revealing a shiny name tag. "Osh Hardware." He couldn't keep a smile from lighting his face. "Tools and Hardware."

Daniel clasped his hands, aimed them at Fang.

"I guess I'm the loser in the group." Big Mac thumbed his nose, blinked a few times. "Lost my job."

X brightened. "He's been taking pity-party lessons from Lil, though, so *that's* good."

Big Mac smirked, and Lil flipped Xochitl off, then seemed surprised by her own reaction.

"Sorry to hear that, Mac," Daniel said. "How's things at home?"

"Solid," he said. "They been solid."

They visited for a time, making fun of one another, reliving some favorite moments. Fang stood up to imitate A-Dre's swagger. "'Member when A-Dre was all like, 'Fighting's fun. I'm . . . ah, ah, ah, I'm *good* at it.'"

"Look at Tools and Hardware, gettin' all cocky," A-Dre said. "Hope you don't have to *talk* in that new job a' yours."

They gave each other five.

X stood up and mock-cleared her throat, blushing at the formality. "We want to thank you." She tugged self-consciously at one of her braids. "For everything you did for us."

Daniel's face grew hot, and he looked down at the tile. "I learned more from you than you did from me."

"We have one more surprise for you," Lil said.

X ran to the door and leaned out into the hall. There was a murmured exchange, and then she pulled gently back into sight holding a toddler. The girl was striking, dark-skinned with loose, sloppy curls. Her long lashes and profile removed any doubt that she was Xochitl's daughter. Though the girl was hardly a newborn, X gripped her awkwardly and with great care, as if afraid she was going to drop her. As she returned to the circle, a middle-aged woman slid in from the hall and stood by the door with her back to the wall.

A social worker. Supervised visit.

Daniel opened his mouth, but nothing came out.

X showed off her daughter. "Isn't she pretty? Far as I can tell, all she does is say sorta words and break sunglasses. Is that what babies do? Break glasses?" She bounced the girl gently on her hip. "I don't get to keep her." She shot a mad look at the woman in the back. "*Yet.* But I get to see her two times a week, and if I line up a job, it'll be more, and then maybe. *Maybe.*"

Daniel stood and said, "May I?"

X nodded and handed him her child. He held her for a moment, fighting to swallow past the growing lump in his throat, and finally he said his good-byes. He went up the corridor to the bathroom, closed himself in a stall, and tilted his face into his hands.

When he cleared up, he came back out into the hall.

Farther down the corridor by the elevator, Kendra was in a heated discussion with a man wearing a sweater vest. She looked up, spotted Daniel, and smiled, and the man took advantage of the distraction to disappear into the elevator. Kendra walked to Daniel and gave him a hug, enfolding him in a swirl of yellow caftan.

"You got my papers, baby?" she asked.

He pulled the termination agreement from his back pocket. Looked down at the paper. Handed it to her. She took it, not happily.

"You see off the graduates?" she asked.

"I did. The new counselor?"

"*She's* great. But the guy for the *new* group?" Kendra gestured toward the elevator. "That was him fleeing midsession, tail tucked. They ate him *alive.*"

"He wears a *sweater vest.*"

"Yeah," she said. "I shoulda known." She glanced past Daniel at the last room down the hall. "They're still in there, gloating." She rolled up his termination agreement, tapped it thoughtfully against her mouth. "Now I gotta find someone *else* to take them on."

Daniel said nothing.

"They're gonna be emboldened now that they scared off *one* counselor," Kendra mused. "It's a big challenge, taking on a room like that."

"You're incorrigible," Daniel said.

"What?" She feigned surprise. "Oh—you thought I was asking . . . ?"

"And the Oscar for Best Actress goes to . . ."

"Well, it's not like it's a full load. It's *one group.*"

"I have a private practice to start."

"You know the good thing about only having *one group*?"

"Lemme guess," Daniel said flatly. "You can fit it in around a private practice."

"That *is* what I was thinking."

He set his teeth. She watched him, her head slightly drawn back. A standoff.

Finally he let out his breath, part sigh, part growl. "*One group*, Kendra. My last. *Really* my last."

"Of course, baby." She folded up his termination agreement, made it vanish somewhere inside her caftan as she turned for her office. "Why don't I just hold on to this for now?"

Daniel watched her go, and then he stood a moment alone before turning to walk to the last room in the hall.

The group members started when he banged through the door. He gave a quick scan around the ring. A rawboned lady wearing wrap-around shades, even in the shitty lighting. Hefty girl with a large-gauge septum pierce and a labret stud in her lip. A rangy kid with cornrows and a fringe of low-hanging braids in the back. Two wispy-chinned gangbangers, Norteños by their colors.

"We're gonna set some new ground rules," Daniel said. "There will be no violence or threats of violence. We meet every Monday, Wednesday, and Friday for two hours. You need to show up on time and sober. You're here for six months, and you cannot miss a single session without a doctor's note. If you're late, it counts as a missed session. If you get asked to or choose to leave two times, it counts as a missed session. Under no circumstances can you share the IDs of the other members of this group. If you're not a threat to yourself or others, nothing leaves this room. No racial slurs. No standing when you're pissed off. No meeting outside group. That includes having sex with anyone from group."

At that, the girl with the labret stud pulled a face.

"The more honest you are," he said, "and the more accountable you are, the more progress you'll make. That's what we shoot for in here—progress, not perfection. It'll be hard, and there will be setbacks and missteps. Change isn't gonna come overnight. It's a process."

The kid with cornrows blew out a breath of annoyance, and the gangbangers slumped in unison.

"Now," Daniel said. "Are there any questions?"

"Yeah," said the lady with the wraparounds. "When can I fucking *leave*?"

He smiled inwardly.

Right on schedule.

He stepped back to the door, yanked it open. "Anytime you want."

She held his stare for an aggressively long time, the others rapt. The rusty heating vent sighed stale air, and the crappy wall-mount clock clicked once and then again.

Finally she folded her arms and looked away.

He closed the door and took his place in the circle of chairs.

"Welcome to group," he said. "I'm glad you're here."

Acknowledgments

While San Francisco is the city of my birth, it was a new canvas for me creatively, which therefore required me to enlist a fresh crew of experts. I would like to thank Officer Rosalyn Rouede of SFPD, a native daughter if ever there was one, for showing me the restricted halls, dark alleys, and hidden secrets of a place both familiar and foreign to me. Vincent Pan was another tour guide to the city, literally and figuratively. With irrepressible enthusiasm, Darra Messing helped fill in the geographic gaps. I should also like to acknowledge Rob Holsen of the St. Francis Hotel, who acquainted me with a wonderful age-old tradition.

I relied on Philip Eisner, Melissa Hurwitz, M.D., David St. Peter, and Maureen Sugden to bring their various sensibilities to bear. This story was fortunate to have you in its orbit—as am I to have you in mine.

Keith Kahla, my editor, was there in all the right ways for this one, as were the rest of my team at St. Martin's Press, including Sally Richardson, Matthew Shear, Matthew Baldacci, Kym Giacoppe, Loren Jaggers, Jeff Capshew, Martin Quinn, Christine Jaeger, Hannah Braaten, and Kevin Sweeney.

Additional thanks are due to Lisa Erbach Vance of the Aaron Priest Agency, Stephen F. Breimer, Marc H. Glick, Rich Green at CAA, Dana Kaye, and last, but certainly not least, Rowland White of Michael Joseph/Penguin Group UK.

Acknowledgments

I would be remiss not to mention Simba the Destroyer, for the brainstorming hikes and loyal hours by the desk; R. and N., capable of making me laugh at any moment, particularly when I least want to; and Delinah, who pulls the proverbial big picture into alignment for me, year after year, with indescribable grace.